I0613112

Solomon Jackson Woolley

Life, Recollections and Opinions of Solomon Jackson Woolley

An Autobiography

Solomon Jackson Woolley

Life, Recollections and Opinions of Solomon Jackson Woolley
An Autobiography

ISBN/EAN: 9783337119447

Printed in Europe, USA, Canada, Australia, Japan

Cover: Foto ©Raphael Reischuk / pixelio.de

More available books at **www.hansebooks.com**

RECOLLECTIONS AND OPINIONS

—OF—

SOLOMON JACKSON WOOLLEY

AN AUTOBIOGRAPHY

1881.
COTT & HANN, BOOK PRINTERS,
COLUMBUS, O.

DEDICATION.

To the thousands in the City of Columbus, and in Madison and Franklin Counties, O., who proved themselves my friends when the day of trial and evil came to my family, who also waited with me for justice to avenge itself, and whose sympathy is yet a benediction, I dedicate this volume of my life.

S. J. W.

PREFACE.

Life is so earnest to any soul, in harmony with the age in which it lives, that it is almost impossible to avoid some sort of record of its memories, impulses and ideas. This book is only one of the fruits of this disposition of a happy life to record not only its joys but its sorrows, and find victories, here and there, in seeming deieats. Friends have asked the publication of the papers, which, like leaves, have tumbled to the earth in these autumn days of my career. The author has yielded to their request, and with the hope that those who are in the spring and summer of life may feel some generous impulses toward a common fruitage in time and eternity.

APPLEDALE, June, 1881.

CONTENTS.

LIFE, RECOLLECTIONS, AND OPINIONS

OF

S. J. WOOLLEY.

CHAPTER I.

BIRTHPLACE AND PARENTAGE.

"I thank Thee that my childhood's vanished days
       Were cast in rural ways,
Where I beheld with gladness ever new,
       That sort of vagrant dew
Which lodges in the beggarly tents of such
Vile weeds as virtuous plants disdain to touch,
And with rough-bearded burs, night after night,
Upgathered by the morning, tender and true,
       In her clear, chaste light.

       "Such ways I learned to know
       That free will can not go
Outside of mercy I learned to bless His name
Whose revelations, ever thus renewed
Along the varied year, in field and wood,
       His loving care proclaim.

" I thank Thee that the grass and red rose
       Do what they can to tell
Your spirit through all forms of matter flows;—
For every thistle by the common way,
Wearing its homely beauty; for each spring
That, sweet and homeless, runneth where it will;
       For night and day;
For the alternate seasons,—everything
Pertaining to life's marvelous miracles."

"THUS, after having lived in the city for twenty
years," says Mary Clemmer Ames, "with not
even a grassy plat of her own on which to rest her feet,

the country sights and sounds, which made nearly
thirty years of Alice Cary's life, faded into pictures of
the past." And, thus, to my readers, I have only to
offer such pictures of the past, as breathe the airs of
the hill-side home and the ample fields, and are sur-
charged with the juices of the soil, forest and orchard.
For my life began in the country, and shall end 'mid nature's harmonies. In no diseased spirit, however, do
I seek to say that "God made the country, and man
the town." But I must also freely acknowledge not
only a love, but a gratitude to the circumstances of
my career, and while I express affection for the innocent grandeur and unalloyed freedom of rural life, I
must add a thankful heart and rejoice that unsuited as
I am to the motley life of the city, my cradle was
rocked under the shadow of forests, and my latest joy
springs from the heart of nature.

My earliest memory goes back to the beautiful hills
and valleys, with their rocks and caves, and ripples of
pure water—to what seem the fancy sketches of the
power Divine, the wild but significant architecture of
Jehovah.

I was born near Zanesville, Muskingum County,
Ohio, on the 12th day of January, 1828. Born
where money was a curiosity, where financial wealth
was almost undreamed of, where great possessions were
unknown, where poverty was tyrannical, I was, nevertheless—despite the paradox—born in the midst of
wealth. I count the first gleam which fell into my
vision richer than if it had shot from a heap of gold.
It was the radiance of a noble woman's eye—the anxious and loving gaze of my mother. Wealth that tran-
scended the somewhat homely garb she wore; wealth,
that altogether outshone any change that might have
been made in the house, or its furniture; wealth, that

put to shame all modification that could have been made of that roof, its largeness, and the things it protected—this was mine in her.

What was this wealth? First of all, a noble soul—tender, loving, but stern for right as well, and full of truth and fidelity. To this nobility of nature, in any human being, all the goodness with which one meets, all the lessons of experience, all the joy of the years, all the teaching of life, all the truth and virtue one may touch—all these will cling. Without it, as a foundation stone, the rest of life can be but a baseless piece of architecture. With it, innumerable things may be preserved, because they may be placed upon it, and builded to it, and thus kept forever. Thus it is, that many men have large commerce with truth, large dealings with noble men, great acquaintance with the great ideas and hopes of their time, and lose them all; because there was nothing for these things to cling to, no foundation stone was there on which they might arrange themselves into a fine building. A noble and true nature is like a magnet, attracting and holding nobility and truth to itself, and an ignoble nature can no more catch and hold these things, than an ordinary piece of pig-iron can gather up fragments of solid steel, as it is passed through such a mixture of elements as is our human life.

My mother had this nobility of soul to begin with, and the difference between her and many other women was, not that they had less to do with human experience than she, not that they had seen less goodness than she, not that they had touched less great and good things than she, but that she had fastened them to herself; they had clung to her, as fragments of steel to a strong magnet, and they became a part of her power to bear and suffer, and achieve.

Through the memory of her, I have looked at men
and women, and have not failed to note how little people get out of life. And I have seen that this power to
get much out of life, does not depend so much on quantity, as quality. Here is a man, for example, great in
sympathies, great in passions, great in appetites, great
in affection, great in will-power, great in thought-power,
great in executive ability,—great everywhere, when you
look at him, as you look at a store when you take an
inventory. But that man comes to a remarkable series
of experiences. Years elapse. He goes through them.
They have silvered his hair. They have furrowed his
brow. He carries a cane now. He is growing old.
They have been terrible, but he has passed through
them. Now you meet him. He is the same man,
weakened, enfeebled, and, perhaps, sour, sad, and idea-
less. He has got nothing out of his journey. He did
not see a glory in all that great route. He learned
nothing. He went, but saw not. He had ears, but
he did not hear. And you feel that, just as a man
who had gone over the sea for pleasure and enjoyment,
and had seen nothing but storm and shipwreck, and
danger and death—that even he ought to know something about a storm at sea, a wrecked boat and the dire
disasters—so with this man who had so much trouble,
you do feel that he, at least, ought to know more than
he did about the difficulties of life, the hardship of living, the nature of sorrow, the truth of trouble, and the
reason of woe. But he does not. And he is a sour,
crusty man.

Here is another. He passed through a like experience. He *would* see every step. No difficulty would
shut his eyes. He thought it was a horrible route,
but he would take in the scenery. He would analyze
the difficulties. He would look out and into the soul

of the storm. He was bound to look at the hand that led him. And you meet him. He is grey and worn. But his eye is clear, and his voice is sweet, and his heart throbs with loyalty. And he can tell you all about it. This sailor can tell you all about a storm, and a wreck, and a fatal disaster. Besides, he is a better sailor. He has not only learned something, but he has won something—the blessing of his experience, a hardier manhood.

The difference between the men was not in quantity, but in quality. One was a magnet to gather all the steel particles of intelligence out of that wretchedly mixed up experience, the other was a big chunk of ordinary iron that saw nothing, and obtained nothing. But there is more. One became a crusty and sour man; the other became sweet and true. The difference is in quantity? No; in quality. One was a block of wood that could not bear the fine chiselings, that would not take on the fine art that the chisel-edge contained; the other was a piece of the hardest marble that bore the strokes, took the chiselings and kept the vision of the artist, clear and true. Greatness is not goodness, but goodness is always greatness. My mother had not the goodness of greatness, but she had the greatness of goodness.

I have since learned that, if the balances of the eras, and much more, if the scales of eternity are to be consulted, there is no poverty in such places as are presided over and influenced by the glow of righteousness and the power of living truth. The civilizations that are to come, reach their roots below trade, commerce, and treasuries, and draw their power from those factors whose dwelling place is eternity. The woof and warp of the future is taken from these elements that no gold can buy, and no lack of it can displace. The future will not be poor, as assuredly the present is not, as long as the forces which gleam from such earnest and faithful eyes are supreme.   John Stuart Mill, to my mind, writes more profoundly than we think, when he says:

"The worth of a state in the long run is the worth of the individual composing it, and a state which postpones the interest of their mental expansion and elevation, to a little more of administrative skill, or that semblance of it which practice gives in the details of business; a state which drafts its men in order that they may be mere docile instruments in the hands even for beneficial purposes, will find that with small men no great thing can really be accomplished; and that the perfection of machinery to which it has sacrificed everything, will in the end avail it nothing for want of vital power, which, in order that the machine might work more smoothly, it preferred to banish."

For all of this signifies and suggests that there is nothing so necessary as the purity and power of *individual*. Well, obviously, no influences nor machineries can make this result certain as the home.   And, as truly may it be said, that the factors of all right home-influence are such as these I have sought to describe.

So I judge that we will see a new political economy dawn.   We will know that it is impossible to substitute, with success, dollars for manhood; that that nation is the richest in the long run, which is conservative and creative of manliness, and that the sources of wealth, therefore, lie with forces great as eternity.

For these reasons, I may say, I am almost grateful that I was born in the midst of poverty, and I hope my life has been a commentary, sufficiently clear, on the fact that *he who honestly makes a surplus, makes personal power and wins personal strength in the making of it,*

to excuse me from any mention of that most potent
reason of gratitude.

My reader need expect no long array of dates and
names. I have descended from no royal house, and
have only such interest in my ancestry as to regard that
royalty with which all men may be invested.

Facts, which it would be immodest for me to mention, have been stated in the " *History of Franklin and
Pickaway Counties,*" as follows :

On her father's side, my mother was of Holland
descent, and her ancestors, including her father and
grandfather, had been people of considerable substance
in Amsterdam, where they carried on a large manufac-
tory of silks, linens, etc. Jacob Askins, her father,
during a commercial voyage to England, some time in
the last century, was overtaken by a terrible storm,
which so disabled the vessel upon which he was a pas-
senger that she drifted for several months at the mercy
of the winds and waves, and was finally driven across
the Atlantic, and cast a wreck upon the shores of
Virginia, nearly all originally on board having perished.
Mr. Askins, then still a young man, was among the
survivors, but was deterred by his dreadful experiences
from again venturing upon the sea, and decided to settle
in the new world, to which he had so strangely emigrated. He settled in Loudon County, in the Old
Dominion, married a Miss Shafer, and after some years,
removed to Washington, Guernsey county, Ohio, where
he reared his family, including Elizabeth, who was my
mother. My ancestors, on my father's side, were
English, but emigrated from the mother country long
before the Revolutionary War, and were among the
first settlers of New Jersey. Jacob Woolley, my grandfather, removed to Athens county, Ohio, when that
part of the State was almost an unbroken wilderness,.

and settled upon what is now called Jonathan's creek. His son, Isaac, my father, was bred a stone-cutter, and afterwards spent most of his time away from the paternal home, working at his trade. After his first marriage, which was to a Miss Stokely, of Muskingum county, he settled on a place of his own near Zanesville, from which he removed, when I was but one year old, to another place, three miles from Amesville, in Ames township, Athens county, on a branch of Federal creek, where most of our family were reared. By this marriage he had several sons, half-brothers of mine, who, in after years, were remembered, as may be more fully recorded. Their mother died while they were young, and Mr. Woolley, in the year 1827, took Miss Elizabeth Haskins to be his wife. Several years afterwards, he sold the Athens county farm, and purchased another in Star Township, Hocking county, where he resided for many years. I was still very young at the time of the removal, but rendered all the assistance I could in the labors of the farm, and in due time, as the half-brothers, one after another, grew to manhood and went away, I had to take upon myself its chief burdens, as my father was absent a large part of the time, pursuing his vocation of stone-cutter. I found little time or opportunity for schooling, nine months in all, or three terms of about three months each, in the primitive country schools of that day, comprising the whole of my formal education. Until I was fourteen years of age, I had never had an hour's training in school. About that time the people of the neighborhood spontaneously agreed that they ought to have a school-house, and forthwith set about the erection of a rude affair, which was ready for occupancy within a fortnight after the vote to build was taken. I preserve this note of this antique structure :

" The architecture of this school-house did not correspond with that of the present day. It was made of round logs, with a clap-board roof, laid on loose, with weight-poles on top, to hold the clap-boards down ; the floor was laid with what we call puncheons—a tree split in wide pieces, from two to eight inches thick, and hewn on one side; the chimney was made at one end, of stone, and we gathered up enough newspapers to paste over the windows, in place of glass ; the paper, being oiled, transmitted a very mellow light. Slabs, or boards, were fastened around the walls, for our writing desks, and pins upon the walls to hang our hats and dinners on. Our seats were made of small trees, split in two, with the split side dressed, and four pins, or legs, underneath, making each of the proper heighth for a seat."

The schools kept in such buildings in those days, were of the kind, long since passed away in this State, known as " subscription-schools." Miss Rebecca Prindle was the first teacher in this school, and so my preceptor, except my mother, from whom I had already received, as I subsequently learned, valuable instruction at home. The old-fashioned spelling-school was held by her once every week in term time. In the summer I attended a Sabbath-school nearly four miles from my home.

I take from a short account of my life elsewhere, a brief extract, which relates a fact more clearly than might be justifiable in myself :

" When but sixteen years of age, young Woolley achieved a notable business and industrial triumph. Through bad management his father's finances became involved, and he was compelled to borrow four hundred dollars at ten per cent. interest, giving a mortgage upon his farm by way of security. A year rolled speedily

2

around, and nothing was realized toward the extinguish-
ment of the debt. It was considered in the neighborhood inevitable that the mortgagee would get the place
by foreclosure. At this crisis Solomon came to the
rescue, and proposed that while his father should continue at his trade for the support of his family, he would
undertake the sole charge of the farm (one hundred and
sixty acres) in a vigorous effort to make enough to lift
the mortgage. It was agreed to. Within eighteen
months the full sum must be raised, and Solomon saw
that with the best of management it was only possible
to effect it by sowing most of the land to wheat, and
that then, with a good harvest and fair price, success
was certain. He had not only the entire responsibility
to shoulder, but almost the entire labor to do, since his
adult half-brothers had now all gone from home, and
his younger brothers were too small to be of much service. He buckled fearlessly and stoutly, however, to
his task. Beginning his day of labor at four o'clock,
he worked three hours until breakfast, and then, with
brief intermissions for dinner and supper, he kept on
until dark, and on moonlight nights until far into the
evening. His faithful toil, though it brought him many
hours of weariness and somewhat impaired his health,
met with its reward. It turned out to be 'a good wheat
year,' and Solomon's crop—'good, well-filled grains, of
a superior quality'—was the finest in that region.
Wheat, too, was higher than usual, and he sold for a
good price. Consequently, when the mortgage fell
due, he had the proud satisfaction of releasing it in
full, and presenting it to his lately burdened and anxious, but now overjoyed and grateful parents.''

CHAPTER II.

I LOOK through the mist of years at the external nature with which I was surrounded. Unconsciously we weave our experience into life and character, even as the plant weaves sunshine into beauty and fragrance. How does the world sweep into us and of that which we give the world how great a part has the world given us. I do not claim all this love of the beautiful and the grand, which I have felt and tried to reproduce, as my own. Nature gave it to me in part, as God gave it all to nature. I only believe that we ought to do for man what nature, and early and late association, have done for us. Those streams flow through my nature as once and even now they glide at the base of those Hocking hills. They are like Emerson's river, *Muskatequit:*

"Thou in thy narrow banks art pent;
  The stream I love unbounded goes
Through flood, and sea, and firmament;
  Through light, through life it forward flows.

I see the inundation sweet;
  I hear the spending of the stream;
Through years, through men, through nature fleet,
  Through love and thought, through power and dream."

They contain streams of thought and inspiration which have their source at the throne and flow into the "river of the water of life."

The scenery of my youth has been an emancipating, inspiring influence upon my whole life. Liberty of thought abides somehow in high and grand

hills, and deep rugged valleys. I do not wonder
that the legend of William Tell finds him free 'neath
the summit of the Alps, and in the regions of eternal
snow. Slavery is intolerable to a man who has once
felt the grandeur of sublime natural scenery. Let
no man own your soul. Let no creed cramp your
spirit. Let no doctrine chain your mind. Let no party,
church, or school, become proprietor of your fetterless
thought. This is the teaching of the magnificent world,
with its rocks and pines. As well might I be the slave
of any creed or idea, man or school, thought I, as for
one of those eagles to fly with a chain, fettered and
bound. Tyranny is unnatural. Oppression is opposed
to splendid heights and gorgeous sunsets, and when
nature has sung her whole psalm of melody into the
soul of man, and man has heard its deep diapason,
every thought and every sentiment, every energy and
every inspiration, of every man, shall have its freedom
guaranteed forever. The rocks showed the abiding testimony they had to give of grand forces. They were
piled one upon another, and kissed with the soft sunshine, they frowned across deep valleys, which were
filled with light. Their torn and fragmentary condition
attested the existence of huge powers. Insensibly I
was broadened in my notions of the universe. I could
not think it a toy. Magnificent energies spoke when
the lightning flashed from crag to crag, and as the
thunder seemed to me to shatter the very skies, and
shake their stars, I was impressed with the importance
of the universe, of which this was a part. Life's loom
takes up these threads, which hang so loosely from the
visible world, and weaves them into our spiritual being,
thus making them realities of the invisible. We all need
the enlarging influence of the presence of great things.
This life has its foundation in the principle of being

grand as the thoughts of God. And when one finds the record of massive energies without him, and is conscious of yet more magnificent forces within him, he feels that again "deep calleth unto deep." There is just as much grandeur in nature to a man as he takes in. To a blind man there is no sun. To some people, the tender grass is not a fine collection of laboratories, and a brave, living energy, but so much hay. They measure a sunbeam by the money which it makes. They see no glory in the colors of a rainbow, because they make no dollars out of it. But the true lover of nature feels that she is valuable not for the seen, but for the unseen, and that her glory is beyond the yard-stick and scales.

> Brighter lights and vaster things
> Have touched my running thought,
> Such are blessings fortune flings;
> Of such our life-work wrought.
>
> Never have the early sounds
> Left the avenues of mind;
> Ceaseless fall the countless rounds
> Of years—the cold and kind.
>
> Still the tender wintergreen
> Strikes my re-awakened sense,
> Still the beauty of the scene
> Hath its own great recompense.
>
> Bosomed 'mid the solid hills,
> Lay the basin, full of stars,
> Fell that confluence of rills
> Over strong and rocky bars.
>
> High above the turkey's nest,
> Builded 'neath the winter sky,
> Here within the sweetest rest,
> Filled with immortality.
>
> Thus the years return and bring
> Fruits of fall and winter's cheer,
> Glory, verdure, love of spring,
> Memories which mould this tear,

The brooks received a most epical significance, as

they dashed from out the bosom of the hills. They held in their quiet, lake-like stillness, when some huge rock impeded their courses, the sun by day and the glittering stars at night, and when they fell over into deep gorges, and rushed along over pebbly and rock-covered bottoms, they shook into beautiful silver haze the mirror their quiet would have given to the moon. Poems, indeed, were these specimens of God's literature.   Tennyson could only read God's thought when he translated into his words of letters those words of God's raindrops, and only by catching the human side of that of which he caught the creative and divine vision, does this our earthly poet reproduce the literature of Jehovah :

> "I steal by lawns and grassy plots;
> I slide by hazel-covers;
> I movo the sweet forget-me-nots
> That grow for happy lovers.
>
> I skip, I slide, I gloom, I glance,
> Among my skimmering swallows,
> I make the netted sunbeams dance
> Against my sandy shallows.
>
> I murmur under moon and stars,
> In brambly wildernesses,
> I linger by my shining bars;
> I loiter 'round my cresses.
>
> And out again I curve and flow,
> To join the brimming river,
> For men may come, and men may go,
> But I go on forever."

From such influences I have never felt entirely exiled.   In my life of business, this peculiar vein of pleasure is omnipresent.

Never have I been able to escape the inspiration of business.   That there is such a peculiarity of mind I have no doubt.   Business has been with me a passion, like the cadence of thoughts and words to the poet; like the idea and colors to the painter. Such it was in my youth, and to the belief that activity, directed by honesty, is the healthful and grand exercise of man, I owe those flashings of success which have crossed my path and now give me pleasure and mental rest. Some of my earliest business ventures have woven themselves into the texture of my very life so thoroughly that I can not reproduce them, but others stand out in bold relief in my memory, and either by a touch of humor or a savoring of tragedy reproduce themselves continually.

In the spring of 1845, I thought I had struck the sources of wealth. I discovered on my father's farm in Star Township, Hocking County, Ohio, a strange porous substance, which I have since learned was one of the countless modifications of iron, and which yielded upon burning, a red result, of a hue between Spanish Brown and Venetian Red. Its strange and beautiful color charmed me, while beneath all the lustre, I sought its possibilities as a source of wealth. All my mechanical genius was aroused. If ever I had felt able to do all things, I felt that then the creatures of the earth were to become my servants. Never had I failed in accomplishing with tools what I tried to do, and I was certain, that, all aglow with the enthusiasm of a new discovery, I could not touch the forces about me in vain. I gathered the old wheels to my new ones, made cogs without number, and brought the remnants of an old grist mill in the shape of two burrs to the aid of my purpose. My poverty made me do without both, and finding necessity the mother of invention, I made of wood what I saw others have in better form. I had made a mill. I hitched the horse to the enterprise. The whole neighborhood for miles around, came to laugh at my lunacy. But the mill *did* go. Then the

grinding begun.   Nearly fifteen hundred pounds of the
raw material, unchanged but by grinding, were brought
out triumphantly.   What was I to do with it?

Cincinnati, a name only larger than my dreams of glory
which had their formation at that wooden mill, rushed
into my head as an objective point.   It was to a Southern Ohio business boy, just what Mecca was to a young
Mohammedan Shiek.   My father was beyond the ideas
of the community in which he lived, because he would
hear my requests that I might go to the city with my
products, and the common sentiment was that a boy,
opinions and all, belonged to the father, until he was
twenty-one years of age.   Before my father, I produced
arguments, unanswerable.   Nothing could exceed my
pertinacity.   At last, what was an enormous sum, two
dollars, he kindly allowed me to make, that this whole
thought, a gigantic enterprise, might have its bud and
blossom in Cincinnati.   At Pomeroy, I gazed upon
the boat which was to carry my great achievement.
The boat was a marvel ; what I should have thought of
that huge institution, if my mind had not been so
full of the idea that the greatest act of its career was to
take that result to the city, I do not know.   I lost all
my wonder in my dream.   I took the cheapest passage,
I "wooded" it ; and thus I paid one-half of my fare.   I
was anxious, and looked at the kegs of paint I had
made, as we went down the river.   I was ready, and in
fact, had been all that day and night, to see any body
who wanted to purchase this load.   We arrived. I saw
the kegs unloaded.   I thought the wharf had never received such an ornament.   After I had quietly refreshed
my pride by gazing for some minutes upon my wealth,
I started to take in the city.   Never since, have I
walked so slowly.   I was confounded with the glories
of civilization.   I was lost in amazement at the stupen-

dous march of man. Only one idea kept me from
losing all thought, except that which possessed me when
some great building, some elegant window, some huge
piece of architecture, or some fine parade of aristocracy
would strike my view, and that was, that I was the sole
owner, proprietor, discoverer, grinder, and agent of that
pile of red dust, down on the wharf, put up in kegs.
This idea was larger than Cincinnati. With it I besieged druggists, cabinet-makers, painters, wagon-build-
ers, hardware stores, and all other men of whom I
might think they could be interested in buying what I
had to sell; but I had no success. The force of my
enterprise began to fail. The city grew in greatness,
and my prospects grew in littleness. Had I struck the
city in a bad time? No! Had nobody any interest in
paint? Yes. Had I not done a good thing? Yes.
Well, what was the trouble? It was only this. I had
to learn that there was a deeper reason than what they
told me when they said: "It is only a cent a pound,"
"we have plenty," and that was, that this was a big
world; it had a great many farms on it, a great deal of
red paint in the raw material, a great many boys who
could make cogs and set burrs;—and that visit taught
me when I left it with the commission merchants sadly,
that, because this world was greater than I had supposed,
it would take all my energies to succeed in it, and that
if I did succeed, that success would be worth as much
more as the world was greater than my boyish notions
of it. The Commission Merchants, Springman & Son,
loaned me enough to get home on. I had lost something in my stock of dollars, but nothing in my stock of
ideas. My inspiration to live and act was as much
greater as the world had become, compared with my
former idea of it. I was bound to enter the magnificent arena of life, and, hearing a thousand trumpet-tones

3

of invitation, I resolved to strike out and alone upon its tremendous issue.   I must touch some tone myself.   I knew of the Cabinet-makers' business; I thought of the trade only as a means to independence, and as a way into the active life of the world.   As a means, such as this, I would have valued anything.   Any road which led to business was for me paved with precious stones. I seized this route, had gone to Chauncey, and had begun to learn the trade, but in the face of a miserable living which—a forceful argument with a country-boy of good health—persuaded me to change my mode of life.   The air was full of the rumor of battle.   The toc- sin of war had sounded, and its echo fell among those hills, and lingered in all our souls.   Ohio was moved by the words of eloquence on both sides.   My friends thought it was the grandeur of heroism to go.

While the Mexican war meant all this to many, to me it meant simply business.   I do not propose to in- flict upon my readers any sham love of country.   While I am a patriot, as I hope, I do not desire to assert a pa- triotism of which I was never conscious.   I believed I could get money enough out of the Mexican war, if I should volunteer, to help me into business.   Evenings at the fireside fled, with my mother (whose affection lingers like a tender benediction).   I tried to assure her that the war would close before I could reach New Orleans.   But love of home was stronger than love of wealth, and I remained to see my friends return from that fragmentary march they made to New Orleans, each holding what I so much desired, their right to a farm and their pay as soldiers.   But this attempt, while it did not cast such rich seeds of experience at my feet as my more serious effort at Cincinnati, also did not dis- courage me, or make life the less attractive to me. Rather did it increase my desire and sharpen my already

acute expectation.   I went to Logan and made a contract with Mr. Kanode; the work I could stand, but not
without good food and of a sufficient quantity.   This I
did not get, and at the expiration of two months I was
again without work.   A gentleman is rare, if even a
thousand such be at one's hand.   There is a certain solitude in all goodness as well as greatness.   And if the
good and the great would multiply, there is a certain
divineness about them both which makes their illustration objects of admiration and love.   Of the rare men
I shall remember, the friend I then encountered, was
Alvin Finney.   With an honesty which was not ashamed,
like the massive rocks of his native State, with a virtue
as pure and bracing in its influence as the breeze
swept from the breast of the ocean upon his boyhood
home, with the love of truth which like an arch setting
upon these two pillars, he, most of all men, filled me
with the idea that life was nothing without honor, that
wealth was valuable only in the clear eyes of truth, and
that he who embodies the principle of manhood in him
becomes the champion of what can never die.   That
descendant of the Pilgrim fathers bore in him the stamp
of his lofty lineage, and how far one human hand can
reach I know not, but I do know that his strong hand
of influences reaches through these years and touch
the strings of my life into new music.

    I aspired to what is termed a business life.   Chilli-
cothe then became an object of attraction.   A slaughter
house was opened, and to this I urged my way.   There
I hired myself, and there—and it proves how fine may
be the sense of kindness when the sense of smell is outraged—I was given a place and sort of work, such as
my physical condition would admit of and endure.
This kindness fell upon me as an argument I could not
resist when a strike was made for higher wages.   When

the hands left and began to receive twenty-five cents
advance per day, I felt that while it was all right for
them, I could not afford to sell my sense of gratitude
for a quarter a day. The efforts of this engagement
crystalized in the shape of about twenty dollars, which
then was the means of my future.

Before this I had written to the publishers of a United
States History concerning the agency. Visiting Lancaster, to obtain a set of harness, I met Mr. Miller and
his sons, who now live in Columbus, Ohio. They informed me of the book and held out inducements. I
engaged to do work for them at such a price, that I
afterward took the amount they must have received into
consideration, and resolving to have no barrier between
the publishing company and my interest, I embodied
my desires in a letter to them. The answer was satisfactory, and my career as a book agent began. The
results of one's life are not to be measured by the conscious successes that have followed conscious efforts.
Many of our best are unconscious efforts. Many of our
most sublime are also unconscious successes. A human being hardly knows the immortalities he touches
inside the mortalities. No man can assert how much of
eternity there is in time. I think of myself as a book
agent. I remember how unpopular he is to-day. I
suppose this is so because the books now sold by sub-
scription are not valuable. He is not only unpopular,
but he is entirely unappreciated as a force in civilization.
How many a dumb soul has spoken first under the news
of the discovery to them of a great world, which would
have been lost without the poor book agent vending
his immortal wares. In the time to which attention has
been cited the book agent was a force in community.
The rough but brave men, and the poorly dressed but
noble women would gather around to look upon the

literary curiosity. And having purchased, it became a family treasure from which were gathered lessons of greatest value. I am persuaded that many hearts have been fired into patriotic devotion by the reading of the book which I sold, and while I sought for money whereby life might be entered upon in security and peace, I "was building better than I knew." My unconscious success was greater than the conscious glory of the renumeration I received, for manhood was being made, and the bands of civilization were being strengthened as by the vast fire places each word of the struggle of liberty fell into their interested homes.

All the money I had was put into the histories. They had been sent to Cincinnati instead of Logan. I managed a way to Cincinnati, but could not get my books. Here I thought of my wealth, stored in kegs, in Springman & Son's commission house. They furnished me, by loan, eight dollars, and with these books I began a march homeward. The proverbial anxiety to get into one's new field of labor had fully taken hold of their new-fledged agent. And the usual fate—such a fate as develop the real agent which may lie all hid in the nominal agent—came to him, for no books were sold that next day. He had exhausted his stock of argument. He had used all his adjectives of praise till they were threadbare. He had over-worked what the publishers told him to say in their private circular. He had killed, by working them to death, all the influence of the pet phrases he had. All this, and not one book had been sold. As such do I contemplate myself as an agent.

The failure to sell my books urged me to Rutland. While I traveled, the men I met and the homes I passed did not escape my earnest solicitation. But Rutland was reached, and that at night, with my sack as full of

books as it had ever been.   They weighed me down as
the evening grew darker into night, not so much because
they were heavy, in and of themselves, as because I
had seen so few prospects of a sale that I was the less
inspired to carry them.   Wagons passed me and I tried
to expostulate with their drivers, beseeching a ride, but
the responses which came were not inviting.   A map,
which I thought ought to strike the noblest chord of intelligence in one fellow's nature, was offered, and though
it was true, as I had divined, that his moral character
lay very near to his intellectual nature, the map moved
neither; for with the ominous gaze of utter ignorance
he fixed his unlettered eyes upon me and the map, and
concluded, I suppose, that, because he had never heard
of one, and the cattle sometimes died unexpectedly,
that "map" and that "fellow" were both to be avoided as a pestilence.

Sunday came and went with the past.   Monday came
with its ill success.   Home began to assume lofty pro-
portions in my soul.   As the glories and greatness of a
newly found enterprise fade, the quiet splendors of the
cradle in which successful thoughts were rocked, appear
and glow with a fresh radiance.   Home became my
chief desire.   Toward that place my route lay.   The
books were nearly all left at Pagetown, and while I only
took with me two or three, I had just that many more
than I could sell.   At home I had left an antiquated
and not beautiful specimen of horse-flesh, and I relied
on this said animal; though it seems now with such an
immediate prospect of death before the beast, I was almost guilty of burdening one who was very near the
grave—to help me out of the predicament.   Security,
such as in those days was placed at the bottom of every
business transaction, was given, and the wood-works of
a buggy were obtained, and with a pertinacity which

astonished the neighbors, I fixed my vehicle and started for my books. Returned, and with them I continued this line of attack, believing that that "tide in the affairs of men" which leads on to fortune "would, perchance, strike me, and I should yet have cause of joy.

Pagetown, Athens, Chauncey, in turn became objects of my care, and with no ray of light. But my time had come. Nelsonville responded to my touch, and like a tone on the key-board, the music then began. Three books sold and a light heart. McArthur was visited; the rest of my books were sold, and with the money I had found expression in joyant expectation. One hundred and fifty copies, so the publisher wrote, lay at Columbus, Ohio. With a one-horse wagon and my companion, who still served me, marvelously, I started; arrived at Columbus; took thirty copies; went north, and began what to me was an era of unexampled prosperity. One hundred miles south did my way soon stretch to the hills of Athens, and there also books were sold, and success was won. But books cannot confine the trading genius of a young man. I caught sight of a man whose trading abilities did not, as I afterwards discovered, equal the honest endeavors I had to guard my own interests. My former "comrade in distress" was exchanged for a new one, with which I was to have some strange experiences. One has not left my thought, though years have intervened. Because life at that time was so full of enthusiasms and its activities were so urgent, whatever touched it became of a nature imperishable. Now, no amount of consideration of the seriousness of life, the value of one's body, and even the fearfulness of death, can chase away some ridiculous hues of humor with which that scene is covered. There are occasions when it is solemn even to laugh, and with this occasion I can only do honorable

service by describing, as the ludicrous affair has since
struck me, the first experience I had with the new
horse.   It is only a very true but irreverent illustration
• of what is a proverb, ''do not put new wine into old
bottles.''   For me thereafter it became ''do not drive a
new horse with an old bridle.''   What a long head had
that horse of which I was now relieved, and what a
short head had this horse of which I was now possessed.
I did not stop to think.   On went the bridle, in the
rush which prosperity had brought upon me.   A few
glances of pride—glances which never see anything,
for pride is blind—and I was ready to start.   That
country is diversity diversified.   Rough, covered with
hills that grow into mountains, deep ravines and large
boulders, made traveling a tragedy.   All this rugged
scenery had for the traveler its climax at Dickey's Hill,
a long descent on the road from Plymouth to Amesville,
whose course was broken by corduroy bridges of unexampled roughness, with deep gulleys at the sides, huge
rocks, which the traveler must dodge in his meandering
way, fallen trees, yet untouched by the hand of civilization, and a loneliness that settled over that new country
like death.   The hill was beyond a mile in length.   I
had began its descent.   Strangely, my horse developed
a strong mouth.   I tightened my grasp upon the reins.
Suddenly the gait of that animal quickened.   I expos-
tulated, in very quick, sharp terms, against this
increased speed.   The wagon bounced from the ground,
and I from the wagon.   I hinted to the steed that I was
not in such a hurry, and I said, very solemnly, something concerning a cessation of such a rapid descent.
Solemnity, words, kind and sharp, efforts at those reins
that tired me out, nothing would stop that beast.
The bits of that long bridle had fallen from her mouth,
and all my pulling only increased her speed.   On, like

the avalanche, we sped. I began to dodge, and think of the "last things." It was a sorry day for the book agent. Where would I land? My horse going faster. Would I land at all? I wished—I wished I was anything but this, and everywhere but here. Crash, through a limb; on, over the pole-bridges; shaking me dumb with their rough surfaces. It was not a pleasant ride. Besides, it was Sunday, and I did not feel that I was in a specially religious frame of mind, for I could see nothing, and as I began to think how foolish I must look, trying to stand up, and falling down, screaming through that wild region, eyes like moons; hair floating, like a flag in a storm from the mast of some ship; just as I thought of this, *crash*, against a fallen tree struck the wagon; away, like an arrow shot from a string, did I speed into the branches. We were stopped at last, but I did not like to be so taken by surprise. There stood my horse looking into the branches for me. Fastened by my torn clothes, I applied for freedom. Solemnly the concern I had rode in awaited my arrival. I took my bearings, for my head was clear, though it was somewhat less covered with skin. I adjusted that bridle, and, looking back over the hill, tried to feel solemn, but I then began a laugh, which has risen again, whenever in the fleeting years I have thought of that horse-trade.

4

CHAPTER III.

ON that trip I passed through Amesville, the home of the family of Bishop Ames, who, as a leader in Ecclesiastical Councils, as a deep and strong thinker into the value of methods and ways, as a statesman of unimpeachable fidelity to church and country, had no rival, and has to-day no critics. I may cherish for the future this fact concerning his home. It was a home of honesty, of thrift, of economy, of piety. Edward Raymond Ames was the child of these forces. Once at a sale made by Edward's father, my father purchased a candle-stick, which, while it holds a source of light, reminds me of that brave man who held in his soul the light of the world. I shall preserve it as a mute but eloquent story of that boy's life.

My book agency comes to its end. My success was so great that I had excited the jealousy of those who were so anxious to obtain my services. The Millers, of Lancaster, were astonished at my sales, and saw that they had dug a pit into which they would probably fall. They simply put an end to my work by securing the sole agency for the whole Western country. Thus ended my first successful venture into the business of the world.

After two months at home, I determined to strike out again for myself. Dreams of New York City, greater than all else but the vision of a young man visited me, and especially since I had learned more of the greatness of the world and its ways. All the West was made to catch and learn what might be found in out of this great city. To Kingston, in Ross County, Ohio, I pressed my way. I hired to a gentleman who was about to take a drove of horses across the mountains. That phrase "across the mountains" just then meant volumes. It was to that day a gigantic undertaking. It also meant much more than distance, for an idea had gained currency that all the civilization of the continent belonged in fee-simple to the Yankee, and he who would see the wonders thereof must visit it at home.

After my engagement I began preparations for myself and my employer. A runaway, and other laughable and dangerous occurrences, and we were off for the city. The route grew in attractiveness and pleasure as we advanced. I was experiencing a gradual enlargement of opinion, and my ideas of the world were undergoing a thorough and systematic expansion. But what was the astonishment of my mind when we entered the grandeur of the Alleghenies. My reader has seen what an influence touched me through that childhood home. But no hint can be given of the great influence of these towering sublimities cast in stone and covered with the glory of that luxuriant season, as I cast my eyes upon these mountains. As my boyhood was impressed with the Hocking hills, so was my early manhood with these bastions of stone. Up and up, they lifted their heads into infinite azure and bathed their broad shoulders in the dewy clouds. Broad foundations knitted to the core of the planet, bearing large forests, crowned with eternal verdure, sprinkled with beautiful flowers—these mountains seemed the name of God written in stone. From their summits one could gaze into the deep blue haze, which like a benediction hung over a large valley, Down, down, down, until the eye is lost in the immense chasm. Up, up, up, until the line which lies between the visible and the invisible seems touched by sight.

There in the green valley one silver thread—a river flowing in silence to the seas.   There in the amazing height
a quiver of sunbeams, shot like arrows from the sun, lie
brokened and fastened against the solid front, amid the
clouds.   The valleys between these huge piles of rock,
seemed like vast cups of sunshine, so full of the glory
that they overflowed.   The everlasting stillness was
solemnity infinite, their eternal solitude was the suggestion of the grandeur of the God who made them.

Especially did the Blue Ridge impress me.   Slowly
we came to their summits.   But as a vision, broke
the splendid panorama.   Great billowy clouds travel up
the valley and break against the mountain side into
fragments.   But over and beyond the clouds I looked
into the mirage of infinity.   Out of a mountain, the
highest of the region, there breaks forth a splendid
spring.   " Where does this head ?" the traveler says as
he looks for a hillside, or a higher point for the location of the vein.   And in that silence the question remains unanswered.   I think of another bursting spring,
upon another but spiritual mountain height, and while
the children of men see dripping down the mountain
sides, the waters of salvation, and ask, " Where does
this fountain head ?" the word of God answers: " And
he showed me a pure river of the water of life, clear as
crystal, proceeding out of the throne of God and of
the lamb."

I also remember the sight of Bedford in the valley,
and standing on a lofty place, I saw great clouds come
against the mountain on the other side, touch and dis-
solve into water, which fell in drops and tiny rills down
the rock-builded sides, and I thought of all the pictures
that I had seen, this was the grandest, since, it now
seems the story of redeemed manhood.   Every true
man feels those clouds touch his life, but he who

embodies the highest truth, keeps his head in eternal light, while they resolve themselves into dew and hang like jewels in the golden light, fall at his feet to, refresh the earth.

The route to New York was enjoyable, and the arrival was to me an intense pleasure. My horse was sold, and the money was soon in forty-eight brass clocks and a pile of books. The books were shipped to Logan, Ohio, and the clocks to Fort Wayne, Indiana, and then began my sight of the great city. It was all that my reader may imagine that such a splendid exhibition of the powers of man could be to a soul all earnestness to find the facts of the world in which he lived.

On the steamboat *Empire* I took passage, on the 19th day of May, for Albany. She was of fine timber, great capacity, and in all a beautiful ship. My eyes lingered long upon the coast, as through the river "we cut our liquid road." Oh, had we known the disaster which hung over and before us, and the doom of men and women who partook with us in the common sentiments which characterize even so short a voyage as this!—if we had seen the skirts of death floating in the Bay beyond us, we had lingered near and upon the shore still more tenderly and with yet deeper feelings of regret.

No description can be given of what occurred upon the peaceful bosom of that Bay of Newburgh. No pen can record the throbbings of any heart. No definition can include or even apprehend the woe which sweeps over human nature when life falls like a star from its place in the skies.

Life has such deep emotions, touches such eternal territory, has to do with such thrilling facts, that he who sees it when its own existence is in danger, sees it in its most terrible phase, and can divine its subtle forces. Such a revelation as I then witnessed held all these elements ; but so personal was it to myself, so frightful, in and of themselves, were the scenes which followed, that instead of what psychological analysis might have gained, I received confused but none the less real and awful impressions.

Night, dark as blackness itself, had settled down upon the river.   Over its surface we seemed to glide from darkness into darkness.   Silence, profound and half-sweet, had lulled the passengers to sleep.   Caught with the novelty and pleasure, alone, I paced the deck and lived life over again in my thought.   Ever and anon came the faint sound of the low-pressure engine.   Sleep, dreams of home, visions of beauty, the march of private cares through these sleeping brains—all these beneath, and soft dark silence covering the world, like a robe let down from above.

A staggering heavy thud that the waves could not hold amid their secrets !   A rush of waves ! plash ! plash !   and we stop the course of eighteen miles an hour.   It is an ominous, awful halt.   The alarm-bell sounds its dread despair.   Shrieks from the awakened passengers almost drown in volume the noise of aggressive waves.   In that terrible counterpoise of motions— it is all seen in the lurid glare of breaking lamps !   *The Noah Brown has run into us !*   The Empire is sinking ! " Help !" " Help !" " Help !" " Oh God !" " Save me !" " My child !"   Agonies deep as the human soul ring their groans through that dark and dreadful sky to heaven.   Heavily loaded with lumber, the *Noah Brown* has struck our death-blow, and that swift breeze has driven her, like an arrow, into the heart of the *Empire*.   I rushed upon the hurricane deck, seized a plank, determined to stand and help unto the last, and then save myself if I could.   Just then the schooner pitched forward.   I rushed to her, jumped on board, and in that act stepped from death to life. The *Empire* gurgled her death groan. Hearts rent with fear, souls torn with agony, cheeks white with terror, expressing the deep and volcanic feelings which also made the whole air a sob, and the world a tear, as the yells of the doomed, the piteous pleadings of the drowning, the gasping prayers of the lost, saluted our ears.

Just then, when the Empire had sunk so low that her hurricane-deck touched the water's edge, just then, like the hand of heaven, came the *Rip Van Winkle*, and many were saved; but as we moved out of sight, I saw the record of the unsaved; I thought of the broken homes, the wretched firesides, the wounded and grief-stricken souls which would never see, but would always partake in that billowy, foaming grave we left behind us.

We reached Albany. No glorified structure could possess my soul, else the state-house there would have displaced in my mind, for the time being, that awful wreck. We passed through the luxuriant Mohawk Valley. Rochester, with all its stately beauty, pleased me. Alone of the survivors of the Empire, did I take passage on the *Baltic* for Cleveland. Another dreadful experience of mind was mine when the *Baltic*, struck with a propeller, staggered in its watery path. I was excited beyond thought, and only saw the bow broken, the guard torn, and heard the deafening crash. I was only satisfied when I learned that the boat was substantially unharmed, and after the delay of inspection, saw speeding toward Cleveland, our imperiled craft.

The beautiful city was reached at three o'clock, but in a very unhappy condition was I to enter any city, and indeed to exist upon the face of a planet, where people charged for lodging and board, where stage-drivers anxiously looked for the fare.

Never before was I so anxious to try the New Testament plan of travel. Never since have I felt the embarrassment I felt through that weary route. The fact was, I was only possessed of twenty-five cents, and a three dollar bill, which bill was a lie of the deepest significance to me, since it was a counterfeit bill. Some vandal, seeing an amount of ignorance proportioned to my anxiety to get home, had put that note upon me, and it was just then a more serious problem than the sinking of the *Empire*.

According to the landlord where I slept, the night's rest was worth forty cents, while I had only twenty-five. My story was told with such earnestness and truth, that I had no difficulty in getting him to take the last named sum for my debt. I was then loose in the world, far from home, and possessed of three dollars in bad money. I had reached Wooster. My heart was heavy. My clothes were dirty enough. I had nothing but that horrible story, and my uncleaned garments, to recommend me. But I met there, what was more than money to me; men of broad shouldered, working charity—a kind so very rare—of great and aggressive kindness, which does not appear largely in census reports;—men who gave me an opportunity to get to my home. The internal experience of that visit at the kind invitation of Mr. Jacobs to his own home, the mental life which silently executed itself as I changed my rusty garment for a clean one, the unseen throbbings of gratitude, when after I had started on foot to Zanesville, was seized by the hand of a true friend and nobleman, J. H. McBride, and made to remain all night, and then set out when morning came with ample funds—all that I felt could not but flow in tears, and to-day it moves my heart. To those men I owed my trip to my home, by way of Zanesville, and their kindness, but when I see life in its issues and know how the destinies are lodged in the smallest acts and occurrences, I feel that the debt can never be paid, and that it is a privilege to be forever grateful.

In a short time after I returned home, I attacked the whole county with my books. I had been born full of energy. I had learned pertinacity and earnestness. I now had lately added to my stock in trade, some experience and enthusiasm born and nurtured by seeing the enthusiasm of others.

When I approached the subject, the people plead ''cholera ;'' and it was a place that had pathetic persuasiveness in its tones. People were dying by hundreds, and the whole country was frightened. Yet, in spite of the fact that many suggested that the death-angel would prevent their reading my books, and others pleaded indifference and woe, I sold them in a few days, and out of regard to my clocks and the people of Indiana, I started to effect their sale at Fort Wayne. What Northern Indiana was at that time, I have thought to leave to the pen of Edward Eggleston. I only have to say, that the " Hoosier School-master" seems to me to be a story true in conception and in detail. There is a depth of suggestion in that word *Hoosier*, which expresses it all. They gazed upon my clocks with stupendous surprise. I could have told them that they controlled the times and seasons with perfect safety. I encountered clock peddlers of all degrees of veracity, honesty and rascality, and never have been so impressed with the total depravity of that section of the human race as when I became one of them, *not in spirit nor in letter*, but as a miracle of grace and of truth, trying to sell an honest clock as an honest man. Human genius cannot be sounded by the critic of Angelo, Raphael and Turner. Ruskin never met an Indiana clock peddler. No

5

idea of the gigantic strength of the imagination of man
can be gained by an elaborate study of Shakespeare,
Milton and Dante.   Macaulay never heard a clock peddler describe the unseen glories of his wares.   Only the
faintest conception of the politician can be reached by
a view of Talleyrand, Michiavelli, and Beaconsfield.
Evidently Froude never saw displayed the tactics of a
clock peddler in Indiana, when before an entranced
band of Hoosiers, he sought to establish the claims of
that marvelous machine.   I, who followed in their wake,
and tried to do with truth and reason what they attempted by poetry and imagination—I, who wished I too had
genius oftentimes, shall not forget how at that juncture
in my life my idea of the abilities of my brother-man
suddenly received an amazing enlargement.

I well knew that there was no use to attempt imita-
tion.   I loved honesty also, and tried to sell good clocks
for good prices, and succeeded where my brilliant com-
petitors failed.   There may be a suggestion in my story
of the proverbial man who told his boys, when they left
home to seize life for themselves : " Now, boys, honesty
is the best policy; I tell you so, I have tried both." But
I assure my readers that I had respect to conscience ; I
never could make myself believe that man could enjoy
any sort of success, who carried a burning conscience.   I
have always had a greater fear of the hells inside than
those outside.   I have always valued manhood as more
than circumstances.   The man who shall think himself
transformed by a change of circumstances, has mistaken
the whole nature of things.   He who is pure within will
see light in darkness.   He who is impure within, even
if he were to sit forever amid heaven's purity, with white
robes, with a song whose tones were purity itself in his
mouth, must feel, as he looks within, the gigantic difference and his heaven would be perdition itself.   He

who preserves his manhood will be preserved. He who keeps heaven in him, can not wander out through the golden gate.

The clocks were sold, and I was at home in November. As I came by way of Lancaster, I there made what was to me a most magnificent purchase, of one hundred and eighty-two acres of land, lying in Star Township, Hocking County, Ohio. For three years I had been watching the destiny of the land; and with all the earnest feeling one may experience who loves a home, and a home of his own, I took possession of it.

To my half-brother, Mr. Isaac Casey, I was glad to give eighty acres of it. While I had been rewarded with the gratitude of all concerned, and with the praise of his neighbors and my own friends, the satisfaction that came to me, as in experience I learned the depth of this sentiment: "It is more blessed to give than to receive," has been more than all.

At this point there begins a chapter of my experience which has given me some amusement, and some cause to think that I then possessed an audacity of which I cannot now feel myself conscious. Faith is as practical as it is pious, though none the less practical because a sentiment of religion. I believe that a conquering faith in the world, in one's self, in the value of life, is one of the prerequisites, the necessities of success. Faith is capital. He who seeks to take the world without it will be taken by the world with it. Its audacity will be honorable and invincible, and its conquests are everywhere. The boy who doubts if he can walk a foot log across a stream, is almost sure to fail and fall in, and experience has taught me, that a man can buy instruments and take pictures with little else but a working faith in himself and in his enterprise.

This is the story. In December, 1849, Dr. H. Jackson amazed my awkwardness, by suggesting that I go into the "daguerreotype business," as it was termed. The proposition that I should become a master of art was to me, and is yet a miracle. My sensibilities were as well suited to the work proposed, as Johnson's mind was to the material of his own poetry, as the soul of Mme. DeStael to the Bay of Naples. Art was to me a palace with closed doors. The country was, however, excited over the possibilities of preserving the human feature, and I was convinced that some fellow who had no more of the art instinct than myself, would astonish the natives with their pictures, and himself with their money. In January, 1850, I learned that if a man would settle in Arkansas, he might become monarch of all he surveyed. "Land" was my cry, like the gasp of a sinking ocean-ranger. Without a thought of the value of it, and of the terrible fate of a man who must live in such a place, I started for this place of "land." Upon my forehead was written "land ahead," and the tendency must have been so strongly expressed, as to give every one the impression that I was bound for the West.

Arriving at Cincinnati, I was not burdened with means, and the fertile thought of my "red paint," which had grown such rich harvests already, touched me again. Soon I was at the house of Springman & Son, and found ideas larger and quite as valuable to me as my paint. The condition of Arkansas was described, and with considerable discomfiture, I went away.

"How about the daguerreotype business?" I thought.

I rushed to the first artist I could find, and was greeted in such a fashion that I should have deemed myself honored to become a member of his fraternity. I asked him for prices.

"How much do the things come at?"

"Well, they come at different prices; they are high, and low, and medium."

"I do'nt want a costly one," said I, "and, to tell the truth, I don't see how I can get any."

"You can't get much of a one for less than a hundred dollars. I guess that is the lowest."

"Wher'll I get one; I don't know where they sell 'em," said I, perfectly amazed at the price, and feeling myself never so poor. I put on my hat and went to Peter Smith's, and with only forty dollars, here I was left—sick of the Arkansas idea, and ashamed of my funds as in contrast with the value of an instrument.

I stammered and asked foolish questions. I had no idea whether what I saw standing there on legs was an "instrument" for this business or a guillotine. But my faith had increased, and I asked questions until I was pretty certain that the institution he had offered me with all the paraphernalia and necessities to run it, was that identical machine standing before me. But "eighty dollars," (for that was his *reduced* price)—thought I. "Forty is my all." I explained the poverty which like leprosy clung to me. I told a long, honest, and it must have been a funny story. He took in the situation. We talked about Arkansas, then "about time on the balance." I told him an incident, and he asked me, "How much can you pay down?" I had a cough, and managed to expel a very poor story from my lips, which were dry with the state of things, and then said, like a half sick lover to his own: "about thirty-five dollars."

There was no trade. I appreciated his feelings, and I guess he did mine. Sixty dollars were necessary, and the hope of it had no soil upon which to grow.

That omnipresent "red paint" again stood in seried ranks of kegs before my mind. I had faith, but more

in Springman & Son, than in the "paint" itself.   I
dodged the sight of the paint, but hunted the gentleman
in control.   That long story was told, and covered with
the enthusiasm I had, but as straight as truth.   The
"truth prevailed."

"You shall not want the money," were the magic
words that had no sooner left Springman's mouth than
my heart fluttered; dreams of great galleries of pictures
fastened upon my eyes, and that instrument seemed
mine.

To Peter Smith the story was told.   A package of
drugs and chemicals, and that instrument were mine.
The way to my home was longer than ever, and if the
vision had been granted me of the ignorant questions
which were to descend upon me, like the Goths upon
Rome, I fear I would have refused to follow it.

But the machine and its equipments were no more
marvelous to them than to me.   I had seen New York
City and the mountains, but they did not seem so
problematic as the newly purchased possession.   I
could not clearly see its beauty, and was altogether un-
decided about its uses.   The application of the drugs
was even beyond this, as a deep question.   I attempted
explanation, and between the desire to say nothing that
would expose the secret and my utter ignorance as to
what the secret really was, the explanation must have
been exceedingly elaborate, trustworthy and clear.
When quiet reigned and silence came, I would quietly
examine the machine myself.   I never dared unscrew
the parts or pull the joints, inasmuch as I might dislo-
cate the affair beyond my remedies, and I was, so far
as this *genus* was concerned, the only doctor in the
country.   I could see the use of this, if it were detached
and in use in the harvest field.   I could understand the
use of that, if it were only on different legs and made the

other side to. But that thing as a whole, so long legged, one eyed, and small bodied, came into my imagination and reason like a sea into a tin cup; it was in and of itself, literally incomprehensible.

And then how the machine took pictures; where the subject or object stood, or walked, or sat; what the artist had to do; and the precise relationship of these horribly scented drugs to the whole enterprise—all these added to the problem. I, however, found that my drugs smelled like the office of my first artist friend, and with that whiff of air, a solid satisfaction overcame my fears, and I went to Zanesville to find the secret.

At Zanesville, I found a man who had as much audacity to display as I had already shown to my own neighborhood. Very soon I got all he knew, which was very little. But I had magnified his services to me, in supposing that I understood the entire fragment he gave of what I ought to have known. If I had possessed one grain less of faith in myself and in the ability of the machine to work of its own accord, and in spite of itself, I never would have allowed that first subject to look toward the instrument.

One occurrence will illustrate my own ignorance.

When I looked over my outfit and counted the drugs, I recollected their names, and felt secure that what I had were all right; but a lingering memory of Iodine had asserted itself, and with these alone I could not make pictures entirely satisfactory to myself, even though the town was loud in my praise. Around the bottle of bromine, sea-sand had been packed, and I leaped to the conclusion one day: "Why, what a fool I have been; this is the Iodine." So, at the proper time, in the history of the genesis of a picture—heaven will forgive the pun I have made so many times—I passed the whole performance over this sea-sand with

with what must have been wonderful but totally invisible effects. Solemnly have I stood, half doubting, and yet not daring to doubt, the use of the Iodine, just like a man when he has seen the nonsense of some idea associated with religion, which he feels it sacrilege to question. But I did not see the influence of *that* Iodine, yet I hung out my card, and told many whom I thought ought to have been ashamed of their ignorance, that *that* was Iodine, and one of the necessities of the art. By that time I could say "Art" with an astonishing liquidness of utterance, which gave the idea that I was its king and lord.

Great questions presented themselves—yet none so great as the running of that institution. Why would certain people desire their pictures? What a joke to inflict upon posterity, was it that certain men and women, with faces of a decidedly Gothic architecture, persisted in having their features for the ages? Whether that country will forgive my perpetuating those faces, I do not know. Women would gaze with rapture upon the homeliest portraits I have ever seen. The joy seemed to come in inverse proportion to the beauty. Once in a while a fellow would see himself as others saw him, and gladly take one and pledge himself, as he left the hall, never to return. All sorts of fun came to my lot. The "Aurora Borealis" had lately received some public mention, and some people had mixed it with my "Camera Obscura," as the old lady cried out, "*E pluribus unum* and *terra firma*," when she was taught to say, as she entered the room, "*Veni, Vidi, Vici.*" I had heard of the man who thought it was dangerous and might "go off," but I want to tell my readers of a near-sighted woman who persisted in moving her chair near to the instrument, and when the artist remonstrated and begged her to go back, and then had to ask her:

"Why do you persist in worrying my life out? Sit where I place you. Why do you get near?"

"Why," responded the old lady, "I must git where I kin see the ' *Aurory.*' I reckon it can see to take me farther 'n I kin."

One beautiful recollection which had its rise as I went down the river, must be chronicled.

While we were going from shore, and out into the stream, a dignified presence fastened my attention. There stood upon that boat a man whose personal following was perhaps as affectionate as it was large, and as devoted to him as it was earnest for the principles their leader advocated. No man who ever looked into that pleasant face, heard the sweet symphonies of that magic voice, and felt the inexpressible charm of that magnetic personality, can forget the earthly lineaments of this spirit divine. I was caught immediately by that form and its genius,

" A combination and a form indeed,
Where every god did seem to set his seal
To give the world assurance of a man.''

Tall and agile, his head is borne upon magnificent but gracefully shapen shoulders. His step is soft, yet majestic. His whole nature expresses itself in that self-poised and benignant carriage; his entire character writes its soliloquy in that finest dignity, the weighty values of which he was in conscious control, and which filled him with an unconscious sublimity. Eyes like the soft and spirit-like windows to the brain of a gazelle; a fore-head, on which might have been written the constitution, and behind which blazed the fires of thought; a mouth, holding the words of destiny; now like a casket of kindness; then, like a ledge of stone behind which justice was held; all these, filled until they trembled with divine enthusiasm, had a tenfold significance when

6

rising to its full height that splendid figure became a *voice*, a net-work of countless melodies; a tone woven of harmonies, and, before an adoring populace gathered upon the river bank, sounding forth the deepest principles of civilization and the loftiest ideals of human government. It was the presence, personality and speech of that popular leader, HENRY CLAY.

He was *en route* from Washington. It was before the statesman had been retired for the captain. Taylor had not yet vanquished him in honors. It was in fact during that great campaign; and while the people would hear him, and desired to hear personal self-defense. It remains a scene in my memory, touched with moral heroism, for Henry Clay preached to them the ideal toward which he fondly desired the nation to march.

Description of Clay's eloquence belongs to no pen. All serious attempt to compass the task and accurately portray the spiritual in him upon the material, and through the material to the spiritual in his audience, are cherished and yet must be called failures. Not even an effort in that direction will be made here. If to other pictures anything may be added from these mixed hues, I shall be thankful; and because, no man can fully realize the greatness of his kind, who has not seen such matchless illustrations in their sublime moments.

I remember above all, one short address. There he stood. His whole bearing added rays of glory to the idea I had of a man. He filled Shakespeare's definition full to overflowing.

Behind that man was history enough to make him seem an embodied message from the skies. The "Millboy of the Slashes," his early poverty, his record as a lawyer, his treatment of the "alien and sedition laws," his silencing the tongue of slander, his advocacy of domestic interests, his war speech, his relations with Jack-

son, his championship of whig principles, his vote for
John Q. Adams, the defense he had made, his whole life
—these with just enough mistakes, with just enough
forgetfulness of right, with just enough affection for the
expedient to make it like a fleecy cloud, which, all baptized in light became fringed with gold as his thought
came in music and fell upon those living souls.   He
stood like a rock-ribbed coast, against this idea and that
notion of political policy.   He fell like a sunbeam upon
this struggling conception of national progress to woo
it into life.   He thundered like Niagara against wrong.
He stretched great loving benediction over the militant
but not yet triumphant right, and as the boat moved
away he became a warm and genial light, to make all
who came near him feel the value of genius with its
great ideas, and a sublime nature.

> " With its droppings of tears,
> And its touches of things common,
> 'Till they rise to touch the spheres.''

CHAPTER IV.

I F ever there was an itinerant, I was that man. One week without taking a picture, almost persuaded me to leave New Plymouth; but I determined on another plan, and this gave me more time with this people whom I did not love, even as they did not love me. They made fun of me and my pictures, and I confess, either because I had utterly no interest in the subject, or because I was afraid, I did not and never shall investigate their grounds of ridicule.

My ignorance of the use of the forces I did *not* have under my control grew with my growth and strengthened with my strength, as an artist. At McArthur I was amazed at myself. I began to have no doubts about my genius; for as I saw the result, and knew how small my information was, I was forced to the conclusion that my abilities must be of a gigantic species. But even here I was glad to sell my instrument. I sold it to G. W. Pilcher, whom I could not violently love, inasmuch as his *finesse* was even greater than his egotism, leaving me sadly defeated at what was then almost a financial Waterloo.

Speaking of egotism, and in connection with this name, I am reminded of a clerical gentleman by that name, whose self-conceit was only equaled by his goodness and truth. Yet once in a while his egotism would overtop all else, and the resulting scene often was excruciating or ridiculous. Once he was preaching at Delaware, Ohio, before an audience of culture, wealth and refinement. Many sceptics sat in the congregation. The occasion was one of which much account was made, since Bishop Thomson—that most gentle and persuasive of pulpit orators—had been expected to preach, and on account of poor health had been compelled to ask Bro. Pilcher to preach in his stead. Now, any other man would have refused. Any other man but Henry Pilcher would have been all mellow with feeling, and weighted with the great occasion. Not so, Pilcher. He tossed his head like a hero. Thomson sat behind him as he arose to speak. With all conceivable pomposity, he announced his text. "The Lord help," quietly, gently, and as a brother, said the great Bishop. Rising to his full height, inflated until he stood the very embodiement of self-conceit, Pilcher said in a fine but squeaky voice, expressing its tones from out distended cheeks and under raised eyebrows: "I—I thank you, yes, I thank you, Bishop. It is a kind prayer. But I—(a cough)—I feel entirely capable for this topic *without any foreign aid.*" I have always thought that this occurrence needed no commentary. It is the scripture of egotism in object-lesson.

Chills and fever attacked me after my sale. These I passed triumphantly. I heard that at Logan there was a regular and very fine artist, and started in that direction. I knew that I did not know it all, but I afterwards found that I did not begin to see the depths of ignorance as others who had names which were known far and wide. I entered this great artist's studio and place of operations, with all the humility I could master. Impressed with my gorgeous littleness as an artist, I looked up into sublime altitudes of art-intelligence to find my great contemporary. When I began to speak, I was met with ridicule. I walked about the establishment, and saw pictures which did not justify his making

any sort of fun.   I knew I could make finer work than
any on exhibition there.   Such a storm of abuse I have
not received—a storm like a fall rain, so pertinacious,
so irritating with mildness—and to it all, I then and
there resolved to respond.

I rented a room on the opposite corner.   I secured a
good outfit.   I charged my pictures with all the sense
and experience I had.   Ladies thronged my gallery.   I
put incessant work upon every detail.   The first gentlemen of the town came and sat for work.   I resolved to
let honesty and hard work do what they could, and they
administered to him a rebuke he could not forget.

My "sensitive" became most ungovernable.   My
pictures began to lack clearness and lustre.   I heard
that a good artist lived in Athens, and although I had
had my faith severely tried, yet I wended a weary way
to Athens, and that for the purpose of getting information.   I arrived and saluted him as a pupil, not men-
tioning this most humiliating fact.   I have not been
more royally treated.   He went to all trouble, and gave
me a feeling of pleasure, which one who has been made
" *at home*" knows and appreciates.   In the morning he
told me what seemed a most pitiful story.   He detailed
his failures, until his story was an Iliad of woes.   He
had not taken a picture for several days.   He had put
all his multiplying customers into an expectant frame
of mind, when he said he could not serve them, by
promising also that an experienced and first-class artist
would be in town soon.   Who he was to be, he never
could tell.   And now he sat with great smiles on his
face, and clapping his hands, he said: "You 're the
man."

I protested as much as I could without showing absolute ignorance, and resolved to bear the burden.   He
escorted me down to the gallery.   He introduced me as

a great artist. As well might a tombstone cutter be called Phidias. I walked up to the situation. I entered the room and said, " Now you let me look around, and see your methods and chemicals." This I did to save myself from exposure. I told him I was not a first-class artist, but I did not tell him that I had come to learn of him. I entered the dark room, and there in a bottle, labeled by Peter Smith, I found the word "Iodine." " By George," thought I, "it aint like mine; mine is dry and like sand. It is sand, sure as heaven." I mused and then thought of the laughable figure I had cut, and then after laughing for a time at the *sea-sand Iodine*, I swore never to tell the story. Reader, your smile is the first.

"Now," said I, " Let us try the thing. Sit down."

A picture, bright as morning! another, and another, and the man worshiped my stupendous genius and great erudition. He wanted to pay me, pleaded to do it, but I could not charge for my ignorance. Yet I very gladly remarked—and little did he know of the genesis of the idea—that when I left, I would take some *Iodine*. His customers returned. His popularity grew, and I found out the difference between sea-sand and Iodine.

I sold my outfit, bought a new one, sent it before me and found myself in Parkersburg, W. Va. If I had taken a catalogue of towns and selected the one least suited to my business, I could not have escaped Parkersburg. The dashing of the Little Kanawha had no prospects of bliss or poetry in store for an artist. The town received me as gracefully as I could expect, having once seen the elements which entered into its life. It was to a new comer, like Charles Lamb's cold spring, with a warm day :

" Unmeaning joy around appears,
And nature smiles as though she sneers."

To Harrisonville, Point Pleasant, Buffalo, Va., Middle-port, Nelsonville and Pomeroy, with competition the most lively, meeting men of all shades of character, fortunes, and prospects, through one fire and much gain and loss, teaching others my art,—I closed for a time this line of work in Ross County, at Adelphi, and Tarl-ton, with a deeper love of truth, and a more profound hatred of wrong, a larger idea of the value of life, and a truer perception of a source of inspiration than I had ever had before.

He who sees only the perishable and loves it, proves his mortality and seals it.   He who fastens to the undy-ing and swears allegiance to it, declares his personal character and proves his own individuality.   There is more in honesty than the " best policy," as there is more in life than breath and existence.

> " And ever something is or seems
> That touches us with mystic gleams
> Like glimpses of forgotten dreams."

In every choice of personal honor rather than and at the expense of circumstantial glory, a man touches the beyond.   He consults the everlasting and the permanent. He may seem defeated, but his defeat is the seed which shall bear flowers of immortal victory.   He seems to be lost in darkness, he shall emerge in light.   The word of a hero at the issues of life, as well as at the issue of death, is Browning's most imposing strain :

> "Though I stoop
> Into a dark, tremendous sea of cloud,
> It is but for a time, I press God's lamp
> Close to my breast; its splendor, soon or late,   .
> Will pierce thy gloom; I shall emerge some time."

We do not appreciate the forces of the life that now is.   We would find that they were fastened to the throne, if our sight were strong.   The world's business is run

on honesty, truth and righteousness. They are higher
than expediency, policy and neutrality; and he who
feels their force has shown the realm to which he belongs. There is a "*sweet by and by*" to any body to
whom there is a *grand* "*here and now.*"

> " Here sits he shaping wings to fly
> His heart forebodes the mystery ·
> He names the name *eternity.*"

I went to Decatur, Indiana, to find that people who
thought I had concluded not to come for the pay for
my clocks were not prepared to pay, and I made happy
a lawyer who took the claims.

November 15, and I have set up, for a second time,
a gallery in Logan. I visited that historic New Plymouth. I thought of my Iodine and enjoyed the growth
of the country. To Pomeroy, McArthur and Cincinnati, with a new stock of necessities, I went down the
river to a somewhere I knew not of.

I was glad to arrive at North Bend. This was the
burial place of that political favorite, Wm. Henry Harrison, ex-President of the Nation he did so much to redeem from barbarism and England's tyranny. The
house which he once occupied is a plain country farm-
house. His grave is a vault of brick, on a beautiful
hillock, in full view of the river.

Here the hero of Tippecanoe lived the solitary life,
out of which the statesman and political leader came
forth, caparisoned for the leadership of that great party,
and the championship of such great ideas.

Harrison's home reminds one of that great man. He
was beyond many of his peers as a politician. He was
greater than most of his contemporaries as a thinker.
His was a mind, which in advance of those about him,
could fly aloft and see the landscape of the past, present
and future. He was a statesman of remarkable forces

7

of strength.   He was a general which knew no hardship, was conscious of no cowardice, and moved into true patriotism, was exiled by the devotion of such great abilities from defeat.   But greater than the general, statesman, thinker, and politician, was the personality which towered above them, and spoke through them. A giant in them all, he was a monarch as a man.

This was the chord which the people struck, and which yielded such music that he became President of their nation.   They admired the gigantic mind, the iron logic, the swift, and almost universal gaze, the mighty intellectual tread of Daniel Webster.   The silvery eloquence of Henry Clay, sending into the abysmal depths of the country's soul that announce- ment, "I had rather be right than President," roused their affectionate esteem.   The metaphysical insight, the colossal argument, the fierce invective of John Cal- houn bended them to his clarion voice.   The laurels which pressed heavily upon the head of Scott were of evergreen, and flowers which the grateful dews of the whole American sky would keep fresh forever.   They were all there; but William Henry Harrison was a thorough, duty-loving, incorruptible man, and the people placed manhood in the chief-seat of modern times.

His name made "hard cider" a phrase of inspiration like the peal of a trumpet.   "Log cabins" were more popular than thrones, and when he fell in one month, having satisfied the people by the selection of his Cabi- net that he sought to be "*chief*" by being "*the servant of all,*" they buried his body here, and his memory in their hearts.

Harrison had many of the popular qualities of our own later Ohio leaders—Thomas Corwin.   I recollect of him, however, as an orator, rather than a leader of a great party. I heard him but once. It was at Columbus, Ohio, while there with one of my friends.

Said I to my friend:

"Let us go and hear Tom Corwin." Shouts of "The Wagoner Boy" rent the air, which was full of hurrahs and greetings.

We found our way with and through the crowd—a crowd whose tumult knew no bounds. There was a certain heartiness in this tumult which was especially perceptible. On that whole vast surge of people was the feeling that Tom Corwin meant honesty and boldness, and that his splendid audacity was the audacity of genius and of the unyielding nature of Right. The City of Columbus had been the witness of that large convocation of his supporters. The enthusiasm of that day knew no bounds. It was fired by an eloquence scarcely less than that of Corwin. When a speaker recounted the efforts of his life, and the audience were ready, the following words swept into shouts of applause: "When the brave Harrison and his gallant army were exposed to the dangers and hardships of the northwestern frontier, separated from the interior, on which they were dependent for their supplies, by the brushwood and swamps of St. Mary's country, through which there was no road, where each wagoner had to make his way wherever he could find a passable place, leaving traces and routes which are still visible for a space of several days' journey in length, there was one team managed by a little, dark-complexioned, hardy-looking lad, apparently about fifteen or eighteen years old, who was familiarly called Tom Corwin. Through all that service he proved himself a good whip and an excellent reinsman. And in the situation in which we are about to place him, he will be found equally skillful."

All this old feeling came upon the multitude. Some

even remembered the old song of that great canvass,
and one fellow struck up the first verse in pristine melody:

> "Success to you, Tom Corwin !
>   Tom Corwin, our true hearts love you !
> Ohio has no nobler son,
>   In worth there is none above you.
> And she will soon bestow
>   On you her highest honor;
> And then our State will proudly show
>   Without a stain upon her."

To one who knew Corwin, it was not even an ordinary
occasion.   For no man so filled the popular idea of a
stump-speaker in Ohio as did Thomas Corwin.   He was
above all things, a gentleman.   Not in that sense, which,
dictated by policy, defines every thing else.   He was
not a man who had no opinions, or if he had opinions,
did not express them.   He was not a man who lacked
strength.   His throne was power.   He was not a *gentle*
man so much as a gentle *man*.   His gentleness was that
of a large-souled, noble, earnest man.   He had the gentleman hid in the man, in another sense, and that had
power with men.   He was, so far as statesmanship can
be mentioned, true, and loved the Right.

Put this behind and let it operate through a great bold
presence—a full exponent of a rich and strong soul —a
voice, strong in its tenderness, tender in its strength ;
an eye, which always meant what the brain behind it
thought, which would glisten with tears, twinkle with
humor, burn with sarcasm, scorch with irony, cut like
a Damascus-blade with wit, beam with hope, shudder in
gloom with despair and gaze into the secrets of the sev-
enth heaven with prophecy; a brain and heart so ac-
cordant as to discover truth together and love it, which,
too, knew the depths of pathos, the significance of woe,
the boundlessness of love, the greatness of truth, the
absolute regnancy of Justice, the omnipotent powers of

Right ;—put a most noble man behind these all in most noble quantities, and you have Tom Corwin on the stump.

All the versatility which came from these was his. His audiences would hiss and applaud, groan and shout, yell and keep silent as the stars above them, hurrah and weep, laugh and get mad, and all because this magician owned the wand which touched them. He would rest an audience on fun, then tire it out with argument; feast it on wit, worry it with statistics ; and, in short, fill those who heard him with the peculiarities of each, that he might control each and all.

His genius compassed the noble instincts of political morality, and the richest humor of the soul ; and, in both, he became pre-eminent. When he made that great speech in the Senate, he showed in lurid outline the hand of Wrong which had been petted by Webster, Clay, and others, under the name of *Expediency*. There was, however, no policy but that of eternity in these mighty words on

" UNJUST NATIONAL ACQUISITIONS. "

MR. PRESIDENT:—The uneasy desire to augment our territory has depraved the moral sense, and blighted the otherwise keen sagacity of our people. Sad, very sad, are the lessons which time has written for us. Through and in them all, I see nothing but the inflexible execution of that old law which ordains as eternal, the cardinal rule, " thou shalt not covet thy neighbor's goods, nor anything which is his." Since I have so lately heard so much about the dismemberment of Mexico, I have looked back to see how, in the course of events, which some call Providence, it has fared with other nations, who engaged in this work of dismemberment. I see that in the latter half of the eighteenth century, three powerful nations, Russia, Austria and Prussia, united in the dismemberment of Poland. They said, too, as you say, "it is our destiny." "They wanted room." Doubtless each of these thought with his share of Poland, his power was too strong ever to fear invasion, or even insult. One had his California, another his New Mexico, and the third his Vera Cruz. Did they remain untouched, and incapable of harm? Alas! no—far, very far from it. Retributive justice must fulfill its destiny too.

A very few years pass off, and we hear of a new man, a Corsican lieutenant, the self-named "armed soldier of Democracy," Napoleon. He ravages Austria, covers her land with blood, drives the northern Cæsar from his capitol, and sleeps in his palace. Austria may now re-member how her power trampled upon Poland. Did she not pay dearly, very dearly for her California? But has Prussia no atonement to make? You see the same Napoleon, the blind instrument of Providence at work there. The thunders of his cannon at Jena, pro-claim the work of retribution for Poland's wrongs; and the successors of the great Frederick, the drill-sergeant of Europe, are seen flying across the sandy plains that surround their capitol, right glad that they may escape captivity and death. But how fares it with the autocrat of Russia? Is he secure in his share of the spoils of Poland? No. Suddenly we see, sir, six hundred thou-sand armed men marching to Moscow. Does his Vera Cruz protect him now? Far from it. Blood, slaughter, and desolation spread abroad over the land; and finally the conflagration of the old commercial metropolis of Russia closes the retribution. She must pay for her share in the dismemberment of her impotent neighbors. Mr. President, a mind more prone to look for the judgments of Heaven in the doings of men than mine, cannot fail in all unjust acquisitions of territory to see the Providence of God.

When Moscow burned, it seemed as if the earth was lighted up, that the nations might behold the scene. As that mighty sea of fire gathered and heaved, and rolled upward and yet higher, till its flames licked the stars, and fired the whole heavens, it did seem as though the God of the nations was writing in characters of flame on the front of the throne, that doom that shall fall upon the weak. And what fortune awaits him, the appointed executor of this work when it was all done? He too, conceived the notion that his destiny pointed onward to universal dominion. France was too small— Europe, he thought, should bow down before him. But as soon as this idea takes possession of his soul, he too becomes powerless. His terminus must recede too. Right then, while he witnesses the humiliation and doubtless meditated the subjugation of Russia, He who holds the winds in his fists, gathered the snows of the north and blew them upon his six hundred thousand men. They fled—they froze—they perished. And now the mighty Napoleon, who had resolved on universal dominion, he too, is summoned to answer for the violation of that ancient law—"thou shalt not covet any thing which is thy neighbor's."

How is the mighty fallen! He, beneath whose proud footstep Europe trembled, he is now an exile at Elba, and now, finally a prisoner on the rock of St. Helena, and then on a barren island in an unfrequented sea, in the crater of an extinguished volcano, there is the death-bed of the mighty conqueror. All his annexations have come to that! His last hour is now at hand; and he, the man of destiny, he who had rocked the world as with the throes of an earthquake, is now powerless,

still—even as the beggar, so he dies.   On the wings of
a tempest that raged with unwonted fury, up to the
throne of the only power that controlled. him while he
lived, went the fiery soul of that wonderful warrior,
another witness to the existence of that eternal decree,
that " they who do not rule in righteousness shall perish
from the earth.   He has found ·" room " at last, and
France, she too has found " room."   Her " eagles "
now no longer scream along the banks of the Danube,
the Po, and the Borysthenes.   They have returned
home, to their old aerie, between the Alps, the Rhine,
and the Pyrenees.   So shall it be with yours.   You
may carry them to the loftiest peaks of the Cordilleras ;
they may wave with insolent triumph in the halls of the
Montezumas ; the armed men of Mexico may quail before them ; but the weakest hand in Mexico, uplifted in
prayer to the God of Justice, may call down against
you, a power, in presence of which the iron hearts of
your warriors shall be turned into ashes.

   When they struck the liberty-loving and anti-slavery
men of Massachusetts, one, who afterwards became one
of the chieftains of freedom—Henry Wilson—wrote to
a friend of Corwin, as follows :

   " The people are delighted with the speech of Corwin.   He has touched the popular heart, and the question asked in the cars, streets, houses, and everywhere
men assemble, is : Have you read Tom Corwin's speech ?
Its boldness and high moral tone meet the feelings here,
and the people of New England will respond to it, and
tens of thousands want to hear more from him.   Tell
him to come out, though, in favor of the Wilmot Pro-
viso.   We all hope and expect it of him.   We can give
him every State in New England if he will take the
right ground against slavery.   How I should like to
vote for him and some good non-slaveholder for Vice

President in 1848. I suppose that Webster, Clayton, Mangum, and Crittenden will be against him, for his speech was a terrible rebuke to them, and I am much mistaken if some of them very readily forget or forgive him. Their position is a most disgraceful one."

Of his wit, Dr. Mansfield, to whom I am indebted for this letter, relates this: His first appearance was in the Ohio Legislature. Some of the primitive laws and institutions still remained in Ohio. Among others, the whipping-post still remained, whipping being an old New England punishment for small offenders. Some member had introduced a bill repealing the whipping law. Upon this, a member from Trumbull County, rose and said he saw no objection to the whipping-post. He always observed that when a man was whipped in his State (Connecticut) he immediately left the State. Corwin arose and said, that "he knew a great many people had come to Ohio from Connecticut, but he never knew before the reason for their coming."

Keener wit never existed than his, and a more true humor, which had all the earnestness of his wit, has not been found.

To illustrate this element of humor: The ex-Governor was in Columbus, Ohio, and, filled with thought concerning an important suit at law, brushed his way along High street. A clergyman, who enjoys any association which may be obtained between himself and the great, walked dignifiedly in front of him, pulling along with him interested friends who thought how great must the preacher be who could speak to Corwin. He addressed Corwin in awfully dignified tones:

"How do you do, Governor Corwin?"

"Ah, very well, sir. How—how are you, to-day? Ah!" answered the Governor, looking him in the face intently.

8

"You do not remember me. I am Rev. ——, for-
merly of ——."

"Oh, yes. I remember you *then*. But," and Corwin's eye twinkled as he looked at him, now half awake
from his deep thought—"I did n't know but you had
been translated long ago, and had been gathered to the
bosom of Beelzebub."

The preacher grew red-faced and confused.

"Oh!" said one of the friends, "you mean Abraham's bosom."

"Do I?" earnestly said Corwin.   "It makes no difference.   I knew it was some one of the Patriarchs."

So my experience ran on—meeting new faces, getting
new ideas.

On the road to Jackson from Vicksburg, I saw another
illustration of the love of authority which possesses
some men.   I had procured a seat in the cars and with
perfect ease set my face like a flint for my destination.
By and by the form and shape of egotism, pure and
simple, came and said: " *Ticket!*"   Having no ticket I
offered him paper money, which was "legal tender for
all debts, public and private."

"No sir!" said he.   "I must have your ticket or
gold.   That 'truck' do n't carry people on this road."

"It is legal tender," said I.   "I offer it to you, as I
do to my boarding-place, for meals, and to pay other
debts elsewhere.   Now, no nonsense about this thing,
here is your money."

"Well, sir, do you hear me?" added he.   "Pay me
your fare or I will put you off."

He went on getting the tickets, and coming back to
me often, he threatened and assured me that the ticket,
which I did not possess, or the gold, must be forthcom-
ing, or I should be "put off."

I stopped at Midway, purchased at that place a ticket

for Jackson, with the same "truck" he sneered at, and again found my seat. He came, when the train moved out, and I handed him the ticket.

"Sir," said he, "pay me the balance."

"No sir," said I. "It is my turn now. I offered it to you once. By this time you ought to know me. I will teach you how to be stubborn."

I went to Jackson with that ticket, and his ire boiled into vehemence.

Coming back from Jackson, I met the same conductor. He seemed more egotistic than ever. I had bought a ticket to Vicksburg, and offered it to him.

"Pay me what you owe me, or I will put you off," growled he.

"No sir," said I, rising in my seat.

He took my satchel and placed it upon the platform, stopped his train, and I said to the gentlemen near us, "What is your name? and yours?" until all their names and addresses were obtained.

Said I: "Understand and remember, I have and do now offer this man my ticket. He proposes to put me off. I want you as witnesses; and," added I, looking straight at him, "I will have you arrested upon your arrival at Vicksburg if you do'nt bring my satchel back."

The satchel was returned. He was again conquered, and we moved on our way, while the "witnesses" laughed, and knew that as all egotists are cowards, they would not be needed in court.

A man's greatness is his capacity for goodness and his ability to be kind and generous.

I was desiring to go from Corinth to Columbus, Ky. This was for two reasons an attractive route; Corinth was a very unpleasant town, and Columbus, Ky., was nearer my home. I never was more anxious to leave and go on my way. I went to the clerk and said:

"Would you please give me a pass to Columbus, Ky.?"

"No," thundered he, "you're too late."

"Why, I cannot think of not going," said I, earnestly but mildly, "I am in no fix to stay, I am all packed up, and it is necessary that I should go. I did not know that"—

"Well," said he, "we have hours for business, you ought to know that."

"I did not know of it," I answered, "and further, I think you could give me the pass as a gentlemanly act, without any rules and regulations."

But he turned his little head—for all such people wear number five hats—and told me, in spite of a long explanation I made of my condition, that I should have no pass. Greatness needs no rules. It is the "spirit" of business that gives "life," not its "letter."

On the wharf stood a number of people. Engaged in pushing a barrel vigorously, was Gen. MacPherson, who was bravery personified. His chivalry was great in little things. He was a knight of generosity and kindness.

"Certainly," said he, "you can get a pass," and forthwith made it known to the clerk. The gentleman conquered the boor. He gave the pass, gruffly, and while I prized the pass itself, I prized more the nobleness that made itself known from a great man, in the eyes of the littleness of a very small one.

CHAPTER V.

IN this connection, I will mention a visit to the home of Zachary Taylor, the seventeenth President of the United States. As purely humble as a home could be, was this of Taylor. A solitary and only pleasant and somewhat small house, on a lofty rise of ground, looking toward the South—this is the old home of the chieftain. I have to note the greatness of Zachary Taylor.

He was not a great statesman. The idea that Henry Clay was retired before him, is not one specially pleasant to the muse of history. He did not even possess in himself the abilities commonly attributed to the politician. His friends, and above all, the enemies of his great antagonist, managed his election, and made out of his splendid career as a general, popular enthusiasm for him as a statesman.

When the clear days shall come, it will be impossible thus to make a great people cast aside the fine heroism and splendid generalship of ideas for the thunder of musketry, the booming of cannon, and the glory of battle. A president of a great nation ought to be that man who has in his brain the greatest ideas of national government. The man who most of all men sees clearly into the mission of a land, who most of all feels the inspirations which blew into the sails that wafted a republic into existence, who forecast the future with reference to the deepest and most abiding ideas, who sees to put into time the greatest portion of eternity—that man ought to be *called* what he really *is*—the president.

"Ideas," said Wendell Phillips, "rule the world." And when the safety of any country is consulted, the men of ideas are in the pilot-house. Let no shoulder-straps either make or break the influence of a man. "The power of a man in the world," says one of the deepest of the thinkers of our time, "is his idea multiplied by and projected through his personality."

But when I speak of his greatness, I do not mean the treatment he gave his great office as a general. In this he was great. "Give them a little more grape, Captain Bragg," said he, at Buena Vista. And with that battle he wrote *chief* on his brow. He obeyed orders like a great man. When he was so chagrined at the news from Tampico, and was ordered to send the best part of his army to Scott, to fall back on Monterey and simply defend it, he showed that, as in private life, it takes more manhood, oftentimes, to *bear* than to *do*. It is what a man can *suffer* as well as what he can *achieve* that makes him worthy his name and blesses the world. He was great as a man holding a sword, because the weapon was not master. Great, not because blood ran in streams, not because men died and he pushed the victory on and on, but Zachary Taylor was great at an armistice, in a defeat, and in mercy. Greatness is large-ness of soul in life and its circumstances. It is not greatness of occasion and accident, but personal and of the man himself.

Ask the citizens of his place of residence, as did I, upon this occasion, and find out that a man may have honor in his own country. Great elsewhere, as a pri-vate friend, a noble soul, a kind companion, here he was great. He was greater as the president of these private affections than as President of the United States. He ruled the "spirit" which "took the city," and added the larger greatness to the less.

Two scenes in the life of Taylor have been related;
one lies in other words, in history; the other in the private soul of a woman living near him.

It was the anniversary-day of Washington's birth.
The American army was filled with the thought which
Lowell has so felicitously thrown into deathless poetry:

> Never to see a nation born
> Hath been given to mortal man,
> Unless to those who, on that summer morn,
> Gazed silent when the great Virginian
> Unsheathed the sword whose fatal flash
> Shot union through the incoherent clash
> Of our loose atoms, crystalizing them
> Around a single wills' unpliant stem,
> And making purpose of emotion rash.
> Out of that scabbard sprang, as from its womb,
> Nebulous at first, but hardening to a star,
> Through mutual share of sunburst and of gloom
> The common faith that made us what we are.

General Wool had, in the absence of Taylor, formed
the line of battle. The battalions of Mexican light infantry struck march for the heights under General Am-
pudia. A large howitzer played death upon the left of
the line. Colonel Marshall secured and held the moun-
tain-spur. Gorges and ravines began to fill with the
dead. But in spite of it all, when dark came, upon the
summits of Sierre Madre and adown its rugged sides,
the Mexicans stood and Marshall retreated. The night
passed.

Dawn came. Beauty and glory, fled from heaven,
descended upon the great combat. Clear and cloudless
were the skies. Breezes, soft as angelic feathers, touched
the aching, fevered brows. Men stood in that glittering
sunshine, who dreamed not of death in darkness. Swept
with flooded radiance, the glow of plain, and tree, and
rock was gorgeous. Grander than all was Taylor, who
had returned to lead the victory.

The action began. Ages will never forget the brave

maintainance of Marshall, the advance of Santa Anna's
huge weapons of war, the rapid fire of Washington's
battery, the pushing of the Mexicans to the feet of those
heights, and the dismay and death in the ravine.   The
muse of history will chronicle the fire of the second
Indiana, the wavering Mexican line, the rally of the
Mexican forces, the awful defeat that looked through
the eyes of the Americans, as under intense fires they
fled before their foes.   While he writes this, she will
seize another pen and write the arrival of Taylor from
Saltillo, the splendid form and noble mien which could
not arrest for a time death and dismay; the final struggle that ensued, and the glory that has since come to
him, who, with less than five thousand men, not five
hundred of whom were regulars, with fourteen pieces
of artillery, maintained their position, though it was
covered with blood, from the breaking until the dying
light.   This was Buena Vista.

Another story I will relate.   It was a common day.
But since the assertion, "the kingdom of God is within
you," it was like all, a grand day because of its opportunities.   Night had fallen about the city.   Alone paced
the hero through the cold and storm.   Visions of his
home invited his anxious, rapid step.   A shriek, followed by a gurgle, succeeded by a gasp!   The hero
stops.   It is the voice of a human being.   Over the
street, into the darkness, through the storm, into the
midst of agony, he pushes his hand, kneels to touch
the forehead, and speaks to hear the secrets of—*a suicide*.
She is not dead.   She persists in dashing her life away.
A grandeur than Buena Vista is here.   Its hero also has
come.   He entreats.   He begs.   He touches the forehead again, and when the death-door opens and she
walks in, and the days of the sadness are gone, little
children growing up receive, in secret, portions of a Pres-

ident's salary, and the great world goes on not knowing how much greater the Zachary Taylor of that dark lane was, than Zachary Taylor of Buena Vista. When I think of it, words great as any the author has written, come to my mind:

> " No dreary splendors wait our coming
> Where rapt ghost sits from ghost apart;
> Homeward we go to heaven's thanksgiving,
> The harvest-gathering of the heart."

CHAPTER VI.

ELSEWHERE I shall speak of my trip to the South, and the observations I then made.

After my return home, I remained six weeks at the town. But I never was idle.

I cannot take honor to myself for not being idle, inasmuch as work seems to be my natural atmosphere. I have no sort of respect for men who sit and gloat over their virtues, when those virtues are simply not vices. And I have no sort of respect for those people who talk eloquently of their achievements, when with all their force, they could hardly have avoided them. That man is unworthy of much more honor, who, against the barriers of his non-constitution, forces his way to success. Work was inbred with me.

Effort has been pleasure. It has always been my joy to do. And I could not think that I could make a greater misrepresentation than to assert that what I did, was done with a predisposition to doing nothing.

There are very many people, who could not avoid being sober, because they never had within them that earnestness of nature, which is often called the passion of a drunkard.

There are very many men, whose piety, likewise, is an indigenous plant. I am accustomed to award glory to those men, who have overcome peculiarities of a nature, which at their full flood, might have driven them to ruin.

Let not my reader think that my constant effort was

altogether a matter of my own will, and purpose, and struggle. Let him rather know, that it has always been more pleasant to do, than not to do. Let the honor, if there be special honor, and there is, be awarded to men who have overcome the dry rot of laziness, and have made their lives living things, organic unities, out of seeming death and chaos.

So as a matter of natural necessity, I began to take pictures in Athens, Ohio. Sixty daguerreotypes were soon finished in the best of style. It is true, very many people received these gems of art, who did not appreciate all the effort, and earnest devotedness to my profession, with which I had made them worthy of their acceptance. Now and then a man would come and receive a picture upon which I had lavished my best thought and work, and would see that it was more than a conglomeration of chemicals, more than an aggregation of the elements of nature upon a hard substance. He would see that it was a piece of *art*. He would know that there was thought in it, with the powers of nature always precipitated the result called *art*. For *art* is a thing, taken in the rough, to which all the powers of one's being has been added.

The *Moses* of Angelo is a piece of marble, to which, with all the energy of his nature, the artist brought the working activities of his being. I simply attempted to make every thing I did, worthy of myself, and I generally found that it was worthy the acceptance of those for which it was made. And such, I think, is the secret of all real success everywhere.

I might have misrepresented to those people, I might have given them work utterly unworthy of my ability. Very many came, as I said, who would have been satisfied with less perfect specimens of picture-making. But this would have been to have reduced myself in my own estimation, and to have lost the use of my best powers. It is by doing every thing with reference to one's best ideal that develops his energies, gives him success, and always wins the day. He who does a thing in sight of public opinion, does it only in a half light. He, who does a thing in the light of himself, and public opinion, does it in the whole light. The greatest praise I have heard to a profound lawyer, is the remark of one of his legal friends: *"He always does his best."*

At Athens, the Ohio University is located. And as a practical man, I could not help observing the methods of education. Here I found dominant, and ruling, the idea, which to my mind, wrecks many an intellectual fortune, and destroys the power of many a human being in the world. For the sin of popular education, seems to me to lie in its being unworthy of the name *education*. *Education* means just what it says :—E–ducation. It means to lead forth, to draw out, to invite forth, to bring from within the latent powers of the human spirit. The critical educational question of our time is, Does so called education do this ? Is it not rather a cramming process ? Do we not seek to get all we can into a boy or a girl ? Are we not trying to stuff our children full ? If we analyze many of our boasted advances in culture, is it culture at all, we are achieving ? Are we not holding fast a large number of pupils with rigor and force, to put into them, by some method or other, all the dates, all the facts, all the ideas, all the discoveries, all the hypotheses of which we know. Is this the true system ?

What are the results of such education ? Does it produce thinkers, men of decision, men of large forecast, men of great ability, men of towering intellect, men of great feeling, men of conviction, men who know how to run conviction into deed—men of power ? Does it not rather produce men encumbered with what they do not understand, men caparisoned with battle-axes which they cannot wield, men who are overcome with an army of facts, dates, other people's ideas which they cannot muster and command? Does it bring to the world natures fitted for the world's work? The fact is, that we have not yet learned the depth of the idea of development. To get a powerful man, we must have a man whose latent power is developed into service. A strong thinker must always be a man who has learned to think for himself, and to think strongly. A man of profound conviction must be a man who has convictions of his own, feels them swelling up from the depths of his nature. A man of action must be able to bring forth an act, and an education which does not bring out and develop into power the as yet undiscovered energies of a man, is not worthy of the name.

I am not decrying the value of facts. I am not asserting the worthlessness of knowledge. I have no designs upon what is known as scholarship. But I believe that the man must be greater than his possessions to give value to his possessions.

What the world needs is practical men. All the professions are demanding these. All of the avocations of life are inquiring for them. This age particularly, is anxious for results. It is a practical time. It inquires after effects. It counts up long columns. It does not ask for ornament so much as for power. It does not lack in theory so much as it lacks in fact. The man who succeeds in it, must be suited to it. He must be a man of scholarship, a man of wide information, a man acquainted with the past, a citizen of the present, but he *must* be a man of power to give these vitality. Facts are always capital. Truth is funds on hand. The experience of the ages is money at interest. But there must be a spiritual financier to manage all these, else bankruptcy will surely come. The work of schools, colleges, academies, and universities, is, as I take it, to develop these resources, by developing to them their masters, and by developing them unto him who shall rule them.

But one month I remained in Athens. A pupil came to me to learn my art. I took the greatest pains in teaching him, and I have the honor to say that S. S. Hitt has never proved unworthy of the idea of that business which I imparted to him.

The twentieth of October found me in Pomeroy. This town never struck me as the embodiement of beauty. It was, on the other hand, the representative of dirt. No charms come with the name of this place. I have heard that I have underrated its inhabitants. I probably was unfortunate in meeting people whose deceit long ago has taken them from the shores of this world forever. I cannot hold the present town, full of good and true people as it is, responsible for the sins of men who have certainly left the world without issue, or were kind enough to remove from the limits of this place to send forward into the future, through their children, the abominable tendencies of the place.

I hope my readers will not understand that I failed in business at this place. For my business was prosperous and thriving when I left.

But business is not all. A man always feels less important to himself when he loses faith in humanity. And if all the faith which I had in my race had come from my residence at Pomeroy, I should have been an exceedingly skeptical creature. We cannot overestimate the value to a man, of a faith, serene and powerful, in the race. It is another element of one's capital. He feels that he is able to do more in the world when he has a cheerful belief in the excellence of its inhabitants.

Here I made a purchase of astounding dimensions. If it had only been the flatboat which I bought, it would have been well. Indeed, if it had only been the flatboat and the burden with which it was loaded, I had fared much better.

But there on the twentieth of December, my reader might have seen me before that flat-boat, loaded as it was, with my new possession; with my hands in my pockets, with my brain in a whirl, with my heart in my mouth, gazing at the spectacle surmounted, as it was, with two families, and gazing into the future,—a future I have never seen—for the profits which were never to come to me. I had paid one thousand and forty-one dollars, for it. I started down the river to dispose of it.

The first day's voyage was against a very hard wind. Many times that day, I wished for the aparatus of the artist, and for the non-existence of this necessity which made out of a successful artist, a most brilliant failure as a seaman. I thought of the ocean-rangers, and did not desire to be one of them. I wondered how a man could persuade himself to a life on the sea. Winds that I had never heard of, tempests that have never been named, storms that would have exhausted all the catalogues, raged about me, made the river a foam, and balked my course. It was a tremendous distance, which we went that day. But somehow, we only got eight miles, when the night came, from our point of departure. The night came gloomily. It was hard enough to go in the day-time, what should we do at night? As the night of sorrow often-times brings the greatest calm, through which one sails to his eternal home, so that night brought with it such opportunities of progress,

that we found in the morning that we had traveled thirty miles.

The twenty-first came. A pleasant day dawned.
Through it, and the night which followed, we traveled
wearily along. The families were there, of Mr. E.
Rose, and Dr. C. N. Maddy. Through the cold night
we suffered greatly. Never shall I forget the sadness
of those chilly hours. At 12 o'clock, we passed Ports-
mouth. On we went until 12 o'clock at night. Then
by a terrific gale we were borne to shore. We had to
remain at the mercy of this blast, nestled close to the
shore, until at 9 o'clock the next night. The wind ceas-
ed, and we began our watery journey. Soon, however,
the wind began to blow again, and a very cold freezing
air added to our serious discomfort. The ice began to
form. The cold was extremely penetrating, and through
the next day we shivered as we rode along. At 12
o'clock we passed Maysville. I was watch every night.
Christmas came at last. Such a lonely, weary, cold
Christmas I have never seen. The festivities of the day
were out of our reach. In spite of all its sacred memories, and its glowing prophecies, the day went in like
a prolonged chill. On Christmas night we arrived at
Cincinnati. Tuesday, and we were off again. Friday
night, and we arrive at Madison. Here a sight came to
my vision which I can never forget. It was so personal
to myself, and so much of my own thought and life was
related to it, that any autobiography I might make
would be incomplete without this picture. Within sight
of the wharf, and a terrible storm rages between us.
Great waves, larger than I had thought could be organized by any tempest upon a river, rose in frightful heaps
before us. At times our whole craft seemed to be
doomed. Heaving waters seemed destined to dash us
into ruin. Great billows, large with the wrath of the

tempest, seemed to laugh our safety into scorn. A storm of woes ruled the hearts of all on board. It was a trying place for me. I knew that if I could not keep calm in myself and in my face, I never should be able to control the affrighted passengers. I soon found that the storm without, although great and boistrous, was not equal, at all, to the storm in my little craft. I tried to rule the two tempests. For once I was compelled to yield to fear. I kept it within my own breast, until passing a mighty surge, I found myself in control, and soon we were at the wharf rejoicing with each other in safety.

The cold increased after we were ashore. The wind gathered in piercing power. Next morning the river was full of ice, and January 1st the boats are laid up on account of their frozen passage-way.

On the 5th, I left Madison for Louisville, on the *Emma Dean*. I remained at Louisville until the 8th, in wait for a boat. At 2 P. M., on the *Mattie Wayne*, I left for Memphis. We laid up at night at Salt River. Nothing but the getting of the money from the passengers brought the captain from his warm retreat. At West Point I took a room for the purpose of taking pictures. Three hundred inhabitants made up the population. A clever and hospitable people did I find them to be. Two weeks passed pleasantly and profitably, when my boat came in sight, and I took my things on board of her.

Through storms of wind and rain, "through perils by sea and by land," we passed, and February 7th found us in Memphis. It had been a terrible ride. It was necessary for me to run when I could, but the elements seemed perpetually against me. The women on board were quite as hard to manage as the elements without. In the midst of a storm, fear and terror ruled them.

10

The monotony of the wrathful elements without, and the affrighted elements within was broken by that melody so peculiarly attractive and so excruciatingly pervasive to the soul of a bachelor, namely, the crying of babies.

All writing and literary work was out of the question. I was too glad to preserve the record of the past.

By this time my sash had got to be a tremendous burden. It was perfectly impossible for me to sell it at any sort of a profit, and the further I went the more I was persuaded that I never should be able to sell it at all. Dr. Maddy, who joined us at this place, was amazed to find his family alive. He expected that we all were drowned. Perhaps in such a short length of time so many flat boats have never been lost on the river. Old sailors gazed on me in astonishment, and I was rather astonished at myself when I realized through what we had passed and found ourselves at Memphis. A few days, and I had sold one hundred and ninety dollars worth of doors and sash. Then we left for Vicksburg. After a trial of two days, we found it impossible to go through the Yazoo pass. Glad was I to see my craft safely landed. I left on the steamer *Mary Agnes* for Vicksburg. Here I sold eight thousand lights of sash. To Jackson, in the cars, did I pursue my way.

A beautiful city is this. Fifty miles east of Vicksburg, surrounded by beautiful rolling country, builded with stately residences, it is worthy to be the capital of this great State.

I returned to Vicksburg to await the arrival of my boat. Here I disposed of more than one-half of my sash. But I was more than glad to give all that I had, boat and possibilities, to Mr. Rose and Dr. Maddy. On the steamer *H. M. Wright* I took passage for Bayou Sara, at which place I landed on the fourth of March.

The woods were green with verdure. The planters were planting their corn. The ravages of the yellow fever had horrified the community, but in spite of it all an artist had been there with some success, and business generally seemed thrifty. Traveling in the South at that time was unpleasant for many reasons. But to me it was especially unpleasant to accustom myself to their diet. The strongest animal food ruled supreme. Highly flavored victuals concentrated into strength, were dominant. A vegetarian was not only unpopular, but was about impossible. Here I remained three weeks. Point Coupee was my stopping place. Six miles back from the river, and directly opposite this place where I had been stopping, is this, which is one of the richest of all the parishes in the State. Splendid plantations line the coast. A beautiful lake, made of the old Mississippi, lies near. It is not a town, but the court-house, surrounded by two or three stores and a hotel. Three miles west is the college. Large and productive sugar plantations lie all along the river, and all this land is cultivated by the inhabitants who are principally creoles of French descent.

Truly, the South is one of the garden spots of the world. The March of the South was the early June of the North. Vegetation is rank, vigorous and green. Potatoes are large enough for use. The flowers that bloom only under Southern skies are heavy with blossoms, and the balmy air is fragrant with their odors. Nature is poetic here. She adds richness to strength, and surpassing glory to her splendid powers. An absolute freedom seems to have taken possession of her genius, and the brilliancy of her show invites the sunbeams of the skies.

To give change to this phase of nature, on the 30th of March a severe storm passed over this region. It blew the fences down, piled houses in ruins, damaged the growing vegetation, bended the beautiful flowers, and washed the low places into unproductive seas. So nature at her grandest puts off nature at her most beautiful and like life itself, often teaches us the greater lesson, because the beautiful flowers which we love are destroyed, and the elements which we fear are shown to be as necessary to the great chain of being, as those which we are accustomed to esteem with affectionate and kindest care.

Twelve miles below on the river lies a small village which was my nearest stopping place. It is Port Hudson, situated on a high bluff, and was, at the time of my visit, a town of great beauty. But its beauty did not keep me. To Clinton I went, twenty-five miles east, which is the parish seat of East Feliciana Parish, and a pleasant village of about twelve hundred inhabitants. Here I found an artist. But to leave had been to retreat. I thought if my art could not stand comparison with his, the business had better be suspended so far as I was concerned, and that I had better enter some other line of work. I did not, however, expect to suspend until I had done my best. My best succeeded, and in spite of the fact that he had a splendid room, precedence in time, and fine opportunities, I soon found myself doing all the business.

Here I saw the most fearful case of drunkenness that it has ever been my misfortune to see. Court was in session at the time, and it seemed to be the especial business of every man connected therewith to make himself incapable of any business at all. Wretched is the view I still preserve of that half-intoxicated town. A picture to which no pen can devote itself successfully has always risen in my mind when I have thought of this unhappy place.

The sash and door speculation gave me not only some very thrilling and unpleasant experience, but the uneasy consciousness thereafter, that, by eight hundred dollars, I was not so well off as when it had its origin with me. I was not only eight hundred dollars poorer, but as every man, after a signal financial defeat, while I stood waiting for the experience to settle over me, I also stood face to face with another opportunity to be a man under any circumstances, and felt the pressing need of doing something.

But I must do something to regain the lost, and prepare myself for the future. I must make a raise somehow. I stood face to face with that fact. There was no escape. I had been a coward if I had desired an escape. Facts such as these, give one's eyes especial keenness, and with great alertness of vision did I gaze about. I saw a large amount of sugar, which, by some strange history, was offered for sale at a very low price. But the price was not low enough to strike me; rather, I was not tall enough financially, to strike it. It could be bought for three cents per pound. Well did I know that it would be worth thrice that sum in one year. The sugar stood unbought, while I roamed the country for a partner. No man could be found who seemed to take hold of the idea with the same vehemence as I did. I wondered why I could not persuade them to my opinion on that sugar problem. I never thought that they were more in doubt, perhaps, about me, than about the three cents per pound or the sugar. As the years fly on, and I learn more and more of men, I can understand that although the sugar did go up as I supposed, it is often more of a speculation to do with one man than to do with a thousand pounds of sugar.

Time followed on wearily, but pleasantly, and when nothing else came to employ me, I used my time in getting important information concerning subjects with which, in life and thought, every man has to do.

The value of general information to men of all sorts, dispositions and tendencies, can not be overestimated. No profession or calling can afford the exclusion of the facts of the world. A man gets into a certain line of business, a profession which has to do peculiarly with a certain line of influences and facts, and is liable to think that this is all the world to him. The universe is in his business. He has taken a very narrow view of life and the universe, and of course becomes narrow himself. He gets to be an ordinary lawyer, it may be, in a quite ordinary man, instead of getting to be a great lawyer by being, first, a great, broad, man. Everywhere we meet them. They clog up the road of life. They have no information outside of their profession or business, and then, taken outside of it, as they will be at times, they fail. What a humiliating sight it is to see the thinker sunk and lost in the doctor, the scholar buried in the physician, the truth-seeker and truth-gatherer overlaid with the facts of one profession in life. Then when occasion comes that the truths of the time are to be defended, discussed or laid down, how perfectly overcome is he who can talk of or act for nothing else than his own peculiar line of facts. The man is lost. Get him into a certain line and he is a strong force, but get him out of his fortress and he is weakness itself. Goethe said a "man ought to be a citizen of his time." And human experience confirms it. It is sheer injustice to himself to lose the great force of facts which comes bounding with life to him, and proposes to fit him for a larger life than his own. There must be a ground of general knowledge upon which men may meet. This gives grace and beauty to the conversation; this gives influence to the social circle. Why do you love to meet your physician in society? Because he can talk of nerves, quinine, bones and acids, operations and fevers? Is it not because he has a general knowledge which meets your own, and you talk and enjoy the day? So the most wretched society which could be called to-gether is that convocation of lawyers, farmers, doctors, and merchants, who know nothing but their respective occupations. There they sit and gaze, and tell to each other the most uninteresting facts. There they dolefully pass the evening, so limited, so bound, so unable to con-fer one with another.

And on the other hand, about the most cheerful thing in this world is a company of congenial souls, of all professions, trades and occupations, with general inform-ation sufficient to make a platform upon which they may all stand. The lawyer lays aside his Blackstone. The physician has left his pill-bags at home. The artist does not smell of paint. The carpenter has no plane. The farmer has no plow. But men, all of them are men; they are free, and the long hours rush by. They enjoy with common love. They part with mutual self-regard. So life is bound together by one manhood, and the air which it breathes through the mind is the acquaintance it is allowed to have with the great interests of men. Every man ought to know enough of every body else's profession, trade and avocation, to see the man in it, and feel his rights as such. What does a lawyer know of a doctor's rights until he gets a general idea of his work in the world. No man will be able to see any thing noble in anybody else's work but his own, if he knows that alone. This is the cause of many foolish bickerings, jealousies and spiteful remarks. Pure ig-norance makes men narrow, uncharitable, and unjust to each other. He becomes a slave to his own part of life. He knows nothing of the great discoveries anywhere else.   He is vacant as an exhausted receiver about the progress the race is making.   He is as careless as a wild man about the problems that are being born elsewhere, which, if he does not understand them, will crush him into failure.

Besides, a man does not, and can not get all there is in his own profession out of it, by living in it alone. He must see its value in the light of the value of others to prize it.   He must see its dignity in the light of the dignity of all human work to approve it.   He must learn that it is related to all the work and activity of men to find out its broad significance and universal importance.

Every man who gets an idea or a fact, is, by that much, the more free.   He has that much more capital. He is possessed of that much more as stock in trade. He will use it all some day in his duty.   It will make him a broader man, if he never uses it at all.

Dark, gloomy days will come.   He will live on ideas, when other men perish without them.   Storms will keep him in-doors, he must be safe in thought.   Winters will come, he must make spring within.   His whole nature will be beautiful and fruitful as he gets acquainted and seeks control of the unknown which lies every where about him.

CHAPTER VII.

The study of the human system had great charms for me. Not without great predispositions did I take to it, and find greatest pleasure in what was afterwards of so much service to me. And, I confess, when I think of what is the truth with regard to the great physiological facts with which the deepest and the shallowest human life has to do, I find that I builded better than I knew, and caught hold of facts which recent scientific investigations have brought out in splendid prominence. Who can be dumb in the presence of facts which seem to speak eloquently for themselves? Who can be unmoved with a feeling in which a great and advancing race takes part, when the whole current of modern thinking is moved and transformed by the attention which has been given to the physical basis and environment of much if not all of our intellectual life!

I am not one who, having dipped into these things, am persuaded that every thought, emotion, and purpose of a human being is physical, and only physical. I have never seen a reason for losing faith in what seems to be as scientific a statement as any ever made: ''There is a spirit in man and the inspiration of the Almighty giveth them understanding.'' That proposition seems exact science, and is a consoling and inspiring revelation. Nothing nas been produced to show that my love for my mother is simply a change of matter within my

11

skull. No reason has yet appeared, why we should
think that our best ideas lie latent in the bread, and
eggs, and potatoes we eat. The study of our physical
structure has gone far, but it has not, and it appears that
in the nature of things it cannot, go so far as that. This
recent study of the human body is only the full exhibition in this particular locality of science, of the spirit of
investigation which has struck and reinvigorated science
everywhere. But I do not know that we have reason to
lay aside any of the great truths in *any* department of
spiritual life. True, many of the gray-headed errors
are gone, and who suffers but narrow creeds? We say,
let them go also. It is only for the health of the race
that we should wish their departure. They have impeded progress, and tied up the angel of the future.
They are tyrants of free opinion, and if the spirit of
fresh scientific thought has buried them forever, nobody
will weep, nobody calls for their resurrection. But
nothing vital, nothing essential, nothing that we need
has gone. Alone with the substantial verities, alone with
the undying truths, alone with invincible facts, shall we
stand, and no man of courage, or thought, will ask for
padlock and key wherewith to hold fast his new-born
ideas and fasten in the fetters of death his new-found
treasures of truth. The excitement has been a little
laughable, and yet serious. But the brightness of the
light now reveals the fact that the truth will never allow
the facts of science and the facts of faith to collide, and
that nothing which we needed, nothing, indeed, but the
old mistakes of the past have gone.

Here was the conception of God. It is an idea that
it is universal. It can not be avoided. When it comes
all is light; when it is absent all is darkness. It is a
necessary idea. But yet, when science began to move
herself, it was funny to see men hunt up their idea of

God, and see if it was damaged. It was ridiculous to notice men trying to hold the ark of the Lord to save it from being carried off by the infuriated cows. It was laughable to notice every young theologue, and every old defender of the faith, shout in the presence of the congregation which did not know what a *Prachipod* was, and could not tell the difference between *Bathybius* and an eclipse of the sun,—his everlasting determination to defend the throne of God, and, bringing down huge and clenched fists upon the dusty bible, add that it must be done now, or it would be too late. Such people as had an idea of God, which was unscientific and unbiblical, have lost it, but God, the absolute, the eternal, Jehovah, He sits upon his throne, and science says: "Yea and amen." People were afraid of Darwinism, and the man who told of it, was said to speak of something which would ruin the idea of God! and yet, the very man who conceived the idea of the theory of Natural Selection, Alfred Russell Wallace, has said that this poetry is "highest philosophy and soundest science:"

"God of the granite and the bee,
Soul of the sparrow and the rose,
The mighty tide of being flows
Through countless channels, Lord, from Thee.

It leaps to life in grass and flowers,
Through every grade of being runs,
While from Creation's radiant towers,
Its glory beams in stars and suns."

They were afraid that when the great laws of the universe were found out, there would be no great First Cause, of all things. But a great scientific thinker, calls science,—from which all the trouble was expected, "the study of the modes of operation of the first cause." They said that it would not do for us to study second causes so much, for then we could not prove our Theism—our belief in God. But the same thinker has said, what seems to be the truest deliverance of our time : "It is evident, therefore, that the recognition of second causes, cannot preclude the idea of the existence of God.   If in tracing the chain of causes upward, we stop at any cause, or force, or principle, that force or principle, becomes for us God, since it is the efficient agent controlling the phenomena of the universe ; thus Theism is necessary, intuitive, and therefore universal. We can not get rid of it if we would.   Push it out, as many do, at the front door, and it comes in again, perhaps unrecognized, at the back-door.   Turn it out in its *nobler forms*, as revealed in Scripture, and it comes again, in its *ignoble forms*, it may be as magnetism, electricity, gravity, or some other supposed efficient agent controlling Nature.   In some form, noble or ignoble, it will become the guest of the human heart."   I therefore repeat, *Theism neither requires, nor admits of proof.*"

The fact is, the moment you speak of the demands of the study of anatomy, you speak of something which calls up materialism to the half-ignorant, half-religious man, and of something which calls up the sublimest proof of his faith to the well-informed and devoted soul. As men were fearful about the destiny of God, when science begun to work in the world, so they have been and yet are, afraid of the destiny of the *soul*, when the anatomist begins his work.   First of all, they have been afraid that by cutting into the secrets of our existence, it might be found that we came of the lineage suggested by Mr. Darwin ; that our grandfather may have been a monkey, and that the other beasts are so related to us that all our talk about our peculiar place and power, our being, the soul, its destiny, nature and outlook,— that all this is even worse than nonsense.   We were frightened at the idea that man might be older than we had supposed, forgetting that it made not the slightest difference whether he was six, or six million years old, as to his greatness and powers. They have taken up the bible and then looked at the knife of an anatomist to be horified, forgetting that scripture and that instrument tell the same story; that man is the crown, the climax—the blossom in an ascending scale of Divine Creation. Science has found out that the deeper she goes into man, and the old earth, the clearer it is that a long preparation has been going on, and that the ages overlapping each other, have been at work by a Divine appointment, to make this world a garden for its occupant. And here the great fact of design, and from that, the vision of a Designer appears. Here are all the capacities of the earth, suited to what the anatomist finds in the nature of man. The world is suited to the citizen, the citizen is suited to the world. Here are organs needing food ; abilities needing place and opportunity. And here is a world all suited to them. The anatomist goes into the human eye, and finds there the same rule which runs its eloquent thread of meaning through the whole body. I borrow an illustration from Prof. LeConte, both because I am better able to make clear to my reader the meaning I want to carry to him, and for the reason that the illustration is so true as to silence forever any objection to the study, I am now advocating, on the ground of its irreligious tendencies.

Comparing the finest piece of divine creation with the finest piece of human ingenuity and workmanship, we shall see the hand of God in design, but *we shall have to use the anatomist* to see His hands.' They are the eye and the camera of the photographer. Notice, the design is the same, *to form an accurate image on a properly adjusted screen.* Now, we might linger with the design which arranged cautiously the covering of these instruments, the design which arranged for the wiping

of them, the design for rapid movements in any direction to get the image—but we should not get at the
glory of either until we found ourselves within looking
at the secrets of those instruments. We could not help
seeing design. We could not help saying: "No design without a designer." And we could not help seeing a human designer for one and a Divine Designer for
the other. We will look at the clear evidence of design
in the proper placing of that screen in the back part of
the small dark chamber, which only admits light from
the front, in the photographer's camera ; we will notice
how cautiously it has been entirely lined with lamp-
black, and how that quenches and prevents the reflection
of any light as it strikes the sides of the chambers, so
that the light which strikes the screen will come straight
from the object to be imaged ;—we will see that and say,
a designer did it. Then we will notice that all that is
true on a finer and more accurate scale with the eye,
that this is Divine art as that is human, and we will say,
a Divine Thinker thought this, and a Divine Creator
made it.

Then notice how this image, which must be distinct
and clear, is made bright in the camera. A simple hole
will not do. The larger the hole, the less distinct the
image ; and it must be distinct. The smaller the hole
the less bright the image, and it must be bright. What
gets us rid of this difficulty? A *lens* is designed. It
can gather light and send it with directness. And the
camera again tells of the human designer, while every
human eye tells of its Divine Designer also.

But there are troubles with lenses. The lens is like
a prism. If you let light shine through it, the white
light is broken into the colors, separated from each other as in a rainbow. Every thing that you see through
that prism is tinged with those colors. Confusion comes.

How shall it be remedied? With design that has been celebrated the world over, a convex and a concave lens were prepared and nicely adjusted, the difficulty vanishes. A designer cleared it away. But long ago, when with the Eden light, the eye of Adam was baptized, a Divine Designer had solved the same difficulty, and whenever a man looks out from his eye and gathers into him images of what lies without, he may know that he is proving the being of God. The crystaline, the aqueous, the vitrous lenses arrange it all—the first two convex, the last concave. This design makes our life beautiful. And so I might follow this out, showing the same great result. The presence of Jehovah flashes in every eye. The same thought which humanly excites the times, once came Divinely to excite the eternities. Anatomy finds the God of the universe in these orbs of vision.

And as surely as anatomy finds God there, does this study find the potency of the soul within their mortal frame. From the edge of the anatomist's knife drops the idea which is accepted as science everywhere. "Organization did not begin life." There is and has been something in us which has formed us according to an idea. It must, therefore, have been a thinking thing. Now this thinking thing is the soul. But Buchner says:

"The naturalist *proves* that there are no other forces in nature besides the physical, chemical and mechanical."

While we have on the side to which I am compelled to say the best anatomy leans, these sayings which contradict it. Says Dr. Elam:

"Once for all, it can not be too clearly understood that this claim is utterly without foundation. No vestige of what can fairly be considered *proof* of the doctrines of materialism has ever been offered. Now, as two thousand years ago, they rest only upon arbitrary assumption and conjecture."

Dubois Raymond has taken up the idea that the brain alone produces thought, and says:

"There is and must forever remain an impassable chasm between definite movements of definite cerebral atoms and the primary facts which I can neither define nor deny. *I feel pain or pleasure, I taste a sweetness, smell a rose scent, hear an organ tone, see red,* together with the no less immediate assurance they give, *therefore I exist.*"

Professor Tait says, concerning those who believe that all our so-called spiritual life is physical:

"On the other hand, there is a numerous group, not in the slightest degree entitled to rank as physicists (though in general they assume the proud title of Philosophers), who assert that not merely Life, but even Volition and Consciousness are merely physical manifestations." But Professor Tyndall goes this far:

"Man is a machine worked only by natural and necessary forces, therefore an automaton; therefore irresponsible, since the robber, the ravisher and the murderer can not help robbing, ravishing, and murdering." And Dubois Raymond, the anatomist of the brain, says:

"I will now prove, as I believe, in a very cogent way, not only that, in the present state of our knowledge, Consciousness can not be explained by its material conditions but that from the very nature of things it never will admit of explanation by these conditions."

So out of it all comes conscious, thinking something we call the human soul.

But has anatomy aught to say against the immortality of this soul (in Miller, Hodge and Alger)? No. The more truly that anatomy does its work, do we find that this nature of man is great in promise. So great is it, and its life here is so short, that science, which believes that there are not wings with no place to fly in, must agree that it has an eternity in which to unfold its trembling destinies. Hence it has eternal life. Hence the soul is immortal.

> It must be so! Plato, thou reasonest well!
> Else whence this pleasing hope, this fond desire,
> This longing after immortality?
> Or whence this secret dread and inward horror,
> Of falling into nought? why shrinks the soul
> Back on herself, and startles at destruction?
> 'Tis the divinity that stirs within us;
> 'Tis heaven itself that points out an hereafter,
> And intimates eternity to man!

Every touch of the anatomist's knife, reveals what is more than the substance by which it acts, and through which it performs the magic of thought. No well-grounded reason has appeared, why Socrates should not say: "I hope to go hence to good men." Or why Paul should not say: "Having a desire to depart and be with Christ," or why there is not truth at the base of the assertion: "Neither can they die anymore." No instrument has been able to find why all over the world, it was not right for men to believe in immortality. But the instruments of the investigator have, on the other hand, shown that this splendid habitation, the human-body—must hold a soul, meant for eternal destinies and careers that out-run the centuries. The fact is that the study of anatomy, has had the best thinkers to an endorsement of Dr. Miller's position: "The properties that we call form, impenetrability, inertia, attraction, no more certainly imply the existence of a *substratum* in which they inhere, and which we call matter, than do the phenomena of thought, emotion, volition imply the existence of a *substratum* in which they inhere, and this we call mind. Matter is an entity. Mind is an entity. If we must doubt the existence of one, it must be matter; for we cannot believe that matter *is*, without assuming that there is a mind which believes it. In and

12

through the wonderful organism called the body, mind becomes tangent to matter—takes a bearing on matter, cognizes it, controls it.   The material pen that traces this line, is moved by the bony structure clasping it, the bones are moved this way and that by the muscles, the muscles contract in response to nerve stimulus, and nerves of muscular motion receive their stimulus from the anterior part of the spinal cord, and the response of this cord to volitions is dependent on its connection with the brain.   Another set of nerves convey impulses inward, from their perimeters up to the brain, and sensations result.   But when the physiologist tells us all this, and measures the rate at which the impulse travels along the afferent and efferent nerves, and solves his own 'personal equation,' he has given us not one ray of light in reference to that something which is susceptible of these suspicions, which compares them as to their intensity, or notes them as agreeable or disagreeable, and which determines when an impulse, and what degree of impulse, is to be transmitted, along what nerve trunk and to what point—that something to which bones, muscles, nerves, spinal cord, and brain, along with the pen, stand in the relation of an instrument.   Now, the further we travel along this path of reflection, the firmer, it seems to the writer, will be the ground on which rest the belief that the mind is, and *must be*, something beyond and above the material organism, and that this something may survive the dissolution of that organism, may take to itself a new and vastly superior organism, and one endowed with immortality."

It was thought that the whole idea of a personal resurrection ought to and must be abandoned when materialism began its seeming succession of triumphs. Men said that materialism was certain in its effect, and that it was well established. But a scholar made fun of it, as follows:

" We witness at this time one of the most determined, and as may be shown, most unjustifiable efforts which the world has yet seen to establish materialism upon a basis of fact and reason. This new materialistic revival is essentially the weakest recorded, and would be simply laughed at if intelligent persons would but carefully and critically examine the facts and arguments upon which it is supposed to rest, and not allow their reason to be subjugated or disturbed by the very solemn demeanor of its chief exponents. Let the reader only think for a moment what would have become of this new materialism could it have been exposed to the intellectual attacks of Socrates. Its chances would now be little better were it not for the polite indolence of many of the educated classes, for the general dislike of critical analysis, and for the ingenuity and audacity displayed by its disciples in assertion, interpretation, and evasion. It is no uncommon thing nowadays to find such questions as the structure, composition, relation, origin and destiny of man, the nature of his consciousness, the question of free-will or necessity, the genesis of man's moral nature, and the probability of a future state expounded, discussed, and definitely determined in an hour's discourse, it may be to working men or women, or done into a magazine article that may be perused in half an hour."

And that same scholar in anatomy, Lionel Beale, after exhaustively discussing the ideas which antagonize the conception of a personal resurrection, and showing that they have no foundation, asserts the following:

" It is not for me, taking up the subject from the scientific side, to say one word in defense of religious truth; but I may, without hesitation, express my conviction

L. of C.

that the main arguments adduced by materialists against religion will scarcely bear thoughtful examination. Many of the more recent observations are very audacious, but that is all. Of the so-called *facts* upon which some of the arguments are said to rest, many are not facts at all, and the less said about them the better. Still, I suppose, that some who disbelieve entirely in religion could clearly state the grounds of their unbelief; but I am sure that many who have discarded religious belief because they fancied that materialism was true, or because they believed and desired that it might turn out to be true, have been misled or have deluded themselves into the belief that certain things are demonstrable and true, which are neither. Such persons have unquestionably accepted doctrines as true which can be clearly proved to rest upon erroneous and unsound data only, and have abandoned what, at any rate, has not been and can not be demonstrated to be untrue."

Nothing can be more absurd than such an objection to the study of the science of the human structure. It has done great harm. It makes narrow bigots, and goes against the health of the world, while the idea of immortality is as clear as the noonday. Dr. Carpenter himself has said very strong words about the study of Nature by theologians, which, I am persuaded, it would be well for them to heed. He says:

"Thus, then, if theologians will once bring themselves to look upon Nature, or the material universe, as the embodiment of the Divine thought, and at the scientific study of Nature as the endeavor to discover and apprehend that thought (to have 'thought the thoughts of God' was the privilege most highly esteemed by Kepler,) they will see that it is their duty, instead of holding themselves entirely aloof from the pursuit of Science, or stopping short in the search for scientific truth wherever it points toward a result that seems in discordance with their preformed conceptions, to apply themselves honestly to the study of it, as a revelation of the Mind and Will of the Deity, which is certainly not less authoritative than that which he has made to us through the recorded thoughts of religiously-inspired men, and which is fitted, in many cases, to afford its true interpretation. And they can not more powerfully attract the scientific student to religion than by taking up his highest and grandest thought and placing it in that religious light which imparts to it a yet greater glory. They will then perceive that, although if God be *outside* the physical universe, those extended ideas of its vastness which modern science opens to us remove him farther and farther from us, yet, if he be embodied *in* it, every such extension enlarges our notion of his being. As Mr. Martineau has nobly said: ' What, indeed, have we found by moving out along all radii into the Infinite? That the whole is woven together in one sublime tissue of intellectual relations, geometric and physical—the realized original, of which all our science is but the partial copy. That Science is the crowning product and supreme expression of human reason. . . Unless, therefore, it takes more mental faculty to construe a universe than to cause it, to read the Book of Nature than to write it, we must more than ever look upon its sublime face as the living appeal of Thought to Thought.' But the theologian can not rise to the height of this conception unless he is ready to abandon the worship of every idol that is 'graven by art and man's device'—to accept as a fellow-worker with himself every truth-seeker who uses the understanding given him by ' the inspiration of the Almighty' in tracing out the divine order of the universe, and to admit into Christian communion every one who desires to be accounted a

disciple of Christ, and humbly endeavors to follow in
the steps of his Divine Master."

But having passed these objections, we come face to
face with the splendid facts of our physical frame with
which anatomy and physiology, has to do. Are they
not of such a nature, and of such beauty as to render it
foolish for one to neglect them?

Here are the subtle harmonies, and rich melodies,
which go to make vitality. All this rush of life within
our bodies, how finely is it connected. What an orches-
tra; what deep-seated preparation for harmony; what
arrangement, this to fit that; what disposition of facts,
what beautiful accuracies; what niceties of structure and
obvious truth of facts.

The bones seem to be a splendid frame-work for a
noble building. How they are fitted each to each, and
how upon them is arranged the great combination of
muscle, nerves, blood, and tendon, which altogether do
a man's work in the world. But with finer facts than
bone and muscle, our physical structures have to do;
with a nobler set of magnificent energies, do these bodies operate. They are the home of the mind, the
workshop of the spirit, the palace of the soul, the dwelling place of the Holy Ghost. This muscular system has
to do duty for all our thought. This blood furnishes
ample force, to allow designs, and these physical organs
supply effort and effect to all our desires. This home
of the mind is wondrously connected with the mind itself, so near, that, as my reader has seen, the question
of the hour is, whether they are not one and the same.
We have seen that question answered, and now see the
deep relation between them. Here is this nervous system and the intellect. So close is the relation that different localities have been made for different spiritual operations. The brain we say, is the seat of all actual ac-

.tivity. All the great art, all the wise statesmanship, all the fine philosophy, all the heart-rending horror, all the noble poetry, all the lustrous chivalry, all the immortal literature, and all of the grand purposes of the human race date to some brain, burning with fervor and bright with effort. But more than this, God comes to human thought, and the fine experiences of Moses on Nebo, Sinai, and Horeb, all the great feelings of Elijah at the place of his heroism, all the experience of Fenelon, John, Paul, Luther, and the untold thousands occurred in human brains, in bodies which were the temples of the Holy Ghost. How grand then, is this study! With what deep devotion ought men to pursue it! It is the physical side of the highest possibility of creation, and who can wonder that it should thus be celebrated by its devotees?

Does not then the study of physiology, as founded on the study of anatomy, lead us immediately into the ethics of hygiene! From the vision point of these studies, do we not gain sight of a set of duties, which will make health sacred, as Divine Capital on which we are to do work for humanity and God, which shall show us that much of the sin, and crime, and woe of the world, has its genesis in a carelessness which overlooks all those facts, and that the pressing duty of the hour is a close study of the ethics of health?

For this is health,—capital, the stock in trade, on which a man does business, for time and eternity. Because it is so, it is his duty to guard it, and protect it. Disease is wickedness, except when inherited or unavoidable. Sickness is wrong, except for the same reasons. A clear head, gives more clear thoughts than a head filled with the results of indiscretion, wrong-doing, and evil. So it is a duty to keep it in the best condition and circumstance. A clear head is so much capi-

tal to do all the business of a human being upon; a sound
body, through and through, has the same valuation.
The world with its duties, demands, pleads, presses upon
each man, and he who is not in the best condition for
duty, cheats not only himself, but the world. "Who
is weak," said Paul : "and I am not weak." We must
learn the ethics of good health, from the anatomy of
our bodies, and their physiology. We there see how
much we are capable of bearing and doing, we then find
the use and abuse of our organs. We there understand
the enormity of a sin against the body, and feel that he
who slights the body, slights the mind. He who slights
the mind slights himself, and he who is unjust to himself, is unjust to the world,

How much of crime is owing to ignorance of the laws
of our bodies. How much evil comes from the fact that
we slight the study of ourselves. Diseases attach to
parents, which they transmit, with their compliments, to
their children, unmindful of the suffering, which must
ensue. Bad habits, which make bad crimes, oftentimes
fall from age to age. Physiology is set at defiance, and
the march of death goes on.

To close this discussion, which I felt must be given,
if my whole life were written, the need of education is
the study of man in his physical nature, without prejudice, without fear, with the assurance that the truth of
his spiritual nature will be seen, as deeper sinks the
-thought of the student into this marvelous connection
of his body, and the duties which we owe to it.

CHAPTER VIII.

OTHER and quite as practical subjects have from time to time touched me and one enforces itself upon my attention while I write.

I was looking at what to-day threatens the life of the republic, yea, the life of the race, more than standing armies or battalioned hosts, more than great navies, more than the shafts of the soldiery of our foes,—when I saw that drunkard. I am not simply reciting dates about myself, nor occurrences, in this volume, but more anxious for my opinions than the recollection of my past, I feel it due to all concerned to present such opinions as I may have formed in a life-work which now looks into the West, and bears the teaching of over a half century of human experience.

I assure my readers that I have not seen these facts which confront the angel of the future so audaciously, without getting well-outlined opinions about the traffic which breaks the hearts of women and damns the souls of men; which steps to the approaching muse of history and hands her a cup of blood, and asks her to dip her pen in that and then write.

The spectacle is awful, if for nothing but its greatness:—a terrible greatness, indeed. The army that every year walks to its awful death, is a spectacle for worlds. It bends the heavens in pity; it woos the tears of the angels in sympathy divine. Every calling has to contribute. Every trade gives its own. Every profession is broken. Every avocation in life yields its

13

men. Every condition is taxed. Poverty with its
rags sends its delegates to the death of the drunkard.
Wealth with its robes of fashion, and jewels, fresh from
the bosom of nature, supplies its aristocratic quota,
who shall have to bury their position, pawn their gold,
sell their glories, to sleep in a common drunkard's
grave. The populations which oscillate between poor
and rich are decimated for the wretchedness which
feasts upon human homes, human hearts and human
souls, and, like a district which is taxed, respond to
their levy which is conceived by fiends in hell and is
executed by fiends on earth. No rank, nor fortune,
no circumstance nor condition, no fellowship nor solitude, no ignorance nor learning, no prospect nor defeat,
no faith of men nor love of women seems delivered
from the audacious attacks of this high-handed tyrant.
No freedom on earth seems to escape the efforts of the
foe, whose army is a band of suffering and wretched
slaves. This grows more awful as we remember that
the tide of intemperance has been going on through the
long, long past. Oh what a world full of tears have
fallen, what a firmament full of oaths which have
been hurled at the eternal One. What a sky full of
wretched darkness has fallen on homes; what number-
less deaths at the cup; what a multitude have gone
staggering down into woe. What a wail reaching
heaven, echoed from the heart of hell, come from the
long, long past. As we look back into the abysm of
time, how many fine characters all blackened and torn,
how many fair futures engulfed in rum; how many
beautiful day-dreams broken into pieces; how many
glorious hopes shattered into fragments; how many
gigantic possibilities perished as they fell, groaned as
they went down into darkness terrible, into the depths
infinite. There are the orators whose voice, all turned

to the splendid ideas which lit their brains, moved nations, raised armies, presented bayonets, saved constitutions, and at last struggled in that death.   There are
the generals whose valor was bright as the noon-day on
battle field, with which history is vocal, who were not
heroic in the place of temptations and fell beneath the
sharp sword of the giant intemperance.   There are the
preachers, whose voices trembled with pathos, whose
eyes were moist with tears, whose hearts burned for
sinners, who pointed to Calvary, who pleaded for the
Holy Ghost, who gazed into the face of God, but who,
at last fell and lost all, and shrieked their foul slanders
on christianity as down into the company of the lost
they rushed, infuriate with rum.   Philosophers, who
gazed into the depths of life, and swept into keen eyes
the heritage of the zenith, poets, whose music lingers
yet among the hills and valleys of human experience,
whose voices can never grow faint, whose tones breathe
of eternity, whose "star-tuned harps" ring yet with the
sounding notes of heaven,—men of might whose arms
shook the cities of the seas—men of thought, whose
ideas made civilization and rocked thrones into fragments, men of love, who builded the image of heaven
on earth over smiling and beautiful children—women—
oh spare the truth—women, who dashed love to death,
and hid the magnificence of motherhood in murder and
sin, children, beautiful, bright, loving children, in
whose nature a drunken father and a bad mother have
sent the secrets of wretchedness which shall make the
years heavy with moans.—*all in the grave of the past,
dug with rum, and sealed with crime.*

But the future comes.   On and on it is to go—all
this infinite wretchedness on, *on* to *eternity.*   Add this
to your thought, if you can.   Just that, enlarged by
the infinities of God, of which every man is full—just

in that infinite proportion is a single phase of the curse of intemperance.

The depth of its woe is not felt, and never can be, until the value of the human soul shall be appraised and declared. This, only the eternal arithmetic can compute. We have no equation for it. No infinities come into our grasp, no measurement can be had. None but God and a soul, which shall have forever and forever in which to learn it, can know the greatness of this curse.

Some of its disastrous work we can know. We can see its devilish work in our common humanity. It blights the best energies.

With fiendish grip it holds fast to the dearest powers of the human being. It takes one's ideal and drags it like a captured banner in its slime and filth. All full of stars, all covered with brilliant stripes, is that flag of our life which felt the gales of heaven upon it, and yielded its beauty to the South wind and the storms of the North. It floated at the summit of our mortal life. It was the expression of our ideal. Intemperance seizes it, drags it with its horrid form through the dust of its vileness, into the midst of its sister vices, where, before our eyes, they sit and tear it into shreds, one strip after another, smear it with their sins, and laugh with horrid screams as we see what we ought to be, what we want to be, what we said we would be, torn into fragments and utterly destroyed.

Love seated on the throne of the heart sees the approach of rum. She is white, clear-eyed, beautiful. She is all aglow with a radiance which ripples against her face as the streams play from the throne of God. She takes but a taste. She has lost her splendor. She touches it caressingly, her clear eyes are coarse and brutal. She tastes again; her soft hand is hard and heavy. She drinks, and her beauty is gone. She cries for more, her face is flushed, her eyes are blood-shot and horrible. She shrieks. Love is gone ; *lust* is here. Home is defiled. Virtue is covered with darkness, and truth and honor are lost in deepest crime.

Aspirations, like angels of God, sit with hopes, who, like other messengers of heaven, invite them to sublimest heights. Rum comes. The war begins. The man yields. These angels are compelled to doff their snowy robes, and in wretched gloom attired, are forced to bring the foaming draught of hell to sink the spirit deeper into lowest degradation.

Rum charges the brain and makes a monster out of reason. Rum assaults the imagination and makes it a wretch to dream of death. Rum seizes the will and strangles it in its snaky fold. Rum catches the instincts, and depriving them of sight, sends them running swiftly on to death. Rum makes the intellect the watch-tower of wrong, and of the heart makes a capitol of evil. Rum is the tyrant of the past, the tyrant of the present, and looks into the faces of men defiantly, and swears with a systematic oath, that Rum will be the tyrant of the future.

Such is the antagonist. how shall we master him? Such is the disease, what is the remedy?

It appears to me that we may see the remedy best by seeing the history of the disease. Where, then, does intemperance begin its work? What is its origin?

Certainly not in the bodily organization. Animals, with a great physical pre-disposition, have no such habits. Besides, as is well known, the most successful treatment does not show that in the physical organism does the sin abide.

Ah, it is a *sin*. That is enough to show that its origin is deeper than the organs of the human body. It begins just where all wrong-doing begins. It has its genesis exactly where all other culpable evil has its origin, in the soul, in the will.   Intemperance is the yielding of the will to the persuasions of its surroundings, as all sin is.   The body adds or not to the force of these circumstances, which, surviving the will, persuade it to yield to the satisfying of itself.

It is saying: "The forces outside of my being are stronger than those inside.   My circumstances are more than I am."   It is a sure sign of lack of inner strength —*manhood*.   All sin, all wrong-doing, all evil, all giving up is that.   The trouble always is at home, within the breast, in the soul, in the will of the man.

Now, if this is so,—and that it is, all experience shows,—what is the remedy?   What is the preventive? The rèmedy and preventive are one: *Keep the man strong*.   Make him greater than all the world has for him.   Fill him with God, and duty, and truth, and a love of righteousness; for nothing can overcome from without what is strong and self-sustaining from within. What does not sustain itself is always weak, and generally at the mercy of its foes.   A hollow globe is weaker than a solid sphere.   The strong man is the full man, the man who is so related to himself and to the source of strength as to sustain himself, and thus be strong.

Such, then, is the preventive, such the cure.

If you want to make people of temperance, make them people of manhood and womanhood   Call out the best and boldest exercise of their best powers.   It is as though you wanted to make a good carpenter out of your boy, you would not tell him to watch and *not* be a preacher, or a doctor, or something else besides a carpenter, but you would tell him how and give him all the opportunities you could to *be* a carpenter.   You would tell him of carpenters, take him to a carpenter-shop, fill him with the idea, call out his ability, give exercise to his powers, get out the carpenter in him, help him to *be* a carpenter all the time. And so if you want a man, do not try to get a human being not to be a demon or a fool, but try to get him to *be* a man. The surest way to keep people from doing what they ought not to do, is to get them to do what they ought to do. And the truest way to get human beings not to be what we do not want them to be, is to get them to be what we want them to be. In all the great work of the world, "the way to resume is to resume."

But in what manner shall we call this latent man out? Certainly, culture shall be a great agency. But are not his troubles deeper than difficulties of the intellect? Does he not need more than the gymnastics of thought? Is it not a fact that some men of the highest intellectual power and scholarship have been ruined by rum? No marshaling of ideas, no array of facts, no collocation of experiences, no tones from the deep-voiced past, no acquaintance with the forces around us, no depth of scientific erudition but has been disgraced by the presence of this marauding foe. We can not, therefore, depend upon the development of the intellect. We believe that that is necessary, but we believe, also, that that is not all. A man must have clear ideas of duty, of the value of life, of responsibility, of his relation to the working ideas of the Universe, to give force to the might of his nature. But something must be behind all these urging devotion with loyalty, filling the recesses of each day's work with their fullness and meaning.

That is, the deep springs of feeling must be touched beneath the rugged rock, and allowed to bubble forth in transparent beauty to refresh the vegetation at its feet, and the Moses' rod that bursts these stone barriers, the unfeeling walls in which these treasures are held is *sympathy*. Mightier than the power of men thought is the power of a human sentiment.   It is a thought to which feeling has been added, and he who can draw these out has enlisted the deeper agencies of our mortal life. Many a man who has felt the advent of the finest ideas, perishes for the grasp of a warm hand filled with the messages of the heart.   Many a human being has staggered into darkness with the profoundest notions buzzing in his brain, while a single touch from a heart-warmed finger-tip, would have led him into light, boundless and supreme.   Abstractions can not catch the deeper powers of man, but a real, visible, living presence, becomes his anchor and guide.   Our theories are far beyond our feelings.   Our thoughts are in advance of our sympathies.   We have cast up columns of statistics, we have tabulated long catalogues of cases, and we have arrived at what we call the scientific view of intemperance.   Our intellect has said it, but our heart has not felt it.

We have sat in our studies and thought the matter out.   We have done less in going with hearts full of feeling to win the wanderer back.   It is an easy thing for us to read the reports of crime, it is an easy thing for us to get the history of woe, it is an easy thing for us to determine the per cent. of murderers who use rum, it is a comparatively pleasant task for us to find and upbraid the reason of our heavy taxes, but it is an heroic thing to send our feelings like so many angels into houses of woe, into homes of disgrace, into the ditches and gutters, into the asylums and penitentiaries, into the dram-shops and stylish restaurants, and keep them there until they bring home again the men who are on their way to ruin, and assist in making their homes places of peace, love, truth, hope and manhood. All this is the work of sympathy.   Sympathy is a more powerful engine for raising man than eloquence, or philosophy, or fear.   It is the warning influence which invites the latent manhood to break through the soil, lift its young verdure into the air, open its leaves at the touches of the light and burst in flowers of fragrance and bear fruit at last to the salvation of men and the glory of God.

CHAPTER IX.

THE study of men is quite as interesting as the study of more abstract subjects. And so I felt it a pleasure as well as a duty to my readers who have come thus far with my story, to give some idea of the men I have met, and with whom I have had to do.

As America is full of Washington, so is Texas full of Sam Houston. He is the household god—and pretty much all the divinity he has Sam Houston is to the ordinary Texan.

While there, to interest myself and to find out the reason of this phenomenal affection for a personal force, I took what I had known of his political career and added to it many facts, which, with the political background with which all students of our history are acquainted, will add something of clearness and detail to the picture of General Sam Houston in the minds of my readers.

On the 2d of March, 1793, this energetic child was born. Strange and suggestive must it ever remain, that on the day of his birth which so many years afterwards he was to celebrate, a new republic also was to be born. For on the natal day of Sam Houston, the independence of Texas was declared.

On the hills of Scotland, led by Wallace and Bruce, fighting for God and Liberty, his hardy ancestry had made themselves conspicuous. Their zealous piety grew on the root of the religion of John Knox and his brave compeers. Driven from place to place, wandering exiles, as it seemed, they finally left Ireland for America, and settled in Virginia, where, near Timber Ridge Church, Sam Houston was born. His father was not distinguished for wealth, but for indomitable manhood. This was the gift which descended to his son. But a powerful motherhood was behind him. That countenance which beamed upon his infancy shed benignant strength upon all his early manhocd, and when history shall have awarded those who have placed the world in debt to them, this matronly and dignified woman, whom the poor recollected with gratitude, shall have a place. Her numerous family did not preclude her giving the necessary attention to the rearing of this boy. No misfortune overcame her. In those unpeo. pled regions, she taught her son the ideas which lie at the base of modern civilization. Young Houston found himself capable of work, and engaged immediately in effort. Near his home there was an academy. For a short time he found his thirst for knowledge growing more ambitious under this auspicious influence. This desire for education, which lies at the base of all true culture, was omnipresent with him. The Texans scarcely know how much they owe to that fire which was fanned into a flame by that heroic mother, and which reached its full power when those two or three books, which he found, became fuel for its future force in the world. He loved History. He looked into History as the chronicle of the race, and found from experience the nature and influence of those passions and sentiments and ideas which make thrones and republics possible. It is a fact, said to be little known, that at this early age he was able to repeat almost the whole of Pope's translation of Homer's Iliad. This led him into the study of the languages. But deeper than mere linguistic attainments did his culture go. He loved to live in the mighty shades of great influences. He loved to feel the throbbing heart of the past, and ascertain the growth and spirit of its ideas and ideals. I am told that a small but effectual tyranny was exercised over him by his brothers, who were only greater in age. They compelled him to go into a store. He compelled them one day to miss him. News came that Sam had crossed the Tennessee River, and had succeeded in becoming a member of a tribe of Indians, whose life he enjoyed at its full. Search was made. Sam was found. A splendid form, blooming with ruddy youth, dressed in the garb and maintaining the airs of a North American Indian, stood before them. They questioned him upon this strange proceeding. I am told that he turned squarely around, uttered the war-whoop of his associates ; that his brothers shivered, as out of his mouth came these remarkable words : "I prefer to measure the tracks of the deer rather than your tape. I want you to understand that I like the wild liberty of my red-faced brothers better than your tyranny. I want you to know, that if I cant study Latin in the Academy, I can at least read a translation from the Greek in peace, here in these woods ; so you can go home as soon as you please."

The family thought he would get sick of it and they left him alone. No tidings of his disgust came. Sam did not make an appearance until his clothes wore out. Then he came home and told them he would take a suit, if they would treat him with propriety. For some time the superior age of his brothers was controlable. But one day, when it did break loose, he returned to the woods to enjoy life with the Indian boys and girls, and to obtain an idea of their rights and the wrongs they have suffered, such as made him the apostle of our duties towards them.

His friends said he was crazy, but history shows that from that insanity this Nation gained that which they would not have willingly lost, and which was clearly seen at the battle of San Jacinto.   In 1840, a picture was seen in Washington, which was not forgotten soon by any who had the pleasure to be present.   General Moore had arrived with forty wild Indians from Texas. At the sight of Sam, who was then General Houston, these dusky citizens of the forest rushed to him, embraced him to their naked breasts, fondled him lovingly with their brawny fingers, and called him by the endearing name of father.

For until his eighteenth year he had remained their companion.   For clothes, he had gone into debt to the pale faces.   This debt he proposed to pay by teaching school.   He who had been taught at an Indian University, was not expected to be able to teach school in the most approved fashion.   But he demanded a higher price than any body else.   His price was eight dollars— one-third to be paid in corn delivered at the mill, at thirty-three and one-half cents a bushel, one-third in cash, and one-third in the homespun cotton cloth of variegated colors, in which he was to be attired.   Imagine him, tall, straight and slim, with a long queue behind, and utter independence in his face ; and you have Sam Houston, the school-teacher.   Not a day after his debts were paid did he teach school.   With a Euclid in his pocket, with which he never seemed content to stock his brain, he heard the bugle note of 1813, when America was preparing for war with her old foe.   With a young recruiting party Houston enlisted.   Some of his friends had a touch of aristocracy, and when they spoke to him about enlisting as a common soldier, he slammed the door of common sense upon it, when he said these words: ''And what have your craven souls to say

about the *ranks?* Go to, with your stuff. I would
much sooner honor the ranks, than to dishonor an appointment. You dont know me now, but you shall
hear of me." These words had an echo in the words
of his mother, when she said at the door of her cottage:
"There, my son, take this musket, and never disgrace
it, for remember, I had rather all my sons should fill an
honorable grave, than that one of them should turn his
back to save his life. Go, and remember, too, that
while the door of my cottage is open to brave men, it
is eternally shut against cowards."

Promotion soon came. On and on they marched,
until we find this intrepid man at Tohopeka, or the
Horseshoe, where some events which this Nation can
not forget, occurred.

Long had the Creek Indians, by stealth, tried to
weary out their foe. General Jackson's army, en-
camped at Fort Williams, contained more than two
thousand men. Their spies were out in every direction. In the bend of the Horseshoe, the Creeks had
agreed to follow the words of their prophets, and engage in open warfare for the settlement of the rule of
the peninsula. A massive breastwork stretched between them and their foes. Jackson no sooner reached
the Horseshoe than he prepared for action. He had
cut off escape from three sides of the peninsula. He
had ordered the artillery to play against the breastworks,
and a mere play it seemed. The Cherokees, who were
friendly, and were under command of General Coffee,
discovered some canoes, captured them, and set fire to
a cluster of wigwams. It was almost impossible for
Jackson to restrain his men when they saw the fire.
They were determined to storm the breastworks. But
that great General was determined to remove all the
women and children to safety. Then the rush began.

Major Montgomery was the first to spring upon the breastworks. He was immediately killed. At the same instant Houston reached the breastworks, jumped with a scream among the Indians, began to make a path of blood. No sooner had he reached the ground than a barbed arrow struck him in the thigh. But on he went, carrying the terrible wound, until in the recoil of the warriors, he tried to extract it. He commanded his lieutenant to do so, not being able to do it himself. Just then he saw that it must be done. The lieutenant faltered. He cried out: "Try again, and if you do not do it this time I will smite you to the earth." The arrow came, leaving a terrible wound. Jackson came, ordered him not to return to the fight. Houston would have obeyed him, under any other circumstances. But he recollected the taunts of the day of his enlistment, and was determined to die in that battle or silence forever the criticism of those what had dare to sneer. In a few seconds young Sam Houston was at the head of his men, leading their valor in a contest which had now become general, and where four thousand eyes were glaring the fierceness of the strife into each other, where two thousand hearts were beating with courage or throbbing with fear. The thousand warriors were select men. Behind them was a strange, ignorant, mighty, religious enthusiasm, and not a solitary warrior offered 'to surrender, even while the arrows were tearing his flesh and the sword was piercing his breast. Dead and dying covered the peninsula. Even when the last warrior had died, the victory was incomplete. For a large party of Indians had hid themselves in the breastworks, and from the narrow holes a most murderous fire had been kept up. Soldier after soldier fell. General Jackson at last called for a body of men to charge upon them. No one responded. He called again. The captains stood

still. Sam Houston could wait no longer. He called
upon his soldiers to follow him. He dashed down the
hill. He jerked a musket from the hands of a hesitat-
ing man. He sounded his order with an almost super-
natural voice. The whole breastwork was bristling with
rifles and arrows. His men hesitated. He stopped to
rally them. Within five yards of the port holes two
rifle balls sped with murderous intent, and his arm fell
broken to his side. He cried piteously for his men to
charge. But they failed. Houston was carried away
beyond the range of bullets, and fell a bleeding hero
upon the earth. Dark night came. What he supposed
to be his dying hour was lonely and deserted. The deep
feelings of disappointment ruled his breast, and he never seemed to recover until when, thirty years thereafter,
Andrew Jackson sent for him to stand at his bedside, while
he died. The wretchedness of his condition can not be
imagined, until we knew that it was only lost when he
reached Knoxville, on his way to report himself ready
for duty, he heard the glorious news of the battle of
New Orleans.

Peace was proclaimed. He was kept in the service
as lieutenant, and stationed at New Orleans. A life
full of variety followed. Honor and suffering seemed
to be his lot, until the next winter, he united with a delegation of Indians at Washington and was met with foul
slander. African Negroes had been smuggled into the
Western States. They had been transported from Flor-
ida, which was then a province of Spain. The friends
of the smugglers were representatives in Congress.
The vindication, before the President and the Secretary
of War, which he made, was complete. He showed
that he had simply in view the honor of his country.
His painful wounds made him an object of pity. He
considered himself unrewarded for his services. He re-

signed his lieutenancy and faced poverty, with a dim prospect of health, resigning all his offices and dignities and beginning the study of law in Nashville. Houston, as a civilian, is very liable to be sacrificed to Houston as the romantic, active, impetuous and daring leader. But a single glance into his character would have revealed facts that the very qualities which made him so sublime a leader, also made him capable of the highest idea of citizenship. The abilities which made him dare, helped him to do. The power which assisted in the bearing of a wound, was present with him in his deepest intellectual investigations.

And as a student of law, young Houston, then twenty-four years of age, was a deep and patient thinker, a strong and agile investigator, and a complete scholar. He sought the philosophical basis of these rules of action. He tried to find their secret spring in human nature, and in finding their springs here he brought to himself a new sense of the dignity of his profession.

I have already spoken of the fundamental defect of what is called education. With this, Sam Houston had no experience. He was developed into a thinker, rather than filled, as a balloon with air, with the facts about him. He was a man of action, and the depth of his spirit was found by a line of development rather than by finding out how much it might hold of dates and names. Sam Houston was never overloaded with the culture of the schools. And even if we must say that he was rough and rude, and scarcely the highest type of our modern civilization, still we must acknowledge that the power of this country in the future will be eminently thankful for the accession of such brawny strengths to the on-marching energies of men. While

15

he was captain of ideas, he was also captain of the forces which they set in motion.

A few month's study had enabled him to pass a brilliant examination. Obtaining a library on credit, he began life as a lawyer, in Lebanon, thirty miles east of Nashville. He was soon made district attorney. He had such success as to explode, with terrible effect upon their authors, the stories of his rawness and verdancy. This district attorneyship he soon found in his way, and resigned it. He was elected Major General in 1821, and in 1823 he was elected to Congress. Twice did he fill the position of a representative, and in 1827, the confidence and gratitude of the people placed him in the Governor's seat by a majority of over twelve thousand. His marriage was unfortunate. An unhappy alliance was the beginning of a short matrimonial career. The darkest jealousy gave foundation and credence to the meanest and most impossible of representation, and the State was filled with the deepest excitement concerning the termination of this alliance. His private character was attacked. The State was divided, and in the meantime Houston offered no word of denial. With a grander manhood than is popular, he heard himself charged with every species of crime. He said : " This is a painful, but it is a private affair. I do not recognize the right of the public to interfere in it. And I shall treat the public just as though it had never happened. And remember that, whatever may be said by the lady or her friends, it is no part of the conduct of a gallant, or a generous man, to take up arms against a woman. If my character can not stand the shock, let me lose it. The storm will soon sweep by, and time will be my vindicator." He resolved, since he had been elected to every office by acclamation, that he would resign instantly, forego all his prospects, and make himself an exile, and the wretched journals of the day pounced upon his innocence and generosity like a fierce eagle swooping from the clouds and tearing an infant from a mother's arms. He fled to the forests. He found a home of which History has said little.

He recollected the old chief, who, in his boyhood exile, had called him his son. This tribe had removed to Arkansas. Eleven years had separated them. But nothing could keep Houston from finding the face of his old friend.

The scene was almost as touching as his separation from his friends at the steamboat, when the leaders of Tennessee saw that beautiful young man resolutely seeking obscurity, throwing aside the wreath of fame, casting off robes of office which he had never dishonored, going into the forest to wait until his enemies had been silenced by tongues which he knew would soon break forth in his praise, and to nurse his mighty strength for the new issues with which he had to deal.

The scene at the home of the chieftain was not less beautiful, suggestive or pathetic. It was the venerable old chief Oolvoteka. Sixty-five years had fled over him, but in the declining day he showed no weakness or age. His grace was the grace of strength, and his dignity was the dignity of power. A large and comfortable wigwam covered his simple but happy life. Twelve servants cared for him on his large plantation, and many hundred head of cattle grazed upon his ample fields. Kindness, hospitality, and love for the oppressed ruled that wigwam.

Here Houston found a home. Here the old chief met him with warm embraces. With the tremulousness, which comes from a soul filled with affection and pity, he uttered to the happy Houston these tender words: "My son, eleven winters have passed since we met.

My heart has wandered often where you were; and I heard you were a great chief among your people. Since we parted at the falls, as you went up the river, I have heard that a dark cloud had fallen in the white path you were walking, and when it fell in your way you turned your thoughts to my wigwam. I am glad of it—it was done by the Great Spirit. There are many wise men among your people, and they have many counsellors in your nation. We are in trouble, and the Great Spirit has sent you to us to give us counsel and take away trouble from us. I know you will be our friend, for our hearts are near to you, and you will tell our sorrows to the great Father, General Jackson. My wigwam is yours—my home is yours—my people are yours—rest with us." Is it a wonder that Houston felt at home after such an affectionate greeting? Three years did he pass among the Cherokees. Truly and faithfully did he serve the cause of the oppressed and outraged Indian. He, somehow, had a natural love for these children of the forest. He was accustomed, years after, to tell with earnestness and enthusiasm many incidents which led him to conclude that very few people had been betrayed or deceived by these citizens of nature. Here he determined not only to keep himself intelligent of their wrongs concerning the character of the red man, but to guard their rights and develop to the nation the humanity which should make it more honorable and them more happy.

Thus Sam Houston began his career, as the relentless scrutinizer of all the Indian agents, the severest opponent of those who did them wrong, the earnest friend of those who sought to protect their rights. Often did the chief counsel him. The closest acquaintance did he maintain with their affairs.

He ascertained, that by the treaty for their lands on

the Arkansas, they were to receive twenty-eight dollars each. He ascertained further, that the agents had made the pretense that they had no money, and instead, certificates had been issued by the agents. These, the Indians had been informed, were worthless, and certain interested parties bought them up at a merely nominal price. Afterwards General Houston, who dared to speak the truth, uttered these pregnant words, before a convocation of men whose successors I am frank to say, have been as faithless to the plighted fidelity of our government as themselves: "During the period of my residence among the Indians, in the Arkansas region, I had every facility for gaining a complete knowledge of the flagrant outrages practiced upon the poor red men by the agents of the government. I saw every year, vast sums squandered and consumed, without the Indians deriving the least benefit, and the government, in very many instances, utterly ignorant of the wrong that was perpetrated. Had one-third of the money advanced by the government been usefully, honorably and wisely applied, all those tribes might have been now in possession of the arts and enjoyment of civilization. I care not what dreamers and politicians and travelers and writers say to the contrary, I know the Indians' character, and I confidently avow that if one-third of the many millions of dollars our government has appropriated within the last twenty-five years for the benefit of the Indian population, had been honestly and judiciously applied, there would not have been at this time, a single tribe within the limits of our states and territories, but what would have been in the complete enjoyment of all the arts and all the comforts of civilized life. But there is not a tribe but what has been outraged and defrauded, and nearly all the wars we have prosecuted against the Indians have grown out of the vast frauds played upon them by our Indian agents and their accomplices. But the purposes for which these vast annuities and enormous contingent advances were made, have only led to the destruction of the constitutions of thousands, and the increase of immorality among the Indians. We cannot measure the desolating effect of intoxicating liquors among the Indians, by any analogy drawn from civilized life. With the red man, the consequences are a thousand times more frightful. Strong drink, when once introduced among the Indians, unnerves the purposes of the good, and gives energy to the passions of the vicious : it saps the constitution with fearful rapidity, and inflames all the ferocity of the savage nature. The remoteness of their situation excludes them from all the benefits which might arise from a thorough knowledge of their condition by the President, who only hears one side of the story, and that, too, told by his own creatures, whose motive for seeking for such stations are often only to be able to gratify their cupidity and avarice. The President should be careful to whom Indian agencies are given. If there are trusts under our government where honest and just men are needed, they are needed in such places ; where peculation and fraud can be more easily perpetrated than any where else. For in the far-off forests beyond the Mississippi, where we have exiled those unfortunate tribes, they can perpetrate their crimes and their outrages, and no eye but the Almighty's sees them."

This was one of the bravest speeches of Houston's life. He had got at the facts by living among them, and he had the inspiration of duty to declare the truth. Knowing these frauds, he visited Washington, and five agents, and sub-agents were promptly removed. These men had their strong friends in Congress. They filled

the newspapers of Arkansas with infamy against Sam
Houston, but he had torn the mask from their faces.
At this time, General Jackson was more unpopular than
he had ever been.   A majority of Congress was against
him and were intent on his ruin, but he had gone
through it all unscathed.   Houston was the dear friend
of the old General, and they swore they would crush
him.   One clearly proven charge which he had made
against them kindled their hatred into flame.   That was,
that they had been contractors for furnishing Indian
rations, and that, as a matter of fact, so scanty were the
provisions to all, that some had even died of starvation.
This roused all their friends in Congress against him.
They selected their leader.   He was a malignant personal enemy of General Jackson, but he wore a mask
of brazen, shameless hypocrisy.   In his place, he rose
and in a vile speech denounced Houston, and boldly
intimated that with him, Jackson and the Secretary
of War were intending to defraud the country.   Houston had borne it as long as he could.   He promised
that he would rebuke such insolence, and careful indeed
was this base man to avoid meeting him.   But one
night the villain under cover of darkness, was about to
attempt to perpetrate his foul deed, when Houston es-
pied him.   He had no weapon but a cane.   He asked
him his name.   No sooner had he answered, than the
cane was shivered into splinters over his head.   A
pistol was snapped at the breast of Houston, but the
missing of that fire saved to the country that brave
heart.

Four processes were commenced against Houston.
The House of Representatives was resolved into a judi-
cial tribunal.   The court sat for nearly thirty days.
Every method of condemnation was tested. The
wretched business went on until the public mind, recol-

lecting the wounded hero, began to plead in his favor. The atmosphere was ripe for Houston's speech. It came in ringing tones. His eloquence was full of chivalry. His speech was long and earnest. Its boldness and ability seized the country with a grip of power. This trial ended in a reprimand to the prisoner from the Speaker of the House, which was full of compliment, and was a signal triumph to Houston.

The second process began. Houston's enemy was made chairman of the committee at the request of Houston, and it was soon found that it would not do to condemn the splendid philanthropy of this noble man. For in spite of every possible array, the committee said, they were *compelled* to report that not the slightest evidence had appeared to sustain the charge.

Another resolution was introduced to exclude him from the lobby, but it met an unhappy death. Another process, and the drama closed. A criminal investigation was inaugurated. He was fined what he was glad to pay for the privilege of shivering his cane on the head of his enemy, and General Jackson remitted the fine.

His return, by way of Tennessee, was a continuous ovation. The public mind was touched with sympathy, and Tennessee was proud to call him her own. Nothing, however, could dissuade him from his purpose of re-entering the forest. The painful occurrences of the past had yielded to the sway of reason, but it was next to impossible to make him believe that civilization had any need of his services.

What was his intention? It was to become a herdsman. To live a life of quietude, out of the reach of slander. Away from the paganism of civilized life. He left his native home, and set out on the first of December, 1832, with a few companions.

This was Sam Houston's entrance into Texas. It is not my purpose to recount here what is known to the civilized world. I have simply spoken of that period of Houston's life in which he received the discipline which filled him to lead Texas into independence. I should be repeating the merest common places of history were I to go farther into the biography of this distinguished man. What I have given, are simply the lights and shadows of which my readers may not be possessed, but which came to me who studied the source of influence which still dominates throughout all Texas. It is as pervasive as it is strong, and my reader will supply the later history of that State which shall show him how great were the elements in which this man worked, how powerful were the forces with which he had to do. A national gallery is not complete without his picture, and I should have deemed it a misdemeanor against my readers had I not made clear to them, with what little information I possessed, the early training of this unique man.

CHAPTER X.

THE following general notice of my efforts and ideas of a life such as my own, may be of such interest as to warrant republication from " *Prime's Model Farms and Their Methods* ":

SOLOMON J. WOOLLEY, HILLIARD, FRANKLIN COUNTY.

Tiling—How to Make Drains—Depth—Laterals—Velocity of Water —Cost of Draining per Acre- -Pastures—Cattle—Sheep—Hogs —Horses—Rotation of Crops—Manures.

APPLEDALE FARM.

Twenty-three years ago, I came to what was then the wettest and most neglected portion of Franklin County, and purchased six hundred acres of heavily timbered swamp land. I deadened four hundred acres at once, and in the course of time rented to all who wanted, from twenty to forty acres of land, for the term of five years, with the understanding that at the expiration of the lease the land was all to be cleared of timber.

TILING.

I at once commenced a system of drainage, which I have continued ever since, draining with tile as I had money to spare, always laying the tile myself, and making sure that every tile was laid exactly right.

Although there are fifteen miles of tile drains on my farm, the low, wet and swaley lands have been drained with round tile, (which I consider the best,) at a depth of from three to six feet, and some of the dry land at a depth of from three to four feet, and laid from six to eight rods apart. On the black, wet, swaley land, it has paid many fold, while on the clay land my most sanguine expectations have been more than realized.

HOW TO MAKE DRAINS.

The distance between drains must be determined by the nature of the soil, their depth, and the amount of fall. A loose, porous soil will permit water to reach the drains for a long distance, while a tough, compact clay is almost impervious to water, and requires them to be made much nearer. In a black, loose soil, drains at the depth of four feet are sufficient at a depth of ten rods apart; but if the land is a hard-pan or a stiff clay, to drain it thoroughly the distance apart should be from four to six rods.

But few persons realize the great advantage that deep drains have over shallow ones. In my extensive acquaintance among drainers, I know of but few that drain to a depth averaging over one and a half to three feet, whereas a depth of three to eight feet should always be obtained. An orchard or vineyard, for example, should never be drained less than eight feet deep. The time is probably not far distant when shallow drains will be taken up and put down again at a proper depth. Persons often say that it costs too much to drain so deep, when the fact is the cost is less. For instance, it would cost but very little more to dig two drains to the depth of four feet than it would to dig three to the depth of two and a half feet, and the two deep drains will drain fully as much land as the three shallow, and will drain it much better, and save the expense of the third line of tile.

BUT THE DEPTH OF DRAINS

Is not always a matter of choice, as very often the outlet is not sufficient, and I have very often noticed that
persons are sometimes extremely contrary about giving
their neighbors above them an outlet. In making an
improvement of this kind, that is to last for all time to
come, it is much better to secure a good outlet in the
first place, if it does cost something more, especially if
the land is flat and you have but little fall; but in all
cases it is best to have a good outlet, so that the water
will fall from six to twelve inches when it leaves the tile.
However, a tile drain that is properly made will not fill
up; if the outlet does fill up fifteen or twenty inches
the water will boil up like a spring and keep the tile
washed out. If you have a good fall, say twelve inches
to the hundred feet, a five-inch tile will carry off as
much water as a six-inch tile will if the fall is but four
inches to the hundred feet; the greater the fall the more
rapidly the water will flow, and a smaller-size tile will
answer. One great consideration in draining land is to
get the greatest amount of water off in the shortest
time possible, with the least expense; but a great many
persons that I have noticed draining do the opposite of
this.

I had an open ditch on my farm which drained a
stream which flowed naturally in the shape of an S; the
ditch was cut six feet wide and three feet deep. In
putting tile in this ditch I commenced at the lower end
as deep as the outlet would allow, which was nearly four
feet. I graded this ditch nearly on a level, giving it
just enough fall so the water would run, and continued
to give it more fall as I advanced up stream, but instead
of following the open ditch in the shape of an S, I cut
the S across, shortening the distance nearly one-half, by

which means I gave the ditch nearly twice the fall it had in following the S-shape, although I had to cut through two ridges, one six and the other ten feet deep, but the amount that was saved in tile by this cut-off more than twice paid for digging this deep ditch. By the time I had dug this ditch three-quarters of a mile it had plenty of fall, and then had a depth at the lowest place, of over four feet; a quarter of a mile further (being my upper line,) I gave it a good fall, making it at the upper end two and a half feet deep; I gave it this fall so that the pressure of the water above would force it rapidly out below, where the fall was less. I continued three six-inch tile in this ditch all the way, branching the other four off as they were needed.

Another big open ditch, that I converted into a tile drain, which carried nearly as much water as the first, I

DRAINED IN A DIFFERENT MANNER,

Which I like much better than the first. I commenced at the lower end, at the depth of four and a half feet. This ditch was so meandering that a straight line would save half the distance. Commencing with four eight-inch tile, which I laid side by side for a few rods, I then branched them off at a distance of about four rods apart, continuing them about this distance until near the upper end, when I brought them nearer together to take all the water of the swale. As I advanced up stream I used smaller tile.

All four of these drains cut across the old open ditch and its tributaries several times. My object in making this drain in this way was to drain a large amount of land with a few tile and get the water off as quickly as possible. If I had put all these tile in one drain they would have carried only the same amount of water, and would have drained only one-fourth as much land as they do now. In digging the drains I had to cut through a few ridges six to eight feet deep, but for all it is the cheapest and best-drained land I have. By tiling the open ditches I not only save thirty feet of the best land on the farm, but save the cleaning of the ditch out every year, which, if tramped with cattle, would cost nearly as much as a new ditch; besides, I get the fields in good shape, and save the lives of a great many sheep, which are lost every year by the open ditches, also the young of other animals.

In draining, always remember that whenever you make a cut-off, although it may cost a little more to dig the drain, you not only save the tile but you get more fall, the water off quicker, and the land better drained; however, in some cases the ridges are too high to dig through, and laterals must be used.

THE LATERALS OR SIDE DRAINS,

As they enter the main drain, should be made to enter at an acute angle, pointing down stream. Experience shows, that if their current enters square across that of the main drain, one or the other stream is liable to be arrested, and sand or gravel deposited, injuring the water-course. The tile drain emptying into the main should have a fall of at least six inches, and the more the better, although, I do not believe in having many laterals, but the smaller the number of outlets the better. In draining six hundred acres of land I have but twelve outlets.

HOW TO LAY THE DRAIN.

Before I had much experience in draining, I would dig my drain the whole length and commence at the upper end and lay the tile down stream, but I have learned from experience that the opposite of this is best. Always begin at the lower end, and lay your tile as the ditch is dug; stand on the tile in laying them, and turn them until the joints fit, hitting them after with your boot-heel so as to keep them close together; lay broken pieces of tile over the joints where they do not fit, and cover the tile as you lay them with a few inches of clay out of the bottom of the ditch, to keep the loose soil from washing in at the joints; after which fill in with as much top soil as possible; it will facilitate the descent of the water.

On leaving the drain at any time, put a board or flat stone at the upper end so as to keep rubbish from washing in, and on finishing the drain at the upper end it must be well closed. The last tile at the lower end should be twice as long as the others, having holes through the end, not over an inch apart, with wires, so as to keep all animals out of the drain; and there should be a stone wall built across over the mouth of the drain, laid up with lime and sand, or cement, so as to keep the muskrats from digging holes up along the tile. I have known them to dig holes on top of the tile to a distance of thirty feet, which would form a water-course in time of a freshet, and wash the dirt from off the tile.

To know the size of the tile needed, learn all you can about drainage, and use your own judgment. One eight-inch tile will carry off as much water as an open ditch four feet wide and two feet deep, and is sufficient for an outlet for fifty acres. Never continue tile of the same size all the way. Whenever a lateral comes in, a smaller tile will do from that point on, and so on. It must be borne in mind that the tile is taking water all the time, at every joint. The tile at the end that has holes in it, should be a size larger than the others, as

the wires will impede the flow of the water to some
extent.

HOW TO GRADE THE DRAIN.

This is the most important feature of drainage, and
should always be done with water, as there is no level
for this purpose equal to water. I have learned from
experience that it is almost a useless expense to get an
engineer; he can tell you how deep to cut through the
ridge to give the water an outlet for a certain depth
above, but this will not help any about grading the bottom of the ditch, and if you get the drain deeper above
than it is below, just that much will it fill up. You
must know that a drain can be very easily ruined by not
being graded correctly.

There can be no question in regard to the best form
of tile. At first, the horseshoe tile was made semi-cir-
cular in shape, and without a bottom. Next, the sole
tile, of the same shape as the horseshoe, but having a
flat bottom. Then the pipe tile, which is circular, and
has many advantages, among them the possibility of
being laid true on the bottom, however it may be
warped or crooked in burning. Horseshoe tile should
never be used, as they will be filled with crawfish and
become useless. Tile are usually made twelve and a
half inches long, or intended to be, but they are seldom
over twelve inches. I have used a great many of this
length, and found, on taking them up, that in several
places where a stone was removed in the bottom of the
drain, that one end of the tile had sunken and the other
end raised up, which would leave quite an aperture for
dirt to wash in. I found a remedy for this by getting
a longer cut-off, and making my tile fifteen inches long,
which I find are superior to the short ones in several
respects.

APPLEDALE · DEVON · STOCK · FARM.   RES. OF *S. J. Woolley*.

Replaced the blocks of workshops.

DEPTH OF DRAINS.

I have often been asked why I drain so deep. I do
so to get the full benefit of my land. After cultivating
wheat I dug down to the tile drain six feet deep, and
found plenty of wheat roots at that depth. Beech land,
which is a hard pan that the roots of none of our crops
can enter, after being drained and frozen, becomes loose
and mellow to nearly the depth of the drain, and twice
the amount of grain can be raised on the same land. I
found a few swamps composed of vegetable mold that
became so light, loose and chaffy after draining, that it
would not produce, but after plowing these swamps
twenty inches deep, throwing the subsoil to the top, it
became the most productive land that I had.

WHAT KIND OF LAND NEEDS DRAINING.

I doubt if a piece of land could be found which would
not be benefited by draining, so that we might truth-
fully say that all lands need it, the only possible exception being those that have a gravelly or sandy subsoil.

On visiting a friend some years since, I found him
draining a wet, springy piece of land at the foot of a
hill. He was digging his drain about eighteen inches
deep; he said that he had read that it was no use to
make the drain deeper than the veins. I tried to get
him to make his drain four feet, as he had a good outlet,
and finally he put them in three feet; and on examining
them several years after, I found that the water veins
had sunk to the bottom of the drain, and this piece of
wet and useless land had become the most valuable on
his farm, and at the end of his tile drain was a living
spring of pure water that never froze over, which was
valuable for his stock.

The water from tile drains is the purest that we have,

and is the best for culinary purposes; and where the land lies in such a shape that it can be used for stock, it is the best water that we have for that purpose.

DRAINAGE FOR HEALTH ABOUT A HOME.

It should be remembered that the well is the outlet for at least ten rods in all directions. I have known whole families to die, and it was said to be the mysterious providence of God, when it was nothing but the cesspools, barn-yards, cow-stables, pig-pens, and slops of the house, all emptying their foulness into the well.

The soil lying between the source of impurity and the well has a certain amount of cleansing power, and while effective, withholds the impurity, but, by degrees, it becomes foul further and further on; and this insidious process of fouling the semi-porous earth with impurity, inch by inch, continues, until, in time, it reaches the well, and then every drop that flows through this soil carries with it its atoms of filth, causing fevers and death. Therefore, deep drains should be made between the well and all places of filth. As the matter is one of great importance, involving doctors' bills, sickness, and death, it should have careful attention.

ITS SINGLE DISADVANTAGE.

Perhaps it is only fair to mention one disadvantage that comes from drainage. If a swampy piece of woodland is suddenly drained, most of the old timber will die; the oaks and hickorys will go first. The change is first noticed in the tops of the trees. However, the young timber soon accommodates itself to the change, and after a time grows more thriftily than ever.

VELOCITY OF WATER IN TILE DRAINS.

From the many experiments that I have made to ascertain, as nearly as possible, the velocity of water in tile drains, I find that in a six-inch tile, with a fall of four inches to the hundred feet, when the tile was running full of water, it was eight rods per minute, when running half full, six rods per minute, and the less water there was in the tile the slower it would run. The velocity of a twelve-inch tile when running full would be swifter than this, while in the smaller sizes it would not be so swift, and in an open ditch of the same fall the velocity is four times less than that of a tile drain.

SOLID AND POROUS TILE.

I do not see any advantage in using porous tile. Solid tile is stronger in all respects, and will not burst and crumble like porous tile from wet and freezing. If porous tile is full of water, and freezes, it is sure to expand, and break and crumble. Some say that tile should be porous, so as to let the water into the drain. If there were no other places for the water to enter the drain except by the pores, the land would be poorly drained. Now, for example, take any sized tile you please, having the sixteenth of an inch at every joint (the space at the joints is really greater than this,) and, count it up for thirty rods, you find that the water can get in at the joints many times faster than it can get out at the outlet; and if your drain is a few hundred rods long, the capacity for getting in, is over a hundred times greater than that for getting out.

THE STOPPAGE OF TILE DRAINS.

I know of a three-inch tile drain that stopped running, and on taking it up there were found over twenty musk-

rats in the drain; they were so swelled that no water
could pass them.   But roots are the most troublesome,
sycamore and willow being the most dangerous, though
elm, ash, alder, and some others are attracted by water.
Old trees are not so apt to injure drains as young and
free-growing trees.   Deep drains are not only the best,
but are nothing like so apt to be closed by animals and
roots.   Shallow drains are very often closed by the roots
of grass and other growing crops.   I have never known
a drain so deep that the roots of growing crops could
not reach it.

WHAT IT COSTS PER ACRE TO DRAIN.

A field of forty rods square, or ten acres, had four
drains put across it from side to side.   In these drains
were laid four-inch tile for the first twenty rods, costing
thirty-five cents per rod; three-inch for the next fifteen
rods, costing twenty-five cents per rod; and the last five
rods were two-inch, costing fifteen cents per rod, aggre-
gating a cost of tile for one drain of eleven dollars and
fifty cents; digging the drain at twenty cents per rod,
eight dollars; laying the tile and filling the ditch, four
cents per rod, one dollar and sixty cents; making the
total cost for draining the ten acres, eighty-four dollars
and forty cents.

I have never known a man to lose his farm by bor-
rowing money at ten per cent. to drain it, but I know
of several farmers who have lost their farms by paying
ten per cent. for money to build with.   However, I
would not advise any one to pay ten per cent. for money
to improve a farm with.

WATER.

The first thing to be looked after is the convenience
and supply of good water.   I have never seen a better

arrangement for a water supply than my own, on Appledale farm. The house stands on an elevation, and the house-well supplies the farm. The water is impregnated with black sulphur and iron, and is very healthy for stock. I have never had a sick animal or called a doctor.

The water is raised by a windmill, which saves a hand, and nearly pays for itself every year. The water is carried in iron pipes, three hundred feet, to the west, and same to the east barnyard, also carried through the milk house to the hog lot.

There are no slops thrown out from the kitchen to ferment in the soil and create sickness. There are deep drains about the well, and the well is cemented from the hard boulder clay to the surface, so there is no possibility of any filth which would breed disease getting into it.

PASTURES.

The best pastures are those that have never been plowed, and blue grass, which is a natural growth here, is the best and richest pasture that we have, and the older the sod is, the more feed it seems to yield. I use clover for hog pasture.

A timothy meadow, which I raise only for hay, will last from eight to twelve years, at which time the blue grass will have possession. There is but little use for hay. In the fall of 1879, my blue grass pasture was well grown, so that I let my milk cows run on it all winter, and they have done well with but little feed. Cattle that are kept up all winter should not have their feed cut off at once and turned to grass. I know some farmers that do this always, which produces scours in their cattle, and results invariably in a loss. I commence to feed my cattle and sheep grain a few weeks before they are turned on grass, and continue the grain several weeks afterwards.

It is well for farmers to be posted on the different breeds of cattle.   The Short-Horns, of recent origin, hold a high place in the esteem of many breeders, having been produced by careful selection, and high-feeding and care.   I have allowed these fine large breeds to run for several years with the common natives, receiving no more care, feed or shelter, and in several years no one could tell the difference between them and the best of the natives.

DEVONS.

But not so with the Devons, which are the oldest distinct breed of cattle known.   The Devons will not run out by neglect or exposure, but under all circumstances, and in all climates, maintain their beautiful form and red color, and uniformity of appearance in every feature, shape of horns, tail, etc.   Their flesh is finely interspersed with alternate fat and lean, and of superior flavor.   The cows yield richer milk, and if properly fed will produce more butter and cheese for the feed consumed.   Although they are not a large breed, they will produce more pounds of beef for the feed consumed than other animals.   Steers, when properly cared for, will weigh from two to three thousand pounds.   They make the best work oxen we have, being fast walkers, docile, and inoffensive, and not inclined to be breechy.

SHEEP.

The most profitable breed of sheep depends on the location.   If near a large city, the South-Downs are decidedly the best.   They hold the same relation to the sheep family that the Devons do to cattle.   They will do well on short pasture, attain early maturity, and are hardy and prolific; they are not long-lived sheep, like the Merinos, but are in their prime at three; for mutton, they are superior to all other sheep. I sold my lambs last July and August, weighing from forty to seventy-five pounds, at two dollars and a half per head. When well kept and cared for, they will average five pounds of combing wool, bringing the highest price. They, like the Devon cattle, transmit their blood in the strongest degree. Wethers, at three years, will weigh two hundred to three hundred and fifty pounds, and are more easily fattened than Merinos. But for wool, the Merinos are the most profitable, as they will herd better than any other sheep.

If I raised but one kind of stock, it would be sheep; they enrich the farm faster than other stock, dropping the manure mostly on the highest places, where it is needed, and return the most money for labor expended. Every farmer should keep a few sheep any way, as they are good to kill weeds and briars.

HOGS.

Although hogs are the most prominent in all the rich corn-growing regions of the West, and will return more money, they require much more labor. It is hard work from beginning to end, and is very exhaustive to the land. A man that has but a small farm will do better to produce hogs only. The Poland, China and Berkshire are the leading breeds.

HORSES.

A bank or basement stable is not a healthy or fit place to keep horses. My stable is at the south end of the barn, with half-doors in the south to let the rays of the sun in and for ventilation, and to throw manure out. The floor is two feet above ground, and is kept clean, with plenty of straw for bedding—the manure pile being hauled away as fast as made.   I never tie my horses up, or imprison them in any way, but turn them altogether, with the stable-door left open, and give them all the liberty of the barn-yard, straw stack and water trough, and they are always peaceable and happy, and ready for their feed.   I feed my horses what fodder or hay they will eat, twice a day, with two ears of corn twice a day, increasing the feed as the working season of spring approaches, but never feeding over nine ears.   Change their feed often in hot weather, and give them a table spoonful of salt, with hickory wood ashes every other day in the corner of the trough, but never on their feed. Never keep more horses than you need.   I keep from ten to fifteen head, and give them no condition powders . or other poisonous drugs, and have never had one of them sick.   A barn-yard well, that takes in all the filth of the barn-yard, is a source of disease among stock.   I always warm the bridle-bits before putting them in the horses' mouths.   If you think the bits are not cold enough to hurt their mouths, touch them to your tongue and see.

ROTATION OF CROPS

Is necessary on all kinds of land, although I have known thirty crops of corn to be raised on our rich lands in succession, the last crop being forty bushels to the acre. I never raise more than six crops of corn on new land, however, and then sow to wheat and grass.   I always sow a wheat crop after Hungarian grass or oats, but never like to sow wheat on a wheat stubble.   On clay land sown to wheat, I seed clover and let it remain two years, then plow under when in bloom, planting to corn the next spring, so that the field will do to seed to wheat in the fall.

PLOWING.

A man should not plow simply to get the best results for the present crop, but should plow to have the best crops in all the coming years ; and the only way to do this is to plow deep, though not all at one time, but keep getting deeper every year. The best results are obtained in our rich clay lime soils, by subsoiling with a regular subsoil plow, except put a narrow mold-board on that will throw a part of the subsoil to the surface. It is best to do this in the fall. You can not, however, plow to much advantage unless the land is underdrained ; but if well underdrained, subsoiling is a great success.

PLANTING AN ORCHARD.

Plant but few varieties of the best apples suited to your climate, and most of them late-keeping, firm, hard, winter varieties, such as bear well. Buy the trees of the nearest nursery. Rome Beauty, Broadwell, Tallawater, Liberty, Seek-no-further, are good winter apples ; Bethlehemite is the best fall apple, and Danvers Winter Sweet is the best fall sweet apple, the former being the best keepers, but small or medium.

Prepare the land for planting by subsoiling, throwing the furrows out at thirty feet apart, and put plenty of the top soil for the roots to feed on ; raise a cultivated crop, potatoes the best, until the trees are grown, but always keep the land level ; plow first one way and then the other. When your trees are large enough, sow to grass. Shape the top of your trees while young, and then trim no more.

MANURES.

It has been said by many farmers that manure was the farmer's capital ; but such is not the case, at least in the

18

great West.   DRAIN TILE is the farmer's capital, and as
I have very fully given my views and ideas upon the
subject, I will now say a few words upon manures.
When I travel over the fair and beautiful land of Ohio,
and behold its fine mansions and well-arranged farms, I
suppose that the farmers possess a vast amount of agricultural knowledge; but on making a close observation
of their farms, and asking a thousand questions about
the high and noble calling that they are engaged in, and
how they manage things generally, I am often surprised
to find that they do not understand the first principle
of agriculture, which is to keep the land up to a high
state of fertility.   I have often seen farmers committing
the suicidal act of burning their straw, and raking up
their corn-stalks and burning them.   A man who does
this is a robber and a thief, who takes from the land its
fertility without returning it.   To keep up such a system of farming as this would certainly impoverish the
coming generations, and destroy any country or any
nation.

HOW TO SAVE AND MAKE MANURE.

The urine of animals contains a very large amount of
nitrogen, the thing most needed for plant food, and,
though the richest and best part of the manure, it goes
to waste on most farms.   To save this valuable manure,
I have the floor of my cow-stable tight, with a close
drain at the back part of it, and have my straw-stack
near to give the cattle plenty of bedding, which will
absorb all the urine; then, as fast as the manure accu-
mulates, both at the cow and horse stable, I haul it to
the fields, and lay it in piles until wanted.   But the most
practical way for the mass of farmers to save the greater
part of the urine, is to let the stock run to the straw-
stack, with plenty of straw for them to stand on while

eating, and lie on.   In this way a great part of the urine will be absorbed and retained by the straw.

If the straw-stack is not all used up by spring, tear it down and let your cattle lie upon it at night during the summer, if possible.   Every thing on the farm that will make manure should be looked after for that purpose. Corn fodder should be fed out in racks in the barn-yard. By this means a large amount of valuable manure is made, with most of the urine retained·in it, as the cattle will keep on the stocks in preference to going in the mud.   I gather all the bones and put them in the bottom of the ash-leachery; they do not injure the lye for soap, but are dissolved, making rich fertilizers.   All the wood ashes should be saved and spread about the fruit trees, especially the peach.   Unleached ashes are rich in potash, and valuable for fruit or potatoes.   Leached ashes contain a large amount of calcium, and are valuable food for crops of all kinds.

CHAPTER XI.

FROM time to time my articles have appeared in the *Ohio Farmer*. Some of the most interesting are published in this chapter of farm notes.

USEFULNESS OF BIRDS.

I see many good things in the *Ohio Farmer;* in fact, it is full of useful knowledge to the farmer. But there is one great farm interest that is not properly looked after, and even some farmers themselves are so blind to their own interest, that they will kill, and allow others to kill, without mercy, innocent and useful birds, their friends, their co-workers and helpers. If the birds were all killed, our land would be worse than a desert, and noxious insects would meet us at every point.

"The disturbance of the proper balance between the feathered and insect tribes, is fraught with incalculable mischief, affecting the food, the health and life of man." They are not only useful in the most material sense, but they are a source of pleasure and beauty, clothed with a softer plumage than the texture of cashmere, and more brilliant than the dyer's richest hues—the flight is the poetry of motion, and their voices are sweeter and more cheering than all instruments of art.

Let the birds live and sing to cheer the farmer. In the sweat of his face he earns his bread. With the genial springs, its balmy airs, sunshine, and gushing bird

songs, his soul rises to new life. Then let the birds live
to help you in your labors. The bird is the Farmer's
poet Laureate—well worthy of the sovereign that
should prove an appreciating friend and patron. The
most useful bird to the farmer is the quail. They are
perfectly innocent; they disturb neither grain nor fruit.
I have seen quails, in immense flocks, foraging in recently planted fields, systematically in sections. On
shooting one no grain was found, nothing but cut-worms
and insects.

Wilson (the naturalist,) says a black bird will destroy
fifty cut-worms daily. Even in winter its food is insects.
A quail will feast her brood on young grasshoppers, taking them in an early stage of their existence, when little larger than a fly. Woodpeckers are constantly seeking insects in the bark of trees. None but the sap-sucker
will pierce the green bark to feed upon its juice. Rob-
ins have been known to eat seventeen caterpillars per
minute. The spotted woodpecker has been seen to
probe the gummy hiding places of the borer in the trunk
and surface roots of the peach, and bring forth and destroy the pest.

While the farmer suspends his operations in winter,
and comfortably occupies the chimney corner, his eto-
mological assistance, reckless of the cold,' prospects
among the trees for insects in every crevice of the bark.
The co-operation of the birds with the farmer, is, therefore, almost uninterrupted by heat, or cold climate, or
season. The quails eat millions and millions of seeds
of noxious weeds, saving the farmer an immense amount
of labor. The birds have been arraigned as plunderers
of the field and garden, by thoughtless and ignorant
persons. The charge is not only unjust, but it is un-
grateful. That they eat a little grain at times, of that
variety which is essential to health, is not denied," and

the red, delicious cherries are, sometimes, too tempting
for the more impulsive.

"The laborer is worthy of his hire," is a maxim that
farmers should respect, and no laborers work so cheap
as the birds.   They provide themselves mainly from
nature's own domain ; yet claim the right to be fed from
man's, in payment for services honestly rendered.

In Ohio, we have a bird law that is strictly enforced;
however, it avails nothing.   It allows birds to be killed
during the winter season, and the quails have disappeared to a fearful extent.   A few years since, where
large flocks of this splendid bird could be seen all over
our land, now there is scarcely a bird to be seen.   Like
the Red Man, they will soon disappear, unless we have
a stringent law for their protection at all seasons of the
year.   If wicked persons are allowed to slaughter our
innocent birds without restraint, our land will be swarm-
ing with insects ; grasshoppers will take our meadows,
cut-worms will take our corn, bugs will eat our vines,
and the discord of the locust will be heard on all sides.

It is really stultifying to see the ignorance displayed
by some farmers ; they kill the robin for eating a few
cherries ; they kill the black bird for the few spears of
corn they imagine he has taken ; their reasoning faculties are so obtuse, that they do not remember that it
followed their plow all the spring picking up all the cut-
worms and other insects that the plow turned over.   I
have been noticing the orchards of these farmers who
kill all birds that are seen in them, and I find them full
of insects, and on the decay with the apples knotty, and
full of moths.

I raise sunflowers in my orchard to toll the birds
there ; it was full of summer birds late in the fall, and
now there are hundreds of chickadees in it feeding on
the sunflower seeds, and hunting the eggs of insects on

the fruit trees. I am not troubled with the tent caterpillar, and my apples are freer from the apple moth and other insect defects than those of my neighbors. This, I will be happy to prove to any and all persons that will visit my orchard at the proper season. I have learned by experience, that those persons who do not respect the rights of birds, neither respect the rights of their neighbors.

A man who could not get leave of his conscience, to go to his neighbor's hen roost, and steal his poultry, will nevertheless range over his neighbor's farm, kill the quails and other game ; throw down his fences and shoot among his stock, if a bird would happen to be in that direction. Mr Lane, a few miles from this place, had a lot of cattle frightened by bird hunters shooting among them, and lost several hundred dollars by it Mr. Richards, near here, had his team shot by hunters, while gathering his corn, which caused his horses to run and do much damage. I have heard of three other farmers who had their stock fired into by bird hunters in this section, and this is the smallest part of the damage done. It is not pleasant to have persons prowling over your farm, making common of your property and violating your sacred rights. The farmer has the heaviest end of the burden to bear, to keep up the laws and institutions of his State ; for this reason, if no other, the laws should protect his rights to the farthest extent. A man's farm and all that is on it, should be his own.

Late in autumn, when the farmer has his team and hands in the field gathering his crop, it costs something to leave his team, at the sound of every bird hunter's gun that he hears, and go to the different parts of his farm and order them off ; it is not only the loss of his time and the loss of his birds, but the vexatious arrogance and loss of temper. I have often felt my equa-

nimity disturbed, and felt nervous, twitching of the muscles of my right leg, and a desire to apply the *argumen-
tum adposteriorem* with the toe of my boot.

The Sabbath day is often made hideous by the yelp-
ing of dogs and bird hunter's gun.   This not only makes
the God-fearing man feel sorrowful, but it is a bad recommendation for the neighborhood.   I could write a
volume about the wrongs and the injustice of the game
laws of Ohio, but, Mr. Editor, I am afraid I will draw
too much on your valuable space.   I have conversed
with a great many farmers on this question, and find
universally that it is their desire to have the game laws
amended, and the time restricted for killing game birds
to about ten days in the year, and then not on the premi-
ses of other persons without the owner's consent.

To make sure of having the game laws amended,
there should be one or more petitions, with a number of
names sent from every township in the State, asking the
Legislature to amend the game laws as you wish, and
should be directed to the Representative from your
county.

———

FUTURE OF CATTLE RAISING IN OHIO.

Farmers who expect to raise beef cattle in Ohio, in
anticipation of high prices, will most likely be disappointed.   Cattle are too easily and cheaply raised on the
sweet grasses of the extensive prairies of the Southwest, and the transportation from there to the eastern
market, will soon be too easily performed for this latitude
to think of competing with.

The writer of this, having spent ten years of his life
on the Texas prairies, considers himself posted as to
the price of raising cattle there.

Those who have not seen these far off regions, can

have but little conception of its vastness, and its adaptedness to the raising of cattle.

As you leave Jefferson, in Eastern Texas, and go west fifty miles through the tall pines, you come to the prairies; and what is the grandeur of the scene that presents itself to you? God's green carpet spread out before you in the vast distance, decked with the gaudy and brilliant wild flowers of this clime. And on the distant green prairies you see herds of cattle, with their large heads and broad horns, grazing with the antelope and elk. Over these vast green plains, five hundred miles to the Rio Grande, interspersed with rippling streams of pure living water, the valleys of which are lined with a thick growth of timber, affording abundance of water and shade for cattle in summer, and shelter from the chilling north winds in winter.

You may leave Galveston and go north, and the same extensive, green, undulating, flowering and fragrant prairies, present themselves to your view for four hundred miles, with plenty living streams of water, and some springs. There is the spouting spring, eighty miles north of Austin, which affords water enough for millions of cattle. This spring is near the base of Cedar Mountain; the water spouts up through a crevice in a rock, nearly in shape of a five pointed star, and is thrown twenty feet high. To see the silver-capped spray ascending and descending, and dancing in the pure light of the sun, is a sight in these wild regions more grand and magnificent than my pen is capable of portraying.

Besides this vast extent of fertile prairies, there is a rich body of wild land extending from Arkansas to the spurs of the Rocky Mountains, in extent nearly equal to Texas, partly settled with civilized, half civilized and wild roaming Indians. We think that in a few years the energy of the white man, will subdue this wilder-

19

ness, to the raising of cattle, for which it is so well adapt-
ed.   It costs no more to raise a bullock in Texas that
will weigh six hundred lbs., than it does to raise chicken
in Ohio.   There is no provision made in Texas for winter-
ing cattle.   They winter themselves on the rich prairie
grass.   There is not much rain in the fore part of the
winter; and the old grass is but little injured, until the
new crop begins to grow in the spring.

The common prairie grass of Texas, is of a less growth
than the grass of our western prairies, and is of a finer
quality.   In the southwest part of Texas the moskete
grass is found.   It is of a luxuriant growth and resembles
the English blue grass, the lower part remaining green all
winter.   The fattening properties of this is equal to our
tame grasses.

Texas is capable of producing, at least twenty-five
cattle, where she now produces but one.   Texas in 1870,
furnished the city of New York, forty thousand cattle.
But four years since only forty-four head of Texas cattle were sent to the New York market.

With the economy of the Texans, in keeping all of
their females to breed from, it will not be many years
until Texas will be well stocked with cattle.   And in
less than two years she will be connected with us by
railroads, besides the many ships that are beginning to
carry cattle by sea to the southern and eastern cities.

In the slaughter houses that are in operation on the
seaboard of Texas, thousands of cattle are annually killed,
and millions more will be packed and shipped to the
different markets of the world.   Eighteen years ago,
steamboat loads of cattle were shipped from Missouri to
New Orleans.   But now cattle are shipped the other
way.

With all these facts staring us in the face, can we of
Ohio expect to maks it pay in the future, raising beef

cattle as a business ? The thinking farmers of Ohio will thoroughly investigate these facts, and shape their future business accordingly.

CULTURE OF POTATOES.

It has been three hundred years since the potato was discovered, but it is now cultivated in all parts of the globe, where civilization has extended. 150,000,000 bushels are consumed annually in the United States as an article of food alone, aside from their extensive utility in occupying so great a part in commerce and the arts.

There are a great variety of opinions in regard to the proper method of their culture. I have tried many experiments in the cultivation of potatoes, and have settled on the following system as being the true one :

If it is convenient, plant your potatoes on new land, sod is next best, and should be broken in fall or early spring, and subsoiled at least fifteen inches deep. Animal or stable manure should not be used on potato ground, it has a tendency to deteriorate and disease ; potatoes thus raised lack the sweet, delicate flavor, that those have which are raised on virgin soil. The crop may be much benefitted with vegetable manure, ashes, lime, salt, etc. I have never succeeded in raising a good crop of healthy potatoes on wet land ; a rich calcareous clay soil that contains a little sand is best, and may be much benefitted by being underdrained.

There are many failures caused by not having the seed properly prepared. There are a variety of opinions in regard to the kind of seed to plant, whether large or small. I am satisfied that large seed not cut in more than two pieces is best, but small seed, if properly prepared, is nearly as good.   Large potatoes should be cut lengthwise, and small ones should have only the sprout end cut off, i. e., the end furthest from the stem. If all the sprouts are allowed to grow, there is not vitality enough in a small potato to make a vigorous growth.   There will be many stalks, and a hill of many little potatoes, whereas, if the sprout end is cut off, there will be a few strong stalks and not more than half the number of potatoes will be produced, but they will nearly all be large ones.

Those that are planted early should be cut at least a week before they are planted, and the heap turned over or spread thin, to dry.   An incrustation of the starch and juices of the tuber, called healing, takes place, which defends the piece against decay.

It is important to have your seed well matured.   If your seed potatoes are not ripe, you need not expect success.   The best time to plant, in this latitude, is about the middle of April, but the time may be extended to the first of July, but early planting, as a rule, is by far the best.   The earlier in the season the potato gets a start the more likely it is to escape the summer drouths, the attacks of the potato bug, and other influences unfavorable to its growth and maturity.   Early planting should be about eight inches deep, so if the frost should kill the tops, the eyes will start again.

If your ground is clear of weeds, I would plant in drills about twelve inches apart, and have the rows three and a half feet apart.

As soon as the plant is about four inches high, run the cultivator close to and between, but not over them. The next time cultivate deep, and thoroughly pulverize the soil, and encourage the growth of the tuber rather than the stalk, and the third time lay them by with the double shovel, not hill them up too much ; cut the weeds out after this with a hoe.

FATTENING HOGS.

The natural climate of the hog, like the negro, is nearer the tropics ; therefore, the best time to fatten this animal is before cold weather sets in. It is only on the rich lands of the West, where corn is easily and cheaply raised, and hogs are raised in large numbers with profit.

A small lot of hogs may be kept on every farm with profit as scavengers. Without scavengers, such as the hog and buzzard, the atmosphere would become a great pestilential effluvium. Corn is most profitably fed to hogs when it is a little too hard for roasting ears ; when in this stage they will often eat corn, cob, stalk and all. Hogs should have a spacious lot to feed in, and never be imprisoned in a pen ; however, they will fatten faster in a close pen ; those fattened on the ground with plenty of room will exercise enough to throw off some of the disease-producing matter, and are more fit for food. But look at the stupid, gluttonous beast imprisoned in his pen, wallowing in his own filth ; at every breath he inhales the foul emanations from his offal. An animal fattened under such unphysiological conditions must be diseased.

A swill barrel should not be tolerated on any farm ; it is always in a state of fermentation ; the strong sour smell indicates rottenness ; swarms of maggot flies revel in such corruption ; let your hogs have the slop before it ferments. The hog being more liable to disease than all other animals, and his flesh being the cause of more disease in the human family than all other causes, should be a consideration worth noticing in producing pork. It is officially stated that the loss from hogs that die of disease in this country, is annually not less than twenty million dollars ; in some counties where distil-

leries are numerous, five thousand have died of disease
in one season.

Some farmers give their fattening hogs salt, which
will make them gain in weight much faster ; but it produces a morbidly increased appetite and occasions con-
stipation.   The result is, the animal fills up with effete
matters which are accumulated in the cellular tissues in
the form of fat.   The animal grows more bulky, and as
its commercial value is reckoned by weight, this process of fattening is profitable to those who sell the
swine, but not to those who eat it ; for the adipose ac-
cumulation is itself a morbid condition, and the more
any animal is fattened, the more unwholesome it becomes.

Farmers who use pork as food in their families, should
produce it as healthy as the nature of the beast will admit of.   Hogs should have range in a spacious lot, and
have the free use of their nose and all the pure water
they want to drink ; and if it is convenient, let them
have plenty of water to wallow in.   When fattened under the most favorable circumstances, there is not more
than one out of ten that is not diseased, if they have
attained the age of eighteen months.

A LITTLE ADVICE TO FARM LABORERS.

Young man, are you a farm laborer ; and do you work
by the month at a stipulated price ?   If so, your calling
is honorable if you make it so.   Many of our wealthy
farmers were once hired to work on the farm by the
month.   You may ask, how did they arrive at such emi-
nence in character and wealth.   It was by a straightfor-
ward course of honesty and industry.   If your work and
conduct pleases your employer, and you take an interest

in his welfare, he is sure to take an interest in you, and the second year you may expect better wages, but the better wages is not always the best part of it; he will speak well of you and give you a good recommendation, and introduce you to his visitors and others, and you will be received and respected as one of the family. Do not try to put on more style than becomes a plain man. To please the family that employs you, must be your study; you must notice and do many little things. It is well for you to know that the things of this world are made up of littles.

At all times, while passing over the farm, if you see any little thing that needs to be done, do it; if you see a few rails off the fence, lay them up; if you see any of the farm stock where they should not be, return them to their place; never wait to be told to do such things as you know should be done. Above all things take good care of the team; never jerk or kick them, if you do, the keen observing eye of the owner will know it, when he takes hold of them. Horses are much more obedient and trusty if treated with kindness and gentleness, and of course are more valuable; they will come when you call them, and save you many steps and much vexation. But if you treat them badly, they will treat you in like manner. See that the harness fits well and is comfortable for the horse to work in, and if broken, mend it. Never rush the team so as to make time enough to rest an hour or so; such work will not do; the team will cool off and be liable to take cold and will be stiff and slow about starting. Let your team rest often and not over two minutes at a time. Never feed or water when the horses are very warm; always clean out the feed box before feeding, and keep the stable clean, and everything in order about the barn; and in winter feed the farm stock with economy and order, and do your work as well, and keep as steady at it when alone as when your employer is with you. It is hard to deceive a farmer in regard to the amount of work a hand should do.

Never go at anything with a great rush, but move as though you were alive. Use the farm tools with care and break as few as possible. If it is necessary to work late in the evening in harvest, to save the grain or hay, do it cheerfully without complaining. If your employer is away, and you have done what he has told you to do, do not await his return to know what to do ; there is so much work to do on a farm, that you cant go amiss for work. It is also necessary to please the lady of the house. To do this, you must never enter the house with mud on your boots. If you are guilty of chewing tobacco, dispose of your quid before entering the house in the evening, and take no more until you leave in the morning. There is nothing so disgusting to a lady as company that is constantly squirting tobacco juice about the fireplace or on the floor.

Observe cleanliness about the house, and manners at the table. Never dip your knife into the apple-butter or any other dish that has a spoon in it. Women notice these things closely, and if you are guilty of them, they will conclude at once that you are of poor stock and have been badly raised. Always get up in the morning before the family rises, and have the fires made ; keep the kitchen well furnished with stove wood. If the women are in the habit of milking, always ask for the milk bucket of a Sabbath morning, or when it is too wet for them to go out. Do not be too officious about the house, and do not have too much to say.

If you will observe the above simple rules you are sure of a good home and good pay, until you are able to purchase a home of your own.

You may say, to observe these rules would be to do

Fannie V. Woolley

a good deal of extra work. Well, would it not pay better to do some extra work, as you call it, and have a good, steady home, with good wages and be respected? Or would it be better to ignore these rules, and spend half of your time in looking for work, and work at low wages, and then be turned off at the end of each month by every new man that you hire with?

LET THE LIGHT AND AIR IN.

That great element of health and life, the sweet, pure and free air that God has given us extending from earth one hundred miles in the heavens; let plenty of it in your houses at all times, don't be afraid of it, it will not hurt you, but will invigorate your system, purify your blood, and give you health. Take the window curtains down and let in the gentle rays of sun, it will take the dampness out of your house and make it more cheerful and less like a prison.

The sun may fade your nice carpet a little, but better that, than have the health of your daughters ruined. A house made dark like a prison with paper or other thick window curtains looks to me like ignorance stalking abroad. If you will have window curtains, get some thin gauze and then have them just so it may be seen you have them.

When I see a cleanly house in the country with open windows to receive God's pure light, I conclude at once that the love of God, happiness and intelligence reign there.

We, with several other families, are compelled to absent ourselves from our own church on account of the vitiated air that pervades the building. The house is closed all the week, Sabbath school at nine, preaching

20

at eleven a. m., all without ventilation.   What do you think of this, reader?   Is it any wonder that the congregation get drowsy and go to sleep?   The most eloquent preaching will not keep them awake.   Is it any wonder that people take cold and get consumptive, take fevers and contract other diseases in such a place?

Dear reader, the country is full of such pest houses in the form of churches, school rooms and dwellings. I spoke to a brother about having our church ventilated. He replied that there was a pane of glass broken out, which afforded plenty of air.   It seems sinful, if not highly criminal, in the officers of a church or any public place, to allow a large concourse of people to breathe the vitiated air, when pure air can be so easily obtained. It is to be deeply regretted that so few understand and appreciate its value, that so many sicken and die for want of it.

Visit your district school some afternoon; you enter the room, your face flushed from a brisk walk in the pure, cold, bracing air; in five minutes a languor begins to creep over you, dimming your faculties, your full breath stops, you breathe a little from the top of your lungs and try unconsciously not to breathe at all, your face burns, and headache begins to creep on, your feelings are like those experienced in a tight room where charcoal is burning. and for the same reason this should convince you of the reason that so many school children are coughing, and sometimes have winter fevers.

BE FRIENDLY TO THE SWALLOWS.

The eave swallows are different in their habits and appearance from the forked tail chimney and horn swallow. The eave swallows only build their nests in the cliffs of rocks or under the eaves of a nice looking barn (they never build about an old rickety barn), they find a location near a pond or stream of living water, where they can get mud to construct their nests. These birds are quite small, but they come in such great numbers that the insects they destroy in a season is enormous and the benefit they are to the farmer who is lucky enough to have their visits, is no very small matter.

Last season, while the measuring worm was making bare the forest and orchard trees, many of my apple trees nearest the barn were kept nearly clear of these pests, and as soon as the mowing machine was started, these birds were seen in large numbers sailing around near the machine, catching the young grasshoppers and other insects as they would fly up from the grass. These birds are also of great value in protecting young chickens from hawks, as they will not allow a chicken hawk to come near the abode.

Early this spring, before these swallows made their appearance, the chicken hawks took from one to four chickens daily, but as soon as these little birds arrived here in numbers, they have kept the hawks away and we have lost no more chickens. The courage of this little bird is an object of admiration, to see them attack a ferocious hawk, twenty times their own size, and drive them away. I am sorry to say that some of our farmers are so ignorant and wicked that they have been guilty of tearing the nests of these birds down from their barn and murdering their young.

CHAPTER XII

DURING my travels in the South I stopped at Fayetteville.

The manager of this post was Colonel Rutherford B.
Hayes, who to day is President of the United States.
He was Provost Marshal at this place.   I never shall or
can forget the courtly manners of this true American.
I have not wondered that at the Capital of this great
nation the kind, yet dignified, gentle, yet courageous
man I saw at Fayetteville is President and leader.   He
was then the most obliging of men.   A clerk he had
was sour, egotistic, short, conceited, a fop, and gave me
no assistance.   I applied to him for a favor, and saw
the haughtiness of his mien, the tremendous self-conceit
which overpowered him. He thundered, and said *"No."*
I accosted the gentleman in command.   I went to head-
quarters.   I saw Colonel Hayes, and of all the specimens of kindness it has been my privilege, personally,
to be interested in and inspect, this touched my whole
nature with the most gratitude.   Besides, I had met a
man—an occasion which every man remembers with
pleasure and profit.   For, after all, nothing is so grand
as manhood, pure and simple. We have so many pounds
of flesh ; so few real men.   So many people we meet,
six feet in height and of full beard, who are jokes—simple and pure jokes on Manhood.   It is such an occasion
of real pleasure to be delivered from shams, to be free
from all the appearances of men, the puns we see on
our best humanity.   Besides all this, nothing is, inher-

ently, so great, interesting, and so full of meaning as a real man. We believe more in the universe—more in God. It is a revelation of ourselves. We think at our best, and so we think more of ourselves. Thus we get regard for men, self-respect, admiration of the universe, and often from these come their flower—the love of God. Who has seen a grand man, and has not felt what the grand-uer of God must be, what the greatness of omnipotent goodness is. Such men there are everywhere. They live grandly wherever they are. On all the long marches they are men; at the camp-fires they are the same. No profession can keep them within its limits. It is a cup holding the ocean. The man fills his profession full of himself, and overflows it with kindness and goodness, that drip down its sides in acts which help men, and bless the world in deeds, that, to us who have seen far too little of the greatness of goodness, are a perpetual astonishment.

> "Life's the true poem, could it be writ;
> Yet who can live at once and utter it?"

Such men are indeed the true poets, and produce, to our minds, the great difference between sham *manish-ness* and genuine manhood. And such men make true patriots.

> "Whom did the people trust?
> Not these, the false confederates of State,
> Who laid their country's fortunes desolate;
> Plucked her fair ensigns down to seal the black man's fate;
> Not these secured their trust.
>
> "But they, the generous and the just,
> Who nobly fell, and truly great,
> Loved steadfast still the servant race
> As masters in a menial's place;
> By their dark brethren strove to stand
> Till owners these of mind and hand,
> And freedom's banners waved o'er an enfranchised land.
>
> These were the Nation's trust,—
> The patriots brave and just."

That man was as dear to his men as he seemed dignified and gentlemanly.   And they had reason to admire
him—yea, they had reason to love him.   Here was no
politician.   He never undertook getting office as a business.   But always was the office glad to get him.
Nothing but the splendid value of the ideas with which
the air was burdened, and the fact that it was a noble,
serious and necessary thing to influence and control
public opinion for the right—nothing but the *duty* which
came to many such in 1856 and in 1860, took him from
his lucrative practice of law in Cincinnati, and put him
into the field with statesmen.   He went into the affairs
of state because he believed it would be self-reproach
to remain out.   It was the martial strain of duty which
made him a power.   He spoke of entering politics to a
friend, much as he did concerning his going to war.
Concerning the latter, he said : " This is a just and necessary war.   It demands the whole power of the country.   I would prefer to go into it, if I knew I was to
be killed in the course of it, than to live through and
after it, without taking any part in it."

He hated slavery with a righteous hatred.   He re-
solved to go.   Lincoln sent him a Colonel's commission.
His friend, Secretary Salmon P. Chase, had suggested it.
Hayes was a soldier.

He made of the literary club of which he was a
member, a company to practice upon.   He bought a
copy of Hardee.   He studied it well.   He refused the
Colonelcy, because he thought himself unqualified, and
in June, 1861, received from Governor Dennison the
Majorship of the twenty-third Ohio volunteer infantry.
He was modest, and would not assume to know more
than he really did know.   He wrote in his journal:
" All matters of discretion, of common judgment, I get
along with easily ; but I was, for an instant, puzzled,

when a Captain of the twenty-fourth, of West Point education, asked me formally, as I sat in my tent, for his orders, he being the officer of the day. I merely remarked that I thought of nothing requiring special attention ; that if any thing was wanted out of the usual routine, I would let him know." When Bull Run came, Hayes was all seriousness, and July 25th, Hayes was going with the rest to West Virginia, to drive out General Floyd. In all this joy and grief, Hayes was a participant. When they struck Virginia, the loyal people came out to meet them. They rejoiced with them. They cried, and laughed, and shouted. The soldiers were all well pleased. They had seen new sights. Some of them had not been from home. They stood on the cars gazing at the country. They all fell back, however, before the rebellion was put down, upon the cool-headed, earnest, but serious man who enjoyed it all, but thought as well about the horrid front of war which they did not see.

All this and much more his soldiers knew, and thus they learned to love him. True, they had not seen him amid thickest bayonets and booming cannon. But they could not forget the valor which lay behind that eye while he marched at their head through the dense laurel thickets after General Floyd.

On the first of September, having had only a few pleasant encounters with the foe, they were ordered to march upon Carnifex Ferry, where Floyd, in gay and strong lines, was occupant and lord. The evening of the 10th came. Floyd fled. Over Gauley river, followed by the Union soldiery, the retreating rebel went. Blinding rains came but the "boys in blue" went on until the whole of Western Virginia was in the hands of the defenders of the dignity of the stars and stripes.

In this operation, Hayes was ordered to follow one of

the aids to General Rosecrans, a full thirty minutes after the action began. He was to take four companies of the twenty-third and make the extreme left of the on-marching force. After crossing at great effort a hill and having gone through a cornfield, they found them-selves within a short distance of the enemies' powers. Another aid departed. Hayes was alone. The aid had no orders for him. He showed his self-command and aggressive earnestness. He was ignorant of the coun-try; did not know the localities; could not appreciate the circumstances he could not see. But he did know that he was there to push the conquests of his country. He seized the most simple direct method, as he has al-ways done. He went forward against the foe. Scramb-ling against and over the rocks, after beating his way through the close laurel thickets of the hillsides, *always in front* of his men, he reached the declivity with a small band. Others soon came. A skirmish line was formed. He pressed on and arrived in time to see and feel the fire of the enemy. Darkness came. Some were wound-ed. The command was broken. They struggled back over the fields until the morning revealed the fact that not only were thirteen killed and seventy wounded, but that the enemy had fled in terror from his works.

All of that circumstance showed the cool headed ar-dor he possessed. It was the circumstance which was faulty, not himself. Often there is more bravery evinced in trying to do than in doing. It is the will and the effort that shows the man, not the success. For success often is cheap. It is often won by accidents and by necessity. But effort and a purpose to do is of the man always.

Then those men were very proud of a man at their head who came to war to fight and not to practice law. He could have practiced law at home with less effort and greater success. They knew that and believed that he came to do big fighting wher they saw him all sad and disappointed on a certain occasion.

They were in camp at New River. Sickness had come. Many died. The joy of the battle and pursuit had fled in care for the unfortunate. Hayes was detached from his regiment at this time—a time he would have loved to have remained in camp with his soldiers, for no man did more for the relief of his sick and wounded men than did the dignified and courteous commander. He was ordered to join General Rosecrans at his headquarters. He was to become Judge Advocate. He obeyed with sadness, and with reluctance did his duty. Yet, as in all things, he put his whole soul to the task. He systematized everything, made improvements in the management and did all things well. But the joy came when in six weeks he was allowed to rejoin his regiment at New River, whence they removed to Camp Ewing and thence to Fayetteville, where I saw him and at his hands received many favors.

I know something of the origin of this letter he sent home. It came from a grand, broad and kind soul. And he sent it as the utterance of his gentleness. Little did he think that all men were not so kind as the loved Colonel of that regiment.

He says : "I am satisfied that our army is better fed, better clad, and better sheltered than any other army in the world. I am now dressed as a private, and I am well dressed. I live habitually on soldiers' rations, and I live well. It is the poor families at home, not the soldiers, who can justly claim sympathy. I accept, of course, the regiments which have bad officers. Government is sending enough, if Colonels would only do their part. We have sickness which is bad enough, but it is due to causes inseparable from our condition." Little

21

did I wonder that they loved him when I was permitted to enjoy his overflowing kindness.   Little did I
wonder that they thought him a loyal and true patriot,
when day after day he made the Fugitive Slave Law
"of no effect."   For he sent no contraband back to his
chains, the auction block and the driver's lash.   He said
all the time "the deadliest enemy the Union has is slavery; in fact, its only enemy; and to strike at slavery is
to strike at the life of the rebellion."

Little did I feel the astonishment of his conduct at
South Mountain, where on the mountain-path he conquered his country's foes in spite of rocks and stones
and their heavy fire.   To one acquainted with him as I
was it was nothing beyond expectation to see him lose
two hundred men, make three successive bayonet
charges, and drive the foe into the woods with a banner
"riddled," as says Whitelaw Reid, "and the blue field
almost completely carried away by shell and bullets,"
and a bleeding wound that after the excitement pros-
trated the gentle but dignified hero behind a log with
the sole companionship of a southern soldier, also
wounded, and a canteen of water.

Cloyd Mountain and Winchester both heard his voice.
He picked up "a small South Carolina regiment entire"
in the valley of the Shenandoah, and Opequan, Fisher's
Hill and Cedar Creek are bound in blood with his
biography.

But greater than all these to me is the fact that purity
places her white hands upon his character and is un-
stained.   Greater than the General, or the Governor, or
the President, is the man.   The call of the head-quarters
is exceeded by the call of duty; the duty makes it all
important to be done. He, of all men, so really honored,
has filled Wordsworth's idea of duty to its full propor-
tions :

''Stern Lawgiver, yet thou didst wear
The Godhead's most benignant grace,
Nor know we any thing so far
As is the smile upon thy face;
However laugh before thee on their beds.
And fragrance in thy footing treads;
Thou didst preserve the stars from wrong;
And the most ancient heavens, though these are fresh and strong.

To humbler functions, Awful Power,
I call thee! I myself commend
Unto thy guidance from this hour;
Oh let my weakness have an end!
Give unto me, made lowly wise,
The spirit of self-sacrifice
The confidence of reason give!
And in the light of truth, thy bondman, let me live!''

No stain has yet been found upon his private character. No hush-words are whispered through the land.
No wise looking on the ground and shaking of the head
have made the fathers and mothers of the Republic unable to say to their children, as our President rode by:
"There goes a boy, now grown to be a man, worthy of
your example." Said Mary Clemmer, the fine corres-
pondent of *The Independent:*

"Meanwhile, as the days go on, as the fight thick-
ens, as human pulses and passions rise higher and higher, a man at the other end of the Avenue sits the long
hours through patiently trying to fulfill the thankless
task of doing his whole duty to millions of people. He
committed an unfortunate offense, the other day, when
he refused to give to a delegation of Washington clerks,
who waited on him to make the request, leave of absence from their desks for three days to join in the
Grant festivities in Philadelphia. He refused, and their
wrath was so severe they went forth and drew up a series of ' resolutions' against him ; and he yet survives.
Imagine it! It was a small matter, perhaps ; but from
it to the greatest, no President of the United States ever
received fewer thanks or more abuse for simply doing
his duty than Rutherford B. Hayes. Were his adminis-

tration like Grant's—false but brilliant, gay with gov-
ernmental pillage, and loud with vulgar display—applause would not be lacking.   The simple uprightness
of the Hayes Administration kindles nobody's imagination, tempts no man's cupidity, feeds no woman's van-
ity.   Therefore I have heard it disdainfully decried, and
the glories of the lost empire of Grant loudly lamented.
The insect of society, the barnacle of office miss the
malaria of that lower air, in which they thrive, in the
pure atmosphere of the White House home.   The outcry against the Hayes Administration is the outcry of
vulgar and selfish minds, the wail of lost power and
place, just as the call for Grant's return is the hope of
returning empire.   Amid the Babel of new presidential
names, one occasionally hears something about 'the
good of the country.'   Does it never occur to the 'eminent' men who are struggling so positively for their
own advancement, so incidentally for their country, that
if they really pursue its 'good' they could in no way
so disinterestedly or so efficaciously serve it as by seeking to leave the Government for the next four years in
the hands of the present Executive?   The truth is, it is
not their country that they seek to serve; but themselves.   If perpetual empire would destroy republican
liberty, so an itinerant Government, forever on the
wing, harasses and torments it.   It is the source of end-
less distraction, as it may be, in the end, its final disintegration."

The fact is we are far too anxious about the commerce
and navigation, the finances and the diplomacy, the
question of appointments and votes, and the success of
our party to care as we ought to care about the purity
of the greatest seat in the nation.   What shall keep
this government from decay if purity goes?   What
shall be more politic than the obtaining of the highest

moral character for the Executive? If that is here the basis of things political, social, and financial, abides, and the greatest capital that this nation could put into the bank of the future would be the fact that it has been, and ever will be, impossible to lead this republic without the loftiest moral character, the most immaculate purity.

I am not writing in the interest of any party or man, but I must say that it is ridiculous to hear the cry for "stalwartness" from men who shouted when the President began to do what they voted for him to do. Pledged to give the South the hand of friendship, elected to do it, having promised on paper that he would do it, is he to be censured for doing it?

When the history of the land shall be written, it shall be seen that there was once a man who did his whole duty in the face of an opposition great and powerful, and that at last the opposition learned to love him.

CHAPTER XIII

I TRANSCRIBE here some impressions of the great Centennial Exhibition.

At that splendid exhibition of the achievements of mankind, I found room for my thought, opportunity for discussion and food for life. I am aware that many volumes have been published on this subject. Volumes, with peans of eloquent description, speak thoroughly of the wonders of that pageant. But one's own eyes see for one's own personality, and therefore it is that just here I seek to give my readers some idea of that splendid exhibition as it came to me. With lessons which I tried to learn for my race, my country and myself, as through these countless avenues of magnificent beauty they came to a single citizen of the republic.

Specialists must write the story and significance of the several departments. Space limits the treatment I would love to give to the details which were of such interest to me. The crowding glories must wait for a larger volume than this. But the feature peculiarly attractive to his readers will receive the present author's attention.

First of all, no man could find himself in Philadelphia and be a self-conscious American citizen without the echoes of one hundred years ago sounding in his ears. And the music of the present was heavy with the gathered melody of the past. At the sight of Independence

Hall I was taken back into the midst of the ideas of 1776, and felt what I could of the air which made an atmosphere of power to liberty and bathed young freedom as a morning cloud while it held this new-born sentiment in its warm embrace. The time was great in interest and significance the world over.

The splendor of the light in which, as a reality, Anson had lately brought the Pacific, was augmented with the closing and crowning act of Cook's notable life. A new world of business, beauty and historical significance, had been opened up by the breaking up of the Spanish monoply over the North and South American coast trade. England was beginning to add strength to it all by the occupancy of these and the refitting of these points for her own great trade. England and France were about to enter the era of their relations which was so different from the one which preceded it, and which was of such meaning to the civilized world. The DuBarrys, Maupeons, and their like had all been sent from Versailes by Louis XIV. and his beautiful wife. George III. had learned many lessons in the history of liberty, and when his mind opened, the soul of England began to grow more capacious and extensive ; but after he had learned much from Junius and Wilkes, he had just began to learn for himself. All England gave the world, from the sword of Washington, the idea that there should be no levies on any land when that land was not blessed in every particular of liberty of which it was capable. Frederick II. of Germany was old. His land was ready for his benediction, and already begun to spread its wings for a flight which is so sweeping and lofty as to be the astonishment and wonder of the civilized world. Clive was protecting from a fierce opposition, in the house of Lords, a child which has grown to contain double the population of the Europe of that day. The young Princess of Anhalt Zerbst had touched Russia, and afterwards Napoleon was to seek the hearts of this land in vain. Liberty was in the air. Freedom hovered beneath and over the world.

Thought, which is the guardian of Freedom, Science and Truth, which are the friends of Liberty, were making the air capable of nourishing a great revolution. Linaeus and Buffon had opened greater secrets than were dreamed. Great worlds swept before the human ken, beautiful and vast. Hutton, Priestley, Cavendish, Lavosier, were to come with the approaching birth of the idea that every man has a right to himself.

America felt the burden and throes of birth. It came. The Declaration of Independence was signed. The lion of England roared. But above the tumult swept the eagle bearing our destinies into the heart of the sun.

The announcement which begun: "When in the course of human events," was the greatest piece of moral courage which had ever been filled so full of profound ideas. Thirteen weak and broken colonies against the mistress of the seas, the queen of the land—England. No soldiers at all, against the English army which so overflowed England that here on American soil, thousands of them stood in virtual possession of the cities.

But the fight developed a still richer grandeur. All the weary years it increased in depth and tone. Through all the Valley Forges, it walked on and ever on to heroism sublime. And at last it came victorious, bearing beauty on its brows that it knew not of, and to-day—I thought as I stood there in the tumult of that glory of a hundred years—it bears the triumphant fruit, sweet, golden, and of a hundred years of liberty.

So I thought of the past as we walked into the enclosure on a day when the hundreds of thousands came.

I enter what is called the Main Building. Eighteen hundred and eighty feet long, four hundred and sixty-four feet wide, forty-eight feet to the cornice, seventy-feet to the roof tree ; this is the enclosure filled with beauty and magnificence. Here in the centre is a dome ninety-six feet above me, leaning on beautiful and graceful posts and trusses of iron, giving a great square at the base of one hundred and twenty feet. There is a significance in it all. It is the exact elevation of the old Capital rotunda. Is there not a hint there, that we will never lose sight of the industries and operations of our countrymen—ten thousand as they are in number—but in the same future they shall be under the same dome ? Let them have equal rights. Let the old measurements be kept. But let the building which shall contain them grow until all the operations of the continent shall be held within the same great enclosure of justice, liberty and truth. Here is a transept, which, by intersection with the nave, forms the pavillion, which is four hundred and sixteen feet long. On each side is one of the same length, one hundred feet wide. The aisles are forty-eight feet each. This great central nave and transept is supported by iron columns forty-five feet in height while the roof rises to seventy feet. Six hundred and seventy-two columns stand here, twenty-two feet apart, and standing upon solid stone. They are made of rolled iron, are bolted together in segments, and can thus be taken apart when it becomes advisable. Here we then travel by the lands of the earth, here we walk through the achievements of men, through the promenades and the aisles running athwart, of ten and fifteen feet in width. There are small balconies or galleries at the sides to which one may retire to study the scene. And many a weary student has taken his note book out in one of those places and looked and wrote,

22

far above the dust, of the beauty of the scene, of the
humorous people he saw, of the lovely days there
given to getting information, of hours in that great college of facts and of the impressions which, without being written, never would pass away from him. Here a
man surveys the world. He sees the globe in its business enterprise and effort. There are thirty-six hundred tons of iron in those trusses, with $1,420,000 in-
vested for our pleasure. With four miles of water and
drainage pipes underlying the twenty-one acres of floor
in this building, it is our great pleasure to see stored
with neatness, taste, and expenditure, the trophies of
nineteenth century civilization.

Now we walk into the Machinery Hall. Here the
music of mechanism is produced. Noise, *noise*, NOISE,
but what infinite quiet is it in comparison with what
would be if no subtle thought nor mighty idea had embodied itself in iron, steel and brass, if no great conception rode triumphant on the steam belts and bars, and
sent its nervous powers through the thousand life-like
activities of that huge convocation. Here is the con-
vention of the forces, here is the meeting place of the
processes, here is majestic strength, and here in delicate
miniature act the powers of the world. Here we learn
the whole history of our pens, pins and needles, here we
read from the operation itself the biography of a ship
held with steel and clothed with iron, or a train of cars
which bears the thousands across a continent. Fourteen
acres are covered by this building. Fourteen hundred
and two by three hundred and sixty feet is its size. It
seems a huge covering for that mighty thing which with
its lungs of flame and sinews of steel throb the life of
motion through and through that whole grand aggregation of power. As we walk along without, we hear that
the main cornice is forty feet in height upon the out-

side. As we walk within, it is ascertained that the interior height is seventy feet in the main aisle, and forty feet with one central and two side aisles. The avenues are each ninety feet in width, and the aisles sixty, with a space of fifteen feet in one and of ten in the other for good free walking such as every tired man wants to do. The hydraulic avenue is a sprout from the hall covering a space of one acre.

To an agriculturist the Centennial was a rich ground and fruitful. We enter into our own place. The Agricultural Building is certainly a home—gorgeous and luxuriant—for the farmer. I was glad to observe its grandeur. It signified that the profession of citizenship and that of agriculture in this country were wonderfully identical. Ten and a quarter, it covered. Five hundred and forty by eight hundred and twenty feet was its size. All the convenience, all the environment, all the advantages were given to those who exhibited what lies beneath our progress—the agriculture of our closing century.

Never did I feel that the hymn of Whittier was so appropriate, as when, full of the recollections of Machinery Hall and the Main Building, I saw nature under the touch of man glow with glory for this great celebration.

From the Philadelphia Times.

CENTENNIAL HYMN.

BY JOHN G. WHITTIER.

. Our father's God! from out whose hand
The centuries fall like grains of sand,
We meet to-day, united, free.
And loyal to our land and Thee,
To thank Thee for the era done,
And trust Thee for the opening one.

Here where of old, by Thy design,
The fathers spake that word of Thine

Whose echo is the glad refrain
Of rending bolt and falling chain,
To grace our festal time from all
The zones of earth our guests we call.

Be with us while the New World greets
The Old World, thronging all its streets,
Unveiling all the triumphs won
By art or toil beneath the sun ;
And unto common good ordain
This rivalship of hand and brain.

Thou who hast here in concord furled
The war flags of a gathered world,
Beneath our western skies fulfil
The Orient's mission of good will,
And, freighted with Love's golden fleece,

Send back the Argonauts of peace.
For art and labor met in truce,
For beauty made the bride of use,
We thank Thee, while withal we crave
The austere virtues strong to save,
The honor proof to place or gold,
The manhood never bought or sold !

O ! make Thou us, through centuries long,
In peace secure in justice strong ;
Around our gift of freedom draw
The safeguards of thy righteous law,
And, cast in some diviner mould,
Let the new cycle shame the old !

Agriculture is to Horticulture "what the man is to the woman," The Horticultural Hall was a blaze of floral glory. Here on a bluff, overlooking the beautiful river, bloomed the garden of the closing cycle. Beautiful nature covered again and dotted with her own robes was the park around. Great heavy building that it was, it was made exquisite without and within by taste. The curved glass sides showed the life within in the sparkling sun. The verandas and porticos filled with excellent and luxuriant foliage make the scene a transported happy place. You enter by a flight of dark marble stairs. A vestibule all gay with bright tiles opens. Forcing houses are at either side, one hundred by thirty feet. The great conservatory is two hundred and thirty by eighty feet, and surrounded with galleries, decorated with faultless taste, but with greatest luxuriance. It seems the beauties of nature fastened for a time willingly and captive to the worshipping genius of man.

We step into the Memorial Building. When the word was sent out officially, that "all works of art must be of a high order of merit," it was supposed that the great walls which had been so industriously prepared would be half vacant and bare. But the work went on. Of the finest stone, the building seemed to imply eternal existence. Massachusetts and Virginia granite held together, and holding together the iron of Pennsylvania —piled up with a cost of a million and one-half of dollars, and decorated with all that architecture could dream, crowded with the work of genius from every clime and coast—this is Memorial Hall.

Crowded—yes, and another building by its side. For when Memorial Hall was being built, it was the thought to get room. Three hundred and sixty-five by two hundred and ten feet, is its size. It is made to afford eighty-nine thousand square feet of wall-surface for pictures. "Enough—for more," said everybody; "for the art which shall come." But genius crowded the century with Art. It came. Another building rose to receive it. Three hundred and forty-nine by one hundred and eighty-six feet was its size, and it was full. Before the ground had been touched, one-half the space was engaged by England, France, Germany, Austria, Belgium and Italy, and the demands at home enlarged it again with such wings that it had the form of a Greek Cross. I shall not detain my reader with any elaborate accounts of the methods whereby comfort and pleasure was secured to every body. I will not worry my reader with long descriptions of the Judges' Pavilion, the beau-

tiful fountain erected by the Catholic Total Abstinence
Union, which delighted every true temperance man,
and seemed a suggestive fact, indeed, with which to
begin a new century.   I cannot dwell with that recep-
tacle of woman's doings—the Womens' Pavilion,—
which, at an expense of thirty·five thousand dollars,
was meant to embody the progress of woman's work in
one hundred years.   We could linger there forever, and
know magnificently little about woman's work and influence.   Nobody heard a sob of Mother's heart.   No
one saw a falling tear.   No one could feel the dwelling
love which sweeps up to God, and bears a race of men
near to heaven.   Woman's Pavilion, it was named ; but
the pavilion she works in is the eternity of God. Heaven
itself is her harvest home.   We could remain with good
results with the United States Government Building,
with the buildings of the several States, with the Japa-
nese Building, Swedish School House, Spanish Building,
British and German Buildings.   They all were gems of
architecture, and of each other fine lessons were to be
learned.

But I pass to the displays within and without those
buildings, which will be of great interest to my reader.
Let us go, first, to the general exhibit of the nations,
that we may look a glance, if no more, into each of
them.

To begin with England, what could be more fitting
than that the mother of this land, who tried so hard to
keep her daughter from running away and marrying
liberty, should be represented here in gorgeous colors.

What is the quality of these goods ? The finest.
What is their characteristic ? Art.   It looks as though
Ruskin's delicate, but purified ideas had dictated the
exhibition.   All the fineness of his art, and that of
Turner, whom he idolizes, is here.   Take, for example,

the glass and silver exhibit. No great, heavy specimens *un*adorn the whole show. Everything is fine,
delicate, and is simply heavy enough to bear all the
ideas which had to do with its conception and manufac-
ture. All of the glory of the old forms of art are there.
All of the delicacy of the new appear also. Angles
have given place to Turner.

And then art has got to be so human. It comes to
adorn our firesides, and make home beautiful. All the
common things are made lovely. The spirit of beauty
has been married to the spirit of use, and the twain are
one. The brush and the chisel are not all of art's tools.
Here are clocks that speak of the finest ideals. Furniture stands before us that seems a canvas for delicate
art instincts and strong power of execution. Carving of
all sorts, made historic by recording famous scenes, and
adding luxuriance to comfort and elegance to necessity.

Woman's needlework was here. The Royal School
of Art Needlework had furnished it. A Terra Cotta
Temple, exhibited by Doulton, was very attractive, and
the cutlery and silks showed how beauty had been made
the bride of use.

I am trying now to give some general ideas which
struck me as I touched nation after nation in my walk
through that main building.

As England showed it under the influence of such as
Ruskin, France developed to my eye an abounding
though somewhat conventional elegance. Everything
France has on hand is of the first quality. The Commission have evidently done their best to make this a
representative exhibit. Here is cutlery of all curious
patterns. Curious as are some of the Paris fashions,
which every American citizen is made acquainted with,
whether he will or no, are the freaks of genius as embodied in these specimens of finer hardware.

More thorough is the art than in England. Deeper fidelity to nature is seen in the English collection, but deeper fidelity to fancy is shown in the French collection.

In matters literary, here is a fine show. The government has loaned everything to the project. Besides, the publishers of the great French works have formed the finest trade specimens of the finest thinking and placed them before us. Great maps, of microscopical accuracy, fine engravings, of the greatest horizon of view, and yet of the utmost refinement of detail; architectural illustrations, which were the glory of the greatest of the French builders—all these make it a place whereto scholars resort.

Science, especially in the department in which the French excel, was well exhibited. In Botany, the most accurately copied small pictures, and large finely painted designs were excellent indeed. It increased the love of many a man for the flower to see there in such open clearness the genuine character and texture of these brilliant citizens of the fields and gardens. All this display seemed to me sufficient to prove to the nations there congregated that France as a Republic had much to rely upon as a self-sustaining nation. And that is the basis of republicanism. A nation must be in reality stronger to remain a republic than to remain a monarchy. We talk of "a strong government." The strong government is that government which most nearly sustains itself. I mean that it must furnish its own ideal and idea, power and will. And that depends upon the many-sideness or rather upon the full development of a people.

Another thing, however, is that its resources must be of great variety. Its strength comes from the unity of these all. And, for these facts, I believe in the future of the French Republic. They are there. Variety of resource and variety of adaption, all united into real strength and operative force by the working intellect of republican France.

All of the Egyptian exhibit suggested age—hoary an-tiquity. It could hardly be helped that the informed looker on should have thought of Lethos and Manetho, of Joseph, the pyramids, the shepherd kings, the musty history and dreamy legend of that ancient land.

Things were sparkling and new, but they had old ideas in them and were ancient. Here was a hint of it,—the silver writing desk appurtenances. Here is an old God, all written over with history, all inscribed with antique fable, solemn, demure, fierce or sorrowful, with his head bowed. Here is an image taken from the deep old past and preserved for the glowing future It is a perpetual dream, the poem of old age.

We step up to the great mantel and the environment of ornaments which are marked "Russia." They are Malachite, beautiful indeed, but looking at their best in a broad great mirror and over an exquisite mantel and grate. But this is the beginning of an excellent ex-hibit.

What a pile of gold, copper, iron, silver and other ores, is that? It is the hint of that which Russia has, piled away in her mountain breasts and the rich resources which are beneath her national life. Besides here is the evidence that can make it all powerful. It is the ex-hibit of Russia's industry and enterprise. Fine draw-ings are those and fine furniture is that. The show in furs is beautiful beyond description. They are rich be-yond any in the whole exposition and they attract all comers. Now and then a lady covered with wealth and adorned with diamonds of amazing brightness walks up, and with the agent makes arrangements for a supply

23

which shall excite the jealousy of all her neighborhood. Let them attend to that now, while we look at furniture made of stag horns.   Silks, that woo the sunbeams as they blush and then fall through upon it relieving it of a glorious lustre ; soap that looks too clean and finely designed to use on our hand even for purposes of cleanliness.   Specimens of anatomical work of the finest sort, and embroidered workmanship of great value.   Majolica Terra Cotta, and a hundred other specimens which show that in Russia is the power of a lofty civilization.

Now as I write, I can not help the thought, which comes from the intelligence of which we are now possessed concerning Russia, and my observation at the exposition, that there is a deep life and a high destiny for that people.   But the state of things is now terrible.

No nation, whose success for the future is not to be lost by any unexceptionable devotion to the glory of the past, or the splendor of the present, can afford to neglect the lesson of Russia.   Her facts are the possibilities of every land beneath the stars.   Her condition and prospect are granted, in fee simple, to any and every other nation, which, by the operation of the same laws, shall find this special story of cause and effect.

Right and liberty are so seemingly concrete to our speech, that they are really abstract to much of our thinking.   The forces which take lands, seas, rivers and mountains, and build, therefrom and therewith, nations, are so loosely spoken of and so familiarly mentioned that it is doubtful if we understand them at all.   The crises of history, catastrophes of politics, and those upheavals of the old and new forces by the elemental powers working toward an end, were, at least, to remind mankind, who mouth these things, that they are basic facts, fundamental realities, in whose fists lie the enchantments, in whose operations lie the destinies which

they do surely organize and control. Such ideas float
on the tide of the latest word from Russia. And other
symptoms of this diseased man will appear and prove
that even a long national illness may develop new phases
of debility every day, and more—that when the body is
in condition to invite sickness, there seems to be so logical a relation between all forms of disease, that, thick
and fast, they come and hunt down the lingering life. I
seek to understand the facts which come into being rather than to be their dreary chronicle. And looking as I
have, to Russia, in the light and by means of such views
of popular rights and righteousness as have been suggested in this volume, it has, as it seems, this duty to
perform: to point out, at least, some casual facts of her
present condition; to mention, at least, some reasons
for that condition of affairs which not only Russia, but
the friends of Russia and popular rights, bewail, and to
thus give full value to those historical forces which in
Russia, as elsewhere, have not lost their power by appearing under new guises, and have never wrought for
liberty and integrity by the mere proclamation thereof.

Serfdom in Russia has and always will have to do with
the problem. It is at least one quantity in the equation.
Of how great power and significance, we may readily
see. It was not, in the first place, of ancient life. Its
introduction into Russia was quite recent. England
must not boast. Praedal servitude had just become ex-
tinct within her own borders when serfdom began in
Russia. Villenage had its last plea in English courts in
1618, and Boris Godunoff gave forth the first edict in
1592, binding the peasantry to the soil. Russian authorities make our modern American historian wild with
ire, when they do not condemn it as an act of tyranny,
but rather do speak of it as an act necessary toward the
civilization of Russia. They speak to-day of Boris Go-

dunoff with reverential love.   His name stands for the
conducting of external affairs with a quiet but potent
success.   He made foreign policy inure to the benefit of
. his country.   But his glory, to the writers to whom we
now refer, is, that he administered with much greater
success the internal affairs of government.   He assisted
in the purification of morals, the improvement of society, ideas, ideals and methods, the enlargement of the
national trade and of international commerce.   The
greatest thing he accomplished, to the end of improving
society, was to take the peasants, who, at stated inter-
vals, were accustomed to migrate from one landed proprietor to another, thus losing much and gaining nothing
—and to break this nomadic, vagrant life, by forbidding,
in 1592, the migration of peasants, cancelling their rights
to move from one estate to another, and commanding
them to stay forever where the edict found them.   The
Czar, the landed proprietors, and the monasteries were
each allotted their portion.

Boris recalled this restriction, in part, in 1601, and
the latter action, in 1606, was revoked by a decree of
Duma.   Nevertheless, history is right in holding that
serfdom proper began with Peter the Great.   He placed
such laws in force, and was the authoritative agent of
such exactions, as, by his capitation tax, "to make each
landed proprietor chargeable for the number of peasants
actually residing on his estate at the time of completing
the census."   Of course, they would not let the peasants go after they had paid tax on them.   And ever
thereafter, unto the date of emancipation, 1861, the
land of Russia was appraised by the number of its serfs.
Landed property decreased in value, and since 1861 a
rapid and unexampled rise has occurred, proving, in addition to the great teaching from Russia, that slavery
everywhere is freighted with loss to the tyrant.

Englishmen would call Russian peasants villein socagers, or socagers *regardant*. They could not be sold
apart from the land they lived upon, and were quite de-
finable from another class corresponding with the villeins
in gross. These were prisoners of war, insolvent debt-
ors, or their children, and were called *Kholopy*, upon
whom, however, no capital punishment could, by their
lord's right, be inflicted.

The Emancipation of 1861 accomplished for them the
following: personal liberty was conferred on the serfs,
who were declared to hold the land by copyhold, paying a fixed rate of rent in labor or money. Arbitrators
were appointed to measure the land and settle disputes
between the proprietors and the liberated serfs; enfran-
chisement of the copyholds was made obligatory on the
landlords on payment of the capitalized value of the
rent, the government advancing four-fifths of the sum
in bonds bearing interest at three per cent., the same to
be paid in installments spread over 49 years, making the
entire operation of emancipation complete in 1910.

But these twenty years which have intervened are
years of the deepest teaching and of great and far-
reaching consequences. The national energies have
been thoroughly aroused from their death-like sleep.
For not only do the rights of men never die, but only
sleep, but the possibilities of men also have never
reached death, though they may have passed another
torpor. Before, Russia was organized calm ; now Russia is organized agitation, and looks towards disorganized
anarchy. Russia under Nicholas was splendid. He
controlled liberalism, and made it conservative ; he was
arbiter of Europe ; he was master of Austria and Prussia, and was surprised at the unlooked-for condition
which shattered his august power. But it was all unreal.
The interior conditions were unnatural, and no foreign

policy could make Russia strong. Says M. Kosheleff,
in his admirable book, published in 1875, in Berlin—
because of the rigor of the Russian censors—"Our
Situation:"

" From 1825 to 1855 we existed under an oppressive
and monotonous system of representation.   There was
no scope for social activity.   Self-government might not
even be alluded to; and the use of the word '*zemstvo*'
stamped a man as unworthy of confidence and design-
ing—yes, even rendered himself liable to danger and
persecution.   The assemblies of the nobles were of no
importance ; scarcely any business was transacted by
them, and scandals were of frequent occurrence.   The
elections to important offices degenerated into the in-
trigues of interested persons.   In the town self-government was a parody of the same, for it was in the hands
of the most ignorant of the inhabitants, and meant ab-
ject subservience to the provincial governors.   The tri-
bunals inspired no confidence, and those among the
judges who were honest and impartial, were, thanks to
the secrecy of the proceedings, suspected of unfairness
and neglect, if not of corruption.   Trade was at a stand-
still, and credit had no existence.   Serfdom weighed
heavily on millions of human beings.   Literature was
fertile in poetry, drama, novels, &c., which might be
quite immoral, provided social subjects and the conduct
of the government were not touched upon.   A Russian
dare not, either in the newspapers or in books, speak of
political questions or the evils of the times.   In a word,
below was the torpor of death, whilst in the upper strata
of society despotism flourished free from all restraint.
The life of a Russian as a man was confined to the secret recesses of his soul. There alone he felt that he
was a being made in the image of God—there alone
could he be conscious of an independent existence, of

a right to freedom of thought, sentiment, and will. But what brought despotism to its senses, aroused a people robbed of its civil rights, and benefited the country generally, was the desolation of the Crimea."

Very true! for the Crimean war aroused her to a sort of national self-consciousness, in which all healthful indignation, personal penitence, devotion to duty, hope for the future, and duty in the present, were born. Disastrous as was the Crimean war to Russia in its immediate consequences, it was the beginning to her of this era of self-consciousness—a self-consciousness so radiant and powerful as to become a means of knowledge to perceive the relations of her national self to all other selves and circumstances. Russia found herself inferior to the neighbors. Her king put his pen, burning with revolution, into the dark chaotic mass, and wrote the death of serfdom on the white conscience of his time. It was done. The tyrannous hand of that powerful and interested faction who are trying to impede its consummation is the witness to the progress made by that single stroke of a pen which averted a revolution of blood and death. The Crimea shook her into life, gave her opportunity to adopt the principle of universal liability to military service ; and cleared the way for the advance of all classes within her lines.

Now, the problem is clear. Actual Russia is seeking to reach ideal Russia, with the weight of so many years of wrong, loss and slavery. It is an awful burden to bear. The civil officials, even, are hampering the progress of this already adopted policy. And 1910 is a date hated by the aristocracy. Free institutions are despised by the officials. "Trial by peers" to every man, is supposed, by them, to be their foe, as it is to all oppression and oppressors. But progress through blood seems sure. The imperial budgets in 1875 began to be published for the information of the people, which seems a great concession to popular rights, and is indeed a great concession to national power by means of national self-confidence. Two things for four years have been lamentable : the insufficiency of the police force, springing from a too lax conception of the relations of liberty and law, and the absenteeism of nobles and landed proprietors. But the deepest fact—since all great facts of politics are primarily ideas—is, that such a sense of despair pervades the best classes, and such a disintegrating social, political and religious faith prevails among the most educated men of Russia. Is government a failure in general? Is mankind a failure? Is there no faithful thing? Has the ideal sort of government been found vicious? Or are there reasons for the failure of only a partial Republicanism in Russia or elsewhere? What are the facts?

The Czar has not for years been able to control his functionaries. He makes free, and they drag back to the fetters. He progresses faster than his government. He does not lead the thought of Russia. Mr. Kosheleff describes the feelings of Russians :

"A man shut up in prison, when he has spent some years there, becomes in a measure habituated to the mode of life. He gets through his time somehow. His emotions become by degrees less sensitive, his thoughts confined; he becomes callous, and ceases to be conscious of the utter misery of his situation. But it is intolerable to a man who has acquired his freedom and tasted its sweets if he is dragged back to prison again from time to time ; more especially if these temporary respites are dependent on the caprice of his jailers, and the concession of more or less indulgence is determined by the same tyrants. The mind of such a miserable being must inevitably lose its equilibrium.

His ideas become confused, and if he do not resolve on some mad act, despair seizes him. He takes no further interest in anything ; his strength wanes ; he is annihilated by this intolerable state of existence.

The interpretation of law is in the hands of the officers. Democracy must take more steps to hold her own. Republicanism must seize the future to make sure of the past.

Since PETER THE GREAT suppressed the Duma, or National Council, there has been no opportunity for the discussion of public affairs. The people could not reach the ears of the ruler. Divided into classes by Peter's hasty reforms, a vast gulf opened between the nobles, superficial and glossy, and the peasants, ignorant and wronged. Between them there was, and, since called to rule together there yet is, no bond of union. St. Petersburg hears no heart-throbs without her walls. Despotism divides; it has never made "the married calm of States."

In spite, however, of it all, the Russian peasant will hear, think and feel for the country. If he cannot speak by personal voice and representation, he will do it by explosions, and back his leaden word with a breath of flame. There is no restricted conversation in the *zemstvo*. The government will garble his speeches. His influence is abated. But he will crowd courts of justice, and he will keep conscience and otherwise prove, that, having the possibilities of self-government within him, it is national disaster to compel him to hold these possibilities in check, and it would be national safety to concede to them the privileges of activity and life. Repression means explosion, education and use mean life, growth, and the fair fruitage of liberty. The only way to keep a man from being a burden to himself is to give him self-government. It is the cure of pessimism. The only

24

way to keep him from being dangerous to others is by means of self-government, which, by making him safe to himself, makes him safe to others. This is the cure of revolutionism. The only way to get out of him all there is in him is by means of self-government, which, by making him valuable to himself, makes him valuable to others. This is the cure for Nihilism, Communism, and this will make citizenship reciprocal, through citizens, to itself, and prevent disintegration. But these are the ideas of Republicanism and Democracy, yet they prove that no Democracy is safe which is not complete ; no Republicanism is safe which oppresses any right of any man anywhere. For four years the complete ideas of Republicanism have seemed to us the only logical safety for Russia. The state of affairs proves the means of Republicanism to be vital. What are they ? *Public because private intelligence.* "*Ye shall know the truth, and the truth shall make you free*"—this is the first utterance of pure Republicanism. *Public because private conscience.* "*The kingdom of God is within you*"—this is the corresponding utterance of the same principles. In these and in their exercise lies the final regeneration of Russia.

But I believe, from the close observation I gave to Russian products at that great Exposition, that Russia is capable of self-government, and that Republicanism is the only method for her people.

In this same light—the light of the past and present, I tried to study Sweden, Japan, China, and the other countries represented. My own country had most to teach, and I listened to her lessons there until the poet's words seemed her own soliloquy :

> " Look up, look forth, and on!
> There's light in the dawning sky;
> The clouds are parting—the night is gone;
> Prepare for the work of the day!

Fallow thy pastures lie,
And far thy shepherds stray,
And the fields of thy vast domain
Are waiting for purer seed
Of knowledge, desire and deed,
For keener sunshine and mellow rain!
  But keep thy garments pure;
Pluck them back, with the old disdain,
From touch of the hands that stain!
  So shall thy strength endure.
Transmute into good the gold of gain,
Compel to beauty thy ruder powers,
Till the bounty of coming hours,
Shall plant on thy fields apart,
With the oak of Toil, the rose of Art.
Be watchful and keep us so!
Be strong and fear no foe,
Be just, and the world shall know!
With the same love, love us, as we give;
  And the days shall never come,
  That finds us weak or dumb
  To join and smile and cry
  In the great task, for thee to die,
And the greater task, for thee to live.''

—A soliloquy which lingered with me, until at Mt. Vernon, I felt that I stood on holy ground near the tomb of Washington, where other words, inspired by the same spirit, came to my recollection :

Minds strong by fits, irregularly great,
  That flash and darken like revolving light,
Catch more the vulgar eye, unschooled to wait
  On the long curve of patient days and night ;
Rounding a whole life to the circle fair,
  Of orbed fulfilment ; and this balanced soul,
So simple in its grandeur, coldly bare
  Of draperies theatric, standing there ;
In perfect symmetry of self control,
  Seem not so great at first, but greater grows,
Still as we look, and by experience learn
  How grand this quiet is, how nobly stern
The discipline that wrought through life-long throes
  That energetic passion of repose.
The longer on the earth we live,
  And weigh the various qualities of men,
Seeing how most are fugitive,
  Of fitful gifts, at best, of now and then,
Wind-wavered corpse-lights, daughters of the fen,
  The more we feel the high stern-featured beauty
Of plain devotedness to duty,
  Stand fast and still, nor paid with mortal praise,

But finding amplest recompense
For life's ungarlanded expense ;
    In work done squarely and unwasted days.
For this we honor him, that he should know
    How sweet the service and how free
Of her, God's eldest daughter here below,
    And choose in meanest raiment which was she.
Placid completeness, life without a flaw   .
    From faith or higher aims, truth's breathless wall,
Surely, if any fame can bear the touch,
    He will say "Here," at the trumpet's call,
The unexpressive man whose life expressed so much."

CHAPTER XIV

A MONG the pleasant memories I preserve, of the happy and not uneventful past, that stand out like beds of flowers, environed with beautiful green, are my days and nights in the great metropolis, my residence near and within the city of New York previous to the breaking out and during the early days of the war.

I shall not invade the respect I have for my reader by writing here all my goings, my mishaps, my private fortunes and misfortunes. I am only glad that I happened to know, and see, and hear certain public men who have such a public interest, and are of such national fame, as that I may serve as an eye and ear for those who would have enjoyed the privilege of making their acquaintance in the times of their greatest service to the race, and their greatest personal triumph. My reader cannot but be thankful that I should retire, therefore, to give him pen-pictures of such men as I happened to know in private and hear in public life.

Prominent among them was one, most written about, misapprehended, misunderstood, loved, honored, and yet not so well loved as to fall its prey, and, on the other hand, not so great as not fall a prey to his own ambition ; I mean Horace Greeley. When I first met him and felt his influence, he was so far in advance of his time and thought that he was not much loved by the masses of the people. Indeed, I doubt if his love of the rights of the masses and their love of him, were not in inverse

proportion one with the other. No heart ever felt
more tenderly the force of a certain set of facts whose
awful pressure they knew and under whose tyranny they
groaned. If Buxton was surprised not to find Garri-
son a black man, thinking that none but a black man
could sympathize with the black man as he did, the
world might have thought Horace Greeley to have been
chameleon-like, inasmuch as he championed the advanced rights of the oppressed of all ranks, colors, and
creeds, as ardently and with as distinguished sympathy
as his great contemporary. His ambition was for the
regnancy of certain ideas. He did not, then, allow
himself even, to stand between them and the goal. He
was a devout lover of principle, and so true was his devotion that their presidency was of more value to him
than his own presidency. The very greatness of the
ideas he entertained made him great. The loftiness of
the conceptions he had, made him lofty, and the stern
nature of the inflexible right added to his sternness, and
made intense his inflexibility for the right when he saw
it imperiled. His native distrust and hatred of aristocracy had been developed by a self-making and self-made
career. His career of life began with the word *industry*
and ended with it. He began to lisp that word on the
lowest round of the ladder, and he lisped it when he
controlled the thought of a great section of a great
country. As he rose from strength to strength, and
attained new power and control over the American people, he lost none of that native and life-grown democracy which always made him not only the thinker for
princes and presidents, but as well the inspiring representative of labor, and the shining example for the
poorest young man on the globe. I knew him first
when, with the face of a big boy and the walk of an
awkward country farm hand, he rushed along the street

in that historic white coat, hurried, with his head bowed with the weight of his idea, and his whole body seemingly following that dome of thought as it led through the rush of people along some crowded thoroughfare, flaxen hair about the base of his skull, bald as his head was on top, thin scraggy whiskers, light eye-brows, impatient, always in a hurry, he defied the photographer, and I think I never saw a fine picture of Horace Greeley.

When he talked you might hear the genius of the Tribune. Full of idealism, ready to hear any fresh generalization or vision of the human soul, anxious for information, believing that there were great worlds to learn, he treated all with respect, had no sacred column, always did regard your dream and heresy, and made the people feel your right to do your own thinking. Of course he was full of vagaries, and dealt with many castles in the air. But great thinkers have to do a great deal of thinking, which never crystalizes into facts, to reach that thinking which shall come to be reality. Besides every fact was once, with God or men, a castle in the air. And every great thing was called a vagary when it lay in conception. The record of Horace Greeley moreover, is enough to prove that besides these considerations—enough to excuse all his vagaries—there was a tremendous per cent of truth and fact, into which his dream, and ideas at last solidified, and few, if any, were the visions he loved which did not cherish in their warm bosoms, the noblest destiny of the individual man, and carry in their sweep to God's throne the enlarging and brightening rights of men.

Nobody doubted his purity of motive and that, like fire, burned as stubble from the fair field of his intellectual endeavor. Such, indeed, was his honesty, that, when mere principle was involved, he counted defeat as only incidental. I have seen him, with defeats enough to have buried a man who did not know that the everlastingly right and the eternally true could not be defeated, as happy and merry as a child. And I have heard him plead for charity, humanity, temperance and the rights of men, when another voice would have been hushed with despondency. On and on he went with his ideas, and in that period of his most triumphant carelessness of the incidents of the campaign of a great thought, it was a grand sight to see Horace Greeley lead it through successive defeats to overwhelming victory.

When we have summed up all that Mr. Greeley has done, what he has left undone, what he made errors in trying to do—his life-work, I think that much must be put down to what has been overlooked, to what became of some common sympathy I saw in him in these heroic days—his intellectual tolerance, aye his intellectual friendliness to the bold, courageous, young, needy, and fresh thinkers with whom he came in contact. Like soft, sweet sunbeams, he fructified many a soul into expression and powerful utterance and if he did much by speaking, he did much more by touching other tongues, inviting other voices, and encouraging other utterances, which, coming from grand and vast natures, still rest and abide with us.

By Mr. Greeley I was led to hear his pastor, Edwin Hubbel Chapin, pastor of the Fourth Universalist Church. After hearing him once, it needed no invitation for me to seek his church again. I at once pronounced him one of the broadest men, in the best sense of that term, as also one of the most truth-loving, earnest, eloquent and soul-inspiring preachers I had ever heard. It is a progressive people led by a progressive preacher. That was my impression on entering church.

His audience room large, central, beautiful, was filled
from Sunday to Sunday, with thinking and active men.
Here was no place for the theological antediluvian.
Here was no rest for the lazy soul who believed that
Jesus had little to do with nineteenth century affairs.
Here, on the other hand, was no room for the mere
dreamer, the loose-jointed liberal, who shrieked for
nothing but liberality, or the tight-fisted soul who
clutched to any creed and its abilities to help men.

One word of such solid sense as trembled from his
lips to the ancient middle age devotee of his creed
would have operated like a thunderbolt. He would
not be bound. He would not bind others. He believed so much in liberty that he would allow you to
do your own thinking. For much so-called belief in
liberty is to this effect; ''you will be free if you believe as I do, otherwise you are a slave.'' Chapin
thundered forth his own liberty to scare nobody else into his creed, and he held his own freedom so sacred
that he loved the sacredness of that of his neighbor,
yet he was, as he yet is, far from being a man who con-
fuses *license* with *liberty*. He has and wants other people to have a very definite feeling on certain matters.

You will hear the exceeding sinfulness of sin, if you
go to Dr. Chapin's church. The everlasting nature of
holiness, the love of God, the grandeur of duty, from
a certain well-defined faith, are fully set forth in his theology, and all these with him bear upon human life.
They have to do with the life of this hour, now and
here; and the glory of his imagination, the clear glance
of his intellect, light it all up with a glow, with a heav-
enly radiance. His culture was orthodox and evangel-
ical. His training has not been lost. He is after men
and their destinies, and with all the faith of the age in
which he lives, he strives to illustrate the only idea

25

which exalts mankind. With all practical men, this poetic man, this orator must stand as a peer. When the
slave was in chains, his voice pleaded in splendid eloquence for him. He has been a marked and great
friend of temperance, and no greater occasions come to
his life, than when this man who would have been a
great poet with the gift of song, who is one of our
greatest orators, at all events, touches these topics.
With a voice like a clarion, he is all enthusiasm. He
smites, and charges, and leaves no tone of human nature untouched, as he deals with the affairs of our life.
Instead of such theological hair-splitting as I heard in
some of the other churches, Chapin would touch these
vast audiences with a sermon on *Home* with such passages as these :

"I have spoken of the family as a Divine institution.
But this should not be a mere abstraction with us. It
should be realized and felt. And the way in which
home is practically regarded by any of us, will prove how
much we realize and feel these claims. Let the father,
the mother, the child, ask—'What is home to me ?'—
and the answer will be the standard by which we may
know how far, in our relations to it, the Divine purpose
of the family is fulfilled. If we make home only a place
to eat and sleep in, a hotel or caravansera; if we are
employed merely in making provision for it, and securing temporal good ; then the Divine purpose is *not*
fulfilled.

"Now it is not necessary for me to speak of gross
violations of the duties of Home, which all would be
prompt to condemn. But I *will* speak here of one
such gross violation, more gross in the very fact that
it is silent and perhaps unseen. I do not allude to
acts of physical violence. I speak of blows that fall on
naked hearts, of violence done to the deepest sanctities

of life. I speak of affections withering from neglect—
of confidence basely abused. I speak of vows that
God has sealed, broken and trampled under foot. I
speak of the shameful profligacy of husbands and
fathers, belonging to hundreds of homes in this very
city. I speak of men with wives and daughters, who
make light of the sanctities of that womanhood in which
those wives and daughters are glorified. Men breath-
ing a moral atmosphere, one breath of which by wife
or daughter would blast her with enduring shame.
Men hiding their sneaking abomination with social
decencies, and living as if they were masked from God.
Men who, if they really felt their own meanness, would
skulk from the face of virtue, and wilt in the light of
innocence. Lepers of domestic infidelity. Animate
plague spots in broadcloth and fine linen. Heads of
families, over each of whose door-posts should be
written the proclamation of 'a deserted home,' and
whose foreheads should be stamped with 'the mark of
the Beast.' "

Instead of the limping ideas of the fashionable godli-
ness of other places, his hearers are treated to such
psssages as this:

" My brethren, we are fond enough of the *spectacle* of
valorous duty—fond of the *romance* of principle, when
we can see it delineated upon some great world-wide
canvas, while we sit comfortably still to look at it.
Then we say—' Duty is a grand thing, and especially
is it a grand thing when men hold on and suffer for it,
and patiently wait for its postponed victory : not knowing whether in their time it will gain a victory at all—
only they are conscious that it is duty, and they suffer
and wait on its account alone.' Permit me to illustrate
this by an instance taken from our own history. There
was no battle, no splendid success, in our Revolution-

ary war, which yields such inspiration as that winter
of dismay and suffering, when that little army of
Washington crouched naked and starving in their miserable huts, sleeping in the frost on the 'cold, bleak hill,'
and with the blood of their bare feet printing the snows
of Valley Forge. No victory to cheer them, there
was nothing to hold them together but the simple bond
of fidelity. To make that hungry, ragged group the
most glorious picture in our Revolutionary annals,
there was nothing but the splendor of devotion to a
principle that absorbed all personal considerations.
Had success actually been in their hands, it would have
been comparatively easy to suffer for the possession of
it. Or even if they could have been struggling for
success in 'the heady currents of a fight,' the object
might have seen near enough to warm and inspire
them. But to stand, as it seemed, far off from the
victory; to see in that leaden winter sky no rift of
promise; instead of the drums that should summon
them to conflict and therefore to hope, to hear only
the wind rattling through the naked woods, and to
behold in that waste of snow as it were the winding-
sheet of liberty; and yet to stand with their frozen
feet unflinching at their posts, believing that in some
way the right would triumph, at least believing that
right *is* right; waiting upon God's will now *they* had
done all they could—it is this that makes that episode
of 1778 so sublime.

"Yes, this is a great thing when represented on the
historical canvas; it is a great thing anywhere, because
it is not an easy thing to do. Man will fight for principle, he will sacrifice for principle; but it is a harder
matter to *wait* for principle. It is a trial of our moral
and religious strength, to do the right thing, and see
no immediate or palpable good growing out of it.

And I say we can do this only as we recognize the fact that we are *bound* to duty; that it is a higher will than our own we are serving, and therefore we are to work and wait, not fretting about results. Work for God, and then wait upon God."

His idea of a man is the beginning of his theology. He often urges that,—

"It is *within* that we look for the distinctiveness of man. Our conceptions of humanity become most perplexed, our hopes most faint, not in the field of comparative anatomy where the dissecting-knife and the microscope lay bare the material tissues that link us to the animal, and weave us in one web of quivering flesh and blood with all this mass of sensuous being that creeps and climbs, that howls and chatters, and lives and dies—not where we trace the life-roots of our manhood twined with those of brute existence and running down into the swamp of common nature. Not here does our ideal of humanity become most depressed; but where the countenance is almost blank of intellectual beauty, and moral distinctions are poured away in dishevelled impulses, and civilizing affections are submerged in appetites. When the light *within* is darkness, how great is that darkness!"

From that he advances, and life is a continual glory under his idea, which so fills him, that, with such wonderful eloquence, my reader must imagine the effect of the extemporaneous delivery of such a passage as this:

"Sometimes the world's form of temptation assumes a truly royal attitude. To some lofty spirit that would stoop to no mean quarry, it promises all the kingdoms of the world and the glory of them, if that spirit will only dethrone God and worship it. It offers honors of place, and majesties of power, and the homage of the multitude. Nowhere is its influence so fearfully dis-

played as when it attacks a nature enriched with large
gifts and capabilities, yet containing no vital germ of
virtue, and bound by no, sanction of religion, and which
with all its splendor of movement gravitates to mere
self-interest. A man like this may walk long in the
path of rectitude and brush away common snares with
his feet. But the moment he encounters something
that touches the leading purpose of his soul, temptation
springs upon him and Achilles is wounded in the heel.
The statesman, the philanthropist, the severe patriot,
is taken captive by 'ambition, the last infirmity of noble
minds.' Is not this a very melancholy spectacle? A
man standing in some high place of intellect and honor,
splendid as ever in the brain, but on one side of him—
the moral side—stricken clear down with paralysis! A
man saturated with the finest culture, with the most
delicate sensibilities playing in his nature, with the
escutcheon pride in eye and forehead, flushed with the
heraldry of genius, scorning the temptations of the flesh,
beating upward like an eagle towards some lofty point ;
yet carrying a hard, cold, selfish heart, and marked as
a deserter from the right. When some great occasion
breaks, and imperiled justice calls to him from the
ground, and far above all mean interests and clanging
factions of the voice of duty summons him like the very
trump of God, he vascillates, he takes up the lance
droopingly, he lets the ark of the righteous cause totter,
he cowers before the dragon of the hour, he falls away
from the good cause, he betrays it, nay, he becomes hot
against it ; and the words of the man that might have
been tones of regeneration and victory, clatter upon
our ears like 'thirty pieces of silver.'

"Ah! a man may chain his appetites, and hold the
realm of knowledge within the cincture of his brain,
and yet in the saddest aspect of all be overcome by the

world. And again I say, how startling is the fact that one may hold on steadfastly up to a particular point, and there all gives way. O my brother man, meaning to live the life of duty, the life of religion! the world is a mighty antagonist, subtle as it is strong ; more to be dreaded in its whispers to the heart's secret inclination than in gross shapes of evil. And let me say to you that it is a great thing in this respect to overcome the world. It is a great thing by God's help and your own effort to keep it in its place, and say to its eager pressure, 'Thus far and no farther.' A great thing, O merchant! to carry the clue of rectitude through the labyrinths of traffic, and to feel the woof of eternal sanctions crossing the warp of daily interests. A great thing, O politician! to withstand the fickle teasings of popularity, to scorn the palatable lie, and keep God's signet upon your conscience. A great thing, O man! whatever your condition, to resist the appeals of envy and revenge, of avarice and pleasure, and to feel that your life has higher ends than these. Strenuous must be the endeavor but proportionally best is the victory of him who in all these issues overcomes the world."

Such was Chapin in those days.

With no other man could I be so much interested. With the preaching of no other man could I have been so much helped, as with that of Dr. Chapin, save that of the best abused, the best loved man in the American pulpit—the greatest man in the pulpit of the world—Henry Ward Beecher.

As I look back upon his past, and, through the glasses of my own recollection of his influence in the East, during these years, I see him, as I am sure history shall see him, as more than the great orator, the magnificent thinker, the powerful writer, the grand reformer that he is—I see him as a noble, heroic man, filling all

these, as a cup is filled and over-filled, and flowing at last
and beyond them into all the tides of our modern life.
Near the beginning of the war, and in its early days, it
was an old heroism which hurled thunder and spoke
lightnings at Plymouth Church, and we who heard him,
felt that, though he spoke in trying circumstances then,
he had spoken in worse days and when graver dangers
threatened his brave heart.   Manhood shone from that
pulpit—nothing more, nothing less.   It was so complete
a manhood that it filled every niche, touched every chord,
and baptized every sentiment with music.   Beecher begun a great man, and this manhood filling a splendid
body made him great with men.   His voice touches all
keys because he has all phases of the entertaining music
within him.   His ideas flow upon every shore, because
the ocean of his soul, of which they are waves, touches
the great human coast everywhere.   He is to preaching
what Shakespeare is to poetry—the myriad-minded.
Beginning with the idea that man is sacred, he feels that
all his work is sacred, and that if he preaches truly he
will preach to all the activities of man.   He is more
than Chapin without being less, and takes the special
greatnesses of his contemporaries to make himself complete.   This completeness of intellectual constitution
must always remain his greatest special talent.   And it
is the highest talent a man may possess.   It makes every faculty strong, since each faculty relieves the other.
It is the strength of a convocation of powers into one
manhood.   I have hinted of the practical heroism of
Mr. Beecher at this time.

A few examples will suffice and illustrate the amazing clearness of his ideas of the New Testament
with relation to the great problem of slavery.   I
need not mention his personal history in connection
with the broken shackles of the slave.   It is known

the world around, and it only came from the same
faith as these words which I quote, as having a great
influence at the time.   Every Sunday was an excited day.   But one Sunday, October 30, 1859, John
Brown lay in prison, and languishingly awaited his trial
for his inaugurating the revolution which freed the slave,
at Harper's Ferry.   The campaign for Abraham Lincoln had just begun and was waxing warm.   The leaders on the other side took advantage of the fact that
Brown had, under those circumstances, precipitated affairs, and represented to the people that such was only
a premature and significant exhibition of what the Republican party intended to do against the rights of the
South.   This was an occasion for Mr. Beecher.   He
saw the need of vindicating the friends of liberty, and
no one who sat in that vast audience will forget how he
arose, and with a voice that spoke the great tender but
heroic soul within him, announced in clear tones the
terrible words in Jeremiah vi, 16—19.   He stopped,
fixed his eyes, shook his head, and said with great emotion: "This is a terrible message."   He pointed out
their history, and eloquently, but in a low tone of voice,
told the circumstance of Harper's Ferry.   Then he said,
in a strong voice, his face quivering with satire:

"Seventeen men terrified two thousand brave Virginians into two days' submission—*that* cannot be got over!
The common sense of common people will not fail to
see through all attempts to hide a natural shame by a
bungling make-believe that the danger was really greater
than it was!   The danger was nothing, and the fear very
great, and the courage none at all.   And nothing can
now change the facts!   All the newspapers on earth
will not make this case appear any better.   Do what you
please—muster a crowd of supposed confederates, call
the roll of conspirators, include the noblest men of these

26

States, and exhibit this imaginary army before the people, and, in the end, it will appear that seventeen white men overawed a town of two thousand brave Virginians, and held them captives until the sun had gone laughing twice around the globe!

"And the attempt to hide the fear of these surrounded men by awaking a larger fear will never do. It is too literal a fulfillment, not exactly of prophecy, but of fable; not of Isaiah, but of Æsop.

" A fox having been caught in a trap, escaped with the loss of his tail. He immediately went to his brother foxes to persuade them that they would all look better if they too would cut off their tails. They declined. And our two thousand friends, who lost their courage in the presence of seventeen men, are now making an appeal to this nation to lose its courage too, that the cowardice of the few may be hidden in the cowardice of the whole community! It is impossible. We choose to wear our courage for some time longer!"

He then sketched in glowing sentences John Brown's life, when he said:

" Let no man pray that Brown be spared. Let Virginia make him a martyr. Now, he has only blundered. His soul was noble; his work miserable. But a cord and a gibbet would redeem all that, and round up Brown's failure with a heroic success."

The occasion had come. Beecher was aroused. He could not save Brown. But he could and did show the Nation's duty to slavery. He pleaded for the Christian spirit toward the South earnestly. He said he hated their slavery. He crushed the idea of stirring up the discontented bondsmen. He made that vast audience weep when he told the bondman's sufferings. But to walk this fine line of truth was not the hardest task of that occasion. He had to tell the North how it could help and ought to help the day of freedom on. He was pale, then flushed; he rose to the grandest heights, and hushed them with his eloquent whispers while he pleaded for a right sentiment at the North. He said:

"If we would benefit the African at the South, we must *begin at the North*. This is to some men the most disagreeable part of the doctrine of emancipation. It is very easy to labor for the emancipation of beings a thousand miles off; but the practical application of justice and humanity to those about us is not so agreeable. The truths of God respecting the rights and dignities of men are just as important to free colored men as to enslaved colored men. The lever with which to lift the load of Georgia is in New York. I do not believe the whole free North can tolerate grinding injustice toward the poor, and inhumanity toward the laboring classes, without exerting an influence unfavorable to justice and humanity in the South. No one can fail to see the inconsistency between our treatment of those amongst us who are in the lower walks of life and our professions of sympathy for the Southern slaves. How are the free colored people treated at the North? They are almost without education, and with but little sympathy for their ignorance. They are refused the common rights of citizenship which the whites enjoy. They cannot even ride in the cars of our city railroads. They are snuffed at in the house of God, or tolerated with ill-concealed disgust. Can the black man be a mason in New York? Let him be employed as a journeyman, and every Irish lover of liberty that carries the hod or trowel would leave at once or compel him to leave! Can the black man be a carpenter? There is scarcely a carpenter's shop in New York in which a journeyman would continue to work, if a black man was employed in it. Can the black man engage in the common industries of life? There is scarcely one from which he is not excluded. He is crowded down, down, down, through the most menial callings, to the bottom of society. We tax them, and then refuse to allow their children to go to our public schools. We heap upon them moral obloquy more atrocious than that which the master heaps upon the slave. And, notwithstanding all this, we lift ourselves up to talk to the Southern people about the rights and liberties of the human soul, and especially the African soul!   *   *   *   *   *

" Whenever we are prepared to show toward the lowest, the poorest, and the most despised an unaffected kindness, such as led Christ, though the Lord of Glory, to lay aside his dignities, and to take on himself the form of a servant, and suffer an ignominious death, that he might rescue men from ignorance and bondage—whenever we are prepared to do such things as these, we may be sure that the example of the North will not be unfelt at the South. Every effort that is made in Brooklyn to establish schools and churches for the free colored people, and to encourage them to educate themselves and to become independent, is a step toward emancipation in the South. The degradation of free colored men in the North will fortify slavery in the South!"

He held that audience under those painful facts for over an hour, and with great applause he closed the argument with such a plea for the slave, and such a withering scorn of "timid priests and lying societies," as seemed to be in keeping with the prophet of the olden time.

As the war advanced his splendid enthusiasm rose, and his solutions of grave problems became more and more clear, and his broad statesmanship was seen more and more inclusive of the best visions of the future.

Before he left college, he had identified himself with

the anti-slavery party, and he was always conspicuous among its advocates. A perfect storm of abuse had been heaped upon him for having had a negro sit upon his pulpit, and he added to its awful darkness by having Wendell Phillips deliver his most eloquent address on "The Lesson of the Hour," from Plymouth pulpit.

Thanksgiving Day, November 29, 1860, he preached another great sermon to a magnificent audience, against any sort of compromise of principle, which was so eloquent that the audience got beyond all control and became noisy in its demonstration of enthusiasm. It was a time long to be remembered, when, standing like an oak which tosses its branches in the gale, he quietly said in mellow, but clear tones, what almost falls into poetry :

"I need not remind you of the year that is closing. Who knew, when January set her cold, calm face toward the future, that she was the herald of such a summer? When was there ever a year so fertile? so propitious to all industry? It has been a procession of rejoicing months, flower-wreathed and fruit-laden—a very holiday year!

"The soil awoke with new ardor; everything that lived by the soil felt the inspiration. Every root, and every blade, and every stem, and every bough has this year taxed itself for prodigal bounty. Except a narrow strip, this continent has been so blessed with husbandry as to make this year memorable even among years hitherto most eminent. The meadow, the tilled fields, the grazing pastures, the garden, the vineyard, the orchard, the very fence-row berry-bushes and wild wall-vines, have been clothed with unexampled bounty and beauty. Nature seems to have lacked messengers to convey her intents of kindness, and the summer, like a road surprised with quadruple freights, has not been able to find conveyance for all its treasures. The seas have felt the divine ardor.   The fisherman never reaped such harvests from the moist furrows of the ocean as this year.   These husbandmen of the sea, who reap where they have not sowed and grow rich upon harvests which they have not tilled, have this year put in the crooked hook for their sickle with admiring gladness for the strange and un-wonted abundance of the deep.''

And then he took up a copy of the paper containing the following proclamation :

'' MAYOR'S OFFICE, NEW YORK,
''*November* 24, 1860.

'' PROCLAMATION.—In accordance with custom and the proclamation of the Governor of the State, it be-comes my duty, as Mayor, to recommend to the people of this city the observance of Thursday, the 29th inst., as a day of 'Thanksgiving and Prayer.'

''While in my judgment the country, either in its po-litical, commercial, or financial aspect, presents no fea-tures for which we should be thankful, we are yet called upon by every consideration of self-preservation to offer up to the Father of all mercies devout and fervent pray-er, for his interposition and protection from the impend-ing evils which threaten our institutions and the material interests of the people.

''Therefore, acknowledging our dependence on Al-mighty God, and deeply sensible of our own unworthi-ness, let the day set apart as Thanksgiving be observed by the people of this city as one of humiliation and sup-plication—not omitting in our prayers the expression of the hope that those who have, in violation of the Fed-eral compact, unpatriotically and unwisely inflicted these injuries upon us, may be the only sufferers by their own wickedness and folly.

''[L.S.]   Given under my hand and seal, the day and year aforesaid.   FERNANDO WOOD, Mayor.''

And with withering, awful scorn, remarked concerning it as follows :

"All the sons of God rejoice, and all good men rejoice. It needs but one element to complete the satisfaction. If we could be sure that this is God's mercy, meant for good, and tending thereto, we should have a full cup to-day. That satisfaction is not denied us. The Mayor of New York, in a public proclamation, in view of this prodigal year, that has heaped the poor man's house with abundance, is pleased to say that there is no occasion apparent to him for thanksgiving. We can ask no more. When bad men grieve at the state of public affairs, good men should rejoice. When infamous men keep fast, righteous men should have thanksgiving. God reigns and the Devil trembles. Amen. Let us rejoice!"

He then began to enumerate other reasons, national, international and human, for thanksgiving. Old Plymouth church literally rocked with enthusiasm when he pleaded against any compromise of principle. And as a great lawyer leaves a jury, knowing their verdict, he left that audience, speaking in their souls his last words :

"When night is on the deep, when the headlands are obscured by the darkness, and when storm is in the air, that man who undertakes to steer by looking over the side of the ship, over the bow, or over the stern, or by looking at the clouds or his own fears, is a fool. There is a silent needle in the binnacle, which points like the finger of God, telling the mariner which way to steer, and enabling him to outride the storm, and reach the harbor in safety. And what the compass is to navigation, that is moral principle in political affairs. Whatever the issue may be, we have but one thing to do, and that is to look where the compass of God points, and steer that way. You need not fear shipwreck when God is the pilot.

"The latter-day glory is already dawning. God is calling to the nations. The long-oppressed are arousing. The despotic thrones are growing feeble. It is an age of liberty. The trumpet is sounding in all the world, and one nation after another is moving to the joyful sound, and God is mustering the great army of liberty under his banners! In this day, shall America be found laggard? While despotisms are putting off the garments of oppression, shall she pluck them up and put them on? While France and Italy, Germany and Russia, are advancing toward the dawn, shall we recede toward midnight?

"From this grand procession of nations, with faces lightened by liberty, shall we be missing? While they advance toward a brighter day, shall we, with faces lurid with oppression, slide downward toward the pit which gapes for injustice and crime?

"Let every good man arouse and speak the truth for liberty. Let us have an invincible courage for liberty. Let us have moderation in passions, zeal in moral sentiments, a spirit of conciliation and concession in mere material interests, but unmovable firmness for principles; and—foremost of all political principles—for Liberty!"

When Fort Sumter was being besieged, April 14, 1861, all hearts were fluttering. Mr. Beecher, on Sunday morning, arose, and after a most wonderful prayer, announced as his text these words: "And the Lord said unto Moses, wherefore criest thou unto me? speak unto the children of Israel, that they go forward." He piled up history and touched the leaves of the past with light. He deduced from the interesting search the idea that "when men stand for a moral principle, their troubles are not a presumption that they are in the wrong. Since the world began, men that have stood for the right have had to stand for it, as Christ stood for the world, suffering for victory. And the whole lesson of the past

is, that safety and honor come by holding fast to one's
principles ; by pressing them with courage ; by going
into darkness and defeat cheerfully for them." He
looked out with a bold, firm gaze, and said, "And now
our turn has come. Right before us lies the Red Sea
of war." He rushed into the full flood of his theme.
The very branches swayed, for the storm had come. A
man stepped upon the platform. A bit of paper lay on
his desk. He halted not. He was most eloquent as he
read the small message. On went the orator thrilling
all souls, until he got them to see that to love liberty is
a thing not to be modified by any change in circumstance. Then he said :

"It is trying to live in suspense, to be in the torment-
ing whirl of rumor, now to see the banner up, and now
to see it trailing in the dust. Early yesterday things
seemed inauspicious. Toward evening all appeared calm
and fair. To-day disastrous and depressing rumors were
current. This morning I came hither sad from the tidings
that that stronghold which seemed to guard the precious
name and lasting fame of the noble and gallant Anderson,
had been given up ; but since I came into this desk I
have received a dispatch from one of our most illustrious
citizens, saying that Sumter is reinforced, and that Moul
trie is the fort that has been destroyed."

The applause was simply deafening. Handkerchiefs,
hats, canes, umbrellas, were all in use, and cheers and
shouts broke forth in an awful din. He saw that he had
not done all. The orator was equal to the occasion.
As no one can forget, he closed by saying:

"But what if the rising sun to-morrow shall reverse
the message? What if the tidings that greet you
in the morning shall be but the echo of the old tidings of disaster? You live in hours in which you
are to suffer suspense. Now lifted up, you will be

27

prematurely cheering, and now cast down, you will be prematurely desponding. Look forward, then, past the individual steps, the various vicissitudes of experience, to the glorious end that is coming! Look beyond the present to that assured victory that awaits us in the future.

"Young men, you will live to see more auspicious days. Later sent, delayed in your voyage into life, you will see the bright consummation, in part at least, of that victory of this land, by which, with mortal throes, it shall cast out from itself all morbific influences, and cleanse itself from slavery. And you that are in middle life shall see the ultimate triumph advancing beyond anything that you have yet known. The scepter shall not depart. The government shall not be shaken from its foundations.

"Let no man, then, in this time of peril, fail to associate himself with that cause which is to be so entirely glorious. Let not your children, as they carry you to your burial, be ashamed to write upon your tombstone the truth of your history. Let every man that lives and owns himself an American, take the side of true American principles;—liberty for one, and liberty for all; liberty now, and liberty forever; liberty as the foundation of government, and liberty as the basis of union; liberty as against revolution, liberty, against anarchy, and liberty, against slavery; liberty here and liberty everywhere, the world through!

"When the trumpet of God has sounded, and that grand procession is forming; as Italy has risen, and is wheeling into the ranks; as Hungary, though mute, is beginning to beat time, and make ready for the march; as Poland, having long slept, has dreamt of liberty again, and is waking; as the thirty million serfs are hearing the roll of the drum, and are going forward toward citizenship—let it not be your miserable fate, nor mine, to live in a nation that shall be seen reeling and staggering and wallowing in the orgies of despotism! We, too, have a right to march in this grand procession of liberty. By the memory of the fathers; by the sufferings of the Puritan ancestry; by the teaching of our national history; by our faith and hope of religion; by every line of the Declaration of Independence, and every article of our Constitution; by what we are and what our progenitors were—we have a right to walk foremost in this procession of nations toward the bright millennial future!"

Another occasion of great interest at Plymouth Church during the war, was when the two companies of the Brooklyn Fourteenth, who were, many of them, members of Plymouth church, met there for the last time previous to their going to the war. The church at the close of the service raised $3,000 for their equipment. The chief source of inspiration was Mr. Beecher's sermon and prayer—which latter is always wonderful. He spoke on the National flag. Passages like these were irresistible:

"This nation has a banner; and until recently where ever it streamed abroad men saw day-break bursting on their eyes. For until lately the American flag has been a symbol of Liberty, and men rejoiced in it. Not another flag on the globe had such an errand, or went forth upon the sea carrying everywhere, the world around, such hope to the captive, and such glorious tidings. The stars upon it were to the pining nations like the bright morning stars of God, and the stripes upon it were beams of morning light. As at early dawn the stars shine forth even while it grows light, and then as the sun advances that light breaks into banks and streaming lines of color, the glowing red and intense white striving together, and ribbing the horizon with bars effulgent, so, on the American flag, stars and beams of many-colored light shine out together.   And wherever this flag comes, and men behold it, they see in its sacred emblazonry no ramping lion, and no fierce eagle; no embattled castles, or insignia of imperial authority; they see the symbols of light.   It is the banner of Dawn.   It means *Liberty ;* and the galley-slave, the poor, oppressed conscript, the trodden-down creature of foreign despotism, sees in the American flag that very promise and prediction of God—' The people which sat in darkness saw a great light; and to them which sat in the region and shadow of death light is sprung up.'   *   *

"This American flag was the safeguard of liberty. Not an atom of crown was allowed to go into its insignia. Not a symbol of authority in the ruler was permitted to go into it.   It was an ordinance of liberty by the people for the people.   *That* it meant, *that* it means, and, by the blessing of God, *that* it shall mean to the end of time !

"For God Almighty be thanked ! that, when base and degenerate Southern men desired to set up a nefarious oppression, at war with every legend and every instinct of old American history, they could not do it under our bright flag !   Its stars smote them with light like arrows shot from the bow of God.   They must have another flag for such work ; and they forged an infamous flag to do an infamous work, and, God be blessed ! left our bright and starry banner untainted and untouched by disfigurement and disgrace !   I thank them that they took another flag to do the devil's work, and left our flag to do the work of God !   [Applause.]   So may it ever be, that men that would forge oppression shall be obliged to do it under some other banner than the Stars and Stripes."

" If ever the sentiment of our text, then was fulfilled, it has been in our glorious American banner:—

'Thou hast given a banner *to them that fear thee.*'

" Our fathers were God-fearing men. Into their hands Cod committed this banner, and they have handed it down to us. And I thank God that it is still in the hands of men that fear Him and love righteousness.

'Thou hast given a banner to them that fear thee, *that it may be displayed.*'

" And displayed it shall be. Advanced full against the morning light, and borne with the growing and the glowing day, it shall take the last ruddy beams of the night, and from the Atlantic wave, clear across with eagle flight to the Pacific, that banner shall float, meaning all the liberty that it has ever meant! From the North, where snows and mountain ice stand solitary, clear to the glowing tropics and the Gulf, that banner that has hitherto waved shall wave and wave forever,—every star, every band, every thread and fold significant of liberty! [Great applause.]

"I do not doubt your patriotism. I know it is hard for men that are full of feeling not to give expression to it; yet excuse me if I request you to refrain from demonstrations of applause while I am speaking. It is not because I think Sunday too good a day, nor the church too holy a place for patriotic Christian men to express their feelings at such a time as this, and in behalf of such sentiments, but because by too frequent repetition applause becomes stale and common, that I make this request. Besides, outward expression is not our way. We are rather of a silent stock. We let our feelings work inwardly, so that they may have deeper channels and fuller floods.

"'Thou hast given a banner to them that fear thee, that it may be displayed *because of the truth.*'

But they forgot his request, when the orator spoke about the closing of the route through Baltimore, and hinted that Washington was reached only by Annapolis, in these words:

"That flag must go to the capital of this nation; and it must go not hidden, not secreted, not in a case or covering, but advanced full high, displayed, bright as the sun, clear as the moon, terrible as an army with banners! For a single week that disgraceful crook, that shameful circuit may be needful; but the way from New England, the way from New York, the way from New Jersey and Pennsylvania to Washington, *lies right through Baltimore;* and that is the way the flag must and shall go!"

Another cheer came with great enthusiasm.

During the war, great occasions were continually coming to this church. A great preacher living in a great time, can hardly keep them off. Indeed it is generally a great occasion twice a Sunday and once on Friday evening, because this great soul pours its life out then. But those who were there, will always remember the occasion when Mr. Beecher preached on Fort Sumpter anniversary days, the Emancipation Proclamation, a sermon demanding energy of administration, and the great statesmen who came there will not forget the deep discussions of the basic faith of civilization as they were given from Plymouth pulpit. For Mr. Beecher, to begin with, is a thinker. He has investigated the problem of government, thoroughly. He is abreast of the times by being abreast with eternity. He understands the weight and bearing of policies, political ideas, and the clearness in which he holds principle and the grasp with which he holds the history of the past, enable him to think in the atmosphere of both. As a specimen of the depth which Mr.

Beecher seeks in these affairs, his sermon preached during the war, on "Liberty under Law," is an example. The whole genius of republicanism lies within its wise eloquence, and the student of the organic strength of our institutions can do no better than to read with thought the sermons of Henry Ward Beecher on subjects connected with government.

But this is only one phase of his many sided genius and his many sided activity. I mention this because his industry elsewhere is better known, because I was familiar with it, because also we are too likely to forget that among the intellectual heroes of our late struggle, Henry Ward Beecher is the peer of any. Slander may touch him, but Liberty will always love him, and eternal justice will keep his name bright forever. History will always see him as did that great audience in the Academy of Music, advancing to a negro, and amid a frenzy of enthusiasm offering his warm hand, and saying; "As the representative of one race, I extend to you, the representative of another, the right hand of fellowship."

I must not, by any haste or over-sight, omit to say that prior to this time, that matchless thinker and fearless apostle, Theodore Parker, had had much to do in giving inspiration and form to my thought. Those who have had any serious regard for the destiny of free institutions, on the one hand, and any profound love for a liberal and earnest religion, on the other, will not fail to point to him as one who blessed both with his warm palms of fervid enthusiasm. It is said of a certain prominent figure in political England, that you may split his reputation up, and each fragment is enough to prove and establish his greatness unto his own and succeeding generations. Such was Theodore Parker. Every struggle of freedom to prevent encroachments of slavery, will

quote his name.   In the history of anti-slavery in this
country, he earned the title of greatness.   On that alone
his reputation for ages is certain.   But he need not depend upon that alone.   For, towering above all others of
his day, with all his faults and eccentricities, he was the
foremost prophet of an absolute religion.   Every struggle
of the spirit against the letter counts in the charm of his
name.   Every combat of ideas as against traditions
calls him one of its Saints.   Every battle of the simple truth against that spirit, which exalts into sacredness its hereditary trappings, names his arguments as
its own.

As time goes on, and the battle becomes more and
more clearly understood, we see the value of that early
heroism of this ardent man.   Many a man who does
not agree with him in his views of God and human sin,
and who would not love to have his name connected
with that of the Boston prophet, has used the better
public sentiment, which Parker created, in which to pub-
lish his ideas.   Many a man within the limits of conservatism, has declined to suspect any likeness unto
this great radical, and yet has done things in public
speech, which, had not Theodore Parker done so much
more thirty years ago, would not have been done safely.
It is half amusing to note how conservatism gradually
comes to accept radicalism, when it is not told that it is
becoming radical.   So that Theodore Parker is far more
near to the heart of this generation than he was to the
generation preceding us.   Indeed, he was so great a
prophet that he not only prophesied the thought of
our time, but that of the time yet to come.   All truth-
seekers are indebted to him, not more—yea, not so
much—for the truth he found, as for the method he inspired, which, in the hands of truth-seekers, can not
but succeed.   That man who gives me truth, has not

done so much for me as He who gives me the method of finding it for myself. This was Parker's mission—to show to the thought of his time that truth was a stern reality and she must be grasped by fearless hands; that courage was demanded in her pursuit; that once having been won by boldness she delighted to live with a brave soul. Unconciously to our time, the method of Parker has become the method of our day. He was called an iconoclast, and now the image-breaking is going on in our time. He was said to be a dangerous man because he insisted on the fundamental facts of religion and laughed at the old tradition, and now our day tends to do the same. If there is more ease in fearless thinking; if there is less friction in the progress of liberal thought; if there is more tolerance to-day than there was thirty years ago, it is largely because of the manly radicalism of that earnest man.

His two reputations blend, because the inspiration of one is the result of the other. There is a good deal of liberalism in theology that is lazy and ineffective. Parker's was a working liberality. Much of our vaunted "breadth of thinking" is vague and not practical. Parker's was as practical as a steam engine. The majority of radicals are destructionists. Parker was a destructionist that he might be a constructionist. He was so practical, effective, and serious with his views of man that he fought the hell-begotten institution of slavery with all his might. He wanted bondage destroyed that freedom's temple might be constructed. He was not as anxious for the death of slavery as he was for the life of liberty. This made his religion and his anti-slavery walk hand in hand.

28

CHAPTER XV.

―――

It has always seemed to me that a strange, though eloquent pathos, lingered about that sentence of our Lord : *" Father, the hour is come."* He had denounced the religious leaders of the nation. He had uttered his brave opposition to the society which hedged him about. As Bengel says, the Greeks had come to Jerusalem at the Feast-time, and had been welcomed by him, "as the prelude of the transition of the kingdom of God from the Jew to the Gentile." Then it seemed to him that nothing remained but his death to make his work triumph. It had been self-sacrificing all the way ; and something, at last, had been gained. But it was only as a simple seed. He must put it into the ground by the greater act of self-sacrifice. It must be watered by His tears. It must be enriched in its growth by His blood. He must *die*, that that for which He had worked so long might *live*. How gladly He opened His heart to the approaching sadness! How joyously He confronts the oncoming doom! How freely He accepts the death which approaches Him ! It is His crucifixion, His cruel murder, His awful agony of suffering that He contemplates ; and yet He says : " Father, *the* hour is come."

Poets have looked through the indifference with which the public received their verses and said, as they

dreamed that they saw a time when men would recognize their genius : " Oh, that will be *the* hour." Heroes
have gazed through battle-heat, and storms of conflict,
to imagine an hour when the laurels would fall on their
brow, and they have said : " that will be *the* hour of my
whole life." Orators have looked through the still con-
tempt of the crowds and the hisses of their audiences
and have found a reason to believe that some day these
same audiences shall wait to crown them ; and they
have said : "That will be *the* time of all." But the
Saviour of the world saw death, crucifixion cruel and
awful, coming over the hills of His life with a cross and
a grave and looking these insignia of defeat in the face,
He nobly said : " Father, *the* hour is come. All my
self-sacrifice was led up to this Calvary mountain. All
my efforts to be and to do Thy will have been paths to
this summit, which I shall have to sprinkle with my
blood. All this life of poverty and conflict with the
world, all this love of my race, all this help I have
given to men—*all* of these lead to this consummate sacrifice, this greatest self-denial, this death of myself. *The*
hour for which I have lived is come."

I have wondered recently if every life of effort and
self-sacrifice has not to suffer one last Calvary that it may
gain one everlasting triumph. I have thought so much
of this that I find, without intending any comparison,
that the life which I have lived, beginning in poverty,
and all the way seeking to help those whom the Providence of Heaven have thrown within my path, would
not have had the completeness it needed to make it a
unit of value to mankind or to God, if in its afternoon,
as the shadows grow longer and the evening comes on,
I had not been compelled to try and bear a cross that I
could not carry, to walk up a mountain that had thieves
upon it, and there on a gibbet erected by the foulest

conspiracy I have known, made by hands which had long been working the dire event, to surrender the life which I tried to live as an appeasing to cruel and wretched enemies.

I am, as it were, this side of the moral victory now. I am where I see the tremendous glory for me which lay in that hour of trial. I can now measure only a few of the blessings of the sacrifice to which I was led, but *the* hour for which I had lived seemed then an hour of cruelest persecution as now I can say it was the hour in which my whole life found its victory.

Because of the organic relation of the whole event to my life, the reader will pardon the length of the story. I shall open it by calling attention to the fact that in the Franklin county court, the following indictment was found:

THE STATE OF OHIO, }
FRANKLIN COUNTY, ss. }

In the Court of Common Pleas, Franklin County, Ohio, of the term of January, in the year of our Lord one thousand eight hundred and eighty.

1st count: The Jurors of the Grand Jury of the State of Ohio, duly elected, empaneled, sworn, and charged to enquire of crimes and offences committed within the body of Franklin County, in the State of Ohio, in the name and by the authority of the State of Ohio, upon their oaths, do find and present, that Thomas L. Moore, Charles Fleming, and John Elliott, late of said County, on the third day of September, in the year of our Lord, one thousand eight hundred and seventy-nine, at the County of Franklin, aforesaid, unlawfully, willfully, feloniously, verbally did demand of one Solomon J. Woolley, with menaces, certain money, to wit: the sum of five hundred dollars ($500.00), of the value of

Five Hundred Dollars, and certain chattels, and valuable securities, to wit : certain promisory notes of the amount and value of three hundred dollars ($300.00), the money and property of the said Solmon J. Woolley, with interest then and there, and thereby to extort and gain from the Solmon J. Woolley said money, chattels, and valuable securities, contrary to the Statute in such cases, made and provided, and against the peace and dignity of the State of Ohio.

2d count : And the Jurors aforesaid, by the authority aforesaid, upon their oaths as aforasaid, do further find and present that the said Thomas L. Moore, John Elliot, and Charles Fleming, on the day and year afore-said, at the county aforesaid, unlawfully, willfully, and feloniously did accuse one Solomon J. Woolley, then and there being of the crime of unlawfully and maliciously procuring a barn of the value of four hundred and fifty dollars ($450.00), the same being his own property, situate in Franklin County, Ohio, and insured against loss or damage by fire, to be burned, with intent thereby to prejudice the insurer thereof, said crime being punishable by the laws of the State of Ohio, with imprisonment in the Ohio Penitentiary with the intent, then and there by means of such unlawful accusation to extort and gain from the said Solomon J. Woolley, certain money, to wit : the sum of five hundred dollars and certain chattels and valuable securities, to wit : certain promisory notes of the amount and value of three hundred dollars, said money, chattles, and valuable securities being then and there the property of said Solomon J. Woolley, contrary to the Statute in such case made and provided, and against the peace and dignity of the State of Ohio.

WILLIAM J. CLARKE,
Prosecuting Attorney, Franklin County, Ohio.

No. 1861. Franklin Common Pleas. The State of Ohio, vs. Thomas L. Moore, Charles Fleming, and John Elliott. Indictment for blackmailing. A true bill.

J. W. DURANT,

Foreman of Grand Jury.

Filed January 16th, 1880.

H. CASHATT, *Clerk.*

WM. J. CLARKE,

Prosecuting Attorney, Franklin County, Ohio.

On this 30th, day of January, 1880, Defendant, Charles Fleming, arraigned, and pleads not guilty to this indictment.

H. CASHATT, *Clerk,*

J. C. GETRUE, *Deputy.*

On this 16th day of February, A. D., 1880, Thomas Moore and John Elliott, defendants, arraigned and plead each not guilty to this indictment.

H. CASHATT,

J. C. GETRUE.

After delays innumerable, in which justice seemed often to be friendless, in which it took the patience commended by the strictest code of morals, John Elliott, having been jointly indicted with the others for the grave offense, and who had, at his own request, been awarded a separate trial at the April term, 1880, of the Franklin county common pleas court, was tried. I well remember to have had no such pleasant sensations as when I heard the words read aloud: "STATE OF OHIO VS. JOHN W. ELLIOTT," by Judge Geo. W. Lincoln. Of course everybody expected the trial. But delays are a part of the scheme of injustice and wrong, and no sooner had the hush come over that court-room, full of my friends, and the few adherents of these criminals,

than an affidavit was made by the attorneys of the defense to continue the case.   Promptly did the Judge,
who, perhaps, had found out that dilatory motions and
legal filibustering had been and would be the main
work of the vigilant and enthusiastic attorneys of Elliott,
over-ruled that motion on the grounds that it was the
second application, and that the court granted the privilege of filing an affidavit, setting forth the matter in accordance with it, that it may be submitted on its merits
and be used as testimony.   To this the defense made
an exception—the first of that remarkable series which
distinguished this trial.   Then the defense filed an affidavit setting forth facts which they expected to prove,
and the defense also took objection as to the ruling of
the court compelling them to go to trial on the affidavit
submitted.   At this point my counsel on the part of the
State made a motion for a special venire which motion
was sustained without objection on the part of the defense—an almost solitary case of harmony as between
the lawyers of both sides.   The day had by this time
been consumed; and at nine o'clock, May 11th, the
court-room was full and the case went on.   Two talis-
men were excluded from the jury on the grounds that
one of them had been on the grand jury which found
the indictment, and the other had formed and expressed
his opinion of the issue.   Two others were called when
the special venire was requested by the State, to which
of course, the defense duly objected.   Mr. Joseph H.
Outhwaite opened the case.   Judge Rankin, as counsel
for the defense, asked to have the witnesses on the part
of the State excluded from the room.   And the court,
to the astonishment of the attorneys for Elliott, ordered
the witnesses on the part of both the State and defense
to be excluded from the room.   To this the attorneys
for the defense objected in strong terms and with great

earnestness. Thereupon the witnesses for the defense were permitted to remain.

The first witness called was Mr. D. E. Seely, of Westerville, Ohio. Mr. Outhwaite conducted the examination in chief, and elicited from Mr. Seely the following points :

In September, 1879, he was acting as an insurance agent for the Ohio Farmer's company. He swore that on or about the 3d day of September, 1879, a man came to Westerville and telling him that his name was Elliott proceeded to talk about his paying a loss to myself on a barn which burned. He was a stranger to Mr. Seely at that time, but Mr. Seely recognized Elliott, who sat near his attorney, as the man. Elliott asked Mr. Seely on that occasion if it was not about four hundred dollars which he paid me. Answering him that it was not that sum. Elliott began a series of questions about the location of the office, and other things, which were quite far from the facts concerning the company represented by Mr. Seely. To use Mr. Seely's words on the witness stand :

" He then said that he was prepared to prove that Mr. Woolley hired a boy to set that barn on fire, and he also could prove that he had paid the boy's father one hundred dollars as hush money. He also asked me —I don't know as he really asked me, but he said : ' I think you have a standing reward for such cases ; do you not ? '

" Said I, ' No, sir.' He then said to me that he was prepared to prove that Mr. Woolley hired a boy to set the barn on fire, and, if we would offer him a reward he would get our money back free of charge. He also said that it did not make any difference how small the reward was, even if it was only a dollar.

" I told him that I couldn't offer any reward, and that

I should not offer even one dollar reward ; that I didn't think there was anything in it. He said he was satisfied it was a clear case and that there was two others with him that had been working up the case, and they were satisfied that they could prove that Mr. Woolley hired a boy to set the barn on fire ; and he went out. As I stated before, I declined to offer any reward, and he re-marked that Mr. Woolley was well off. I told him I supposed he was. I said I believed he had five or six hundred acres of land there, I didn't know much about his circumstances, and he intimated that Mr. Woolley would pay pretty well.

" He wanted me to offer a reward, and I declined, he wanted me then to go in with them—to take a fourth interest in what they could obtain from Mr. Woolley. I said to him then : If you attempt to exact money from Mr. Woolley, in that case, you will get yourself into difficulty.

Mr. Seely testified that he took the same train for Columbus on which Elliott came from Westerville to the city. ' Mr. Seely thus related a conversation that Elliott had with him on the train :

" I had some conversation with him on the train ; he said to me, he wanted to know if I was going to stay in the city over night, I told him I didn't know but what I would ; he wanted to know where I would stop ; I told him if I staid in the city I would stay at the United States Hotel. He said then that he would meet me there about eight o'clock. I told him that I had some busi-ness in the city, and if I got through, I had some business at or about Reynoldsburg. I didn't know whether I whould stay in the city or not."

The cross-examination of Mr. Seely by Judge Rankin, the attorney for the defence, was exceedingly severe. In every way that this notorious cross-examiner could

29

invent, did he attempt the circumvention of the witness. He had listened with critical caution to the examination in chief, and the very clearness of it irritated him even more than the fact that it was evident to him that he had a desperate cause, which must be won, if at all, by besieging witnesses and breaking down statements of those who testified. With surpassing ingenuity, and with an earnestness born of that desperation, the attorney went in upon this first witness for the prosecution, with a sort of vengeance known only to the profession, when it sees itself the champion of so wretched a cause. He tried hard to make Mr. Seely show to the jury that he himself believed me a rascal, and having been somewhat stirred up about the matter by Elliott, proposed that night to go to my home and make matters right. As Mr. Seely said, he did come that very evening and saw me. As Mr. Seely was telling this, it was sought to make evidence that he had too good a memory about some certain facts, and too poor a memory about certain other facts, and that, therefore, he was not a good witness; but this ended in complete failure. Mr. Seely proceeded to tell how he came to my house to inform me that a man by the name of Elliott had been to see him and had told him that story and that I ought to know it. But objections were argued and speeches were made with such earnestness and at such length, that it was some time before he could make the following statement :

"I went to Mr. Woolley's and said to him that there had been a gentleman to see me at Westerville and said his name was Elliott, that he was a stranger to me. And I described him to him, and I told him that he said that he was prepared to prove that he, Mr. Woolley, had hired this boy to set the barn on fire, and that there was two others of them that had been to work in the matter ; and I told him I didn't know what they proposed to do ; and I didn't know as they would do anything, but yet the substance, perhaps, was, whether it was better for him to pay the money over into our hands ; that I didn't know what was best for him to do. I told him that the money would be in safe hands and he said all right. That was the substance of the conversation between Mr. Woolley and myself, as near as I can recollect."

At this point, there was brought in the fact that J. A. McCoy, an adjuster of the company, had been to see Mr. Seely, and that Seely had said that there was some doubt as to one of his losses, meaning that on my barn. The effort of the attorneys for Elliott was a strong one to make out that McCoy, the adjuster, was recommending some course to be pursued against me. But it succeeded in bringing out this clear statement from Mr. Seely :

"I don't think he was recommending on the part of Mr. Woolley. We were talking up some other matters, simply, and I had said to him that there was a case down in my territory that looked a little dark, 'but,' said I, 'I don't know as there is anything in it ;' said I : 'I don't think there is ;' but he said : 'if there is, or you think there is, and the gentleman is willing to pay the money over into our hands, you receive it.'"

And when he was asked about what information he had that I had been guilty of foul play, he made this very full and satisfactory answer :

"Mr. Woolley came to meet me at Westerville, in the spring of 1879, and said to me that the barn that we paid for, as we supposed, was struck by lightning, or was set fire, as he supposed, by a boy that was living with him, and I said to Mr. Woolley, 'how did you ascertain that fact ?' He said that the boy told

some person, whose name he told me, but I don't recollect it—and that person told his wife ; that is the way
the knowledge came to him ; and he said that he had
taken the boy to raise, but he didn't know who was responsible for his acts, and if the money did not belong
to him he did not wish to retain it.   And I said to him,
' Mr. Woolley, if you had no information of that boy
setting the barn on fire, or knowledge of it, in the least,
and was not implicated in the matter whatever, you are
entitled to the money, no matter if it were your own
son that did it.' "

When the attorneys pressed him to answer the question, why he told McCoy that there was something
dark about this transaction, the prosecution made objection which the Court sustained ; whereat the defence
made exception, and so violently was the subject discussed, that, to the chagrin of the defence, the Court
informed them he would rule out all that was related
by the witness as to the conversation between McCoy
and himself.   Then all that was left for the defence was
to get him to say that he had some suspicions of his
own as to my conduct in this matter, to all of which
efforts he gave a decided negative.   The questions and
answers are so interesting that I give some of them as
they occurred, transcribing from the stenographer's
report:

Q. Now, Mr. Seely, if you, to that moment, believed
Mr. Woolley to be an innocent man, what interest had
you in the matter in his paying over to your company
any money !

A. I would say this : so far as my idea went with
Mr. Woolley, that I took him to be a staightforward
man, and after Mr. Elliott had stated what he did to
me, and seeing that other man, I thought there was
something wrong somewhere, but I didn't know where

it was ; that was what prompted me to go out and see Mr. Woolley. In connection with the other, as I told you, I considered it my duty, as he had been to see me and always acted the part of a gentleman with us.

Q. Didn't you say yesterday, upon your examination, that, before Elliott was there, you had communicated to a member of the company the fact that you believed there was something dark in a transaction in your territory, and it was the Woolley matter?

A. I didn't say,—but that man, I believed—

Q. (Objected to, objection over-ruled. (Question repeated.)

A No, sir; I didn't say that I believed, and I didn't refer to any one—that is, I didn't give him any person's name ; I didn't tell him it was Mr. Woolley, or Mr. Roebeck, or anybody.

Q. That may be good as far as it goes, it don't suit me. Didn't you say on your examination yesterday, that it was the Woolley matter you referred to, whether you communicated to him or not ?

A. In my mind, yes, sir.

Q. Now then, will you explain to this jury here, when that impression was on your mind, and you admitted that you communicated the fact that there was something dark in a transaction in your territory, will you explain to the jury, why you now swear that you, after seeing Mr. Wooley, thought and considered him a just and upright man ?

Objected to. Question repeated.

A. I say this : that after Mr. Elliott had been there to see me, and when I saw this other man, I didn't know but there was something wrong in the matter, and I was unable to tell, or make up my mind in the matter.

Q. But didn't you say yesterday that you had in

your own mind marked out in your territory a dark transaction which related to Woolley?

A. I don't know that I said it was a dark transaction. I think my idea was it appeared to my mind that there was something wrong somewhere. I don't think I used the word *dark* as he has it there.

Q. Why did you say to McCoy that there was a dark transaction in your territory, without communicating it to him as to who you thought it was?

A. I said to him, I thought there was a matter in my territory that there appeared to be something wrong with, but I didn't know that there was.

In many ways, did the defence seek to break down Mr. Seely. Objections were interposed and argued, and exceptions almost innumerable were taken. The cautious eyes were meeting each other, and, if I had not been so personally involved in the whole proceeding, I would doubtless have taken still greater interest in the war which these men waged against one another. After the cross-examination closed, the State began the re-direct examination to strike no point of value but that was objected to, and to bring out no facts more important than those I have already detailed.

The next witness called was Robert Snapp, who, on examination, said that he was acquainted with John Elliott. He had seen him one night about September 3d, in company with Henry Alton. He lived on John Elliott's farm, and saw him when he was on his way going from 'Squire Norris's office in Prairie township. Elliott halloed and asked Alton if he had any handcuffs with him, and Alton said he had. Elliott obtained the loan of them.

At this, of course, the defence again objected, but the Court over-ruled, and all that they could do was to accept the ruling.

Henry Alton, very properly the next witness, said he was constable at the time in Prairie township. He told substantialy the same story about the hand-cuffs, adding that Thomas Moore was with John Elliott when the latter returned the hand-cuffs, next morning.

The testimony of the next witness was the more personally interesting because the next witness was myself. My name, residence, business were asked, and then I had to tell the story of that terrible night of September 3d, 1879, and of the meeting there with John Elliott. I shall transcribe the exact language I used before the court:

"He came to my house about nine o'clock. I think the dog barked or something. I went out on the porch and three men came up. One of them had a paper in his hand, I believe, and touched me on the shoulder and said, 'You are my prisoner.' Standing there on the porch he asked me if my name was Woolley. I told him it was. He said, 'you are my prisoner.' I think he said it was about burning the barn.

"I went into the house and they followed me in and inquired something about it. It seemed as though they wanted me to go to Columbus or somewhere. I said, 'gentlemen, if you have authority or a warrant, I have no objection at all; you can arrest me and I will go with you.' I went into my bed-room to put on my clothes.

"I was just getting ready to go to bed. I went to put on better clothes and went into the bed-room. They followed me in and stuck right to me; I couldn't get away from them at all.

"There was so much said in the bed-room that I can't tell all that was said, but will tell all that I recollect. Sometime, while we were in there, somebody spoke about the warrant, and I think it was Fleming, who said

he would read it to me; I think it was he.   He said,
'come into this room and I will read it to you,' to the
best of my recollection.

"I went in and took a light and went back into the
bath-room; the door was open.   I believe Elliott went
along, and they read the warrant.

"It purported to be a State warrant, issued by
Squire Brown, calling for my arrest for hiring a boy to
burn a barn.

"After the warrant was read we went back into the
room, and I continued dressing.

"About the time I got through dressing, one
of them pulled out what I supposed to be hand-cuffs,
and turned them in this way (showing).   My wife saw
what it was, and my wife begged him not to put them
on me.

"Fleming said he was a deputy United States Marshal; and the other said they were detectives.

"I got my clothes on, and got ready to go, and we
started, immediately, and went out into the lane.

"Having gone out into the lane, there was a man
sitting in the buggy.   I didn't know who it was,
only as I was told.   I didn't know him, and Elliott told
me to get into the buggy.

"So I got in and then Elliott got in, also.   We went
up on the pike, and started in the direction toward
Hilliard.

"I was on the left side; there was scarcely room to
sit on the seat.   He wanted to sit on my knee and I
wouldn't allow him to do it.

"I can't recollect what was said; there wasn't much of
importance until we got on the road.   I think I asked
them where they were going; I think they said Columbus.   After we got on the road, Mr. Elliott said: 'Mr.
Woolley, there need be nothing serious about this mat-

ter.' He added, ' You can have a chance to settle it.'
Said he, ' We knew you was a man of considerable
wealth, and respectability, and good standing in the
community here ; we didn't want to come here and arrest you in the day-time and ruin your character ; so we
thought we would come in the night, so as to give you
a chance to get out of it.' Well, I wanted to know
what they meant, and I believe they said they had been
to a good deal of expense and trouble, and they had
been working at this thing for about a year, or nigh
that ; they had been to a good deal of expense in hiring
buggies, etc., to get information, and that I could afford
to pay them a thousand dollars. I just hooted at the
idea and said, 'you don't get any money out of me.'
About that time they took a drink of whiskey, or something ; it smelled like it.

" They drove on in the direction of Hilliard, and they
kept driving very slow ; they let the horse walk the
whole way to Dublin.

" After we got started, they said they were going to
take me to Dublin, and try me before 'Squire Tuller.
I said ' all right.' When they got to Hilliard they pretended not to know the way. I told them. I don't
know whether they knew or not ; they had been drinking considerably. So they went on. I wanted to stop
in Hilliard, but they would not allow me stop at all. It
was considerably after nine o'clock when we got to Hilliard ; we left home about nine o'clock and drove very
slowly.

" After we left Hilliard they kept talking with me all
the time ; saying how much better it would be for me to
pay the money and be discharged, and go to Brown and
get discharged, and nobody would know anything about
it; and said that that was the reason they went over
there to get the warrant; it would be so far that nobody

30

would know anything about it.   It seemed they didn't
want to injure my character, or want it known.

"When we got on the other side of Hilliard, and they
found they couldn't get a thousand dollars out of me, or
any thing like that, they said they would take five hundred dollars, and said they would give me a letter. I utterly
refused to give it, and said I was not guilty of anything,
and hadn't anything to settle.   Then they accused me
of counterfeiting.   I said, ' how's that, what have I
been counterfeiting ? '   They said, ' You know.'   I told
them I didn't know anything about it.   ' Well,' said he,
' you needn't try to deny anything now, we have got the
evidence ; your neighbors know it ; they went before
the justice of peace and swore to it ; you needn't try to
deny it now.'

"I tried to find out who it was—who my neighbors
were around there, who went before the justice of the
peace and swore that I had been counterfeiting, or anything of the kind, and they wouldn't give me any information.   They said if I would give them five hundred
dollars I would get a letter stating who ; that I had better get rid of such persons—so and so.

'There will be no name signed to it ; but you can
take the hint though.'   So they went on to Dublin.

"When we arrived at Dublin, they stopped at a
saloon.   They got out and one went in, and when he
came out, the other went in ; I suppose they were
drinking.

It must have been eleven o'clock ; it was fully that
late.

" In Dublin I saw Pearly Mosure.

"They took him in the saloon, I believe.

" Fleming brought him and I saw him go into the
saloon.

" They said they would prosecute me there, and

talked with me there about settling; that it would be much better to settle it. And I said take me down to Tuller's and try me; and I said don't fool your time away here. I didn't want to stay there all night. I heard a good many things.

"It seemed to me that it was a very long time that we were there; I couldn't say how long. It seems to me it was an hour and a half or two hours.

"We went from there home. While we were there I saw there was no way of getting away from them, and they didn't take me to Tuller's to try me, and finally wanted to know what I would give. I said, 'I have no money, but will tell you what I will do; I have some notes'—but they had made that proposition before. They said, 'Woolley, you are manufacturing tile and must have some notes from the people around.'

"I said 'Yes.' And they said if I hadn't the money they would take the notes as security.

"First they wanted to know if I couldn't borrow the money. I told them yes, I thought I could in the day time—the next day; and they finally concluded they would take three hundred dollars, and go back to Jefferson, and no witness would appear against me there; I would be discharged. When they first arrested me at my home, I supposed it was a genuine thing, and thought so until I got to Dublin; and when they would not take me before Tuller, I supposed then there must be something wrong. I didn't know what to think of it.

"When we started from Dublin we started to go to Jefferson; we went by the way of home—where I lived —and went in there to get my horse and buggy.

"Elliott came in the house with me and stuck right close to me all the time. They drank several times on the way from my house to Dublin; they took a drink of whiskey some four or five times probably.

" And then I had an object in going into my house
to get my own horse and buggy. I came to the conclusion about that time, that I had better get away from
them, that I was in a dangerous crowd ; that is, judging
from what I saw when I was in Dublin , one of them
had a revolver.

" He had it in his hand in front of him.

" It was Moore ; he didn't make any threats or point
it at me, or anything of the kind.

" We stayed at my home a few minutes.

" We went out to the barnyard to get my horse and
hitch up. Elliott followed me everywhere I went. If
I had had an opportunity I would have gotten away that
night and at that time. And another object in getting
my buggy was that they had an old horse, and pretty
well played out ; I concluded if I got my buggy and
horse I could drive off and leave them, but when I got
in Elliott jumped in and said, ' I will ride with you ; '
and so I couldn't say anything.

" He seemed to be pretty happy along the way and
got to singing Methodist hymns.

" It was just a little before daylight when we arrived
at West Jefferson.

" They said they would wake up Brown and get him
up in his office, and they did so.

" When we were ready to proceed with the case I
asked them if they were ready, and I told them then I
would make a statement then of the case. They said it
was of no use to make any statement, ' all you have to
do is to say whether you are guilty or not guilty.' I
said, ' I am not guilty.' ' Well,' they said, ' that is the
end of it.'

" Then the notes I had promised in security for the
money I should give them, I should give them notes
then, and went to do it. We went to the window, for

Brown had some screens there, such as they have in saloons in front of the door. We went up to the window where there was a light, and I had a book of notes and expected to take out three hundred dollars of notes to give them as security ; but as I was looking over them Elliott said : ' You needn't tear any out, but we will take the whole of them ! ' and took them and put them into his pocket, making in all about eight hundred dollars of notes.

" They were all on good men, at least the most of them. My purpose in giving the notes was, that I was satisfied they could not collect the notes and I was going to look into it and see about the matter.

" They said they would go and have some breakfast. It was about day light.

" They said I would have the costs to pay, and I asked them how much it was ; they went to figure up and they said it was twenty dollars and a few cents ; I gave Elliott a twenty dollar bill and they changed it and gave be back five dollars and I gave it to Brown and Brown took that.

" Brown claimed five dollars and twenty or thirty cents, something like that.

" The fifteen dollars was divided around among them.

" I saw them making change among themselves.

" My horse was a little lame—his shoe was off.

" So then I said I would have to get my horse shod, it was lame; and I believe Elliott went with me around to the shop, and then left me at the shop and went and got breakfast.

" I didn't take any breakfast at all ; they wanted me to take breakfast with them but I refused.

" While I was there I saw them going to the telegraph office pretty often and I heard Fleming say that they had some business down toward Columbus.

" A very short time after they got done eating breakfast we left West Jefferson.

"Elliott went with me.

"I told them we would go to Evan Jones', I thought
I could borrow the money of him.

"My object was in going there, for I didn't know
whether he had any money or not; it would not have
heen any trouble for me to raise a thousand dollars or
two thousand dollars without going to Jones, for that
matter— I only just went there as a blind.   I didn't in-
tend to pay them any money.

"Jones lives down on a lane.   When I got to Jones'
I concluded they would stay for me outside and I would
go in and get the money and they would remain out
there, which they did, and said for me to be quick about
it, and I said I would.

"I struck out then west.

"I left Elliott at the road which runs nearly east
and west.   I went south down a lane to the house;
when I got to the house I went down south toward
Reese's—I think his name is—and I struck up west
toward the creek.

" When I left them, I concluded to go around home,
and went over to the creek and started up the creek.
I guess I went up the creek for a mile or three quarters
and studied what I had better do, and finally came to
the conclusion if I went home they might possibly over-
take me and they would kill me, for, if this thing was
not genuine, they had laid themselves liable, and the
probability was they would kill me to get me out of the
way; so I sat down there and studied a while; and I
had some business at Indianapolis, had to go there anyhow, in a short time, whether this thing had occurred
or not, and I concluded while this thing was up I would
go there anyhow, and hear from my family how this

thing stood, and then would come back, and I did so.'

"I went to Mechanicsburgh and got on the train.

"I remained in Indianapolis several days.

"It was the next day that I sent word back, I sent a package; I thought I would send it by express, and as I didn't have time to write a letter and go to the office to mail it, but would send a package, so they would know I was not murdered.

"I remember that when on our way to Dublin, and I protested in giving any money at all, they said, with an oath to it: 'it is no use to try to get out of that, you have got to wear the stripes anyhow; you know you burned the barn to get that $400; now there is no use for you to try to get out of it; you have got to wear the stripes anyhow.'

"They were pressing me so hard for money, and threatened me that I would have to wear the stripes, and that I was a man abundantly able to give them plenty of money; I had better give them a thousand dollars than go to the penitentiary. That was in burning the barn, and they said that they could make more charges more serious than that. I said: 'What are they?' and they said: 'counterfeiting money.' I wanted to know to whom I had passed any such money and they would not give me names, but said I had passed it, and they had men who had gone to the Justice of Peace and testified to it and swore to it. I said: 'Are you quite sure that you have men that will swear to that?' They said: 'yes, we know what we are at; we mean business, and we hardly undertake to do anything unless we know what we are at;' and I didn't know what to think of it."

The cross-examination was all that might have been expected. Of course, the energies of the defence were

focalized on me.   It seemed as though every device was
employed, that could be employed, to trip me up, and
confuse me in my relation of the facts as they
occurred.   Mr. Rankin, who has an extraordinary reputation as a cross-examiner, though not a reputation such
as lovers of truth would envy, conducted the ordeal,
and by all his efforts and inventions to suppress the
truth, advanced from point to point, expecting to carry
consternation whither he went.   I cannot understand
how some assaults which are made perpetually in court-
rooms upon the truth-telling tendencies of witnesses,
can be allowed, where even the worst of men, let out
of jail, or, it may be, covered with stripes, is said to be
believed innocent until he is proved to be guilty.
What is to be gained to good manners, justice, or truth
by that systematic way too often allowed, by which a
witness is questioned as though he were a murderer
and he himself knew it, I do not quite see.   I could
have thought, and did think, that, in this case for which
there was no shadow of foundation as against me, the
desperate character of the cause, its utter lack of
righteousness, and its complete poverty of probable
truth to recommend it, demanded such insulting efforts,
and suggested, if it did not necessitate, that bull-doz-
ing style of inquiry.   My reader may judge that the
person who had been imposed upon as I had, as related
by the testimony, had no relish for these methods.   It
seemed strange enough that that was a part of civilization.   It seemed no stranger, however, than that,
almost within sight of the capitol of Ohio, there should
have been organized, set into motion, and operated,
such a damnable scheme as that of which I had been
the victim.   I could have no such time for thought, as
I have now, when those armed men, with the semblance
of law and authority, dragged me through that dreadful

night, the victim of their wretched schemes. As I look back upon it, as I write these notes, I find how perfectly unable any pen is to describe my feelings ; how futile it is to attempt the portrayal of of my pertubed soul. The testimony offered by myself in that trial could only relate to facts as they occurred in their boldest outward form and shape. No testimony that I shall be able to give on earth can, in any way, sound the depths of those inner facts, whose occurrence shall be remembered only as unutterable. As it was then attempted to bandy me about by the forces of evil, in the defence of that man Elliott, the old feelings came again. I remembered the horror of that night, and the pain of spirit simply indescribable, with which its devilish details went on.

These feelings were trampled upon, it may have been in due process of law, but they were nevertheless outraged by the methods of counsel on the other side, to whom a desperate case had suggested such abominable means. Not for my private sake, nor for any flush of individual victory, would I have dreamed of submitting to such a public rasping of my feelings, or to such a scene of studied insult as went on in that Court. But I thought, and think yet, that every man in some sense is his brother's keeper. I owed a duty to every citizen of my community to prove to them that the trust they had reposed in me so long had not been misplaced. I owed it to every man who, in poverty, had given me a hearty shake of the hand and encouraged me. I owed it to the fond mother who bore me. I owed it to that cloud of witnesses with whom Paul suggests we are each of us surrounded. I owed it to every citizen of Ohio to expose the direful wrong that had been organized in these breasts. I owed it to every citizen of the commonwealth to make the moral atmosphere purer by uniting

31

public indignation upon such fiends.   I owed it to every human being, the earth around, to do my part toward the removal of such allies of hell to places where their revolting schemes would have to live only in their heaven-forsaken breasts, and where their frightful inroads upon the rights of men and society would be impossible.

For these things, either of which had been enough to have made it a duty, I bore that distinguished effrontery and cunningly conceived persecution which marked the trial of these men.

The first question asked by Judge Rankin was: "Mr. Woolley, you were inquired of a minute or two ago as to whether something was not said on your way to Dublin ; then you told us something about wearing the stripes and going to the penitentiary.   How was it that you did not think of that this morning ? "   That question illustrated, perhaps, the method which the defence was to use.   It illustrated, perhaps, the fact that I did continually come to other facts in the story as that trial brought up afresh in my memory those terrible details.   Any fair mind will know that no human being in the simple narration of that strangely involved and perplexing story could touch all the points. But of this the defence sought to make capital against me.   As if, forsooth, that whole night wandering, under the guidance of armed desperadoes, those threats, . those deep-laid schemes, the conversations, could be caught up from the frightened soul of their victim and suddenly be brought out from all that wild chaos of fear and suspicion and desire to escape them, and put into a thread of interesting romance !   Nothing could have been more silly than the idea.   And yet, as I say, much was sought to be made out of the fact, that I had to gather the story of events from that dim and wild atmosphere of memory. Just as much capital against me would have been attempted to have been made, if, as they seemed to desire, I could have told the story as if it were dry and uninteresting, and not colored by all the mighty meanings which made that night hideous. But the trouble with this cause was that I told my story with perfect truth to the facts of that night, the feelings of my mind at the time, and with consistency to the several parts of it.

Yet I could not tell that story—nor can my pen— as it grew with those feelings which the awful occurrences of the night brought to me. My reader may judge how they were outraged, how my whole life and character was insulted, and how the defence tried to get me excited to madness in the early portion of the case where the following dialogue occurred before that jury, between the cross-questioner, Mr. Rankin, and myself:

Q. Tell us something more that was said?

A. Yes, sir; I think of things occasionally. There is one little thing——

Q. Out with it?

A. Speaking. When I protested my innocence that I hadn't counterfeited any money or anything of the kind, he said, "it don't make a bit of difference, if we have the proof we will send you up anyhow."

Q. Did you think at the time that was pretty nearly true?

A. No, sir; I knew it was not.

I was then asked if I had been arrested for forging or counterfeiting, and that matter was pretty well ventilated, I have no doubt, for the purpose of making the jury believe that I was a desperado myself and that I was persecuting such saints as Elliott and Moore. I was then questioned closely, but only with the effect of

being able to state truths unpleasant to the other side,
concerning which of the three men entered my house
first, and as to why I could not see who came in first
when they were behind me. My acquaintance with
Elliott was asked about, and capital was tried to be
made against me because I did not know him until he
told me as he entered the house who he was. Every
action was inquired of. I was compelled to review the
whole proceeding until the jury must have been tired of
it. But it all seemed to fix the story in their minds
favorable to the truth.

The reader may obtain an idea of the line of
defence when I give him a partial list of Judge Rankin's
questions, which were evidently prepared to make the
jury think Mr. Elliott a very white-souled and much
persecuted man. Of those referring to Squire Brown I
shall have more to relate as I proceed with the story.
Concerning the hand-cuffs, he asked: 'Didn't Mr.
Elliott and Moore say right there to Fleming: "I would
not put them on. I think he will go without them.
There will be no resistance here.'" One of the other
questions was: "Was it not announced then distinctly
and honorably, within the hearing of everybody else
around there, that they were going to have the
witnesses while you were going to Dublin, and so you
could have a hearing," to which I answered, "*yes.*"
Another question was put in that self-assertive manner :·
"Now, Mr. Woolley, I will ask you if you was not the
first man, after Elliott and Moore had started to Dublin,
to speak about money?" He pressed the inquiry:
"I will ask you whether you did not make the proposition?" "Did not Mr. Moore say in reply to you, 'No,
sir; we don't want a cent of your money or property;
we expect to get our compensation from another
quarter," He asked also if when I saw Pearly Mosure

I did not say to him : " Well, Pearly, I suppose you have told these men all about this burning business? " to which I answered "*no*." After I said no to this the following sharp colloquy occurred :

Q. And he said " yes, I have told them all about it " ?

A. No, sir ; I didn't speak to the boy that night.

Q. I will ask you whether Mr. Fleming then after they had got there a little bit and had young Mosure there, whether he didn't start off (Fleming) to walk up to 'Squire Tuller's ?

A. No, sir.

Q. He didn't?

A. No, sir ; not that I know of.

Q. I will ask you whether you don't know it, and asked Mr. Elliott to call him back ?

A. No, sir.

Q. And whether you didn't give as a reason that you didn't want a trial in your own neighborhood and to get into the papers of this county, and that you preferred to go before 'Squire Brown where the warrant was issued, as it would not become so public ?

A. No, sir ; I didn't say anything of the kind.

Q. Was Pearly Mosure taken before 'Squire Brown in West Jefferson ?

A. I didn't see anything of him there.

Q. Do you know why ?

A. No, sir.

Q. I will ask you whether you didn't tell those men that it was not necessary to take Pearly there, that you would either plead guilty or waive examination and be bound over ?

A. No, sir ; I didn't say anything of the kind.

The attorney, on the other side, Mr. Rankin, tried to make something out of the fact that when I was in West Jefferson I had opportunity to have obtained justice elsewhere than at the 'Squires, and that I might have made my escape.   This was the testimony :

Q. I will ask you, when you were dismissed by the 'Squire, whether you went away anywhere ?

A. Yes, I went to get my horse shod.

Q. Why didn't you go where you pleased, or did you go where you pleased, to get your horse shod ?

A. Elliott went with me and showed me where the shop was.

Q. Did he go with you where you took your horse to be shod ?

A. He showed me where the shop was.

Q. Wasn't that before you took your horse there ?

A. I am not sure of that.

Q. And if he didn't go there with you before you took your horse there and neither of them or either of these men went with you when you took your horse there ?

A. He wasn't with me at the shop when I got him shod.

Q. Wasn't you at liberty to go where you pleased when you were at 'Squire Brown's ?

A. I didn't know anything about that; they kept pretty close to me, I noticed.

Q. How far is the blacksmith shop from 'Squire Brown's ?

A. Not very far.

Q. How far ?

A. From 5 to 15 rods.

Q. Isn't it several squares ?

A. It is probably two squares ; not further than that.

Q. How long was that smith putting on the shoe ?

A. I don't know how long it was ; just one shoe.

Q. Did he make the shoe ?

A. He put an old one on he had there.

Q. Just nothing but that?

A. Yes, sir.

Q. Now, when that was done did you attempt to go home?

A. I went to the office of Brown.

Q. Did you attempt to go home; was there any restraint upon you; was there anybody there to prevent you from going where you pleased?

A. No, sir, I didn't try to go home, because I knew it would be no use.

Q. What was you afraid of?

A. I had given them some notes until I got some money for them, and they seemed to want to stay by me until I got that money; they stayed with me all the time until I got back.

Q. Didn't you say you were at the blacksmith's?

A. Yes, sir; but as soon as I got back from the blacksmith shop they stayed with me right along till I got to Jones'.

Q. When these notes, amounting to seven or eight hundred dollars were grabbled out of your hands and taken possesssion of by Mr. Elliott, and against your consent, you was in the presence of a public officer—in the presence of Brown, Justice of the Peace, did you make any complaint to him that your property had been taken from you against your will?

A. No, sir.

Q. Why didn't you?

A. I had no confidence in the man at all.

Q. Do you know 'Squire Brown?

A. I am not acquainted with him; I have heard of him.

Q. He discharged you that morning, didn't he?

A. Why, he pretended to.

Q. He told you that you was discharged, didn't he?

A. He told me so.

Q. Then you did go?

A. Yes, sir.

Q. Now, you say there was a high-handed wrong there upon you, and you didn't complain to the Justice of the Peace that stood within a few feet of you?

A. No, sir, I didn't say anything to him at all.

Q. Did you know whether there was a Mayor or not?

A. I asked 'Squire Brown if there was a lawyer there, and he said, "no; not to amount to anything."

Q. Was there a Mayor?

A. I didn't say anything about that.

Q. Was there a Marshal there?

A. I didn't inquire.

Q. Nobody there in particular for you to complain to?

A. No, sir; I didn't say anything about it; I was very well satisfied that the notes would not be any use in their hands; I didn't think they could collect them.

Q. Why didn't you just quietly go home, or go to town, when they were not disturbing you, and take steps to recover your notes?

A. I concluded to do that at the proper time.

It was sought to make capital out of the fact of my leaving and going to Indianapolis. That dreary route was traveled over again for that jury and to answer the question of counsel. It was broken by questions such as this: "Did you not go away and leave for Indianapolis, not because you had business there, but because you feared arrest from another quarter"? I answered, after being interrupted by other questions, with a decided *No*, and desired to explain my feelings and what prompted me to that course. Yet that was not the place, and since no pen can describe them I leave these to the thoughts of my reader.

On the re-direct examination, I had opportunity to

make the following explanation of the whole accusation, as to counterfeiting:

"In 1855, while at Henderson County, Kentucky— the Southern Bank of Kentucky is located at Henderson, in the south part of Kentucky—while in the year 1855, or near that, I was making photographs, and I had heard that money might be counterfeited. I went to the bank—the cashier—and got a $20 bill and set it up before the camera and took a picture of it and put it on paper and took it to the bank, and asked them what they thought of it, and they said it was pretty good, and wanted to know all about it, and asked me a good many questions about it, and I showed him how to detect it. I says, 'you take cyanide of potassium, it will take the color out; if one of your bills is genuine, it will not do it. Take a weak solution of cyanide of potassium and it will take the whole color out. It is the easiest thing to judge it in the world, and I thought you ought to know it, and I made one to show what the thing would do.' The State Fair was held at Kentucky at that time, and I was awarded the first premium on my photographs and a good deal was said about my fine photographic work, and also how nicely money could be detected in that way. A short time after that, the bank had the books and all their notes colored so it could not be counterfeited. Merchants there wanted the bill to see if they could pass it or not. All of them had it there for a few days, and one of them said some of them would take it and some wouldn't. I have told several of my friends here in this county and different places, that I had done that thing in Henderson, without any intention that the bill should go out at all."

Oran Clover was the next witness. He had lived forty-two years in Norwich Township; he said he had known John Elliott for twenty-five years; he saw him

32

on or about the third of September, in Alton, while he
(Elliott) was standing in a saloon door; Elliott came
and asked him if he had seen Woolley; he said they
had arrested him the night before for burning his own
barn; he said they took him to West Jefferson and
settled the matter. Clover then went on to testify
concerning what Elliott said about the notes. Elliott
said, "We have got $180 or $190; in the settlement
we are to have $300 more." Elliott then said to Clover
that Woolley had given him $700 of notes to hold in
the place of the $300 to be paid. Clover went on to
say: "He put his foot on the hub of the buggy and
said, 'these are the notes;' it was a note book, a black,
cloudy book." Elliott told Clover, "If Woolley don't
come with the money by sunset, or six o'clock in the
evening, I will make my money out of the notes." Mr.
Clover saw Moore that day standing in Elliott's door,
and he saw Flemming drive up, with his horse very
much abused by fast driving.

The cross-examiner immediately saw that this was
dangerous evidence for them, and tried to confuse the
witness as to times and places and as to the recollection
of words uttered. The whole geography of the scenes
described was exhaustively inquired of. Every particular thing was dilligently asked about, but the cross-
examination yielded them nothing.

Samuel Hunter was the next witness. In September,
1879, he was living in Dublin, Franklin county; he had
known John Elliott twenty-five years, quite well; on
the night when it was said Mr. Woolley was taken from
the neighborhood he saw John Elliott at Cook's saloon,
at Dublin; it was in the night; he did not know
exactly what time it was; he had been asleep and
awoke up; he judged it was about twelve o'clock; in
the crowd that he saw there were Flemming and Elliott

and Moore and a person whom he supposed to be Mr. Woolley. I heard Moore say that he had "Mr. Woolley" and the boy; this boy was Mosure's boy. Flemming and the rest of the party talked so loudly that it woke him up; he couldn't hear all that was said; he opened the door between where he was in the room five or six inches wide, and listened as close as he could; he heard Elliott say in the presence of Mr. Woolley, "Charley, come back here," twice; "O, Charley, come back here." He was alluding to Charley Flemming; Charley Flemming had started to go; he said he would go and wake 'Squire Tuller up; Elliott called him back and said, "Charley, come back here, I guess we can fix that up." This crowd was there about one hour; there were two vehicles. Mr. Hunter thought Flemming was intoxicated. He heard Moore say that he had got "Woolley." On the cross-examination no such heavy attempt was made to confuse this witness as had been made with the others. Mr. Rankin asked him if he might not be jumping at conclusions, to which the witness answered, "Mr. Elliott called him to come back." Mr. Rankin then asked, "Isn't it possible in a night, when you couldn't see him, and at about 200 feet at best, that he might have arrived at 'Squire Tuller's residence and made a knock or two?" "Yes, sir," said the witness. "Why did you say that you didn't believe it, then?" The witness answered, "Well, I don't believe it yet; I didn't hear that knocking." "Why did you volunteer that you didn't hear it, and don't believe it yet"? The witness answered, "Because I heard him answer."

George Hann was then called. He lived at West Jefferson; about the third of September he saw John Elliott at his (Hann's) meat store; he was constable and marshal; Elliott and Moore came to his store together; Moore spoke first and wanted to know where Brown was; 'Squire Brown was sitting there, and he and Moore and Elliott went out and talked. To use the witness' own words he testified as follows: "After Mr. Moore and 'Squire Brown went out, I believe I asked Elliott what was up, or something as to whether he was after somebody. He said they were. He asked me if I sat up late, he said he might want to put a man in jail; I told him I would get up; it was after dark; I saw Fleming the next day; I saw him early in the morning at Grizley's saloon, and pretty drunk, with a very muddy buggy there; I saw nobody with him; it was about sunrise; it was the night before Woolley was reported as mysteriously disappearing." There was no cross-examination.

The next witness was J. M. Johnson. He said that his business was that of a tile-maker, and that he was living on the farm of S. J. Woolley; he said he recollected the night that Mr. Woolley was taken from home; it was the second day after he was taken that he saw Elliott and Moore; it was at Moore's place of business on Broadway at Columbus; they were both together at that time; Elliott said that he had some notes in his possession belonging to Mr. Wooley; he said he took them as security for some money that Mr. Woolley was to pay him; Moore said for him (Johnson) to go down about the Penitentiary to meet Mr. Woolley, that they wanted to get hold of him before the others did; Elliott pointed out some men to Johnson and said that they were looking for Woolley. One was Mosure and one was Dan Flemming. Elliott had said that Woolley had promised to pay him $300. He said if Woolley attempted to play any game on him he had more notes than he had promised to pay him money.

When Johnson asked him why Woolley gave him

the notes, he said they had arrested Mr. Woolley and they had a case against him, and they gave him to understand that it was best for him to pay them some money. He saw Moore and Flemming the same day in the afternoon at Mr. Woolley's house. Mr. Woolley's horse was returned home that second day. Mrs. Woolley requested Johnson to go and see where Mr. Woolley was; that she understood the evening before he was in the neighborhood and didn't come home, and the next morning she thought it was strange that he was so near and didn't come home.

Judge Rankin conducted another earnest examination, which was as long as it was useless to the other side. The times of his arrival, the times of his leaving one place and coming to another, the way that he went, the mode of his journey, the recollection of his conversation, the whys and wherefores of every step—all these were thoroughly recanvassed.

A short re-direct examination followed, then a re-cross-examination, and the witness was excused.

The next witness made for herself a name not to be forgotten in the memory of all present. Perhaps the tenderness of her relation to the family, the earnestness of her devotion to the severe truth in this as in other instances, the fact that all these were, as it were, trod upon by the operation of the fearful conspiracy, made her testimony a thrilling episode in the trial. It was my niece, Miss Emma Woolley. She testified to the same terrible facts with the glow of her nature. She recited detail after detail. As a woman's character is all the more open to impressions, somewhat different from the soul of a man, so was her story the gethering together of those peculiar facts which would fasten themselves upon her attention. She said, "When they came into the house my uncle, Mr. Woolley said, 'get my clothes, I have got to go to Columbus with these men.' She said, 'Why what is the matter.' He answered, 'Why, I suppose they have arrested me; I suppose it is on that barn burning that has been reported around.'"

There were several such passages as this in her testimony, which showed not only the unaffected truthfulness of her story, but that she, in her loyalty, caught phases of the tale which a man would have forgotten. She said, "My uncle started toward the door and he said, 'Come on, I am ready,' and we put our arms around him and kissed him, and they took him and started. I saw him the next morning at two o'clock; Elliott came with him to the bedroom door; nothing was said that I heard; the clock struck two just as they came in. It wasn't more than a minute or two."

There was no cross-examination. That simple story, so affectionately told, would have turned the edges of whatever lances might have been hurled against it.

The next witness was my wife. She told, in her way, the same story. It was not colored *from* the truth, but made all the more truthful because an affectionate wife related the operation of a disgraceful conspiracy directed against her husband, as it occurred before her eyes. Now and then in the midst of the testimony, there would shoot forth fires which must have been kindled into flaming indignation, when those desperadoes, in their mock of law and authority, entered that quiet home. There was no explosive anger; there was no foolish sentamentalism; there was nothing flippant, nothing silly, everything was dignified. It was the composure of a noble hatred of such baseness and of such men which was behind every word. If now and then there was a tremulousness of voice, it was because the voice was not able to bare the weight and burden of indignant scorn. Let my reader imagine her feelings. A quiet home, where books and pleasant conversation ruled the hours of rest, invaded by men, the despera-tion of whose eyes, the irresponsible wickedness of whose hearts, the black infamy of whose characters and the apparent seriousness of whose mein would astonish a prison or thrill with new instincts of crime the occupants of a penitentiary. This woman knew my life had been a struggle for what I thought was right and that our mutual care had at last ripened into our innocent home. Then to have such men enter with the idea of fastening a crime upon her husband in such manner as this, was enough to have made reason stagger on her throne. It was no wonder that she earnestly spoke in tones of love for me and deep indig-nation toward them, when the handcuffs were produced, begging, "You won't put them on, now promise me you won't put them on him." It was not strange to me, who knew her moral force and calmness, that when in the court room she was asked these questions, her emotion was evident and yet so thoroughly under control, that not one sentimentalism occurred. The story itself was marvelously straight, clear and precise, and to its bold consistency and remarkable fidelity to the story as already told by others. No cross-examina-tion was attempted.

Mr. Clover was recalled. I was asked one question. Mr. Clover was recalled again. Mr. James M. Johnson was recalled, then the plaintiff rested.

The testimony for the defence opened amidst the wonder of all in the court room, except the criminals and their attorneys. This wonder was, by what possi-ble method there could be any defence. As the defence, like a wounded serpent, "dragged its slow length along," its character and method were clearly seen. Very naturally the first witness was T. D. Brown, the Justice of the Peace before whom the farce of the trial was acted.

In the examination of 'Squire Brown, Judge Rankin asked him to tell the jury what took place concerning the warrant. After some wordy delays concerning the matter, and various efforts on the part of the defence to avoid the issue, the Court said : " If the warrant is in existence it should be brought in." Brown said that no trial was had before him, because he had no jurisdiction in the case. He said Mr. Woolley requested to be sworn to make a statement, and "I swore him and he made a statement." Brown was then asked : "You say you dismissed the case, and discharged him on the ground that you had no jurisdiction in the matter?" To which he answered : "Yes, sir." The Court detected the effort at impeachment, and informed Mr. Rankin that the question he was asking was not a good one for the purpose. Mr. Brown was asked : "Tell the Court what Mr. Woolley said to you, and what you said to him, on the subject of being arrested by the Mosure's, whether he consulted about their liability about what had taken place before you ?" To which he answered : "After we got up stairs he asked me if Mosure and his son could arrest him after his making this sworn statement. I told him certainly they could, that wouldn't hinder them from having him arrested. I told him if he was afraid of arrest by them he had better get Moore and Elliott and Fleming to watch them fellows a little for him, and see what they were going to do."

The cross-examination was so pertinent that I transcribe the most of it from the printed testimony as filed in the court.

Cross-Examination.—Examined by Mr. Outhwaite.

Q. Upon what principle did you recommend him to get Moore and Fleming and Elliott to watch them fellows, Mr. Brown?

A. I thought they were all friends of his, they appeared to be there in the office—all friends.

Q. You thought they were all friends of his?

A. Yes, sir.

Q. They appeared to be good friends?

A. Yes, sir.

Q. How long had you known Mr. Elliott, Mr. Brown?

A. Well, sir, I couldn't tell you.

Q. Well, about how long, 20 years?

A. No, sir.

Q. How long have you lived in West Jefferson?

A. About 16 years.

Q. Well, 16 years?

A. I have been personally acquainted with him about 6 or 7 years.

Q. 7 years.

A. Yes, sir.

Q. Wasn't this the statement you made him: that he had better pay Mr. Fleming and Mr. Elliott and Mr. Moore some money to watch them fellows?

A. I made the statement that he had better get them to watch them fellows if he had to pay them some money.

Q. If he had to pay them some money?

A. Yes, sir, if he had to pay them some money.

Q. Where were you at the last term of this court when this case was called?

A. I don't know, sir. Which time do you mean?

Q. I mean in February.

A. Well, I couldn't tell you.

Q. You couldn't tell?

33

A. I don't know what day it was called.

Q. You don't know just what day it was called?

A. No, sir.

Q. Where did you start for just after you learned it was set for trial?

A. I never knowed it was set for trial, sir.

Q. You didn't?

A. No, sir.

Q. Don't you know you left the county in which you lived and got out of it at about the time this case was set for trial at the last term?

A. No, sir.

Q. Do you know when the last term of this court began?

A. No, sir.

Q. Didn't you leave and get away at the time this case was set for trial?

A. Well, I went away, but I didn't know when the case was set, I told you.

This is not a specimen, but only a mild beginning of that searching cross-examination which was made. It was exceedingly interesting to notice how a Justice of the Peace who had served twelve years, suddenly found out that he had no jurisdiction in this case, even after he had issued the warrant. A very interesting portion of the cross-examination was that as to his whereabouts February 25th, as to what he was doing at Jamestown and Xenia when the trial was first on hand. It was interesting, also, to hear the account he was made to give of a visit to Indiana. He said he left on election day; that he was at home in the morning, when he received a subpœna to the trial. When he was attacked again concerning the subject of jurisdiction, the following colloquy occurred. I transcribe from the stenographer's notes.

Q. How long did you say you had been a Justice of the Peace ?

A. 12 years.

Q. Now, tell the jury how you learned, after 12 years' service, within 12 hours, that you had jurisdiction over this case ?

A. Well, I made the warrant returnable to the Justice of the proper—the Justice of the proper county.

Q. What county was that?

A. Madison county.

Q. You made it returnable to Madison county ?

A. No, sir.

Q. You said you did.

A. To the Justice of the Peace of the proper county where Mr. Woolley resided, in Franklin county.

Q. Well, go on with your explanation ?

A. I found that I had no jurisdiction over Mr. Woolley.

Q. Why ?

A. When they brought him back there he wasn't in my county.

Q. Did it take you 12 years' service on the bench of Justice of the Peace for you to find out you had no jurisdiction over a man living in Franklin county ?

A. No, sir.

Q. Did you know it at the time you issued that warrant, that you had no jurisdiction over a man for a crime committed in Franklin county ?

A. I didn't understand when they made the affidavit, I didn't understand where this man lived. I never knew Mr. Woolley ?

Q. Didn't you say a minute ago you issued your warrant to Franklin county, to any constable in Franklin county.

A. Yes, sir.

Q. Returnable before a Justice of the Peace in Franklin county for an offence committed in Franklin county?

A. Yes, sir.

K. Well, now then, explain to the jury how it is you, with 12 years' experience as a Justice of the Peace, should learn in less than 12 hours what you failed to learn in 12 years?

A. I stated before that I issued the warrant, thinking he was a man that was trying to get away.

Q. Does that confer jurisdiction on you?

A. Well, I thought it did.

Q. You didn't learn in 12 years that you had no jurisdiction over a man living in another county for a crime committed in another county?

A. Yes, sir, I have.

Q. How did you learn this very important fact in a few minutes after you had issued the warrant?

A. Well, sir, I learned it by finding out the constable couldn't make any return to me.

Q. What constable?

A. Mr. Fleming.

Q. Was he a constable in your jurisdiction?

A. He claimed to be a constable.

Q. I didn't ask you what he claimed, sir?

A. No sir, he was no constable in my county.

(It was agreed between counsel for the State and defence, that what Fleming claimed to be, should be striken out.)

Q. Why did you make that returnable to Franklin county?

A. Because I thought that was the place for him to be tried.

Q. Why did you think it was the proper place for

him to be tried—because the crime was committed in Franklin county?

A. Yes, sir.

Q. Why did you issue the warrant and take jurisdiction of the case in Franklin county?

A. I didn't.

Q. Didn't you take jurisdiction when you issued the warrant?

A. I took jurisdiction when they made the affidavit and issued the warrant under the affidavit. They said that this man was a man that was trying to get away from the clutch of the law.

Q. You thought that these men had come from Franklin County over to West Jefferson for the purpose of getting out a warrant to catch a man that was fleeing from the law in Franklin county?

A. I did.

Q. You did.

A. Yes, sir.

Q. You are still a Justice of the Peace in Madison county?

A. No, sir, not now.

Q. What was the reason you didn't bring the papers in this case with you?

A. I didn't know that they were necessary, I didn't have any notice to bring them.

Q. Have you got any record of it?

A. Nothing only just what I had written on the warrant or affidavit. The statement that he made me. I wrote it on the warrant and affidavit.

Q. Also the fact that you dismissed him for the want of jurisdiction?

A. Yes, sir.

Q. Don't you make record of cases whether you dismiss for want of jurisdiction?

A. I didn't make any record of the case at all.

Q. I asked you if you didn't make a record, and if the law don't require you to make a record of every case brought before you?

A. Yes, sir, in my county.

Q. Now, tell the Jury why you violated the law?

(Objected to, objection overruled, exception taken by the defence.)

Q. Did you ever have a case brought before you out of your county before?

A. Not until this one happened to me.

Q. Answer my question.

A. No, sir.

Q. What is bringing a case before you, according to your idea?

A. Filing a bill of particulars and making an affidavit, &c.

Q. And here was a case, according to your statement now, in which an affidavit was filed and the case brought before you in your county, now tell the Jury why you didn't make a record of it?

A. Simply because I had no jurisdiction in the matter.

Q. I will ask you if the law does not require you, if you didn't know the law required you to make a record of your proceedings in cases in which you dismiss for want of jurisdiction as well as any other cases?

(Objected to.)

Q. Do you mean to say—I don't care what you think now, but at the time you dismissed this case, that you thought that the law didn't require you to make a record of cases which you had dismissed for·the want of jurisdiction?

A. I thought the law wouldn't require me.

Question repeated.

A. Well, I considered that I had no right to make any record of this case.

Q. That is not an answer to my question, I will have an answer to my question, if you please.

Question repeated.

A. Well, I didn't know; I didn't hardly know about it.

Q. Do you know a book called Swan's Treatise?

A. Yes, sir.

Q. How many years have you had it in your office?

A. I have had one most of the time.

Q. What does that require in regard to the fact of entries?

The Court: I don't think that this is proper.

Mr. Outhwaite:

Q. At the time, you knew that the commencement of a case in a criminal action was the filing of an affidavit?

A. Yes, sir.

Q. This case was commenced in that way?

A. Yes, sir,

Q. And a few minutes afterwards you learned that you had no jurisdiction?

A. Yes, sir.

Q. How did you learn that?

A. I told you because he was a resident of Franklin County.

C. When did you learn that?

A. Right away.

Q. Did you learn that before you issned your warrant—didn't you learn that from the affidavit itself?

A. I didn't know where Mr. Woolley lived when I made it, but I learned afterward where he lived.

Q. Why did you make it returnable in Franklin county?

A. Wait till I get through if you please.

Q. Yes, sir.

A. And they made the affidavit and then when I made the warrant I made it returnable to the proper officer of the county where he lived.

Q. Why didn't you stop there?

A. I thought I had a right to issue a warrant of that kind.

Q. You thought you had a right?

A. Yes, sir, and I thought this man Woolley was trying to get away from justice.

Q. You thought that he was in Franklin county?

A. No, sir, I thought that he was trying to get away.

Q. Why did you issue a warrant to the county?

A. Returnable to Franklin county if they got him.

Q. Didn't you issue to any Constable in Franklin county?

A. Yes, sir.

Q. Why did you issue to a constable in Franklin county?

A. The constable claimed to be from Franklin county.

Q. Had you ever read this in Swan's Treatise: "The criminal docket must be a good and substantial blank book in which must be entered all proceedings on any complaint for a violation of the criminal laws of the State." Had you ever read that?

A. I expect I have.

Q. Your practice gave you an opportunity to look at that more than once, didn't it?

A. Yes, sir.

Q. Don't all proceedings include the filing of an affidavit?

A. Whenever we enter the case on the docket it does.

Q. Doesn't all proceedings include the issuing of a warrant and to whom issued?

A. I didn't consider this a case at all.

Q. About proceedings now: Don't all proceedings include that?

A. Yes, sir, where a person has jurisdiction.

Q. What do you call the jurisdiction?

A. Jurisdiction of the case.

Q. What is jurisdiction?

A. When the parties live in the county where he is stopped from fleeing from justice.

Q. How far did you have to go in the case according to your understanding of the law before you took jurisdiction?

A. No reply.

Q. You went so far as to issue a warrant, take an affidavit first, and issue a warrant, and hear the statement of the witness, and discharge him for the want of jurisdiction, and perhaps collect your fees, how was it?

A. No, sir, it was his request to make that statement.

Objection made to the question and answer, objection sustained, exception taken by the State.

Q. You took the statement of Mr. Woolley?

A. Yes, sir. I told him before he made his statement that I hadn't no jurisdiction in the matter and that I couldn't try it, and he wanted to make a sworn statement before me, and I swore him and took his statement.

Q. That statement was made after he was dismissed, was it?

A. Yes, sir. I told him when he came into the office that I hadn't any jurisdiction in the matter, and that I couldn't try the case.

Q. And that statement was made then after you had discharged him because he was not guilty of any crime known to the laws of the State of Ohio?

A. I hadn't any right to hold him.

34

Q. You didn't discharge him because he wasn't guilty of any crime known to the State of Ohio, but because you didn't have jurisdiction?

A. Yes, sir.

Q. You didn't enter upon those papers over in your office that he was not guilty of any crime known to the State of Ohio, but you discharged him for the want of jurisdiction, how is that sir?

A. I told him that I had no jurisdiction.

Question repeated.

A. I discharged him for the want of jurisdiction.

Q. The first part of the question: Did you enter upon those papers or in your docket that?

A. No, sir; I understand it now.

Q. Oh, yes, sir.

A. One statement that Mr. Woolley made to me.

Q. Tell the jury what you entered upon the book of those papers, if you made any?

A. Well, sir, I don't believe I can do it.

Q. How soon did you make up your entries?

A. I made them partly right when Mr. Woolley was in the office.

Q. Where are they now?

A. They are at my house.

Q. At your house.

A. Yes, sir.

Q. Did you ever make a copy of those papers for anybody?

A. I did, sir.

Q. You made a true copy, of course?

A. Yes, sir.

Q. I will ask you if you know anything about those two papers (showing him papers); is that your handwriting at the bottom of those papers?

A. Yes, sir.

Q. Turn them over and see whether it is your handwriting and signature?

A. Yes, sir.

Q. It is?

A. Yes, sir.

Q. I will ask you what was the amount of your fees in that case?

A. Three or four dollars.

Q. They were paid at the time?

A. Yes, sir.

Q. And were true copies made at the time of them, September 16th,—copies at the time?

A. I didn't read them over; I made true copies of them—true copies at the time.

Q. These were the notes that you made at that time?

A. They are in my hand-writing; that is my signature—I think it is. I wrote that in pencil; that may be changed, probably. I don't know anything about it.

Q. You have several times stated that that examination was made at the request of Mr. Woolley?

A. Yes, sir.

Q. You haven't said at any time that the prosecuting witnesses joined in that request, have you?

A. I couldn't tell without seeing my answers.

Q. Can't you tell the jury how it is that Woolley made the request, but don't recollect that the prosecuting witnesses didn't make no such request, as a mere matter of memory?

A. I believe the parties, Mr. Moore or him, did request. Mr. Woolley wanted to be sworn and make a statement; I think Mr. Moore done that, too.

Q. How does this sound (counsel commenced reading from the paper)?

(Objected to.)

The Court: Do you offer that as testimony?

Mr. Outhwaite: Not yet.

The Court: I guess you hadn't better read it.   .

Mr. Outhwaite:

Q. You still say you have no jurisdiction?

A. That is what I said.

Q.' That is the reason you didn't examine into the complaint at all, is it?

A. Yes, sir.

Q. Do you recollect of meeting a man by the name of Cromwell about the third day after the trial of Mr. Woolley at your office in West Jefferson?

A. No, sir; I don't.

Q. Cromwell?

A. There was one there, but I can't recollect the name; some man there on this particular business, but I can't recollect his name; he was there.

Q. Was he there on this business?

A. Yes, sir.

Q. He was there in order to have you make up your record?

A. I don't know as he was there on that or not; he was there speaking about Mr. Woolley.

Q. Did he ask you if you had made up your docket yet?

A. I don't know that he did.

Q. How long did you say you had known Moore?

A. Oh, I have known him eight or ten years.

Q. Are you related to him?

A. No, sir.

Q. No way whatever?

A. No, sir.

Q. Had either of these men been there to see you within a few days before they came this time?

A. No, sir.

Q. Did you learn what this gentleman's name was

that came to see you about the docket shortly afterwards?

A. I didn't; he might have told me his name at the
time he was there to see me, but I don't recollect anything about his name.

Q. What time in the morning was it that this man
came there?

A. Well, sir, it was pretty early in the morning.

Q. It was before day-break, wasn't it?

A. No, sir, it was after daylight, just after I
got up.

A. Well, now, hold on; which party do you mean?

Q. The three men that came back there with Mr.
Woolley.

A. That was after daylight.

Q. September, about what time in the morning?

A. Indeed I couldn't tell you.

Q. Where were you when the men came there, at
your office?

A. No, sir; 'twas in my house; they came and went
out of the house.

Q. What, if anything, was said when they came back
by Mr. Moore or Mr. Elliott or Mr. Fleming in the
presence of Mr. Elliott?

A. They wanted to go up to the office.

Q. Do you recognize this gentleman (pointing)?

A. No, sir.

Q. You are not short-sighted, are you?

A. No, sir.

Q. Now do you recognize this man coming to you
within a few days afterwards and asking you if your
docket was filled up?

A. No, sir, I don't know as I ever saw him.

Q. Well, this is Mr. Cromly. I will ask you whether
this gentleman, Mr. Cromly, met you within three or

four days after the trial of Mr. Woolley, north of Jefferson on the pike?

A. I met some man north of Jefferson on the pike.

Q. In company with some young man?

A. Yes, sir, there were two of them in a buggy.

Q. Did that gentleman ask you whether you had made up your docket in the Woolley case yet?

A. I don't think he did.

Q. Did that gentleman tell you (Mr. Cromly), at that time and place, that this was the third day and he would like to have that docket made up right away?

A. I don't think he did.

(Objected to.)

Q. You say he did not?

A. Not to my recollection.

Q. Did that gentleman ask you whether Mr. Woolley was before you or not, and you said that he was?

A. Well, sir, I can't recollect that he did.

Q. Your recollection is that he did not?

A. No, I won't say that; he might have done it, but I can't recollect.

Q. You can't recollect that he did?

A. No, sir.

Q. Did you tell him, at that time, that you didn't know these parties that had brought Mr. Woolley there?

A. I don't think I did.

Q. Did that gentleman ask you what the testimony was on the trial, and you told him that there was no witnesses produced and that you put Mr. Woolley on the stand and examined him, and found that he wasn't guilty on the charge and discharged him?

A. I might have told him that I swore him and didn't find anything against him.

Q. Didn't you tell him that you found him not guilty and discharged him?

A. I may have told him that ; I don't know, sir.

Q. You don't know ?

A. No, sir.

Q. You might have told him that, and it wasn't the fact ; why did you tell him that ?

A. I don't know that I did tell him, because I don't recollect.

Q. You don't recollect what you did tell him ?

A. No, sir.

Q. Did you say to that gentleman that Woolley had better give them men a little money to keep the other party off him ?

A. I don't know, sir ; I couldn't tell you.

Q. You can't recollect ?

A. No, sir ; I might have told him that ; I won't say whether I did or not.

Q. When these men came back in the morning, why did't you tell them the conclusion that you had come to a few minutes after you had issued the warrant, that you had no jurisdiction ?

A. I did tell them.

Q. Why didn't you tell them when they came to your house after you ?

A. They didn't ask me; they wanted to go up into the office, and I went up with them.

Q. How far did you have to go ?

A. A few steps, it is right on the same lot, it is—it is on the same block.

Q. What do you call a few steps ?

A. Fifteen or twenty steps.

Q. From your house to your office ?

A. From my door to my office stairs.

Q. Didn't that gentleman that you met on the road tell you distictly that he was a brother-in-law of Woolley's, and that his name was Cromwell ?

A. He told me he was a brother-in-law of Woolley's, but I can't recollect his name.

Q. Didn't he tell you his name, now, whether you recollect it now or not?

A. Yes, sir, he told me his name; yes, sir.

Q. Now, I will ask you in regard to the indorsement on this warrant at the request of the defendant and prosecuting witness: "I examined into the complaint and hereby order the defendant discharged from further restraint under this writ." Is that an exact copy made at the time this was taken?

A. Well, I suppose it is if there is no change in it.

Q. Don't you know, when it was written by you and to the gentleman that came after it, and one was written by one and the other by the other?

A. I say that this is an exact copy if there has been no change in it.

Q. "Jackson Woolley, by his request, was sworn and made the following statement: First, that he did not by any manner or any means coerce Pearly Mosure to burn his barn, and no evidence appearing to me that the defendant was in any way guilty, as charged; or guilty of any offence against the laws of the State of Ohio, the defendant, Jackson Woolley, was ordered by me to be discharged from custody at the cost of T. L. Moore." Is that correct, sir?

A. Yes, sir.

Q. Where is there in that for the want of jurisdiction?

A. No reply.

Q. Didn't you tell this jury that you had examined into this complaint?

A. I didn't examine into the complaint at all.

Q. Why did you put that on the back there at all? "I examine into the complaint"?

A. By his request, I said.

Q. You said, to this jury, didn't you, you didn't examine into the complaint?

A. I didn't examine into it as a Justice of the Peace. And having tried is what I mean.

Q. Didn't you say—isn't this signed T. D. Brown, J. P.?

A. Yes, sir; that is his sworn statement after I told him I hadn't no jurisdiction.

Q. Is that your sworn statement, too?

A. Yes, sir.

Q. "And no evidence appearing to me that the defendant was in any manner guilty of any offence against the laws of the State of Ohio, the defendant, Jackson Woolley, was ordered by me to be discharged from custody at the cost of T. L. Moore." Is that Mr. Woolley's sworn statement?

A. That is what he swore to, all except the last part of it; that I put in.

Q. The part that I read to you is his sworn statement?

A. All but the last part of it, that part.

Q. Didn't you say you put on the back of these papers that you discharged him for the want of jurisdiction?

A. No, sir, I don't know as I did; I don't know that I swore that I entered upon the back of those papers. I told them when they came into the office that I had no jurisdiction.

Q. Didn't you, a while ago, in the presence of this jury, repeat several things that you had entered on the back of the papers, that you discharged him for the want of jurisdiction, and not because he was not guilty of any crime known to the State of Ohio?

A. I don't think I did, I might.

Q. If you might have done it, what do you mean

35

now; if you made the statement then, what do you mean now?

A. I discharged him. I told them I had no jurisdiction when we came to the office, and then afterwards he made that statement.

Q. After he was discharged?

A. Yes, sir.

Q. How does it come you entered up the statement first and then go on and enter up the discharge?

A. It is all the same thing.

Q. It is all the same thing?

A. Yes, sir.

Q. We will read it over again: "Jackson Woolley, by his request, made the following statement: First, that he did not by any manner or any means coerce Pearley Mosure to burn his barn." Is that his statement?

A. Yes, sir.

Q. "And no evidence appearing to me "——

A. Who is meant by that me?

Q. "That the defendant was guilty as charged, or guilty of any offence against the laws of the State of Ohio." Whose language is that?

A. Mine.

Q. "The defendant, Jackson Woolley, is ordered by me"; is that Jackson Woolley or you?

A. That is me.

Q. "To be discharged from custody at the cost of T. L. Moore"?

A. That is me.

Q. "I hereby certify the matter above to be the proceedings had by and before me." Is that a falsehood?

A. No, sir.

Q. It is not?

A. No, sir.

Q. That is the truth, is it?

A. Right as it is written there is what I done there.

Q. It is all the proceedings?

A. Yes, sir.

Q. If it is all the proceedings, where is your entry of having discharged this man for want of jurisdiction?

A. I never had jurisdiction in the matter.

The re-direct examination of Mr. Brown was either mere repetition or the assertion of unimportant matters. The defence then called D. R. Hill. He swore that he saw Elliott about the third of September, and that he had with him at the time Moore, Fleming and myself. He said two of the party took breakfast at his house in West Jefferson that morning. They were Moore and Fleming. Elliott came to Hill's house, but did not eat breakfast there. Moore and Fleming were there about an hour and a half. Elliott was there about twenty or thirty minutes. Mr. Hill said he was not certain, but it appeared to him that I, also, was at his house for a short time. "When they all got ready to go," said Mr. Hill, "Woolley was in the buggy in front of the house." It was, of course, the policy of Mr. Rankin to ask Hill: "Did you hear, and if so, state who invited, if anybody, Elliott to get into the buggy with him?" He did not know; he was certain only that Elliott got into my buggy.

The interesting points in the trial were many, but the curiosity of the court-room was intense when Pearly Mosure was called. Mr. Rankin began in a bland way to ask the boy unimportant questions, when the boy in response said he was thirteen years of age, and that he had lived at my home, that he had left there about six months ago, and then he had been there about one year. His mother was dead; his father was living. Part of the time he was "about here," and part of the time his father was in Michigan.   His father was in Michigan when he left my home.   He then said that my barn burned during the time of his residence there; it occurred in July.   Then, in a peculiarly paternal tone, Judge Rankin thus addressed the boy: "Now, Pearly, the next question, the question I am going to ask you; now these gentlemen may think it ain't proper for you to answer it, and don't answer it until they determine whether they shall object to it or not.   You said you knew how the barn took fire?"   Said Pearly, "Yes, sir.".   "Now," said Mr. Rankin, "I will ask you this question: whether it was accidental, or whether it was fired purposely?"   To which question, of course, objection was made, and the objection was very properly sustained; to which the defence did themselves the delight of taking an exception.

Mr. Rankin was not to be defeated in his plan to get what he so much desired out of that boy.   He began in a half-sympathetic tone again, with this query: "Now, Pearly, if you know who set that barn on fire, tell who it was and whether he did it on his own account or at the instigation of somebody else, and if so, state who that somebody else was?"   This was objected to by my faithful counsel.   Judge Rankin arose and said: "I state professionally to the Court, as an attorney of this defendant, that if objection is sustained because of some other testimony that ought to precede it, we will at a subsequent state of the case, produce such testimony.   I propose this offer in open court."   The objection was sustained, and the defence contented themselves with another exception.   Then the Judge asked: "Now, I will ask you another question, but you need not answer it until the Court tells you to: tell the jury whether, to your knowledge, that barn was burned by the direction of Mr. Woolley?"

When objection was made the witness was withdrawn.

A very interesting personage also came next in the person of Thomas L. Moore, one of the criminals. He described himself as one of the persons "who made the affidavit upon which a warrant was issued, and by virtue of which Mr. Woolley was arrested." He very dignifiedly asserted that before this, he was possessed of information and was in the possession of facts which satisfied him that I was guilty of the crime with which I was charged. The craftiness of the defence was shown when the witness said only that *he was satisfied in his own mind.* Judge Rankin said : "The question went farther than that. I asked you whether you were in possession of information which operated upon your mind that brought you to that conclusion." I do not know whether Moore took in the labyrinthine meta-physics of that query or not, but as if he had been called to a special burst of intelligence, he meekly said, "I was." How it operated upon the lower hemisphere of his gigantic brain, I think my readers will judge. He was then asked if Fleming and Elliott had this informa-tion, and he said he had told them of it. But he went on to say that they never dreamed of such a bad thing as a conspiracy, or had in their saintly souls the evil thought of blackmail. He did not know whether he went into the house or not on the night of the arrest. He then testified as to distance, and went over the route, telling, also, how Fleming went with Frank Davis for Pearly Mosure. He asserted, to use his own language, that on the route to Dublin "there were no demands of any money in my presence, or property, or anything said." He said there were no "threats or menaces," and went on to explain with great clearness how "there couldn't have been any, because we rode there in a buggy and he rode on my knees most of the

time." He asserted that there were no mentionings of
forgery or counterfeiting, or passing counterfeit money
—"not a word about it." He said that Elliott and he
spoke of money in only one connection. He then went
on to say that I said to them, when we were going out
of the lane: "Gentlemen, I suppose it is money you
are after," and that he (Moore) answered, "No, we
ain't after your money, we expect to get our pay elsewhere." He then went on to testify that I told him
that they could not get it out of the insurance company,
because Mr. Seely had just been there and had just gone
away, and that matter had been settled with him; that
I had paid back to Mr. Seely the money with interest
which he had paid me for the burning of the barn. He
swore that he did not think Elliott mentioned money on
the whole ride. "Not one cent" was demanded by
either of them. He then detailed the occurrences at
Cook's saloon in Dublin, and testified that on his
(Moore's) asking Elliott what was to be done, Elliott
replied that "Woolley wanted to be taken back to
West Jefferson to be tried there; that he (Woolley)
would waive examination and save the taking of the boy
over to West Jefferson, and be bound over to the court
and would go up there." Judge Rankin failed in the
attempt to get from Moore any reason that I assigned for
this self-imposed and delightful programme. Moore
proceeded to say that at Cook's saloon, I talked with
Pearly Mosure; that I said, "Well, Pearly, I suppose you have told these men all about this business?"
and that Pearly said, "Yes, sir, I have." Moore
said that he himself spoke about taking the boy to West
Jefferson, and remarked at the time "that it would be
bad to drag that boy away over to Jefferson." Within
five minutes after that, they had started, said Moore, to
West Jefferson. The route was detailed. He told

of the midnight visit to my house. No menaces, as usual, were heard or dreamed of by the pure-minded Moore. Brown's office was reached, and that intelligent Justice was represented to that jury as saying: "Moore, what did you bring this man here for? I have no jurisdiction over him. Mr. Woolley, I will have to discharge you." Then the matter of costs was inquired into. He saw no money divided, and did not remember any request to make a statement.

In the midst of this, 'Squire T. D. Brown was recalled by the prosecution, and examined by the attorneys of the State and myself, concerning Mr. Sherwood's coming to see him, inquiring about the case of myself before him a day or so before. But poor Brown couldn't recollect anything about his saying to Sherwood that he gave me a "trial." The 'Squire hid it all behind the constant assertion that, as he said, they had "a heap of talk" and he could not remember. He did not remember that Hann, the Marshall, told him, when he stayed in his house a whole day, that he must come out and explain the matter to the people. He did not even think that it was of any importance that he should conduct himself in any particularly careful manner after the trial. He had brought his papers with him, and Judge Rankin looked carefully at them, while Mr. Outhwaite went on with the questioning of Brown, as to Cromwell and Sherwood, who came to his office after I was missing, and hoped to satisfy the excited community and the hosts of friends who had assembled at my house concerning my whereabouts. Reference to the city papers, as quoted in the appendix, will give the reader some idea of the feeling of those succeeding days.

Moore was recalled, and the direct examination went on. He then told about the statement which I made, the tavern scene was re-stated, and a description of the

way we took was given.   From his testimony one would
have supposed that I was running away with the three
confederates, when the cross-examination begun.   Sav-
agely did they pierce the illusive fabrication.   It was
unfortunate for Moore that he had appeared before the
grand jury to seek an indictment against me for arson,
for this ground was traveled over.   His statement to
that grand jury was brought in shining contradiction to
what he had just spoken.   Witnesses, who were members of the grand jury, were called upon to testify, and
did freely record the confusing absurdity of the truth of
two such diverse stories.

The ignorance which Moore displayed as to the obtaining of money from me was only equalled by the ignorance he professed to have of the arrest of myself before it occured.   And the notes—why, he knew nothing of them.   He never saw any notes at all.   He did
not know "that Mr. Woolley was to pay anybody a
cent."   Nobody had any revolver to his knowledge.
But the next day, when he went to my house, he said
he did have one.   He did not start out from home expecting to make any arrest.   He was only going to
David Howard's near West Jefferson.   And John Elliott got into his buggy at, or near, Patty Cummin's saloon, in Franklinton.   There might have been some arrangement about their meeting there.   Fleming naturally enough was met between Howard's and Big Darby.
Frank Davis was with him.   "They saw us," said
Moore, "and kind of stopped."   He swore he did not
represent himself to be a U. S. Detective.   He could
not remember that two days after he told Mr. Harting-
ton at Alton that he was a U. S. Detective.   But he
probably did, as he said, state in the presence of Lynn,
Mr. Sherwood, or Mr. Johnson, or in the presence of
some one of these, that he was a U. S. Detective.   The

"mob," he termed the hosts of my friends, which had gathered about my house the next day to seek my whereabouts. Moore said he told some of that "mob" that he was employed by the government to work up that case. He swore that he was not with Elliott when the handcuffs were obtained, and saw none. Moore said he first learned of the notes the day after they arrested me. It was probably two or three days. He got to Columbus certainly before he knew of the notes at all. When he was asked concerning my escaping them, he earnestly said: "He never got away from us." He then said that the three men, of whom he was one, stayed so long at Evan Jones' gate because they wanted to let their horse rest; the horse had given out. It was all that persuaded them to stop. It was under a shade tree, and an excellent place to let a horse rest. They stopped about one hour. He saw young Evan Jones that morning, but he denied having heard John Elliott tell him that if Woolley did not come to Alton and pay that money by two o'clock, or come to Columbus and pay it by three o'clock, that he would dispose of that property he had. Here he saw a pair of handcuffs. The witness was pressed to embarrassment and perfect consternation with regard to the notes. He was then followed to the grand jury room where he was caught in the meshes of his own fabrication. The question of costs was brought up, and ignorance and absurdity were obtained in answer. He said that as he and Elliott drove toward Jefferson, they met Fleming, and, to use his words, "we just drove along and he (Fleming) asked us where we were going. I said we was going over to Jefferson, and they pulled in behind us and went along." Moore affirmed again that he had no idea that day of having me arrested. Until they got to West Jefferson, not a word was spoken on the subject. Moore said he had

36

no particular reason to give for his going to West Jeffer-son, after he left Mr. Howard's.   He said : "I often go there ; I was very close there, some two and a half miles from West Jefferson, and I drove over there."   He de-nied having said to Mr. Johnson, at my house, when, amidst the excitement, he came out to show where I had escaped them, that he had himself already converted those notes into money, and if they would come down with the cash to Columbus, the notes would be procured and returned to them.   He denied having put his hand on his pocket and saying : "We have the money al-ready for those notes."   He said : "there was only one place that I spoke to Mr. Johnson ; that was in there, when we got into the barn-yard.   Johnson opened the gate and let us in.   Johnson went away, and this crowd of men, or *mob*, as I call it, came up around the buggy with knives and I don't know what else, and asked a thousand and one questions, and I don't know what all, and made threats at us.   I thought we was in a pretty tight place.   I don't remember just what we said. They undertook to arrest us ; I fought my way out, or the same thing, to the gate, and after I got at the gate, Johnson called me to come, and said : 'Mr. Moore, I want to see you.'   Says I, 'As soon as I get out of this mob, so they can't get me, you can come to the buggy and I will talk with you.'   And Johnson came up to the buggy, and says I : 'I will listen to what you have got to say.''   He said he would like to have these notes kept where they could be likely to get them.   I said I didn't know anything about the notes, but I would use my influence to get the notes for them when they came down.''

Moore made objection to having to answer whether he went to the Prosecuting Attorney, Mr. Clarke, and spoke to him about Mr. Elliott's selling his property.

He was not allowed, by the objection of his attorneys, to answer concerning his having said to Mr. Clarke: "Elliott is in this so deep that he can't get out, if he stands a trial. He dragged me into it, and (with an oath), he wants to leave me in the lurch." His attorneys would not let him answer if he saw a revolver the next morning in front of Evan Jones'. Nor did they desire to have exposed the black infamy of their witness, by having him answer as to the fact that the next day, when he was to my house, after I was missing, he drew his revolver, and Mr. Lynn said that he thought him to be more of a man than to draw a revolver on an unarmed man, to which, then, Moore replied: "We always carry our revolvers."

It was fitting that the next witness should be the defendant himself, John W. Elliott.

He began by telling the jury that he was one of the persons who went from West Jefferson on the night of September 3d, to my house. There was no conspiracy, he said, among those, or between any two of them, to extract money or property. He had information that I had burned my own barn. It was such that it produced the belief upon his mind that "Mr. Woolley had been guilty of arson.". "On the fore part of the day," to use Mr. Rankin's words, Mr. Elliott said he went to Westerville to see Mr. Seely, an agent of the company. Elliott thus related the conversation with Mr. Seelly: "I met Mr. Seely after I got over there on the corner of some street—right close to the corner, rather; a gentleman showed me who he was, and he said, 'there goes Mr. Seely, now.' I had inquired for him; I did not know him at the time. I went down to meet him, and introduced myself and said: 'I have come over here to see whether they have offered any reward for the parties that had burned Woolley's barn,' and he

said : 'there was none issued or offered as he knew of.'
And he said more than that, that he had wórked that
case up himself, but did not think there would be any,
and if there was anything in it, he was going to get it
himself.   I don't know as we had much more conversation about it.   I asked him if there was any reward.
I says: 'can't you offer any reward?' and he said he
had no right to offer any reward, that the reward would
have to come from the board or secretary direct.   And
then I asked him where I could find those men, and he
told me at the time, but I have forgotten now.   He
said if he offered a reward it wouldn't be binding.
He had no authority to do it.   I never asked Mr.
Seely to offer a reward of one dollar.   Seely said to me
that he had a man here in Columbus, or up there, I
think he spoke of it, or up to Columbus, looking after
that case for him, and had just received a letter from
him the day before, and he said he was satisfied in his
own mind that Mr. Woolley had burned his own barn
from the evidence he had gotten, and wanted to know
then what evidence I had then, but I would not tell him.
I told him that 'I had not come here to give you any
information I have got,' and he went on to state that
Woolley had been down to see him, and that he had got
track of more information himself, and that he had paid
him ; that he believed there was something wrong in
the burning of the barn, and that he had only paid him
a part of the policy now ; that Woolley was abundantly
good, and he could get it back, and that he could ferret
it out and finish up the matter before he would pay the
balance of the policy.   He didn't name the man to me
who had been working up the job for him, but coming
down to Columbus on the train, he asked me if I knew
a man by the name of Carr in the city, and I told him I
knew an old gentleman, and he said this man worked

up at the freight depot here in Columbus. I didn't know him. When Seely and I separated, he went up to see this man Carr.

"The night of Woolley's arrest," he continued, "Chas. Fleming, Frank Davis and Thomas Moore and myself went in two buggies from West Jefferson to Woolley's. Mr. Davis, Fleming and myself went into Woolley's house. Moore stayed with the buggies and horses. Woolley was on the porch; I went up and bid the time of evening, and Fleming was the one that had the warrant, and he said to him : ' Mr. Woolley, you are my prisoner.' Mr. Woolley's reply was, says he : ' What is this, the Mosure business?' and Fleming said, ' No, it is about the burning of the barn.' ' Then,' says he, ' come into my house till I get my clothes on ; I will go with you.' "

In this way the whole affair was detailed. Fleming said he would go after witnesses. Elliott said : "I could not tell the road. He asked Mr. Woolley which was the nearest way to go, and where the boy stayed, and he told him, ' I don't just know where the boy is.' But Fleming learned that he was on some other road, and we came through on to Hilliard and from there to Dublin, and Fleming had to take the other road where the boy was—the boy Pearly Mosure. Fleming and Davis took the road for the boy, and Moore and I took Woolley to Dublin. On the road to Dublin, not a word was said about one thousand or five hundred dollars. There were no charges or accusations brought against him concerning forgery or counterfeiting money. There was no talk about the ' proof among the neighbors.' Nothing was said about the coming in the night to keep it secret ; nothing of these, from Woolley's to West Jefferson." He then repeated Moore's fabrication about my conversation, and the talk concerning the

insurance company.   At Cook's saloon they were waiting, he said, for Fleming.   It was half amusing to hear
Elliott tell the jury that, " when they came up with the
boy, Fleming said : ' here is Pearly.'   We stepped off
a little to one side ; 'now,' I says, ' *my son*, I want
you to tell me the truth about the burning of the barn ;
I want you to tell me the truth, just as it is ; now be
sure to tell me the facts.' "   Elliott repeated what
Moore said about my conversation with the boy.
" About this time," said Elliott, " Fleming started to
wake 'Squire Tuller ; I called him back.   Woolley said
to me, ' call Fleming back,' says he, ' I don't want to
be tried here.   I will go over to Jefferson.   I don't
want '——I wouldn't be positive whether he said he
would plead guilty or waive examination ; I won't be
positive which he said, but that ' he didn't want to be
tried here ; that it would get into the newspapers in this
county, and he didn't want to have it there.'   Woolley
said it wasn't necessary to take the boy along.   He said
he would plead guilty or waive examination.   Fleming
was to take the boy back home.   I rode with Woolley
to Jefferson."   Moore's story of the occurrence in West
Jefferson was substantially repeated.   He said : " After
Fleming and Woolley had been behind the screen
awhile, Woolley called me to come around, and said to
me : ' Mr. Elliott, will you take these notes and hold
them as collateral ? '   I said, ' I will if it is your wish,'
and I wanted to know what they were for, and he said
it was ' expenses that *we men* had been to."   Woolley
said there were some five or six hundred dollars worth
of them."   Elliott said he knew nothing about the costs.
" Moore pulled the money out of his pocket."

The tavern affair was canvassed.   The horse-shoeing
was related.   He asserted that he showed me where
the shop was, and that no one went with me to the shop

where the horse was shod. After that, Elliott said:
"Woolley drove right up in front of the tavern, and
called for me; and I went out to the buggy, and talked
a little bit; and he asked me to come and get into the
buggy and go with him, and that he would go and borrow the money to pay the expense; and I says: 'Mr.
Woolley, you go and get the money and come down to
Alton; it is nearer for us to go to Alton than to go
around that way.' And he said the second time: 'No;
come and get in with me,' and I got into his buggy with
him and started off, and Mr. Moore and Fleming followed until we got to the first road to turn North, after
we left Jefferson, the Plain City pike, I believe, and
there Mr. Woolley motioned, and even called for them
to come up. We drove up I don't know how far on
that road, and there was some road to go across, some
by-road. We did not halt until we got in front of Evan
Jones'. Right here, he said: 'I will go down here and
see if I can get some money of Jones.' I got out and
opened the gate, and said, 'it was not necessary for me
and the rest of us to go in, and will wait until you
come back.' And we let our horses graze along the
road, and sat down under a shade tree that stood in the
road. We stayed there until a little after 11 o'clock in
the forenoon. Mr. Woolley did not return. I did not
see him any more that day. I don't know, probably it
was a month after that—a good while anyhow—before I
seen him any more. Fleming started, when he left us,
to go back to Woolley's house to change horses. He
said that his horse had given out, and that he would
stop at Woolley's house and there borrow a horse—he
returned to get his own horse that he left there. Davis
and Moore returned to Alton. I didn't see Frank Davis
after we was in Dublin. I heard the testimony of Oran
Clover. I had a conversation with him. I told him

that I had received one hundred and eighty dollars in money. I told him that Mr. Woolley had paid Mr. Seely $180 back that he had received on the policy. I did not tell Clover that I was to receive three hundred dollars more. I did not say that if Woolley did not come there, or to Columbus, and pay it before sundown that I would dispose of the notes. I told Oran Clover that I went to Evan Jones' with him to borrow some money to pay the expenses we had been to. I did not tell Mr. Seely that Woolley was rich, and that he should go in and take a one-fourth interest, and that I could make him come down. I saw no revolver during the whole time."

The cross-examination was conducted by Mr. Clark. I can not too highly commend the wisdom of the people of Franklin county in the election and re-election of this excellent young lawyer to this responsible position. In this case he was a model of industry and sagacity. I shall not be able to put into words what I feel of personal gratitude to him for the generous devotion he gave to the cause, the unbounded enthusiasm he evinced in the looking up of evidence and the scholarly sagacity which characterized everything he did. His plea was an extraordinary word picture, and was so knit with logic and loaded with argument that it seemed irresistible. He and his co-counsel deserve great credit, and the assurance is at least worth mention that the people may know that so long as he is at the head of the department of justice in Franklin county a vigilant pair of eyes and a noble devotion will serve the rights of men as against the criminals who may be unfortunate enough to fall into his hands.

Mr. Clark had him repeat that I gave him no money in 'Squire Brown's office. He then gave the gentleman the benefit of the following dialogue:

Q. Did you testify before the Grand Jury, last January term, in the case that came there upon complaint against S. J. Woolley, filed by yourself and Moore?

A. I was there; yes, sir.

Q. I will ask you if at that time—

A. The complaint of whom?

Q. Yourself and Moore.

A. I was a witness there.

Q. And didn't you and Moore come to me with a list of witnesses and ask to be subpœnaed.

A. Yes, sir.

Q. I will ask you if, at that time, you didn't testify in the Grand Jury room that S. J. Woolley gave you $20 to change and that you did change it, and that you gave $5 to 'Squire Brown for the costs?

A. I never testified to such a thing.

Q. Then I will ask you if, at the same session of the Grand Jury and at the same time when you were testifying, you didn't enumerate what the balance of that $20 was for?

A. I don't know.

Q. After testifying once of giving it to Woolley, and then further along in your examination you said you kept it for expenses?

A. No, sir.

Q. And if I didn't then examine—

A. I could not have testified to such a thing as that, because I didn't handle a dollar of the money.

Q. Didn't you enumerate then that you had two buggies, and they were worth so much, and the horses worth so much, and breakfast, and go on and enumerated your expense, and say it was $20?

A. You might have asked me there what the expenses were, and I might have went on then and explained what the expenses were.

37

Q. And if you didn't answer and said, enumerating the expenses, that is $15 ; the balance of the $20 *was* kept for expenses?

A. That Woolley should have given to me ?

Q. Yes, sir.

A. No, sir.   I never testified to any such thing.

All of which will be the more interesting if the reader will but refer to the testimony of the Grand Jurors, Messrs. Staley and Durant, on a subsequent page.

Mr. Clark then attacked him with reference to when he first saw Moore on the 3d of September, and Mr. Clark obtained the following facts from the unwilling witness: "I saw Moore in the morning before I started to Westerville.   I stayed a part of the night at his house. I got there some time in the night and went to bed and stayed there until morning at his hotel.   A part of the night Fleming was there; the latter part of the night. Fleming and I came in together.   I don't know as Moore knew where I was going.   Fleming knew that I was going there.   When I came back from Westerville, I got off the train at the depot.   I came along High street, and stopped at one or two places and finally went down to Moore's.   I don't know just exactly where I was, but was at Moore's.   Then crossed over to Cummins', on the other side of the river.   I don't know as I told Moore that I had been to Westerville."

Then Mr. Clark called up the recollections of Elliott about what he said before the Grand Jury.   It was unfortunate for the criminal that on the stand in his own trial, he forgot what he had said to the Grand Jury, in the desperate effort they made to make me a criminal. Madness itself seems to have come over them in their intent, at any cost of consistency or probability of truth, to place me behind the bars and thus accomplish their own freedom.   Mr. Clark worried him with the fact of his having sworn before the Grand Jury that on the morning before he started to Westerville he told Moore that he was going up to find out if he could not get a reward offered; that when he came back he recited to Moore what conversation had occurred between Seely and himself; that he got into the buggy with Moore at his place on Broadway and started for West Jefferson. Elliott said his intention in getting into Moore's buggy was that he was going home, and Moore said he was going to Howard's. "I went to Jefferson to keep Moore company. That was the first time I thought of going there."

Here the questions and answers are reproduced, which is but justice to the interested reader:

Q. That was the first time you had thought of going to Jefferson?

A. That day, yes, sir.

Q. Did Moore tell you what his business was at West Jefferson?

A. No, he didn't tell me what his business was over there; he told me what his business was at Howard's, the reason why he wanted me to go with him.

Q. He just said he had business over at West Jefferson and wanted you to go over there?

A. Yes, sir.

Q. And you went over there for company's sake?

A. I thought I would rather ride over there in order to ride back.

Q. What time did you get into Jefferson?

A. Well, I don t know.

Q. Where did you get your supper that night?

A. I don't think I eat any supper that night; I think I eat when I got back. I think I got my dinner at Columbus before I started out; I don't think I eat any supper that night.

Q. You got along with one meal that day?

A. Yes, sir.

Q. Where did you get your dinner that day?

A. I couldn't tell you, probably at Hart Shrader's, I often do when I am down that way.

Q. It was dark when you got to Jefferson?

A. Well, it must have been somewhere along pretty near there, I don't know, I wouldn't be positive.

Q. When did Moore first make known to you his business in Jefferson?

A. I think that he didn't say anything about it until after we stopped at Howard's.

Q Until you had stopped at Howard's?

A. Yes, sir, and had went to Howard's.

Q. I mean did he then tell you what business he had down to Jefferson?

A. No more than what he had said.

Y. When did Moore tell you the nature of the business that he had in West Jefferson?

A. He didn't tell me.

Q. You don't know to this day what it was?

A. No, sir, I didn't ask him.

Q. When did you meet Fleming that day?

A. Between Howard's and Big Darby.

Q. How did Fleming happen to turn around and go back with you?

A. We was driving along and hollowed "whoop", and he just turned right around, and followed us right along until we got to a man by the name of ———, and we stopped there.

Q. He understood what that whoop meant, didn't he?

A. I don't know as he did, he just stopped and went along.

Q. Suppose you met Judge Rankin in a wagon out there, and hollowed "whoop," and he followed you right along to West Jefferson, would't you think it strange?

A. Oh, no, sir, if his business wasn't very important; I have been out riding and wasn't very particular where I was going.

Q. As the boys say, he tumbled to it?

A. Well, he turned around and came back.

Q. You rode on to Jefferson, didn't you?

A. Yes, sir.

Q. And had a procession of two vehicles at that time?

A. Yes, sir.

Q. What did you first do when you first got to Jefferson?

A. We stopped at Millard's and got a drink.

Q. Then what was done, all four of you together?

A. Yes, sir.

Q. Did Fleming ask you what you wanted of him?

A. No, sir, I don't think he asked me about that; there is where the conversation came up about Mr. Woolley. We had no idea about meeting Fleming until after I had caught him; I found that Fleming had been there; some one was talking about it.

Q. This was that afternoon?

A. No, sir, this was while we were at Alton; we wanted to serve a subpœna on Mr. Fleming as a witness. That was the first that I knew that Mr. Fleming was out that way.

Q. Answer my question. You say in the saloon was the first time you discussed about this matter of filing an affidavit against Woolley?

A. Yes, sir.

Q. Who mentioned it first?

A. I don't know exactly who mentioned it first. Mr. Fleming and I got to talking, but I couldn't tell you who mentioned it first.

Q. Did Fleming ask you what you meant by whoop, and you tell him you went over there to swear out an affidavit against Woolley?

A. I didn't, and he didn't ask me any such question.

Q. You didn't; who mentioned it first?

A. I don't know, now, sir; no, sir.

Q. How long were you in Jefferson altogether that evening?

A. Well, sir, I couldn't answer. I don't know what time it was when we left there; I don't know what time it was when we got there.

Q. Well, were you there an hour?

A. We might have been and might not have been, or longer; we might have been a little longer.

Q. How long were you in 'Squire Brown's office?

A. I don't think we was there a great while; proba-bly long enough for him to draw up an affidavit and write out a warrant.

Q. All four of you came there?

A. I believe we did; there was all four of us there.

Q. Then you all four started to arrest him?

A. That was after we got the warrant issued we started for Woolley's house.

Q. Mr. Elliott, I will ask you if this wasn't your lan-guage in your testimony before the Grand Jury, that in Columbus here, at Moore's, when you got back, after talking with Moore and telling him what had transpired between Seely and yourself, and if you didn't say then, "we then got into the buggy and started for West Jef-ferson to swear out a warrant for the arrest of Woolley?"

A. I couldn't have said that, because we didn't start there for that intent.

Q. Then you say you didn't say so?

A. No, sir, I don't think that I did.

Q. I will ask if you didn't say before the Grand Jury

that in 'Squire Brown's office, the next morning after you brought Woolley there, while these costs were being paid and so on, that you was sitting back and didn't see what was going on at the table?

A. No, sir, I will tell you what I said about it.

Q. Did you say that?

A. No, sir; I said I wasn't there at the time the costs was figured up was the reason that I couldn't tell you how much the costs was.

Q. Where were you then?

A. I think Fleming and I was standing a little back at the time the costs were spoken of, and then we stepped up to the table, but I didn't see how much it was figured up at.

Q. Did you see Moore lying down in the 'Squire's office on the counter, reclining?

A. He might have been on the table; I don't know; I couldn't say positively now.

Re-cross examination:

Q. How often were you before the Grand Jury, Mr. Elliott?

A. Once.

Q. Did you see Woolley down here in the hall waiting to be called as a witness, at the session that you appeared to testify against Woolley?

A. I saw him in the hall.

Q. Was that before you had testified?

A. I don't know that.

Q. Don't you know as a matter of fact, that it was after you testified?

A. No, sir.

Q. Didn't you know as a matter of fact, that your charge against Woolley was considered first by that Grand Jury?

A. No, sir, I didn't.

When Pearly Mosure was re-called by the defence, the same effort was made upon him as had been so ardently attempted before. Judge Rankin asked him in various forms who burned the barn, that the conspiracy might say the last word. Here occurred the long argument upon both sides, which engaged the Court for some time. Authorities were quoted, and some very eloquent talking was done, but the objection which the State made to such questioning was sustained. It was then in order for the defence to introduce some letters which I had written to William Fleming, the brother of one of the conspirators, and Emma Fleming, the wife of Clark Fleming. The argument was deferred until further along in the closing hours of the case. Mr. M. W. Stutson was called by the defence, and for the purpose evidently of proving that I invited Elliott to get into my buggy at Jefferson ; but when, by circuitous routes that point was reached, and the question was asked : " If you heard any person invite Elliott to get in, state who it was ? " he said : " I couldn't so state." " Didn't hear anybody say ? " asked the questioner. " No, sir," said the witness, " not to the best of my recollection."

At this point the State brought in two witnesses in rebuttal. E. C. Hill testified that in front of his hotel on the morning of the fourth of September, Thomas L. Moore said in his presence that he had made one hundred dollars that night. Andrew Miller said that on the same morning, at Hill's hotel in Jefferson, Moore told him confidentially that he made one hundred dollars very easy that night.

Here came the argument of counsel on both sides, as to the admission of those letters in testimony. It was a long and fierce struggle, and ended by the Court saying : " I don't think the letters can be admitted, as the matter stands." Judge Rankin then put in an affidavit for the continuance of the case. The absence of Mat Grace was lamented in the paper. But the Court sustained the objection to the movement, and the defence had to except. The jury which had been out during all this argument, was recalled, and I was asked to testify. Judge Rankin seemed greatly exercised concerning my prejudices against this amiable man Elliott, and could not avoid his questioning me on that point. I gave him to understand that I could tell the truth and at the same time be exceedingly severe in my judgment concerning evil men. The matter of the letters was traversed, and the whole meaning of my letters was shown when they were found to be answers to letters received, and that I did desire by Fleming to exibit the foulness of the conspiracy. John S. Cromwell, called by the State in rebuttal, was examined by Judge Rankin, who objected to him. He nevertheless yielded the following facts to the prosecution: He met 'Squire Brown on the pike, north of Jefferson; he knew him; he asked him about the Woolley matter. He found out from Brown's lips that he (Brown) had examined the testimony against him, and had found him not guilty and had acquitted him. He (Cromwell) went to Brown's to find out some facts about the mystery. Nobody could tell anything, and my reader need but refer to the extracts from the papers to find what was the feverish excitement at the time. Judge Rankin pressed him on this point, until Mr. Cromwell gave him this quick and clear reply: "Well, sir, I will tell you: Mr. Woolley was charged with a crime, tried by the Justice and acquitted, as he represented. The public opinion at that time was that Mr. Woolley had been dealt with foully. My object in making that investigation was to enable me to come to some rational con-

38

clusion upon that point; to know whether the circumstances would justify me in concluding that these parties
had dealt foully with Woolley. Brown said nothing
about any want of jurisdiction."

Thomas Sherwood swore, also, that Brown told him
that he "tried the case, and found him not guilty and
acquitted him." He thought, as a neighbor, he ought
to go up to West Jefferson and see about the matter.

Then, to the consternation of Elliott, came Mr. Frank
Staley and Dr. Frank Durant, members of the Grand
Jury, who gave the Court and jury some little insight
into the effort of Elliott and Moore to indict me for
arson. They detailed the evidence of these men so
that it was evident that desperation had been yoked
with wickedness, and the jury must have felt that the
foulness of the conspiracy had hardly been reached.

May 20th had been reached in the lingering progress
of the trial, when Judge Rankin tried to quote one of
the articles from the daily *Dispatch*, published in the
appendix. The Court refused this privilege to him, and
the testimony on both sides closed.

Through the story I have thus given of this trial, I
have made reference to the excitement of the people
over the whole matter, and the growing interest of the
community, and the city of Columbus in the finding out
of all facts connected with my experience that night.
I make the following extracts from the *Ohio State Journal*,
which are only examples of the spirit of inquiry in
many other papers. The extracts themselves will relate
the story without personal prejudice of my own. They
will correct their own mistakes and I can only ask the
reader to read them all in the light of the result of the
trial of these base men. Under each date, I put the
extracts which I copy from the *Journal*:

[*September 6th*, 1879.]

MYSTERIOUS DISAPPEARANCE.

THE CITIZENS OF BROWN TOWNSHIP IN A STATE OF EX-
CITEMENT—S. J. WOOLLEY, A PROMINENT FARMER,
GONE — A STORY OF ARSON, ARREST, SETTLEMENT
"HUSH MONEY"—PROCEEDINGS WHICH ARE LINKED
TO WESTERVILLE, DUBLIN, ALTON, HILLIARD, WEST
JEFFERSON AND OTHER OUTLYING PROVINCES.

Brown township, this county, is all torn up over the
mysterious disappearance, since Thursday last, of S. J.
Woolley, a prominent farmer and owner of a tile factory. The particulars of the affair did not reach the
city until a late hour last night, and even then came in
a disconnected manner so that it was difficult to secure
a true run of the story. A man named F. E. Linn, a
neighbor of Woolley's, called on the Chief of Police
shortly after 9 o'clock last night, and just after the
Police Commissioners had adjourned, and gave an account of the disappearance and related a few other circumstances connected therewith which gives the story
more than a local bearing.

The result of Mr. Linn's call was an immediate order
for the arrest of Thomas L. Moore, keeper of a saloon
and hotel on West Broad street, and Charles Fleming,
of West Jefferson, who was found at Moore's house.

At the station house suspicion was entered opposite
their names. The story of Linn is that Moore and
Fleming came to Woolley's house Wednesday evening,
the former claiming to be a United States detective and
the latter a deputy marshal, and arrested him, as they
alleged, on a charge of arson. They said they were
going to take him to Dublin for trial, and seemed to be
in a big hurry to get away. The distance to Dublin is

about nine miles, and they were gone, says Mr. Linn, some four hours, when they came back to the residence of Mrs. Woolley and told her they had to go to West Jefferson. Mr. Linn says they proceeded to West Jefferson the same night and claimed to have had a trial before 'Squire Brown. They then came back in the direction of Woolley's residence until within about three miles of his farm, where Woolley stopped at the house of a man named Evan Jones and tried to borrow $300, as is supposed for the purpose of settling the case. Not being able to secure the money here, Woolley left his horse hitched to the fence and started across a field and piece of woods to the house of a man named Thomas Rees, where he thought he could secure the money. Woolley has not been seen since he started across the fields in the direction of Mr. Rees's house, which was some time during the forenoon of Thursday, and the whole country is excited over his continued abscence, and of course numerous stories are afloat in regard to foul play, suicide and, least of all, that he has left the country. Mr. Linn states that Moore and Fleming came back again yesterday, and a crowd of the neighbors who had gathered at Woolley's house, undertook to arrest them, but were resisted at the point of a revolver. The two men left and started in the direction of the city, arriving here between 7 and 8 o'clock last night. Mr. Linn's effort was to get in ahead of them, and secure their arrest as soon as they reached the city.

As an evidence of the strong feeling that exists against Moore and Fleming, the following precaution was also taken last evening, in addition to that of sending Linn to the city:

HILLIARDS, OHIO, September 5.

To Charles Engelke, Chief of Police, Columbus:

S. J. Woolley has been mysteriously missing some

time.   Arrest T. L. Moore and Charles Fleming on suspicion of maltreatment.

FANNIE WOOLLEY.

The foregoing was received shortly after eight o'clock
last evening, but did not reach Captain Engelke until
he had seen Mr. Linn and ordered Sergeant Lingo and
roundsman Lee to make the arrests.   A call was made
on Moore and Fleming at the Station last night, but
they had very little to say.   In fact they were extremely reticent, and looked at the efforts of the reporter to get the facts in the case as a "set up job" to
do them some injury. On being approached with "What
are the facts in this case, Mr. Moore?" the man looked
savage, fairly gritted his teeth, and replied :

"Open that door and I will soon show you all there
is in the case."

Mr. Moore, however, soon quieted down, but not to
the extent of giving any detailed account of his business
up in the country.   He, however, said he had gone up
there with this young man, at his request, and so far
as he was concerned himself he was on private business.
Mr. Moore was very anxious to learn what the reporter
had picked up from other sources, but was not in the
business of giving out himself.   He ventured the opinion that there was something behind all the alleged
arson business, sufficient to cause Woolley to leave the
country.   The most of which Mr. Moore gave out
would not be sufficient to furnish a full connected account, as he preferred rather to tell what he knew about
it when the case came up for trial.

Mr. Fleming was even more backward on the subject of talking and did not care to enter into any detail
of the cause of the arrest, even if he knew.

As learned from two or three sources, the alleged
arson part of the business is somewhat as follows :

About one year ago Woolley had a barn burned, which
which was insured in the Ohio Farmers', of which D.
T. Seely, of Westerville, is agent.   It is stated that
there were suspicions at the time that Woolley had the
barn burned for the insurance, but nothing definite
could be secured in regard to the matter.   One source
of information has it that the neighbors believed him
innocent of the charge as it is claimed that the barn or
stable, as it may have been, was struck by lightning
during the daytime and fired, and the same was put out
by a tenant of Mr. Woolley.   It is claimed that the
same tenant at night awoke and saw the barn burning,
and believed it to be from the old fire, which he had
failed to extinguish entire during the day.   The other
part of the story in regard to the burning is, that Mr.
Woolley had in his employ a boy named Pearl Mosure,
whom he ordered to fire some rye straw in the barn.
He was first offered compensation, and afterward did
the work under threat.   A falling out took place
some time afterward between Woolley and the boy,
the latter leaving.   The foregoing is given as the
story which comes from the boy, and it is further
stated that the boy's father, who is a shop-keeper in
Dublin, has received hush money in the case.   It seems
that Mr. Seely has been working up evidence in
the case, and had several parties assisting him, among
them Officer Carr, watchman at the Short Line Yards,
and it may be that Moore and Fleming have some authority in the case from Seely.

The most connected story of the whole affair was
secured last night from Mr. John Elliott, of Alton, who
came to the city Thursday with Moore and Fleming.
He says the warrant was issued by 'Squire Brown of
West Jefferson, charging Woolley with arson, and that
Fleming was authorized to serve the summons.

Fleming came to town Wednesday, and he and Moore went out with a hired rig to Woolley's house Wednesday evening, when the arrest was made. They changed horses at Mr. Woolley's, taking one of his, while the prisoner rode in a buggy by himself, and they proceeded to Dublin, expecting to have the case tried before 'Squire Tuller. At Dublin, however, the matter was settled with the assistance of Lyman Cook, attorney, Woolley agreeing to give back Mr. Seely the sum he had received as insurance money, defray all expenses that had been incurred in the case, and what further Mr. Elliott did not state. After the agreement had been entered into at Dublin, the three men started back in the night, going to Woolley's house, and arriving in West Jefferson some time in the after part of the night. Matters were here arranged before the 'Squire, the suit withdrawn, and about 8 o'clock Thursday morning, the three men started in the direction of Woolley's house, *en-route* to which the latter expected to borrow the money to make the settlements. When they came near the house of Evan Jones, Moore and Fleming waited for him to go in and transact his business. Not securing the money here he started across the fields and woods to see Thomas Rees, as before stated, and has not been heard from since.

Mr. Elliott states that Fleming went on a distance of two or three miles to get the horse which he had left at Mr. Woolley's, and Moore, after waiting some time, went to Alton, where the three had arrangements to meet at 2 o'clock, and all matters would be adjusted. It seems that Fleming, after getting his horse, reached Alton by some other route, instead of coming back the same way. They waited at Alton until 4 or 5 o'clock in the afternoon, Thursday, when they came to the city, Mr. Elliott coming with them.

Yesterday morning early, a young man named John-son, who resides in the vicinity of Woolley's, came to the city to see if Woolley had turned up here, but find-ing he had not, went back, and was soon followed by Moore and Fleming. Mr. Elliott states that they started out about 2 o'clock yesterday, going to Woolley's house, where a dozen or more of farmers had gathered, and were in an excited state of mind over the situation. Captain Sells, of Hilliard, who was one of those present, ordered Mr. Linn to arrest Moore and Fleming, but the latter refused to be put under arrest unless the proper papers had been issued. The result was they drove back to the city and were arrested as stated.

The absorbing topic in Brown township is, of course, the disappearance of Woolley. Whatever suspicions may rest against Moore and Fleming as regards the mysterious disappearance will be developed on a hearing of the case. This may be the principal charge which will be lodged against them, as the tone of the telegram indicates. As regards the personating of officers, there are two sides to the story. Moore and Fleming may be able to explain away this part of the proceeding, pro-vided it happened as stated.

The peculiar feature of the whole theory of the arson and disappearance business is, how Mr. Woolley could afford, in the light of his standing, to allow such charges to rest against him. He owns a farm of over six hun-dred acres, is the owner of a large tile factory, and is said to be one of the substantial men of Brown town-ship. People from that quarter will be in the city to-day, when, probably, further particulars can be had. It is a mysterious affair all around, and seems to be with-out intelligent beginning or end.

[*September 8th*, 1879.]

FURTHER PARTICULARS OF THE MYSTERIOUS DISAPPEAR-
ANCE—LATEST PHASE OF THE ALLEGED ARSON—IN-
TERVIEW WITH SEELY, THE INSURANCE AGENT—
WOOLLEY REFUNDS THE MONEY WITH INTEREST.

S. J. Woolley, of Brown township, an account of
whose mysterious disappearance appeared in this paper
Saturday morning, had not been heard from at last accounts. There are several peculiar features in the case,
which remain yet to be developed. Moore and Fleming, who were arrested and placed in the city prison on
Friday evening, on suspicion of having foully dealt with
Woolley, are still held, and have nothing to say in regard to the affair. Constable Linn, of Brown township,
who was one of the party making an effort to arrest
Moore and Fleming Friday afternoon at Woolley's residence, and were resisted at the muzzle of a revolver,
appeared in the city Saturday morning and swore out a
warrant charging them with assault with intent to kill.
On this charge Moore and Fleming were bound over to
court, but did not give bail, although claiming to be
able to do so. They are now being held for further
developments in the matter of Woolley's disappearance.

The excitement still continues in the neighborhood
of Hilliard, and the people are slow to believe the
theory that Mr. Woolley is guilty of arson, but rather
look upon the proceeding of Moore and Fleming as a
scheme for blackmailing. The theories are either that
Woolley has been foully dealt with or has been hounded
about by these men until he concluded to leave the
country, for a time, at least, until matters became settled.

As regards the arson, Mosure, the saloon keeper of
Dublin, says that Woolley did lure his son to burn the
barn. He denies having received consideration for

39

keeping the matter quiet.   It is stated that Mosure was
in the city Saturday and told Carr, the man who helped
to work up the case, that he would take $1,000 and
push his boy out of the country, then Woolley would
come home and there would be no one to prosecute
him.   This little conversation, if true, would indicate
that it is a money grabbing game all around.

A reporter of this paper had a talk with Mr. D. S.
Seely, of Westerville, Saturday, the agent for the Ohio
Farmers', the company in which the barn was insured.
The information received from Mr. Seely puts a rather
different phase on the entire matter, and one that will
be a matter of regret to those who believe Mr. Woolley
innocent of the charge of arson.   Some time after the
barn was burned and the insurance money, about one
hundred and eighty dollars, had been paid, Mr. Seely
heard of the arson charges and paid Mr. Woolley a visit.
The affair was talked over.   Mr. Woolley seemed willing, at the time, to pay the money back and save all
further trouble, but Mr. Seely did not care to involve
himself in any questionable transaction, hence it was
concluded to let the matters develop themselves.

An agreement was made, however, that the money
should be refunded on certain conditions, together with
interest thereon from the date of payment.   As near as
could be gathered from Mr. Seely's remarks, he desired to give Woolley a chance to settle the matter without exposing himself and injuring his reputation.

Mr. Seely says that he never told any person that
suspicion rested against Woolley for burning the barn,
and further that he had no person in his employ working up the charge of arson.   On last Wednesday, Mr.
Seely says, John Elliott, of Alton, came to his house
in Westerville, and told him that they had the case
worked up and wanted him to offer a reward, even if it

was not more than a dollar. He says that he refused to offer a reward of any character whatever, and further, refused to make affidavit for Woolley's arrest; hence, what was done was without any authority from him. After Elliott had gone away, Mr. Seely drove across the country to see Woolley, which was some time during the afternoon, Wednesday. He told Woolley that the shape things had assumed, he believed it would be better to pay the money back with interest. Woolley was of the same opinion, and paid the money back. This was a transaction between man and man, and Seely left for home with the understanding that the affair had been settled. In the evening of the same day was when Moore and Fleming appeared on the ground and took Woolley on the wild goose chase to Dublin, West Jefferson, etc., and finally lost him Thursday forenoon, the particulars of which have been given in this paper. From the rapid manner in which the business was transacted, it would seem that the effort was to secure Woolley's arrest before Seely would have a chance to see and make a settlement with him.

[*September* 9, 1879.]

THE WOOLLEY CASE.

LATEST PHASES, RUMORS AND DEVELOPMENTS—THE STATEMENT OF SEELY, AND WHAT IT MEANS WHEN DIAGRAMMED—THE MOORE AND FLEMING SUITS CONTINUED TO WEDNESDAY.

The Woolley case still remains as much a mystery in its several departments as it was last Saturday morning, when the publication of the several theories was first made. The missing man has not been heard from and the populace of Brown township is on the tip toe of excitement. Last Sunday the citizens of that and adjoining townships turned out in force to hunt for the body of Woolley, which was supposed secreted somewhere in the vincinity of where he was last seen.

There was over three hundred engaged in scouring the country, but their efforts were without success. The most that is to be said about the disappearance proper, has to be taken from rumor and the statements of parties, almost every one of whom has a different theory. They are, however, made none the less valuable for this reason, and the public is entitled to all shades of developments.

The account given in this paper yesterday morning relative to the statement of D. T. Seely, of Westerville, the insurance was correct as given to the reporter in an interview on Saturday, and one of the most responsible and respected citizens of Franklin County, who was present at the time of the conversation, is willing to vouch for the same as he understood it.

Mr. Elliott, with whom Mr. Seely had the conversation embodied in the interview, says that it is correct in the main, the probable single exception being that Mr. Elliott says that he did not ask Seely to swear out a warrant for the arrest of Woolley, or make any such suggestion to him. This is a matter between themselves and one of minor importance at any rate. The following was furnished for publication yesterday evening, but owing to a chronic press of jealousy, a desire to suppress news and find fault, it failed to appear and is given herewith:

To the Editor of the Ohio State Journal:

In reply to the matter of S. J. Woolley, of Brown township, this county, which I noticed in your paper of the 6th inst., I would say so far as him having a barn insured in the Ohio Farmers' company, and destroyed about a year ago, is correct. I would also say that I never said to any one that I suspected Mr. Woolley of arson, and that I have never employed any one to ferret out the matter, and the gentlemen referred to are strangers to me. D. T. SEELY, *Agent.*

WESTERVILLE, O.

A card containing the same points and in about the sume words, was handed to the *State Journal* Saturday, but owing to a more complete and satisfactory statement being obtained from Mr. Seely himself—the same was not used Monday morning. The point made in the card is the same as that made in Mr. Seely's fuller statement, being that he did not make a business of going about the country and telling every person he knew that he suspected Mr. Woolley of arson. This we believe, is all that Mr. Seely claims is incorrect, and it is a late day now for him to say that he did not suspect Mr. Woolley of anything, after insurance money has been refunded and accepted in good faith. The refunding of the money is the unfortunate feature in the case for Mr. Woolley, and is a source of no small pain and regret on the part of prominent citizens and business men, who had learned to confide and trust in him. The simple fact that the money was refunded should not lead persons to the mistaken conclusion against Mr. Woolley, because as yet it is nothing more than an open charge, without probably any person sufficiently interested to go ahead and establish the same by evidence, even if such a thing could be done. A man from Brown township told a reporter of this paper yesterday that Mr. Woolley had other reasons for paying the money back to Mr. Seely, reasons which are entirely private and known to but few. It can only be hoped that such is the case, and the true statement of the affair will appear in due time. The immediate friends of Mr. Woolley, who claim to know and were in the city yesterday, were not slow to express the opinion that Woolley has either been foully dealt with, or is being held at some private place for purposes of extortion. To substantiate the last theory they cite the round-about offer which was alleged to have been made last Saturday to the effect that $1,000 would clear the country of important line of prosecution, and leave Woolley free to return without fears of being molested.

The particulars of the arrest have been pretty well developed, with the exception of the West Jefferson end of the affair, where the trial and settlement was alleged to have taken place before 'Squire Brown. The following was received last night and may throw a little light on the subject :

WEST JEFFERSON, O., Sept. 8th.

The town has been in fever heat about the disappearance of Woolley. Your article of Saturday's issue was the first we knew of this place being interested in the case. Quite a number of our citizens saw Woolley, Elliott, Moore and Fleming when they were here, but no one knew of any case being tried. 'Squire Brown says Woolley was acquitted of the charge. Parties who have seen the docket say there is nothing of the case at all. A report came last evening that Woolley's body had been found in the Big Darby. It stirred our good citizens up, and two men were sent out to Jones' to see if it was correct. At 1 A. M. they returned with word that his body had not been found.

It will be remembered that when Moore and Fleming were at Woolley's residence last Friday, an effort was made to arrest them, prominent among whom were Constable Linn, who it is stated was resisted at the point of a revolver. Linn appeared in the city on Saturday, and while the two men were being held on suspicion, Linn filed an affidavit charging them with an assault with intent to kill and murder. It was arranged for the case to be heard yesterday afternoon before Mayor Collins, but owing to some misunderstanding in getting service on witnesses for the defense, the case had to be continued to Wednesday, and the time for hearing 1 o'clock in the afternoon. Ex-Prosecutor Outhwaite appeared for the State yesterday, and attorney Castle for the defense. There was fifteen or twenty persons present from Brown township, and all seem to be much interested in the proceedings. The Mayor fixed the appearance bond of Moore and Fleming at $500 each, and last evening they succeded in securing the required bonds and were released.

[*September* 12, 1879.]

THE WOOLLEY MYSTERY.

Nothing has yet been heard of the whereabouts of Woolley, the man who so mysteriously disappeared in Brown township one week ago last Thursday. The many responsible farmers in the vicinity of Woolley's home about all have a theory of their own, and the time has been taken up exhausting each. The favorite theory now is that Woolley is alive and has left the country until the storm of excitement blows over.

There was a report yesterday morning that tracks . had been discovered leading across a corn field and down to the edge of Darby creek, which would answer to the size of Mr. Woolley's foot, but there is no further evidence than this in that direction, and the complete search that has been made, not only of the country round about, but also of Darby creek, leaves very little ground for the theory that the body of Woolley is at any place in the creek.

It was also reported yesterday that Woolley's wife had received a couple of letters the evening previous, and that they probably contained some evidence of his whereabouts. Captain Sells, of Hilliard, who is a justice of the peace and also postmaster at that place, was in the city last evening, and states that Mrs. Woolley has received no letter since her husband went away or disappeared. He is under instructions to deliver her mail to a certain person and no other, hence he would be apt to know if any letters should reach her in the regular manner.

[*September* 16, 1879.]

WOOLLEY INTERVIEWED.

He Runs Against a Reporter and Says Briefly.

Mr. S. J. Wooley, of Brown township, concerning whom so much has been said and written in connection with his mysterious disappearance several days ago, was in the city yesterday, and, in the course of his perambulations, ran across a *State Journal* reporter. Mr. Woolley is rather aged in appearance, and has the look of a man with considerable force of character, although he seems down and troubled in mind. He seems like a man who has been thoroughly frightened, and looks upon the movements of every stranger who approaches with a sort of dread and suspicion.

Mr. Woolley did not seem talkative on the subject of his disappearance to the extent of taking up the story from the beginning and giving a complete account of the same from his standpoint. He said he had business to attend to at Richmond, Ind., and he went there in part for that purpose, although it was not his intention to remain silent about his whereabouts and thus give his family trouble. He sent an express package to a member of his family, and expected that in this manner his wife would receive information of where he was, but somehow the package was mislead, and failed to come through. As regards the going away in the manner he did, all of which is known to the public, Mr. Woolley says that nothing induced him to go but one thing, and that was the mortal fear he entertained of the men into whose clutches he had fallen. After being hauled over the country all night, and undergoing the ordeal of a mock trial, supposed settlement, and increased demand for money, he concluded to make his escape the first chance he had. The men who had him in charge were all drinking, and with this condition of things he could expect nothing else but foul treatment, should the occasion present itself in good shape.

Mr. Woolley has made up his mind to stay now and see the thing through. He says there was no occasion for his leaving beyond the reason already assigned. In regard to what has been said in the papers, Mr. Woolley did not seem to find objections, with the exception of the intimation at the photograph business, and he said he must have that straightened up. There are numerous friends of a substantial kind who will advise Mr. Woolley to stand his ground. The exact business in the city is not known, but it is safe to say that in a few days there will something drop.

[*September* 17*th*, 1879.]

Mr S. J. Woolley, whose disappearance caused so much excitement in Brown township, was in the city yesterday. He says he is ready to stand any investigation that is asked on his account, and that he has already taken measures to prosecute those who were attempting to blackmail and extort money from him.

40

CONCLUSION.

After examining these reports and notices of the press, my reader, no doubt, will be interested to look at that portion of the testimony upon which so much depended, and which has come into my hands since the writing of the foregoing pages. I therefore beg leave to incorporate here a synopsis of questions and answers which brought out the special fact which rose above all the rest in this remarkable controversy :

I was asked to what point I went after reaching the railroad, in my escape from the desperadoes, and after answering " Richmond, Indiana," and stating in reply to a question that I waited there until the passing of the Indianapolis train, my attention was called to the statement that I had made to the effect that I communicated with my family the next morning after I left the house of Evan Jones. I then had opportunity to state the manner of that communication. I sent a large envelope containing some things by express, directed to J. M. Johnson, the gentleman who was in my house on the night of the 3d, and who was the foreman of my tile works. The whole affair was done hurriedly by the necessity of the case. I went to Indianapolis and seized that opportunity to inform my family of my whereabouts. I remained at Indianapolis until I heard from my family. So soon as I reached that city in the evening, I wrote another message to my home. The day afterward I sent a telegram to James Fleming, Secretary of the Ohio State Board of Agriculture. It was eight or ten days before I heard from home. These were answers brought out by the questions of Mr. Castle, who also gave me occasion to say that a short time after the trial of Elliott, Mr. Seely repaid the money to me from the insurance company.

My wife was called. She testified concerning the let-

ter, and said that she got a letter out of the office addressed to Mr. Johnson ; that she brought it home and
very naturally put it up, and that the letter remained
where she put it until the next week. This was the
letter I wrote at the office of the *Drainage Journal.*
Mr. Billingsly, the editor, kindly gave me an envelope,
and I asked him to address it for me, sitting at his desk
as he was, and being a fine penman. The envelope had
his card printed thereon, and addressed as it was by him
to Mr. Johnson, being of the same sort as many other
envelopes containing circulars to me concerning the tile
business, it would have been very strange if my wife
had opened it. The next week I wrote to my wife another letter, addressed by myself, though I used that
sort of an envelope. This my wife opened and read, as
she would, naturally enough. She received this letter
on the 11th or 12th of September. My wife proceeded
to state that she told Mr. Johnson that she brought a
letter for him like the one she had from me, from the
office, and saying that he would like to see it, he read
it and was astonished to find a letter from her husband.
She then told of my sending some keys and notes to
her, whereupon I arrived the next day after she had
received them.

Nicholas Kœhler testified that he made a mistake in
reading the address on the package and gave it to J.
M. Robinson instead of J. M. Johnson, who gave a
receipt for it. When Robinson brought the package
back to the express office Dr. Seeds was there, and he
said he was confident that the writing was that "of Mr.
Woolley." He told Mr. Johnson, and Johnson came
to the office and recognized the writing.

I have thus called attention to this testimony to show
how truly I made every effort to make communication
with my family. Such a set of untoward circumstances

and events intervened that, as has been shown, they did not hear from me; but I trust that as the jury found, so will my readers find, that it was no fault of mine that they had not the fullest information of my whereabouts.

All the testimony in these cases was taken by the efficient official stenographer, Mr. C. H. Lander, and the cases themselves were in the hands of the excellent prosecuting attorney, Mr. W. J. Clark, and the Hon. J. H. Outhwaite and Col. J. H. Holmes, to whom I here return my sincere gratitude.

Throughout the case, every effort was made on the part of the defense to avoid trial; I have referred to these efforts to postpone justice. In February, when the trial of Moore came, the defense asked for a postponement, because an important witness could not be obtained. I happened to know that the "important witness" was in reach, and he was placed before the Court with this result: that he knew utterly nothing about the case. Again they attempted to postpone, because important witnesses could not be obtained. I then found what they expected to prove by them, and simply admitted that they could *prove* these things by these witnesses (for they would swear to anything), and the case went on.

The trials of both Elliott and Moore, were noted by the press, and had I not already showed the interest which the public took in the matter, I should put before my readers some specimens of the just interest which the press of the city of Columbus and the State took in the progress of the trial.

The trial of Moore developed more facts and brought to the surface more malevolence on the part of the defense than that of Elliott. A certain Mr. Castle became the champion of these men, and what the defense lost in brains in the fact that Judge Rankin forsook the case, was perhaps compensated in the gain of low pettyfogging in the fact of this other acquisition. The conduct of that attorney with regard to my wife, while she tried to relate the story of that night, was exceedingly ungentlemanly and beneath either the dignity or the honor of a lawyer.

Yet, in these closing pages, I am glad to say that I have learned to forgive. I cannot and will not go down into old age with a rankling, unforgiving hate in my soul. I come to these last words, therefore, with charity for all. My creed will not admit of that vindictiveness which casts a gloomy shadow upon him who cherishes it. It is ungenerous, while my enemies are both in yonder penitentiary, to let a fierce hate climb over their walls to attack them with this last episode. I have thought to stop, and with my reader shake hands of farewell, repeating to him, as I have to my own heart, the words of Emerson :

" Lowly, faithful, banish fear,—
Right onward, then, unharmed ;
The port well worth the cruise is near,
And every wave is charmed."

FINIS.

GREAT INDUCEMENTS TO DRAIN YOUR FARM !

A Sure Gain of from Twenty-five to Fifty Bushels of Corn to the Acre, with Half the Work of Man and Team.

DRAIN YOUR LAND AND MAKE YOUR SOIL FROM TWO TO FOUR FEET DEEPER.

Drain Your Land and Go Dry-shod, and Save Your Health and Doctor Bills.

At Appledale Farm, three miles west of Hilliard, O., I have a large amount of SUPERIOR DRIAN TILE, of all sizes, and will sell on a year's time, without interest, or discount ten per cent. for cash

All that purchase $20 worth of tile hereafter will receive this book as a premium. I give liberal measure ; they over-run three and one-half rods in one hundred.

My tile are the cheapest in the county, considering the quality of the tile.

I will sell, from my Appledale herd of Devons, Calves of either sex.   S. J. WOOLLEY.

HILLIARD, O., 1881.